William Clark Russell

Round the Galley Fire

William Clark Russell

Round the Galley Fire

ISBN/EAN: 9783337192921

Printed in Europe, USA, Canada, Australia, Japan

Cover: Foto ©Andreas Hilbeck / pixelio.de

More available books at **www.hansebooks.com**

ROUND THE GALLEY FIRE

BY

W. CLARK RUSSELL

AUTHOR OF

"THE WRECK OF THE GROSVENOR," "AN OCEAN TRAGEDY,"
"ON THE FOK'S'LE HEAD," ETC.

A NEW EDITION

London

CHATTO & WINDUS, PICCADILLY

1893

These stories and sketches originally appeared in *The Daily Telegraph*. No further preface to them is needed than this statement; for the title under which they are collected will fitly express their character, if the reader can imagine himself one of an audience, in a cold Dog Watch, listening to the yarns of a man who has planted himself in the galley, where he delivers his memories and notions to the little company who have gathered round to listen.

CONTENTS.

ROUND THE GALLEY FIRE.

A DANCE AT SEA.

A LARGE Australian passenger ship, homeward bound from Sydney, New South Wales, lay becalmed in about two degrees south of the line. She had carried the trade-wind to that point, but it had failed her at daybreak, and all day long she had hung upon the whitish-blue of the oil-smooth sea, slightly leaning with the swell that ran through the bosom of the deep with the regularity of a restful respiration, her white canvas softly beating against the yellow masts, which were radiant with lines of fire, and the water bubbling like a fountain under her counter, as the stern of the great fabric was depressed by the heave of the swell under the bows.

She was tolerably well crowded with human beings, carrying a large number of passengers in the cuddy and steerage, and some thirty or forty people in the 'tween decks. The poop was sheltered by an awning, and under it, seated on chairs or lounging upon the skylights and the hencoops, were such of the passengers as were privileged to use that portion of the decks, reading, talking, smoking, casting languid eyes upon the breathless ocean; ladies fanning themselves, gentlemen

B

in the airiest possible costumes, and at the extremity of
the shadowed deck the steersman grasping the wheel,
his figure in the pouring vertical sunshine rising and
falling against the rich sapphire of the tropical heavens
with the swaying of the ship, and the brilliant brass
of the binnacle-hood flashing into flames as it slowly
lifted and sank under the eye of the burning luminary.

The quarter-deck was partially sheltered by the folds
of the mainsail, which hung from the great yard in the
grip of the leechlines; and there, wherever the shadows
rested, congregated the steerage and 'tween-deck passengers, lolling red-faced and open-breasted. In one
place a knot of women with children gathered about
them, in another a number of men in their shirt-sleeves
sprawling in many postures; and, forward, glimpses of
Jack could be caught at work at some job in the waist,
or on the forecastle, or in the shadow of the break of his
big parlour, or popping his head through the scuttle
with a sooty inverted pipe between his teeth to have a
look around him, or enjoying a wash-down, stripped to
the hips, in a bucket of salt water, screened from the
passengers' eyes by the galley; while the live stock in the
long boat filled the air that way with rumbling and
squeaking noises, which harmonized with the hoarse
pipes of the boatswain standing betwixt the knightheads
and bawling instructions to a couple of ordinary seamen
on the foretopsail-yard.

The day passed with never so much as a shadow upon
the sea to give the officer on duty an excuse to sing out
to the watch. But nobody could reasonably complain.
The ship had rushed grandly into this stagnant ocean
under topmast and topgallant studdingsails, and for days
and days the roar of foam speeding furiously past and
the thunder of the trade-wind sweeping into the spacious

concavities of the gleaming cloths had been familiar sounds. This calm was only like giving the ship a little breathing-time. Besides, it would directly serve a very pleasant purpose then in hand, which was simply this. It was the birthday of the daughter of one of the passengers, a rich Australian gentleman. The girl was pretty, charming in manners, and universally liked; indeed, four gentlemen were seriously in love with her, and one of these had suggested that they should celebrate the occasion by a dance. The skipper came promptly into the scheme, and so did the rich Australian papa, who merely stipulated that the dance should be general from one end of the ship to the other, and that he should be at the charge of enough wine to keep the heels of the forecastle and 'tween-decks nimble and up to the mark. They could dance in a calm like this, and the light and regular swell would be rather a help than a hindrance, as the heave of the deck should put additional alacrity into the swing of a waltz or the stampede of a gallop round the hencoops and hatchways. They could muster a little music: a flute, a concertina, and two fiddles, and they also had the cuddy piano. So all that was needful for a sea-ball was at hand, and in the second dog-watch, before the sun went down, they began to prepare for the festivity. There would be a bright moon, and the question whether they should dance in its light, like the Buffalo girls, or keep the awning spread, had been earnestly debated at luncheon and dinner. It was decided, however, to let the awning stand—first, because it would keep the dew from the deck; and, secondly, because the lanterns would show to advantage in its shadow.

At the appointed time, therefore, the sailors came along to rig up the lanterns, as many as they had, side-lights, cabin-lamps, and the like. Any departure from regular routine delights Jack, and his grin is never broader nor his whispered jokes more explosive than at such times. Besides, he was to dance presently, and he tumbled through the preparations like a man in a hurry to enjoy himself. The sun went down—a mass of glorious splendour—flinging up the glass-smooth water until the western horizon all that way looked to be twenty leagues distant, and shedding a haze of purple gold far to the eastward of the zenith that tinted the mighty expanse of ocean with a delicate crimson which yielded fast to the eager stride of the tropical night, though darkness was in the east, and the large tremulous silver stars were sparkling upon its deep ebony bosom, and the white snow-like moon was floating in the pure deep shadows in the south and whitening the water with a slender stream of icy light, when the west was still ardent with the fires of the vanished day-beam.

The cool of the night was immediately felt in the air, and now the circling draughts thrown down upon the decks by every flap of the lower canvas could be felt and enjoyed. With the row of lanterns along the poop, here a red and there a green one, mingling with the yellow radiance of the other lamps, the lustrous pearl of the moonlight on the main deck and forecastle, and the drowsily-flapping sails lifting their pale heights to the stars, the ship was a picturesque object indeed. The musicians posted themselves against the rail at the break of the poop, so that all hands could hear their strains and dance to them ; and everything being ready, they dashed into a waltz, keeping very good time, and accompanied (after a fashion) by the piano in the cuddy, the notes of which rose very clearly through the open sky-lights. Aft, of course, there was the necessary decorum, ladies and gentlemen gliding over the smooth

planking and skimming along with great propriety, and
with a more or less tolerable exhibition of art. But on
the main deck and forecastle shore customs were not very
strictly adhered to. Women danced with women, men
with men; the children hopped to and fro, clapping their
hands and getting in the way; here and there a sailor
would be showing off his paces in a lonely dance, slap-
ping the deck with his heels in a hornpipe without the
least reference to the music, which, so long as it kept
going, was all the same to him, no matter what dances it
played. The steward and his mates bustled about with
wine and glasses; but the wine was light, and Jack, and
many of the steerage and 'tween-deck passengers too, no
doubt, were seasoned, and the mild refreshment did no
further mischief than impart a sense of festivity.

They say, and I can well believe, that a prettier
sight was never seen than all those people dancing, and
laughing, and enjoying themselves on the decks of that
becalmed and sleeping Australian vessel. You must
figure yourself taking your stand on one of the poop-
ladders, say, clear of the awning, where, looking aft, you
could see the row of lanterns and the dancers shifting
their colours as they swept round into the rays of the
green and red lamps, with little floods of moonlight here
and there upon the deck under the awning; and beyond,
the man at the wheel, standing there like a bronze
figure, the binnacle lamp softly touching his shape with
light, and making his image clear against the stars which
slowly slided to and fro, past him; or where, looking
forward, you commanded the vessel to the very eyes of
her, whence the great bowsprit and long jibbooms forked
into the gloom like a spear pointed by a giant, on which
the row of jibs glimmered as they soared into the pale
obscurity. On those decks the moonlight lay broad; but

in places shone a yellow light which, with the moonshine, threw twin-shadows upon the silvered planks, and the shadows of the rigging were sharp and black, and scored the sails as though they were ruled with lines of India ink. The crowd of big spare booms over the galley, the outline of the huge windlass barrel under the forecastle, the solid masts piercing the night and bearing on high their vast stretches of symmetrical canvas, from which an occasional shower of dew would fall when the sails came in to the masts, loomed large and vague in the moonlight; there was something of shadowiness, too, in the figures of the dancers as they swayed in crowds between the bulwarks, and frollicked on the forecastle, with frequent bursts of hearty laughter and loud calls, which were thrown back in light echoes from the lofty sails.

The musicians varied the dances often, but it was all one to the sailors and the steerage passengers, and whilst the cuddy people were staidly stalking through quadrilles or decorously gyrating in waltzes or hopping gravely through a mazurka, the company on the main deck kept steadily to galops and polkas—this last, a beloved dance among sailors—floundering against each other, capsizing over the children, spinning around the main hatch and through the galley, and awaking the echoes of the forecastle with their active toeing and heeling.

But it was impossible to look abroad upon the vast and vague distances of the dark sea, upon whose horizon, down to the very water's edge, the stars were shining like fireflies, without a mingling of melancholy in the thoughts. How small a speck that ship made in the midst of the lonely leagues of ocean! how minute a theatre sufficed for the revelry of near upon two hundred human souls! The contrast between the sounds in the vessel and the deep silence upon the sea was defined to a degree such as no pen could give expression to. The silence was like the night itself, a near and impervious envelopment which absorbed the shouts and laughter of the dancers as a stone flung at a mound of snow vanishes in it. The water against the ship's side looked thick and black and sluggish as liquid pitch, but now and again the wash of the swell would set it on fire with phosphorous, that poured away under the surface in bright illuminated clouds, which sparkled and faded until they vanished utterly and the water was black again. Once an exclamation from the second mate, who was looking over the rail at the sea, brought several dancers to his side, and, following the indication of his outstretched finger, they perceived a fiery oval shape sneaking stealthily along towards the bows of the ship. "Only a shark, ladies, hoping that some of us may waltz ourselves overboard;" and, merrily laughing, the dancers drew away and fell to their prancings afresh.

But presently, and in the midst of all this gaiety, the stream of moonlight in the south-west sea—a reflection that had hung like a cone of solid silver without a breath to tarnish the exquisite polish of its surface—trembled, and the water on either hand of it took a deeper shadow. Overhead the sails were silent, and a faint air streamed athwart the poop under the awning. The skipper, a fine-looking, hearty seaman, swung himself abreast of the officer in charge, with his arm still clasping the waist of his partner, said something in a low voice, and whisked off again. The officer walked to the break of the poop, and his loud cry startled the dancers on the main deck for a moment.

"Trim sail, the watch! Lay aft some hands, and man the starboard main braces. Wheel, there; how's her head?"

" North-west by north, sir."

And now some new strains were added to those produced by the musicians. The rough voices of seamen
rounding in the braces rose harshly, and the measures
of the dance music were somewhat perplexed by the sharp
cries of " Belay all that ! "   " Haul taut to wind'ard ! "
" Too much the royal yard.   Slacken a bit to leeward ! "
But the dancers, to whose ears those cries were as
familiar as their fingers were to their eyes, went on
footing it bravely.   The decks grew steady and slightly
inclined ; the sails had fallen asleep, and there was not
a stir among the pallid folds ; a pleasant sound of tinkling water came up from the ship's side, and under the
counter a narrow wake of green fire crawled away, with
little eddies of foam twinkling among the ghastly sparkles
of the phosphorus.

But the musicians began to slacken ; the piano had
given over, and Jack had lighted his pipe forward, and
was beginning to remember that his watch below would
be up in two hours.   By-and-by a bell was rung in the
cuddy, and those who looked through the skylight saw
that the grog and the biscuits were on the table.   The
music ended suddenly, and the fiddlers and the others
gathered around the cuddy door, where they were received by the steward, who handed them each a glass of
liquor.   In twos and threes the steerage and 'tween-deck
passengers went below, and in half an hour the ship's
decks were deserted save by the steersman, the pacing
officer of the watch, and some dark figures leaning over
the head-rail, visible from the poop under the arched
foot of the foresail.   Up through the booby and main
hatches would come fitfully the sound of a child crying,
or a woman's voice talking low, or the growling hum of
men ; otherwise the silence was profound, the ship like

phantom in the moonlight, and nothing audible aloft
it the moan of the tropical night breeze in the rigging,
ith now and again the creak of a sheave as the light
ving of the swell hove the great ship very gently to
indward, and brought an extra strain upon the taut
ieets.

GOING ALOFT.

Some time ago, when the Queen was at Osborne, her Majesty visited a troopship in her yacht the *Alberta*. Her Majesty's ship *Hector*, lying in Cowes Roads, manned yards in honour of the royal presence. One of the men got as high as the main truck and stood upon it. The main truck is a small circular platform—varying in diameter, of course, according to the size of the ship·· fixed on the royal masthead, the highest point of the mast. Sometimes it has holes in it, through which halliards are rove for hoisting flags. The trucks of the *Hector*, I was told, are furnished with iron staffs, so that the sailor who stood on the main truck had something to lay hold of. But this diminishes nothing of the wonder of the feat. The nerve required coolly to stand upon a small circumference at a prodigious elevation is one thing; the more extraordinary feature of that achievement lies, it would strike a landsman, in the man's getting over and on to the truck, and then kneeling and swinging himself off it and down upon the royal rigging. In the fine old song of the "Leap for Life," the skipper's son gets upon the main truck and stands there, holding on with his eyelids. To save his life he is ordered to jump, and the dog follows him overboard and picks him up. The order to that boy was a sensible one, for though it is perfectly true that he had managed to get upon the truck, it was really impossible that he should get off it without falling.

In truth, going aloft is one of the hardest parts of the sea-life at the first start. Seamen who were active, courageous men enough, have told me that it took them months to vanquish their nervousness; and many a young fellow has given up the sea after the first voyage simply because he never could overcome the purely physical infirmity of giddiness the moment he had his feet in the ratlines. In "Redburn," one of Herman Merivale's delightful sea tales, this weakness is illustrated in an incident narrated with wonderful power. A young man, named Harry Bolton, ships for the return voyage from Liverpool. He is rated as an ordinary seaman, but his friend notices that when any work has to be done aloft, Harry is always busy about the belaying pins, making fast the clewlines, etc. At last he candidly owns to his friend that he has made a private trial of it, and that he cannot go aloft; that his nerves would not allow of it. But this does not save him. One day the mate ordered him to mount to the main truck and un-reeve the short signal halliards. Where the ends of the halliards came is not stated, but one might think that the royal yard would have been high enough for the unfortunate young man to have clambered, even if the crosstrees would not have done. Be this as it may, Harry Bolton hesitates, is rope's-ended by the mate, finally springs into the main-rigging and gets as high as the maintop. When there he looks down, and his heart instantly fails him. The pitiless mate thereupon orders a Dutch sailor to follow and help him up, which the Dutchman does with his head, butting at the base of his back and hoisting him along in that way. "Needs must," continues the narrator, "when the devil drives; and higher and higher, with Max bumping him at every step, went my unfortunate friend. At last he gained the royal yard, and the thin signal halliards—scarcely bigger than common twine—were flying in the wind. 'Unreeve,' cried the mate; I saw Harry's arm stretched out—his legs seemed shaking in the rigging, even to us down on deck; and at last, thank heaven! the deed was done. He came down pale as death, with bloodshot eyes and every limb quivering."

Sailors will know there is no exaggeration in all this. Some beginners will run up aloft like monkeys, others will get into the shrouds and stand there, hanging back and looking up, and holding on as if they meant, to use an old sea phrase, to squeeze all the tar out of the ropes. There is not, perhaps, any worse cruelty practised on board ship than that of driving a nervous lad aloft. In former times there was a custom called pricking—a sailor got behind a boy and forced him up by digging into him with a pin or a "pricker." It is, perhaps, scarcely worth while, nowadays, to speak of such things —the sailing ship is dying out, and the steamer gives but little work to do aloft; but there are few men who have followed the sea who cannot recall cases of exquisite suffering in nervous boys hurried and pricked and thrust up the rigging. One instance I remember—that of a lad of thirteen, who was shipped in an Australian port. He was ordered on to the foreroyal yard along with another youngster. It was his first journey up the masts, and when he was half-way up the shrouds he came to a dead stop. The boatswain sung out to him to look alive and go on. The poor little chap, with shaking hands and a face like the foam alongside, footed it as high as the futtock shrouds, where he halted, looking up at the overhanging platform of the top. "Over you go," shouted the boatswain from the forecastle. "I can't, sir; indeed I can't, sir!" cried the little fellow piteously. "We'll see about that," said the boatswain, and called to an ordinary seaman to help him up. This youth was a brute, and when he reached the clinging boy he began to pinch him in the legs, and pulled out his sheath-knife and threatened to stab him if he did not go over the top. It was a big top, the angle of the mast—the wind being abaft the beam—was a small one, and the futtock shrouds stretched away from the boy like the ribs of an open umbrella from the stick. The miserable little fellow, terrified by the sight of the knife behind him, laid hold of the long irons and made a swing with his legs at the ratlines, missed them, vibrated a moment or two like a pendulum, and then dropped past the outstretched hand of the sailor below him like a flash, striking the shrouds, and rebounding as a ball might overboard. He was drowned, of course.

But as steamers multiply and the number of sailing ships decreases, going aloft will become the least and most infrequent of sea duties. Practical seamanship, in the old sense, is bound to die out, because there is no need to preserve it. It was only the other day that an old skipper assured me that he was acquainted with the mate of a steamer who did not know what a harness-cask was, "and, worst of all, sir," cried my friend, "he's not ashamed of his ignorance." It is true that harness-casks have not much to do with seamanship; but one may excuse a shipmaster of the old school for taking a very gloomy view of the contemporary marine when he meets a man holding a master mariner's certificate, ignorant of the receptacle in which Jack's salt horse is kept when he is at sea. Most of the steamers nowadays are monkey-rigged, many of them with pole-masts, which are useful mainly as derricks upon which a little bit of fore and aft canvas will be hoisted to steady the vessels. What should men who serve in such ships know about going aloft? Even a landsman may comprehend the emotion excited in a seaman who has passed his life in sailing ships when he sees sailors without any spars or rigging to attend to, and with nothing to do but to wash decks down. Nearly all the work of the traditional mariner lies aloft, and to reflect upon Jack without dead-eyes to turn in, chafing gear to look after, reef-points to knot, rigging to tar, masts to stay, studdingsail gear to reeve, and the like, is almost as confounding as to think of him sleeping aft, eating fresh meat throughout the run, and going to the steward for a can of filtered water, instead of to the capstan for his eight bells caulker of fiery black rum. No doubt things are pleasanter as they are. It must be nice to turn in with the certainty of having the whole of your watch below, instead of going to bed in your sea-boots in readiness for the thundering of a handspike, and the cruel roar of "All hands shorten sail!" And yet, to the true sailor, going aloft is so much the part of his life, it is so complete a condition of his vocation, that when such a man finds himself aboard a steamer with nothing to take notice of above his head, it may be supposed that at the first going off he is as fully bewildered as a steamer's man—that is, a man who has never served in anything but steamers—would be among the ropes of a full-rigged ship, taken aback with her studding sails abroad. He will miss the old songs at the reef tackles, the flapping of canvas, the thud of coils of halliards and clew-lines flung down on deck, the springing into the shrouds, the helter-skelter for the weather caring, or the ascent of the topgallant mast that jumps to the flogging of the clewed-up sails.

There is a touch of wild excitement in going aloft in heavy weather, which no seaman can be insensible to; just as in a calm day or night a man may find a strange pleasure in lingering a few moments aloft after he has done his work, and looking down. The labour of reefing has been greatly diminished by the double topsail yards, which halve the great sails, so that when the halliards of the upper yards are let go, the ship is under close-reefed topsails. Moreover, there is only half the weight of the sail to handle in reefing or stowing. This valuable contrivance makes the task of shortening sail light in comparison with what the labour was in the days of the whole topsail. Old seamen will remember what that kind of canvas involved in a ship of fourteen or fifteen hundred tons, manned by about eighteen or twenty men, capable of doing sailors' work aloft.

It is the second dog watch. The royals and mizzen-topgallant sail have been furled, but the wind comes in freshening puffs, the sky has a menacing look away out on the starboard beam, and at eight bells all hands are kept on deck to roll up the mainsail and topgallant sails, and tie a single reef in the fore and mizzen topsails. The sea washes noisily against the weather bow, and the night settles down as black as a pocket; but the ship is tolerably snug, there is no great weight of wind as yet, and the watch below are dismissed to the forecastle. They have been an hour in their hammocks or bunks, when, on a sudden, the scuttle is rudely flung open, and a loud cry summons them on deck. They are up in a moment, scarcely waiting to pull on their jackets, for the instant they are awake they perceive that the vessel is on her beam ends, and they can hear the thunder of

a gale of wind raging overhead.   All three topsail
halliards have been let go, and the watch are yelling out
at the reef-tackles, the skipper shouting at the mizzen-
rigging, the chief mate bawling from the break of the
poop, and the second mate and boatswain roaring in the
waist and on the forecastle.   The sea is flying heavily
over the weather rail of the prostrate ship, and adding
its peculiar bursting noise to the din of the furiously-
shaken canvas, to the deafening booming of the wind,
and the hoarse long-drawn cries of the sailors hauling
upon the ropes.   You can barely see the weather shrouds,
though to leeward their black lines are plain enough
against the washing heights of foam which swell up as
high as the rail of the bulwarks.   You do not feel the
force of the gale until you are in the rigging, and then
for a spell the iron-hard pressure of it pins you against
the shrouds as if you had been made a spread-eagle.
The rain drives along in slashing horizontal lines, and
you see the sparkle of the deluge over the skylight where
the light of the cabin lamp is shining; or, maybe, the
gale is charged with sleet and hail, and the cold so
tautens your fingers that you can scarcely curl them to
the shape of the rope you grasp.   Over the top you
swarm in company with the rest of your watch, perhaps
getting a blow on the head from the heel of some fellow
above you as you lay yourself backwards to swing over
the futtock shrouds; and then, finding the weather side
of the topsail yard with as many hands on it as are
needed, you pass over to leeward, where you find the
boatswain or third mate astride of the yard-arm, ready
for the cry of " Haul out to leeward," to pass the earing.
At such a time as this a man has too much to do to
look about him; the ship is brought close to shake the
sail, that the men may get the reef-bands against the

yard, otherwise the canvas stands out to the force of the gale in a surface as round as St. Paul's dome, and so hard and tense that it would serve as a platform for a ball-room.

In the whole-topsail days I have seen half a dozen men standing upon the canvas in the slings and quarters trying to stamp the sail down to bring the reef points within reach without so much as dinting the wind-swollen convexity. Still it is possible to knot a reef-point, and take a look round and below. It is a wonderful scene; no landsman can conceive of its wild and awful majesty. The ship surges heavily through the black heavings, and with every headlong plunge fills a wide circumference of the far-down ebony waters with a furious swirling of foam, in the midst of which her long narrow shape is distinctly visible. Overhead is a dim vision of naked spars and yards, reeling in the boisterous void in whose gloom it is just possible to trace the outline of huge black clouds rushing past like folds of swiftly-carried smoke. The yard on which you stand is at an angle of thirty or thirty-five degrees, and every lean-down of the slender fabric that supports the immense superstructure of masts threatens to submerge the point of it, astride of which—riding it as a horse—sits the seaman who takes the lee-earing; and his figure and that of the fellow beneath swinging on the flemish-horse, and those of the row of men who overhang the yard, and who chorus with a kind of shriek that rings athwart the yelling of the gale to the cry from the weather yard-arm of "Light over to windward!" are marked like pen-and-ink drawings upon white paper against the snow of the seas which stretch from the ship's side into the darkness.

But this is only one aspect of "going aloft." Another

—if the bowsprit and jibbooms may be included under the head of the word "aloft"—is that of laying out to furl, let me say the outer jib, when it has come on to blow hard enough to make the stowing of that sail necessary. From the masthead you see the ship under you; you can watch her hull flying through the sea, mark the glorious white of the foam that bursts from her bows and races in a broad band astern, and behold the ship in her noble solitude amid the tenantless world of waters whose pale green skirts lean against the hazy azure of the remote heavens. But on the jibboom you have the ship rushing at you, as it were; her cutwater seems to bear right down upon you; you see her coppered forefoot gleaming with a greenish tinge through the glass-clear water whose surface it divides into two feather-shaped fountains, whose seething and hissing and prismatic summits arch away from the glossy bends. And now, as she dips with a glorious rush into the hollow over whose yawning gloom you are poised as you overhang the jibboom, the half-buried bows break the sea into smoke, and yeast, and snow; the white and hissing mass, splendid with sunshine or rendered more vivid yet by the dark green of the seas along which it is sent rolling, roars and runs ahead of the ship as far as the flying jibboom, where its impetus fails and the soaring vessel swings over it, rising almost noiselessly over the thick froth, and in a breath it is passed, whilst you look down along the sloping deck from the forked-up boom and mark how like a creature of instinct the noble ship seems to be gathering herself together for the next headlong jump, her copper shining to windward, her black sides lustrous as a curried hide with the whirling spray, her leaning masts full of thunder on high, the white sails hard and still as carven marble, no sound reaching you but the regular wash of the spurned and trampled waters under the bows, the rude and clear moaning of the wind in the rigging, and the complaining of massive timbers as the stem of the ship lengthens in a steady upheaval, and then crushes down until the torn and sobbing billows of foam are flashing their white feathers over the head-boards. Or jump aloft to loose, let us say, the mizzen royal after the tropical squall has gone away to leeward, and left the clear moon shining in a purified heaven of indigo, and striking a cone of silver glory in the dark sea whose northern waters are studded with flakes of light from the great stars. It is the middle watch; you have overhauled your clewlines, the yard has been hoisted over your head, you come down the topgallant rigging into the crosstrees, and linger there a few moments. All is silent on deck; the helmsman stands motionless at the wheel; you hear the faint jar of the tiller chains; you mark the delicate nimbus of light round the binnacle hood. Nowhere is the mystery wrought by the magical beams of the moon felt so much as at sea. The pearl-like radiance steeps the fabric of the ship in an atmosphere of soft light as illusive as the clouds of phosphorescent fires which break from her sides as she leans with the swell. The movements of the sails are like the flapping of phantom wings; and not a sigh of air, not a sound of chafing rope, not a voice calling suddenly from the distant deck, but seems to take from the moonlight and the measure. less and impenetrable spaces of the deep, and the immense and enfolding silence of those far-off waters, a character of unreality that makes them seem the very phantasm and mockery of the things they veritably are.

A man might linger a long hour at the altitude of the crosstrees among the shadows of the moonlit, placid ocean night without weariness. Better than the loftiest and loneliest cliff is the mast head of a ship for the surveyal of the sublime and mighty surface on which she floats, for you rock in unison with the breathings of the deep; you are upon her great heart, and every beat of it is marked by a stately motion of the towering masts against the stars; phosphoric outlines of huge fish haunt the sluggish wake; or a sound as of a long, deep-drawn respiration denotes the neighbourhood of a leviathan whose vast proportions, as they heave in the broad silver stream of moonlight, resemble the hull of a ship keel up, driven to the surface by some hidden power and slowly settling downwards again.

These are some of the excitements and some of the quiet pleasures of " going aloft." It is, no doubt, a highly sentimental view of the duty, and sailors who have had to let go the reef points, and beat their hands against the yards to drive life enough into their fingers to enable them to hold on, may consider that a very different representation of that kind of work would recommend itself a good deal more than this to their experience. Very possibly. But retrospection is apt to make us tender; and since " going aloft" must in the course of time—unless the shipbuilders change their minds—become a thing of the past, it is worth while spending a few minutes in trying to discover what there was of poetry and the picturesque in that old obligation of the marine life in the discharge of which the English sailor has always proved a shining example to all mariners. Even now—in these days when the steam-engine has so eaten into our maritime habits that a sailing-ship is looked upon as a kind of wonder of other times—do we not find Jack doing honour to his Queen by standing erect upon the main truck? But, oh! master mariners,

mates, boatswains, and able seamen, all you who have
youngsters under your charge or among you as shipmates, have mercy upon the timid lad, give him time
to feel his way aloft, show him the lubber's hole, and
remember that many a first-rate sailor has faltered at
the outset, and gazed with horror and despair at those
giddy heights whose summits seemed to his boyish gaze
to pierce the sky.

I REMEMBER a seaman, who had served for years both in sailing and steamships, telling me that never in all his life did he remember the like of the impression produced upon him one night when he was at the helm of a large ocean passenger steamer. He described the darkness; the occasional scattering of red sparks blown low down upon the sea on the lee beam; the glimmer of white water here and there out in the windy gloom; the silence aboard the vessel, disturbed only by the muffled beating of the engines and the seething of water washing in snow from under the bows; and he told me how all these things, combined with the thought that under his feet there lay sleeping a whole crowd of men and women, made him feel as though he and the ship and the great wind-swept shadow through which she was speeding, were portions of a phantom world, and that nothing was real and sentient but the compass, whose illuminated card stood out upon the gloom like a composant at a ship's yard-arm.

I can conceive of many a strange, fanciful thought coming into a sailor's mind as he stands grasping the wheel in the lonely night watch, and I say this with a plentiful knowledge of the seaman's prosaic and unsentimental character. A man must be but a very short way removed from a four-footed animal not to feel at times

the wonderful and subduing spell which the ocean will
fling over the human soul; and being at the wheel will
give him the best chance of yielding to the nameless
witchery, for at such a time—in most cases—he is alone,
no one accosts him, the gloom falls down and blots out
the figure of the officer of the watch, and completes the
deep sense of solitude that is to be got from a spell at
the helm on a dark and quiet night at sea. I cannot
but think that the spirit of the deep is brought, at such
a time, nearer to you aboard a sailing than aboard a
steamship. The onward-rushing fabric that is impelled
by engines demands incessant vigilance; she may be off
her course even in the time that a man takes to lift his
eyes to mark a flying meteor; there are no moments of
rest. But in a sailing-ship you have the moonlit night
and burnished swell heaving up in lines of ebony out
of the visionary horizon, where the stars are wanly
winking, until it rolls in billows of sparkling quicksilver
under the wake of the bland and beautiful luminary;
there is not a breath of air aloft, though little creepings
of wind circle softly about the decks as the pallid surfaces of canvas swing in and out with the leaning of
the ship; the moonlight lies in pools of light upon the
planks, and every shadow cast upon those pearl-like
surfaces is as black and sharp and clear as a tracing in
ink; the after portions of the sails are dark as bronze,
but looking at them forward they rise into the air like
pieces of white satin, soaring into a stately edifice full
of delicate hurrying shadows which resemble the streaky
lustre on the inside of an oyster-shell as the cloths swell
out or hollow in with the drowsy motion, and crowned
with the little royals, which seem to melt even as the
eye watches them like summer clouds upon the heaven
of stars.

Moments of such repose as this you will get in a sailing-ship. Who that has stood at the wheel at such a time but remembers the soft patter of reef-points upon the canvas, the frosty twinkling of the dew upon the skylights and rail, the hollow sob of the swell under the counter as the ship heaves her stern, and the tiller-chains rattle, and the wheel jumps to the echo of the groan of the rudder-head? It is the middle watch; eight bells were struck a quarter of an hour since; the watch on deck are forward, coiled away anywhere, and nothing stirs on the forecastle; the officer on duty walks the starboard side of the deck, for the yards are braced to port, and that makes a weather deck where the mate is pacing, sleepily scratching the back of his head, and casting drowsy glances aloft and at the sea. The moon is low in the west, and has changed her silver into copper, and will be gone soon. The calm is wonderfully expressed by the reflection she drops; the mirrored radiance streams towards you like a river of pallid gold, narrow at the horizon and broadening, fan-shaped, until it seems within a biscuit's throw of the ship, where it vanishes in a fine haze; but on either hand of it the water is as black as ink, while the lustre of the moon has quenched the stars all about her, and left the sky in which she hangs as dark as the ocean.

The setting orb carries the mind with it. The eye will seek the light, and it is a kind of instinct that makes a man watch the sinking of the moon at sea, when there is a deep repose in the air and nothing to hinder his thoughts from following the downward-sailing orb. Many a time have I watched her, and thought of the old home she would be shining upon; the loved scenes she would be making beautiful with her holy light. There is nothing in life that gives one such a

sense of distance, of infinite remoteness, as the setting
of the sun or moon at sea. It defines the immeasurable
leagues of water which separate you from those you love
with a sharpness that is scarcely felt at other times. It
is the only mark upon the circle of the ocean, and courts
you into a reckoning which there is something too vague
in the bare and infinite horizon to invite. As one bell
strikes the moon rests her lower limb upon the horizon,
and her reflection shortens away from the ship's side as
the red fragment of disc sinks behind the black water-
line. In a few seconds nothing but a speck of light
that glows like a live ember is visible ; and when that is
quenched the faint saffron tinge that hung about the sky
when the moon was setting dies out and the whole circumference of the ocean is full of the blackness of night.

The ship makes but a ghostly shape. The stars are
there, but a haze floats like a veil under them ; the
diamond-dust that glittered in the hollow caverns of the
firmament is eclipsed, and the planets are rayless and
sickly in their defined and blueish-coloured forms. A
fold of deeper darkness seems to have swept along in the
wake of the vanished moon, and the officer of the watch
coming up to the binnacle takes a brief look at the card,
and then goes to the quarter and stands there softly
whistling, while the canvas aloft echoes with a louder
note, and the rolling of the ship breaks the water under
her counter into foam that seethes sharply and expires
quickly. Black as the water is out on the starboard
bow you notice a shadow upon it that gives a fresh
shade, a further profundity, to the jetty obscurity, and
in a few moments the sails aloft fall asleep as though
the wand of a magician had been waved over the
swaying spars and a soft air comes blowing over the
rail.

"All aback forrards!" rings out a hoarse voice, and the cry finds an echo in the hollow canvas. The mate runs along the deck bawling out orders to flatten in the head-sheets and square the after yards, and so forth; the men come out of a dozen corners, coils of rigging are flung down, songs are raised, sheaves squeal as the yards are swung, topsail sheets rattle, and all is bustle and hurry. Meanwhile the wind freshens with a moan in the gathering gust, and the ship leans under it as her headsails fill, and she pays off. Presently the yards are braced round, the vessel brought to her course, and the wind is found to be a point free. The decks are still full of life, tacks have to be boarded, "small pulls" are wanted here and there, and the running gear has to be coiled away; the light from the binnacle lamp puzzles your eye, and when you lift your gaze from the illuminated card the darkness seems to stand around you like a wall; but the compass is there to tell you that the ship heads her course. You would know with your eyes blindfolded, by the mere feel of the helm, that everything is drawing, and amidst the calls of the mate and the songs of the sailors you can hear the sloppy sound of flat falls of water under the weather bow, and the hiss of exploding bubbles, and the faint wash of froth churned up by the rudder below you.

Two bells are struck, and all is quiet once more. The skipper has been on deck, talked with the mate, pushed his bronzed face betwixt you and the binnacle, and after a few turns and several prolonged looks aloft and around the sea, has gone below again. The wind has steadily freshened, and the ship, under all plain sail, heels amid the darkness like a leaning column of white vapour. So softly she sweeps through the snow with which she girdles her shapely length, curtseying with queenly

grace as she runs over the long-drawn undulations out
of whose inky coils the wind is striking phosphoric
sparks, that she steers herself; you have nothing to do
but keep hold of the spokes, and let the breeze blow the
noble fabric along. The deep gloom is full of strange
sounds now that the seamen are forward, and all is
silent aft.

A spirit-like minstrelsy echoes down from the glimmering inclined heights like a far-off chorus of human voices;
the wind is full of the mysterious sound. It does not
appear to come from the ship, but from a group of invisible ghostly creatures sailing through the air over the
mastheads, and setting the moaning voices and sobbing
wash of the ocean to melodies which may easily seem
to make this darkness belong to the night of a world
peopled by phantoms and creatures without similitude
in human knowledge. Hark! how plaintive is the song
of the bow-wave that falls in an arch of green fire from
the shearing stem, and rolls aft in a white swirl, inter-
laced with fitful and sullen flashes of phosphoric light!
But the breeze freshens yet; you cannot count a dozen
stars in the void of gloom overhead, the music aloft
takes a clearer note, straining sounds are audible as the
passing swell rolls the ship to windward, the white water
under the main sheet rises closer to the scuppers and
flashes fast and far from under the counter into the
blackness over the stern. An order is sharply bawled
out, and some hands come tumbling aft and jump into
the mizzen rigging to roll up the cross-jack. A hoarse
song reaches you from the forecastle as the flying jib
downhaul is manned, and at the same moment the fore
and mizzen royal halliards are let go. You hear this
canvas flapping in the gloom amid the chorus of the
men on the crossjack yard as they trice up the bunt.

There must be no more wool-gathering with you now. The wheel is giving you as much work as you want; every now and again a smart kick stiffens your arms into iron, and you begin to feel that your jacket will have to come off soon.

For some time nothing more is done, but the watch keep on their feet and stand about ready for the next call, which they know will not be long delayed. The sea to windward is full of white glancings, and the breaking heads make a vague light of their own which gives you a sight of the water for some distance. The canvas that has been taken off the ship counts for nothing; the main royal is still on her, and she is heeling over like a racing yacht, striking the bow swell with a stem that hisses like red-hot iron, and shattering the coils of liquid jet into foam, which widens out on either hand of her into a storm of snow, in the midst of which the flying hull of the vessel is as clearly traced as were the shadows of her rigging in the moonlight, while her iron-hard distended canvas is full of the low thunder of the pouring blast, and her forecastle is dark with flying spray that sweeps over the rail and strikes the deck like a hail storm. It is noble sailing, and this booming and hooting ocean night wind is something to be made the most of while it lasts; but it gives you at the wheel as much occupation as you relish. It is like drawing teeth to " meet her " as the swell sweeps the ship round; and at last the captain, who is again on deck, and who has been standing at the binnacle for five minutes, sings out for another hand to come aft to the wheel. A figure tumbles along in a hurry and stations himself to lee-ward of you; and thereupon your work, though it is by no means half as easy again, becomes considerably lighter than it was. " Hold on a minute, Bill," says your mate, and he feels over his pocket for a chew of tobacco. The quid found and properly stowed away in his cheek, your companion resumes his grasp of the wheel, and in the haze of the binnacle lamp you may see his leathern jaws working like an old cow chewing the cud as he mumbles over the black fragment, sometimes directing a doleful squint at the compass, sometimes looking astern, while he helps you to put the wheel up or down, that you may keep the course swinging fair with the lubber's mark.

But the ship is being overdriven. At one bell it was a dead calm; it is not three bells yet, and here is the sea white with wind, and the vessel roaring through the smother with the blast thundering like a hurricane in the sails.

"In main royal and mizzen topgallant sail."

The canvas rattles like an old waggon over a stony street as the clewlines are manned, and whilst furling it the foretopgallant halliards are let go. What other sails are taken in you do not know, for the ship wants much clever watching, and the skipper is at hand to bring you up with a round turn if the vessel should be a quarter of a point off her course. Being eased, she steers more comfortably, but whole topsails and courses and main-topgallant sail are rushing her through it fiercely; the water on her lee quarter is pretty nearly as high as her main brace bumpkin, and the billow there goes along with her as if it were a part of the vessel; the main tack groans under the tearing and rending pull of the huge convex surface of canvas; now and again the blow of the swell which the racing vessel hits laterally makes her tremble fore and aft like a house under a clap of thunder. But she is to have all she can bear; the spell of dead calm is to be atoned for;

and so on through the shrilling and echoing darkness rushes the great fabric, sweeping her pallid canvas through the folds of gloom like the pinions of some vast spirit of the deep, making the water roar past her as she goes, breaking the dark swell into fire and foam as she rushes through the liquid acclivities with her powerful stem, with notes of mad laughter and lamentable wailing in her rigging, and with streaming decks which hollowly echo the fall of the solid bodies of water which shoot up just before the weather fore-rigging, and roll in a rush of creaming white into the lee scuppers as far aft as the break of the poop.

At last you hear the welcome sound of four bells; your trick is up, the wheel is relieved, and catching your jacket off the grating abaft the helm you walk forward, wiping the perspiration from your forehead; and, dropping down the fore scuttle, grope about for your pipe, which you light at the slush lamp that swings from a grimy beam, and returning on deck squat somewhere out of the way of the wind and wet, earnestly hoping that if it is to be a case of "reef topsails" there will be time for you to have your smoke out before the order is thundered forth.

THE BAILIFF AT SEA.

SOME time ago I heard that a bailiff had been carried off to sea whilst in the execution of his duty. Anxious to learn the nature of his voyage, how he fared, and what condition he was in, mentally and physically, when restored to his anxious relatives, I made inquiries, and my diligence was at last rewarded by meeting the mate of the vessel that had sailed away with the man. Truth obliges me to own that this mate was not what might be considered a very gentlemanly person. It was not his velvet waistcoat, nor a rather vicious squint, nor a striking-looking bald head ringed with a layer of red hair like a grummet of rope yarns; the want of genteel-ness was noticeable in his abundant use of what is called "langwidge." "If I were a bailiff," thought I, as I glanced at his immense hands and huge arms which swelled out his coat-sleeves like the wind in a sailor's smallcloths drying in a strong breeze on the forestay, "I should not like to be put 'in possession' of a house occupied by *you*, my hearty."

I took a seat opposite him and said, "So you're the mate of the vessel that stole away the county court man?"

"Right," said he looking at me, without a move in his face; "but don't you go and say that I'm the mate

as gave him up again. If I'd had my way he'd be in
charge o' any goods he might have come across in the
inside of a whale by this time. I'd ha' chucked him
overboard, as sure as that there hand's on this table,"
and down came a very leg-of-mutton of a fist with a blow
that jerked his tumbler into the air. It was as good as
a hint that the glass wanted filling; and when this was
done, my companion opened the top buttons of his warm
and tight velvet waistcoat, and composed himself into a
posture for conversation.

"How," asked I, "came your skipper to have a
bailiff aboard his vessel?"

"You may ask how," he growled; "what I say is,
what right had he to come? I've got nothing to say
against the law as it works for them as lives ashore—
for them as are in fixed houses, and can't sail away with
any blooming old rag of a chap, in a greasy coat, as
come in with a bit of paper, and takes a cheer, and says,
'Here I sit, mates, till I'm paid off.' But what has the
likes of such scowbanks got to do with sailor men when
once they're aboard? What I say is, that when a man's
on the water, his chest stowed away, articles signed, all
the law that consarns him is in the cabin. The capt'n'
the law; and not only the law, but judge, magistrate,
bailiff, husher, registrar, high chancellor, and Lord Mayor
o' London on top of it; and my argument is that any man
as takes the liberty to walk over a wessel's side and
order the captain about, and sing out contrairy orders,
and threaten to have him purged (I heard that very word.
'Ye'll have to purge for this,' says the bailiff. Did ye
ever hear such language applied to a captain?)—any
man, I say, as takes such a liberty as that ought to be
dropped overboard without asking 'by your leave,' and,
as I said before, left to take possession of any goods he

come across in the inside of a fish or at the bottom of
the ocean."

I waited until he had partially quenched his excitement by a long pull at his tumbler, and then asked him
again how it happened that his vessel had been boarded
by a bailiff.

"I'll tell you," he answered. "The wessel was a
brig of 300 tons. Coming home she plumped into a
schooner. It was the schooner's fault; we sung out to
her to get out of the road; instead of doing which she
ported her helm as if to provoke us, and in we went,
doing her a deal of damage and carrying away our own
jibboom. Well, we arrived in port and discharged, and
then filled up again with coal. It was Toosday afternoon, the sky middling dirty, and a fresh breeze of wind
blowing. We hauled out and lay at a mooring buoy,
waiting for the tide to serve. I was talking to the
captain when I took notice of a boat coming along, rowed
by a couple o' watermen, and a chap in a chimbley-pot
hat sitting in the starn sheets.

"'Is that boat for us?' says the captain, looking.

"'Why,' I says, 'it looks as if she meant to run us
down. Is it a wager? Bust me if hever I saw watermen
pull like that afore!'

"They were dragging on their oars as if they would
spring 'em, lying back until nothing but their noses was
to be seen above the gunwale, and making the water fly
in clouds over the cove in the starn as if prompt drowning was too good for him, and he was to be smothered
slow. They dashed alongside, hooked on, and the fellow
in the chimbley-pot hat comes scraping over the rail,
shaking himself free o' the water as he tumbled on to the
deck like a Newfoundland dog.

"'Just in time, captain,' says he, with an impudent

D

kind o' smile, rummaging in his side-pocket; and with that he houts with a sort of dockiment, and hands it to the skipper.

" 'What's this?' says the skipper, smelling round the paper as it might be, but never offering to touch it.

" 'Only a horder for you to return to the bosom of your family,' he says, ' as the date o' your sailing's not yet fixed.'

" 'Isn't it?' says the captain, breathing short. ' Who are you, and what d'ye want?'

" 'I'm a bailiff,' says the man; ' and I'm here to take charge o' this wessel, pending the haction that's been entered against her in the Hadmiralty side o' the County Court by the schooner as ye was in collision with.'

" 'Can ye swim?' asks the captain.

" 'Never you mind whether I can or not,' says the bailiff, looking round at us, for all hands was collected and listening their hardest.

" 'Because,' says the captain, ' if you can't swim you'd better turn to and hail that boat to come back again and put ye ashore.'

" 'No, no,' says the bailiff, ' I'm not going ashore, my friend. I'm here to take charge o' this brig and stop her from going to sea.'

" Had the captain chosen then and there to give orders for that bailiff to be dropped overboard, I believe I'm the man as would have executed the command. Taking the temper I was then in, I don't know anything that would ha' given me more satisfaction to perform. The aggravation of being stopped when we were all ready to get away was the least part of it: it was the bailiff's cool grins, the impudence in his eyes as he looked round, as much as to say, ' All what I see is mine,' his taking the skipper's place and saying ye shan't do this, and I won't allow that, that made me want to lay hands upon him. The captain stared at him a bit, as if considering what he should do ; then turning to me, he asked me the time. I told him.

"'In another quarter of an hour,' says he, 'loose the torpsails and make ready to get away.'

"'You'd better not,' says the bailiff ; 'it'll be gross contempt of court if you do.'

"'Court!' says the skipper. 'Court! there is no court here, Mr. Bailiff. This is a brig, not a court. Don't talk of courts to me. The gross contempt is of your committing. How dare you stand there ordering of me ?'

"'Rest assured,' says the bailiff, 'you'll be punished if you don't do what I say. You'll have to purge in open court, and that's a job that may cost ye enough to lay you up in the union for the rest of your natural days.'

"'Stow that,' says I, doubling up my fist and stepping close to the fellow ; 'if the captain stands that kind o' jaw, *I* won't.'

"'I'm here in the hexecution of my duty,' says the bailiff, dropping his confident grins, and beginning to grow whitish. 'Whatever you do contrairy to my orders you'll do at your peril.'

"And so saying he walks right aft, and sits on the taffrail with his arms folded.

"Never was any quarter of an hour longer than that which the captain told me to wait. I had my watch in my hand, and all the time I was afraid the skipper would change his mind and give in to the bailiff, who sat aft with his hat over his ears, looking at the shore with his little eyes.

"'Time's up, sir!' I bawled to the captain.

"'Loose the torpsails,' he sings out, and in a moment

all hands were running about, sheeting home, and yelling
out at the ropes, being as much afeard as I was that if
we were not quick the sight of the dogged bailiff 'ud
operate upon the skipper's hintellect and stop our just
rewenge upon that funkshonary's audacity. The bailiff
seeing the men at work, tumbles off the taffrail and comes
running forrards.

"'D'ye mean to say you don't intend to obey the
law?' he shouts out, holding on to his chimbley-pot.

"'Out of the ways!' answers the skipper, 'there's no
room for law here. We're full up, mate; and since ye're
bound for a voyage, blow your nose and wave your hand
to them as ye're a parting from!' and, as he says this,
the wessel, catching the wind that was coming strong
enough to make nothing above our topsails necessary,
lays down to it, and we heads for the open water.

"I saw the bailiff staring wildly around him, as if he
really *would* jump overboard, and it was worth a month's
pay to see him looking like that, and holding his hat on.

"'Why, man,' he shouts to the captain, 'you're
never in earnest: d'ye know what you're a doing of?'
and, finding that the skipper took no notice, he calls out to
the men, 'You'll work this vessel at your peril if you
obey your captain. My orders are to stop this brig, and
if you don't allow me to execute my duty——' But just as
he came to this the wessel met the first of the seas which
were rolling outside the harbour—stiff seas they wos, for
it was blowing half a gale o' wind; she put her nose into
it, and then rolled over, fit to bring her lower yardarms
into the water; away flew the bailiff's chimbley-pot hat
clean overboard, and ye may boil me alive if I didn't
think he meant to follow it; for the send o' the wessel
tripped him over the weather hatch coamings, and he
seemed to shoot—ay, as neatly as if he'd been kicked by

one of them giants I used to read about when I was a little 'un—clean into the lee scuppers, where he lay stunned as I thought, until all on a sudden he jumped up and went clawing along till he come to the lee o' the after deck house, where he squatted down, looking with his yaller face and blowing hair like a Madagascar monkey recovering from a fit of intoxication."

Here my companion broke into a loud laugh, which he repeated again and again, as if the thoughts awakened in his mind were of too exquisite a kind to be dismissed with a single guffaw.

" I don't know," he continued, after a bit, wiping his eyes, and then fixing his dismal and malignant squint upon me, "whether on the whole we should ha' done better by dropping him overboard. The brig was as deep as pretty nigh twice her tonnage in coal could make her ; she was a wet boat at any time ; but now she tumbled about as if she had made up her mind to drown herself. I reckon she knew she had a bailiff aboard. Every dip forrards threw the water over her head in oceans ; she'd roll to wind'ard almost as heavily as to leeward, so that the decks was all awash, and I was looking and hoping all the time to see the bailiff fetch away. But there was enough law left in him to keep him holding on. I was standing to wind'ard of the house—the skipper being aft agin the wheel—when Mr. Bailiff comes staggering round, his breeches clinging to his legs like wet brown paper, and his shoes full o' water.

" ' Hallo, shipmate ! ' I sings out, seeing him making for the cabin door, ' where are you bound to ? Aren't you happy where you are ? '

" ' I'm going to lie down on one of the lockers,' says he. ' I feel half froze, and I shall be sick presently.'

"'You may be half froze and sick too,' says I, 'but smother me, Mr. Bailiff, if you shall use the cabin.'

"'Not use the cabin?' says he, gaping at me, and talking as if there was something in his swaller; 'd'ye mean to keep me on deck all night?'

"'Don't ask no questions,' says I. 'You're here by French leave. Nobody wants you. If I had my way you'd be towing astern, with your neck in a bowline; and if all the rest o' your tribe and the blooming 'tornies you sarve were tailed on in your wake, I'd be willing to woyage round the world, and never grumble if we took years in reaching home.'

"I was in a passion, which rose my woice, and the skipper, hearing me, comes over.

"'Hallo, bailiff!' says he, cheerfully; 'not drowned yet, my lad? What d'ye think o' the weather?'

"'Captain,' says the man, 'you've carried me away by force. D'ye mean to freeze me to death by keeping me on deck all night? Your mate here says I'm not to use the cabin.'

"'Why should he use it, capt'n?' says I. 'Could a sailor man sit with the likes of him? I've messed afore now with Chaneymen; I've slept along with Peruvian beachcombers when the air's been that thick with the smell of onions ye might have leant agin it; but ye may boil me, skipper,' says I, 'if ever I occupied a cabin along with a bailiff afore, and if he's to share that crib along with us, I'll sleep forrards.'

"'You hear that, bailiff,' says the skipper. 'I can't let my mate live forrards to oblige you. If you're cold I dare say the cook 'll let you warm yourself in the galley. But noboby wanted you here. You were not invited, consequently it's not for you to grumble if you don't find yourself perfectly comfortable and happy.'

" But as he says this, Nature fell to manhandling the bailiff as if she'd taken his own trade upon herself, and making one rush he lay over the lee rail so ill that I never saw the equal of it, even in a Frenchman; he twisted himself about just as if he'd been revolving on a corkscrew; the water blowing over the forward weather rail hit him neatly, and he was like a streaming rag in five minutes.

" We left him enjoying himself and went on with our work. It was falling dark, and not only blowing hard, but there was the look of a whole gale of wind in the south-west sky. The brig was making desperate bad weather of it under lower topsails and reefed foresail, taking in the water fit to wash every movable thing overboard, and shoving through it very slowly with a surprising sag to leeward. The skipper went below for some supper, and after a bit he calls me in.

" ' Where's the bailiff?' says he.

" ' Don't know exactly,' I says. ' To leeward somewheres. There's a figure half over the rail just abaft the fore rigging, if that's him.'

" ' I've been tarning it over in my mind,' says the skipper, ' and I've got a notion, William,' says he, ' that we'd ha' done better not to bring that bailiff along with us.'

" ' But he wouldn't go ashore when you told him,' says I.

" ' Quite true,' says the captain; ' but that won't make it better for us. After all, the law's not a thing ye can take liberties with, and there's something in his threat of making me purge in open court, William,' says he, ' which mightn't matter if I knew what it meant; but, being ignorant, I'm willing to think it alarming.'

" ' Pooh,' says I, ' it's only a lawyer's word. There's

nothing in it. They use onintelligible words to scare plain men; but there can't be anything more terrifying in language ye don't understand than in language ye do.'

" ' I wish I had some book aboard that 'ud explain that word,' says he. ' The bailiff 'll know; but I'll not ask him for fear he should think me afraid. But we can't let him starve. Better send him here and let him get something to eat.'

" I was going to argue, but he wouldn't listen.

" ' No, no,' says he, ' send him here; ' and I knew by that that the fear o' the law was beginning to master him.

" Well, it was my duty to obey, so I went on deck, and after rummaging about I found the bailiff sitting up to his hips in water against the scuttle-butt abreast of the galley.

" ' Come along,' says I, ' supper's in the cabin, and the captain wants you there.'

" He stood up, but was so cramped in his timbers that he could scarcely shuffle along, and I had to drag him by the collar. When the captain saw by the lamplight the plight the fellow was in, his heart failed him altogether. There was no more proper dignified scorn.

" ' Why,' says he, looking at him, ' I didn't think it was such a bad job as that,' and he jumped up and fetched him a suit of dry clothes, and then poured out a dose of brandy. This was regular knuckling under. He had gone on con-sidering and con-sidering until he was in an out-and-out funk. There was no use in my saying anything. The bailiff had growd on a sudden to become the strongest man aboard that brig, though as for me, when I tell you that had I been the captain I'd have sent the fellow aloft, and kept him there all night, as a hint

to leave sailor men alone on future occasions, ye'll allow
that *my* caving in wur only because I wasn't skipper,
and that's all. Well, sir, to cut this yarn short, luck
turned in favour of that bailiff with a wengeance. At
midnight it was blowing a hurricane, and the skipper
said there was no good going on facing it, he must put
back.

" ' There's a handier port,' says I, naming it, ' than
the one we're from to make for.'

" ' Ay,' says he, ' but since we're bound to up keeleg
it'll look better to carry the bailiff slick home than to
give him a railway journey.'

" It would have made a hangel growl to hear the
captain, all through fear, placing this bailiff afore the
werry hurricane that was blowing, and thinking of him
only whom he'd ha' gladly drownded a few hours earlier,
instead of the wessel and the lives aboard her. But
reasoning was out of the question. The brig was just a
smother of froth, the gale roaring like thunder, the seas
as high as our maintop, and the old hooker shivering
with every upward heave, as if she must leave all the
lower part of her behind her. It was a job to get the
vessel round, but we managed it, and at half-past five
o'clock in the morning we fetched the harbour we had
started from and brought up, nothing having carried
away but the bailiff's chimbley-pot."

" And what was the result of all this ? " said I.

" Why," said he, with a loud rumbling laugh, " the
skipper had to find out what purging in hopen court
means. He was brought up afore an old gentleman, who
lectured him for about half an hour, said that the law
was meant to be respected and that it would be a bad
job for any man as sneered at it ; and after having talked
out all that lay in his mind, he up and fines the captain

ten pounds and fifty shillings costs. It served him right. He'd no business to bring that bailiff back. But he was hoperated on by the fear o' words, and depend upon it the man who allows that sort of alarm to wisit him is not a fit person to carry a bailiff to sea."

THE passage of the Horn has long ceased to be a thing to boast about. Time was when a man who had doubled that formidable iron headland reckoned he had performed a feat that entitled him to a good deal of respect. This is characteristically shown in "Two Years before the Mast," the author of which dwells at great length upon the struggles of the *Alert* among the ice in latitude 58 deg. South, as though he considered that part of the voyage to be something proper to hand on to posterity in a bulky form. Not so much notice is taken of the achievement nowadays. It still confers privileges; it qualifies a man to "spit to windward," for instance, and no doubt it inspires many a youthful midshipman or apprentice with much big talk and nautical airs in the presence of lads who have yet to see with their own eyes what an Antarctic iceberg is like.

But the passage of the Horn is much too common an occurrence in these days to inflate anything but a boy. In Dana's time a ship was a wonderful object down there; it seemed almost a deserted ocean; nothing was to be met but an old "spouter" jogging along with stump topgallant-masts, and her sides full of boats; or a cargo-ship, with a freight of "notions," bound to the Peruvian or Mexican ports. Now, if it is not so full as the Atlantic,

it is pretty nearly as busy; for since those days Australia
has grown a mighty and populous continent; towns
have sprung up as if by magic along the western sea-
board of the Americas; even the little remote South Sea
Islands have lent a hand in the thronging of the great
Cape Horn highway; and the most desolate, sterile
region in the world—such a harsh, forbidding, icebound
piece of coast as no man who has passed within sight of
it can ever forget—is skirted, week after week and year
after year, by scores and scores of great steamers and
sailing ships, bound west, and east, and north, if never
south. The Panama Canal threatens the famous old
route; and should that waterway ever be completed, the
Horn will probably fall even more out of date than the
Cape of Good Hope has. It is not to be expected, however, that even the most ancient mariners will be found
to mourn over the desuetude. There are many uncomfortable spots to be encountered in a voyage round the
world; but a turn off the Horn, in the months which we
call summer here, probably beats anything in the shape
of marine discomforts to be found on the ocean. Of
course this is speaking of it as sailors find it—as it is
experienced by the men who have to remain on deck, go
aloft, stand at the wheel, and whose shelter is a forecastle with the scuttle closed, and not a dry stitch of
clothes to be found by groping.

For it is off the Horn where the galley-fire gets washed
out, and where, therefore, the streaming and hungry
watch below have nothing to eat but what they may
find in the bread-barge; where the tears freeze in a
man's eyes faster than the most pitying angel of a
woman living could wipe them away; where one is glad
to keep one's seaboots on for fear that one's toes may go
as well as the boots when they are hauled off; where

everything is like sheet and bar iron aloft ; where the
very cockroaches turn in to wait for the Equator, and the
hardiest rats are so put to it with frost that they watch
in the gloom until a man goes to bed and falls asleep, in
the hope of getting a meal off his nose.   Unhappily the
Horn does not improve.   It blows and snows as hard
there now as it did when the old *Wager* rounded it, and
when Drake or Anson was rolling among its stupendous
combers. Other places are more tractable. For instance,
Dana, twenty-four years after he made his memorable
voyage, found that the climate off Point Conception had
altered, that the south-easters were no longer the curse
of the coast, and that vessels anchored inside at Santa
Barbaro and San Pedro all the year round.   No one
could have told him this of the Horn.   Had he chosen to
beat to the eastward or westward a second time in the
months when the attempt was made by the *Pilgrim* and
the *Alert* he would have found the same blinding snow-
storms, the same hurling seas, the same sunless, melancholy sky, the same plunging, washing, straining, roaring
tumblification he recorded forty-two years ago.   Let the
story of a brig of 300 tons' register bear witness to this.

It was in the month of May that the vessel in question was bound to Callao with a cargo of coal, but a
strong north-westerly gale had driven her much further
to the southward than the captain had any desire to
find himself.   The gale left them on a Wednesday
morning, rolling their yardarms into it on a real Cape
Horn swell.   What is there to which to liken these
prodigious heavings ?   The actual altitude of those liquid
hills may seem small in comparison with the appearance they present when viewed from their hollows ;
but whatever may be their height, to lie dipping and
wallowing among them in a vessel of the tonnage of

that brig is to undergo an experience hardly less formidable than what was devised by the Mohocks, when they shut up old women in empty casks, and sent them spinning down Ludgate Hill. What straining and groaning and complaining of the tortured fabric, if it be of timber! Every beam, carling, tree-nail, transom, knee, stanchion, and futtock lifts up its dismal creaking and wailing voice as the bewildered craft, with her top-sails rattling in the motionless atmosphere, is swung like a pendulum up the shoulder of the swelling mass of green water, leaning down as she goes until she is fairly on her beam-ends, with pots and pannikins, sea-boots and sea-chests, dishes, books, furniture, and whatever else may be inside of her, fetching away with dreadful noise to leeward, amid a volley of sea-blessings from skipper, cook, and steward, and muffled shouts from the watch below in the forecastle.

Luckily Cape Horn calms do not last very long; indeed, there is nothing but " weather " down in those regions, and a calm is only a short pause among the gales and squalls whilst they are considering whose turn it is next. Within an hour from the time of the first gale failing them, another gale from a little to the north-of-west was bowing down the bothered and beaten brig, which, under lower topsails and fore-topmast staysail, manfully struggled to look up to it with her head in the direction of Cape Horn and her wake streaming away over her weather quarter. It was one of those pictures of storm which are rarely seen in like perfection out of the parallels that divide Terra del Fuego from the South Shetlands—an ocean of mountainous seas, raising each of them a note of thunder as their arching summits crashed from a dark, oil-smooth ridge of green water into huge avalanches of snow: a sky of gloomy slate,

along which masses of scud—torn, ragged, and tendril-
shaped—were flying with incredible velocity. The
horizon was broken with the incessant rising and falling
of the pyramidal billows, dark as the night, against a
ring of sooty clouds, from which, ever and anon, one
would break away, like a winged messenger of evil,
whitening and veiling the air with a kind of boiling
appearance as it swept its furious and blinding discharge
of snow and hail along. No wonder that in olden times
the man who had passed these tempestuous and in-
clement seas should have considered himself an object
of importance. Stand, in fancy, upon the deck of that
labouring brig, and survey one of the countless aspects
of marine life. The seas are breaking heavily over
the port bow of the vessel, deluging her forward and
racing aft in a foaming torrent as she sinks her stern to
mount the huge surge that almost lays her yardarms
level. The bitter, raw, flaying cold of the wind there is
nothing in language to express. The flying spray smites
the exposed face like a volley of sail needles. Now and
again a squall of snow and hail comes along with so
much fury in it that it takes the breath away from the
strongest of the seamen cowering with their backs to it.
The rigging crackles to every strain put upon it like
burning wood. The snow upon the yards makes them
glimmer like lines of pallid light as they furiously sway
against the dismal ground of the dark and rushing sky.
There are spears and arrow-heads of ice upon the bulwark rail, upon the catheads, upon the scuttle-butts
lashed amidships; and though the seas repeatedly break
over them they are always left standing. The helmsman, with his hard fists wrapped up in mits, rigged out
in oilskins from his head to his huge, well-greased sea-
boots, and with the after-thatch of his sou'-wester blown

up by the gale, and standing out from his head like the tail of a gull, gets the full of it. Nothing of the man is visible but a fragment of mahogany face showing between the flannel ear-covers of his head-gear, and a pair of watering eyes, which he now and again wipes upon his mit when a pause in the yaws and come-to's give him a chance to raise one of his hands from the spokes.

How would some of our summer-water mariners appear beside that salt-water sailor were they to have stood their trick at the helm on such an occasion as this; gazing to windward as yonder skipper is doing, holding on like grim death to a backstay, with the salt drying in crystals in his eyes; or making one of that oil-skinned group there to leeward of the galley, stamping their boots upon the deck to put life into their frozen toes, ducking as a shriek in the wind warns them of the passage of a green sheet of water over their heads, biting doggedly upon the tobacco in their cheeks, and growling as they reflect that another three hours must elapse before they are privileged to quit the deck and take such warmth and comfort as they may find in the forecastle, whose darkness is scarcely revealed by the sputtering slush-lamp, and whose beams and stanchions are decorated with draining clothes?

It was already blowing two or three ordinary gales in one, and the lower topsails were more than the brig could safely stagger under, though the captain held on, since by ratching to the northward he might hope to get clear of the ice, of which, on the previous night and that morning, some monstrous specimens had hove in view. Indeed, at one bell in the afternoon watch, during a flaw in a heavy squall of snow that was blowing in horizontal lines along the sea, they caught sight on the lee bow of the greenish marble-like glimmer of a berg that looked to be a mile long and as tall as St. Paul's Cathedral. It vanished, but reappeared broad on the lee-beam when the squall passed, and stood out in its complete shape against the smoke-coloured gloom of the sky over the horizon, where, though it was four or five miles off, the men on the brig's deck could see the white, steam-like haze of the spray that flashed in clouds from its base, and fled past it in eddying volumes, and almost imagine that they heard the thunder of the smiting surges reverberating in the hollows and caverns of the mighty frozen mass. But when it had drawn on the lee-quarter another squall blew up and smothered it, and after that it disappeared entirely.

It was at this time that the gale increased in fury, and the sea grew terrible. The weather was enough to blow the masts out of the vessel, and all hands were turned up to stow both topsails and bring the brig to the wind under a small storm staysail. How is the aspect of that Cape Horn ocean to be described?—the rage of its headlong acclivities; the long sweep of olive-green heights, piebald with hissing and seething tracks of foam, blown along their gleaming sides; the hard iron-grey of the heavens, out of which the storm of wind was rushing, bearing upon its wings masses of vapour, which it tore to pieces in its fury; and the cold—the piercing, poignant cold—of the gale, with its lashing burden of sleet and spray and hail?

The men had come off the yards after having struggled, each watch of them, for hard upon three-quarters of an hour with the frozen topsails, when the brig shipped a sea just abaft the weather fore rigging. It was a whole mountain of green water, and it fell in a dead weight of scores of tons upon the deck, beating for awhile the whole life out of the devoted vessel, and

E

making her pause, trembling and stunned, in the roaring hollow in which it had found her, whilst above the thunder of the dreadful stroke could be heard the crash of breaking wood, of splintered glass, and the rending noise of deck furniture torn from its strong fastenings. A heavy upward send drove the water off the decks, and all hands were found to be alive, holding on like grim death to whatever was next them; and then it was seen that a long range of the weather-bulwarks had been torn down flush with the deck, the cabin skylight broken into shivers, the long boat amidships stove, and nothing left of the port-quarter boat but the frame of its keel and stem, dangling at the davits. The loss of the two boats was a bad job, but still worse was the terrible straining the deeply freighted vessel had undergone, and the destruction of the skylight that left the cabin open for the floods of water that rolled along the deck. The benumbed and half-frozen crew turned to to secure what remained of the skylight and to cover it with tarpaulins; but whilst they were in the midst of this work the brig gave a heavy lurch, which made the men believe it was all over with her; and before a single cry could have been raised, a portion of the weather fore rigging carried away, and in a trice the fore-topmast broke off at the cap, and fell over the side—a horrible muddle—with all its raffle of sail, yards, and gear.

The early Antarctic night was now drawing down over the furious sea, and it was already so dark that the men could hardly discern one another's faces. Some active fellows sprang forward at the risk of their lives to cut away the rigging, and release the wreck alongside before the yards upon it should pierce the brig's bottom; and this being done, the helm was put hard up, with the idea of wearing ship, in order to secure the foremast.

But the storm-fiend had marked this unhappy brig, and the successive blows came thick and fast. Scarcely was the wrecked spar sent adrift and the helm shifted, when all the rest of the port fore rigging carried away, and the foremast fell down, carrying with it the bowsprit, main topmast, and a portion of the port main rigging.

By this time it was as dark as the bottom of a well; the brig wallowed before the seas with a mass of wreckage over her side, pitching miserably in the fearful hollows, and huge surges curling their white heights around her. A man had need to be a seaman indeed, and to have a seaman's heart in him too, to act at all in such a moment as this. The full extent of the mischief could not be guessed. Nothing was certain but that the brig was dispossessed of all but her mainmast, and that there were some heavy spars over the side, pounding at her like battering-rams with every hurl of the raging seas. The first business would be to get clear of this mischief, and the men went to work with their knives, feeling for the lanyards and hacking and cutting with a will. Darkness gives a peculiar horror to disasters of this kind at sea. In the daylight you can see what has happened; you can use your eyes as well as your hands and make despatch, and the worst is evident. But the darkness leaves everything to be guessed at. You shout for help for some job too heavy for you, and it does not come. The outlines of the sea grow colossal by the illusion of the faint light thrown out from their breaking crests; you cannot perceive the flying water so as to duck away from it, and in a breath you may find yourself overboard. It is all distraction and uproar, loud and fearful shouting, and blind groping. When at last the wreck was cleared, the vessel seemed little better than a sheer hulk, nothing standing but her mainmast, upon

which the mainyard swung helplessly. That she should
have lived through that long and fearful Antarctic night,
the seas combing over her, icebergs in her vicinity, and
draining in water with every roll, must count among
the miracles of the deep. Her people had discovered
that the mainmast, having little to support it, had
worked loose, breaking away the mast-combings, and
starting the planking all around it; so that through
this large aperture the water poured into the hold in
torrents. The port pump had been disabled by the fall
of the masts, and the only other pump was manned and
worked with such energy as dying men will put into
their arms; but in less than an hour the coal choked
it, and now nothing remained but to lighten the vessel
by throwing the cargo overboard and baling with buckets.
All through those black and howling hours, amid freezing falls of water, and in the heart of the raging Cape
Horn storm, this severe labour was pursued, so that
when the bleak and melancholy dawn broke upon the
desolate ocean it found the brig still afloat, and the brave
hearts in her grimly fighting death, though faint,
famished, and frozen. Help came shortly before noon.
A sail was made out heading dead for the wreck, and by
the time she was abreast, the wind and sea had so far
moderated as to enable her to bring all the men safely
off. It was not a moment too soon, for twenty minutes
after the crew had been transferred to the ship the brig
was observed to give a heavy lurch, and so lie on her
beam-ends, never righting, but slowly sinking in that
position—so slowly that after her hull had vanished
her mainmast remained forking out like the lifted arm
of a drowning man.

When this story was told me I could not help thinking of what the Horn route was in Dana's time, and the

very small chance that brig's crew would have had for
their lives had her name been the *Pilgrim*, and had she
been beating to the westward forty years ago. Certain
it is, that however ships may come and go, and change
the nature of their material and the form of their
fabrics, the weather in the Pacific down there is very
much what it was in Anson's time, and as it has been,
in all probability, since the creation of the world. Other
climates may vary in the lapse of ages, and south-
easters may in places be found to work themselves
into north-westers. But the Horn remains always the
same harsh, tempestuous, frozen headland, echoing at
this hour the hurricane notes which reverberated over
it centuries ago, and grimly overlooking the stormiest
space of waters in the world. Who, then, does not
hope that the final construction of the Panama Canal
may abridge the bleak and icebound horrors of that
point of continent which looks on the chart to stretch
its leagues and leagues of tongue into the very heart
of the southern frozen waters? To be sure, the passage
of the famous cape has long since ceased to be a wonder;
but none the less is it full of perils to vessels which, like
the brig I have written about, are at the mercy of the
monstrous seas and furious gales of that formidable
tract of Pacific waters.

ONE is sorry to hear of the growth of the very un-English habit of sheering off and scuttling away after a collision. The first duty of a shipmaster who plumps into a vessel or is run into is to stand by, if the condition of his ship will permit him, and render all the assistance in his power. There is nothing more despicable and cowardly than running away after a disaster of this kind. We know what came of such conduct in the case of the *Northfleet;* and week after week one reads in the shipping papers how such and such a vessel was run into, and how the other ship made off, and how so many people were drowned in consequence. Darkness, that is fruitful of collisions, is also, unhappily, favourable to these mean and unmanly escapes. At night it mostly happens that the utmost you can tell of the vessel that comes grinding into your ship is that she is big or little, a steamer or a sailing-vessel, and rigged in such and such a fashion. The letters on her nameboard cannot be deciphered; she will not answer your hail; and her reply to the melancholy shout of "For God's sake don't leave us, we believe we are sinking," is to shift her helm and vanish in the gloom. The obligation to record such casualties in the log-book or to depone to them before receivers of wrecks does not, it is to be feared, always imply the sort of accuracy that would be useful to sufferers. From time to time a buoy is sunk, a lightship run into, and the Trinity Corporation offer a handsome sum of money for information, but without avail. The absence of all reference by shipmates to such occurrences must make one hope that they are mainly the work of foreigners. But whatever the flag under which a captain sails, his sneaking away from a disaster in which he has had a hand expresses a species of cowardice that presses heavily upon the humbler order of shipowners. A little coaster is run into by a fine large vessel, which stops a minute or two and then proceeds. The master of the coaster may be her owner, and all that he has in the world is in his little ship. She is not sunk, but her masts are over the side, and she looks as if she had been for some hours under the guns of a fort. Whether or not the master be to blame for the collision, he is pretty sure to consider that the fault was not his; and his hardship is, that whilst he stands a chance of being ruined, he is unable to discover the name of the ship that ran into him, so as to be able to bring her owners into a court of justice, and take his risk as a litigant.

I was amused and interested some time since by hearing the story of the resolute behaviour of Mr. John Whitear, master of the schooner *Jehu,* a vessel of about 150 tons. Giving chase, if you can, is one way, at least, of clearing up the mystery of the paternity of an offending ship that sneaks off in the darkness in the hope of saving her owner's pocket. Any way, Mr. John Whitear's conduct illustrates a spirit pleasant to come across in the homely prosaics of the marine life of to-day. Eighty and a hundred years ago it was men of the stamp of Mr. Whitear who commanded British privateers; otherwise how should the maritime memorials of that kind of

vessel be so full as they are of the unflinching obstinacy
and the grim courage which followed the fleeing enemy
over leagues and leagues of ocean, through storms and
through calms, finally overhauling and boarding the
breathless chase in latitudes so remote from the point
of departure that the span between the two places might
even now be reckoned a long voyage ?

Not very many days ago, then, the *Jehu*, with 230
tons of coal aboard, was quietly jogging along on her
way to her port of destination. The afternoon had been
fine, and the night came down very clear and bright,
with starlight. The water was smooth, though a merry
wind was blowing, and the little vessel under easy canvas
lay softly leaning in the gloom, with the white water
rippling and crisping past her sides in a hollow, brass-like
tinkling. Starlight gives beauty even to a coalman; and
I have known stump topgallant-masts and sails yawning
upon sheets hard upon a fathom from the points in the
yardarms through which they lead, make as dream-like
and dainty a picture in the tender sobering shadows of
the night as the tall and tapering rig of the handsomest
yacht now afloat.

At all events, the *Jehu* was Mr. John Whitear's sea-
home, and as he paced the weather side of the deck,
sometimes squinting into the windward darkness where
the loom of the land hung low upon the vague greyish
softness of the water that way, or sometimes aloft where
the stars, like so many benign and encouraging eyes, were
tipping him cheerful winks through the black squares in
the shrouds and over the main gaff and among the dim
tracery of the standing and running rigging, whose
heights seemed to bring near the sweeping enfoldment
of the glittering heavens, as though the vast star-laden
shadow were revolving and was weaving its circling

burden of gloom closer and closer yet round the lonely schooner journeying slowly along with a bell-like resonance of broken water around her, he was no doubt as well satisfied with his little hooker as the captain of an ocean steamer could be with his stately ship.

His pipe being smoked out, the weather looking as steady as a church, and all being well in every possible sense of that marine expression, Mr. John Whitear thought that no harm could come of his going below for a spell to take some rest. Accordingly, after exchanging a few words with his mate, and taking another good look to windward and then aloft, he walked to the companion and disappeared down the steps. But instead of going to bed like a landsman, he kept on his boots and his coat, merely removing his cap as a preliminary to turning in, and stretching himself upon a locker, within easy hearing of the first shout that should come down through the companion, he closed his eyes, and was presently contributing to the other creaking sounds raised in the plain and quaint little cabin by the occasional movements of the *Jehu*.

How it came about he could not say, not having been on deck at the time; but whilst he lay dreaming such peaceful dreams as should visit a master mariner whose whole professional life is dedicated to the careful attention of the three L's, he was suddenly aroused, and in some measure startled, by a loud and fearful cry in the companion of "Below, there! here's a barque running into us."

Fortunately, Mr. Whitear had no occasion to stay to dress himself; in a breath he was up the ladder and on deck. The first thing he saw was a large barque on the port bow, apparently paying off, having just gone about. Fresh as he was from a deep sleep, Mr. Whitear had all

his wits about him in a moment; and he immediately
perceived that, let him do what he liked and shout as he
would, a collision was unavoidable.   The barque loomed
up large and massive in the darkness.   Her lights were
as plainly to be seen as the stars, whilst the *Jehu's*
burned as brightly.   The wind had freshened somewhat,
and both vessels were heeling under it.   All was silent
aboard the barque—not the least sound could be heard;
and in that thrilling and breathless moment all other
noises took a startling distinctness—the washing of
water, the creaking of spars, the squeak up in the darkness of a sheave upon a rusty pin.   There is no sensation
comparable to what is felt in the few minutes which
elapse between the approach and shock of two meeting
vessels.   A railway collision gives you no time.   If by
chance you look out of the carriage window and see
what is going to happen, before you can sing out the
thing has come and is over.   But a collision at sea
furnishes you with leisure to think, to anticipate, and to
make an agony of the disaster before it actually befalls
you.   Whichever way the helm of the *Jehu* had been
jammed would have been all the same; the barque was
bound to come, and in a few moments there she was,
with her bows towering like a cliff over the low bulwarks
of the well-freighted *Jehu*, her jibboom and bowsprit
arching across the little schooner's deck like a great
spear in the hand of a giant.

The *Jehu* heeled over under the blow until the rail of
her starboard bulwarks was flush with the water.   The
men came skurrying, half-naked, out of the forecastle,
thinking she was sinking, and rushed aft to be out of the
way of whatever might tumble down from aloft.   You
heard the grinding noise of crushed wood, the thud of
falling gear, the tearing of canvas.   The weight of the

barque, that was a big vessel in ballast, swept the stern
of the little *Jehu* to windward, rounding her in such a
manner as to free them both. But by this time there
was plenty of noise and activity to be noted aboard the
barque. Orders were rattled out in plain English, and
you could hear the scampering of feet and the songs of
the seamen as they ran to and fro and pulled and hauled.
She heeled over like a great shadow with her mainyards
square and her fore-sheets flattened in. It was impossible
to know what mischief she had done ; and, running to the
side, Mr. Whitear shouted to her at the top of his voice
to stand by them, as he feared the schooner was sinking.

No answer was returned.

"They're leaving us !" cried the mate. "Look!
they're trimming sail ; they're swinging the mainyards ! "

Again Mr. Whitear bawled to them not to abandon
the schooner; but no answer was vouchsafed, and in a
few moments it was not only seen that she was leaving
them, but that she meant to get away as fast as she
could, for they loosed their fore topgallant-sail and main-
royal, and sheeted the canvas home with all expedition.

Under such circumstances most men would have contented themselves with bestowing a sea-blessing on the
stranger, and then turned-to to sound the well, and, if
the schooner was leaking fast, get the boats over. But
Mr. John Whitear was made of the old, and, as some
people might think, the right kind of stuff.

"Bill," says he to William Dart, A.B., who was at
the wheel, "keep your eye upon that old catermerang
while me and the mate overhauls the schooner. Follow
her without a wink, William ; for if there's a creak left in
this old bucket, we'll stick to her skirts and have her
name, though she should go all on sailing till we comes
to Australey."

Forthwith he and the mate went to work, sounded the well, looked over the side, peered at the damage done aloft; and then, coming aft again, " She's tight and she's right, boys," said Mr. Whitear. " Now, bullies, here's a mess that's to cost some one pounds and pounds. That some one's not to be John Whitear ; so, William, starboard your helm, my lad ; and the rest of ye all turn to and make sail forrard, every stitch ye can find, and then we'll repair the main rigging, and get a new mainsail bent ; " for he had discovered that the barque's jibboom had cut through the centre cloths of the mainsail, ripping it open from the head to the second reef-band as neatly as if a sailmaker's knife had done the job.

They all went to work with a will, putting uncommon agility into their limbs and spirits by calling the shadow ahead many hard salt names, and swearing they would catch her if she carried them into the Polar regions. The labour was severe, for there were not many of them to " turn-to ;" nevertheless, they managed, in a time less by three-quarters than they would have occupied on any other occasion, to repair the damaged shrouds, set up preventer backstays, bend a new mainsail, and cover the little vessel with canvas. The barque was close-hauled, three or four miles ahead, on the port tack, lying over, as a light vessel will in such a merry breeze as was then blowing, under both royals and gaff topsail; she was trusting to her heels and running away, like a big bully from a little man whom he has accidentally hurt, and is afraid of. Her people would probably ridicule the idea of the deep-freighted schooner chasing them ; indeed, they had left her apparently helpless, her port main rigging hanging in bights over the side, her mainsail in halves, and the whole fabric looking wrecked and stunned from the shock of the collision.

Meanwhile, Mr. John Whitear stumped the quarter-deck of his little craft, often pausing to point an old leather-covered telescope at the leaning shadow out away under the low-shining stars just the merest trifle to leeward of the lee knighthead, and then cocking the glass under his arm afresh, and swinging round with a sharp, obstinate stamp of the foot to resume his walk.

"Boys," he sung out, "there's no occasion for the watch below to remain on deck."

"No, no," was the gruff answer; "there's no going below till we've found out that wessel's name."

The wind came along with a fresh, strong sweep, and a deep moan in the gusts as they blew over the bulwark rail into the hollow glimmer of the great mainsail; there was a kind of flashful light in the breaking heads of the little black surges, and a regular rise and fall of fountain-like sound from forward, where the stem of the driven schooner was hissing through the dark water, and the wake ran away astern like a snow-covered road, until, looking at it, you seemed to see the dark water on either side stand up as if the white vein were the frothing stream of a cataract rushing into darkness betwixt the shadows of hills.

"Why, smother me, if she's not got the scent of us!" suddenly cried Mr. Whitear with the glass at his eye; "she's off three points, and there's no luff left in her! Boys, did any of you take notice if she had her stun-sail booms aloft?"

"No," answered William Dart; "her foreyards were just up yonder" (pointing into the air), "an' I'll take my oath she'd got no booms on 'em."

"Then we'll run her down yet; we'll have her!" cried Mr. Whitear, fetching his knee a slap that sounded like the report of a pistol. "Keep her away a bit; ease off the sheets fore and aft. Hurrah, my lads! the *Jehu* knows the road! We'll weather the sneak, boys!" And so he rattled on, sometimes talking to his men, sometimes to the schooner, and sometimes addressing the barque ahead.

Shortly after two o'clock in the morning, however, four or five sailing-vessels hove in sight and bothered Mr. Whitear exceedingly, for there was a chance of mistaking the chase among them and pursuing the wrong vessel. All hands were implored to keep a bright look-out, and the glass was now much more often at the skipper's eye than under his arm. It is strange enough to think of a little collier with 230 tons of coal in her bottom pursuing a vessel three times her size. It might really pass as a most satirical travestie of the old maritime business, were it not for the very strong commercial instincts at work in it. The purse was always as great a power on sea as on land, and the flight of the big barque from the little coalman was only another illustration of its supremacy.

To the great satisfaction of Mr. Whitear, the schooner turned out to be more than a match for the cowardly runaway. It was quite clear that the barque had no more sail to set; as it was, she was bowling along under a press of canvas that must have made her decks mighty uncomfortable, to judge from the sharp angle of her inclination. Had she chosen to put her helm up and bring the wind well aft, she would no doubt have walked away from the schooner, whose fore-and-aft canvas then would not have much helped her. But the barque could not forget that she had to work her way to windward, and that her port lay N.E. and not S.W.; and though she might slacken away her lee-braces in the hope of making the obstinate little schooner give up, it would not answer her purpose to do more than that.

Inch by inch the *Jehu* crawled up to her. Just before daybreak the wind breezed up like a squall, though the sky was clear, and Mr. Whitear, who all through the night had watched the chase with the intentness of an old British commodore following a squadron of flying Frenchmen, shouted out that she had taken in her royals and gaff topsail, and that, as it was, she was nearly out of water to windward. But not so much as a ropeyarn was touched aboard the *Jehu;* she had never been so pressed since the hour that she was launched. She hove up the foam as high as the head-boards; every bone of her trembled; the wind boomed away from under the foot of her sails in a thunder-note, and the sheets and weather standing rigging stood like bars of iron. There seemed as much eagerness in her shivering, rushing frame as in her skipper, whose excitement deepened as the square and leaning shadow ahead loomed bigger and bigger. Earnestly was it to be hoped that the port main rigging would stand all this straining; and yet such was the temper of the captain and the men of the brave little *Jehu*, that, I believe, had the mainmast gone overboard, they would have held on after the barque with a single spar, just as I once saw a man with one arm and a wooden leg give chase to a rogue who had sneered at his misfortunes.

The faint grey of the dawn was in the sky when the barque was brought to the wind again, and, after holding on for a short while with a close luff, went about. Before she had her foreyards braced round, the schooner had stayed and was on the starboard tack, savagely breaking the quick seas which were rolling in the wake of the wind, and finding all the advantage she needed in the weathering she had made upon the barque, who, with the rising of the sun, appeared to lose all heart, for no more sail was made, and when she was braced up she was kept so close that the weather half of her fore top-gallant-sail was aback. The white sunshine that had flung a deep blue over the stars, and transformed the ocean into a tumbling green surface full of sparkles and white lines, and a horizon so clear that it was like the sweep of a brush dipped in bright green paint along the en-folding azure of the morning sky, gave stout-hearted Mr. John Whitear a good sight of the tall vessel he had been chasing all through the middle and morning watches. She was what he called " a lump of a barque," so light that half her metal sheathing was out of water, with very square yards and a main skysail mast, and she tumbled with such unwieldly motions upon the running seas that it seemed no longer wonderful that the *Jehu* should have been able to weather and forereach upon her. Her way was almost stopped by the gripe of her luff, and within an hour of the time of her going about the schooner was on her weather quarter.

Mr. Whitear had already deciphered her name upon her stern, but he had some questions to ask; so, jumping on to the rail and clawing a backstay with one hand, whilst he put the other hand to his mouth, he bawled out, " Barque ahoy ! "

" Hallo ! " was the answer.

" What's the name of your vessel ? " sang out Mr. Whitear.

" Have you forgotten how to read, skipper ? It's under your nose," came the reply.

" You're the barque *Juno*, of Maitland, N.S.—that's clear enough on your starn," shouted Mr. Whitear, whose temper, inflamed by the long pursuit, was not improved, as may be supposed, by this reception; "and you're the vessel that ran into us last night, and carried away our shrouds, braces, and running gear, the main-rail, topgallant bulwarks, and split our mainsail."

"No, we ain't," was the reply. "We know nothing of the job you're talking about; so sheer off, will ye, and take care to spot the right party afore letting fly."

Without answering, Mr. Whitear shifted his helm so as to bring his vessel to leeward of the barque; and then, running forward when the schooner had forged abreast of the other vessel, he shouted to the man who had answered his hail to look over the port bow of the barque and there he would see the marks of the schooner's chain-plate bolts, whilst further evidence of the barque being the culprit lay in particles of her planking adhering to the *Jehu's* chain-plates. This was too decisive to admit of further denial; and Mr. John Whitear having obtained all the information he required, walked aft again, once more shifted his helm, saluted the barque with a farewell flourish of his fist, and then gave orders to his men to trim sail and head for the port to which they were bound.

AMONG the most picturesque and lively incidents of the sea are those of the encountering of abandoned vessels, and the struggles of the people who board them to carry them into port. Were it not for the imperative injunctions of owners, and the various obligations imposed upon shipmasters by the terms of charter-parties, policies, and the like, there is no doubt that we should hear very much oftener than we now do of the preservation of derelicts and their cargoes. The mariner often stumbles upon some substantial prize in this way. A ship is sighted, low in the water, with nothing standing perhaps but the stump of her foremast. A spell at the pumps eases her, she is overhauled, and her hold seen to be full of valuable cargo. She is taken in tow, and after several days, or perhaps weeks, of manœuvring, she is carried into port and found to be worth some thousands of pounds, a goodly portion of which goes to the men who navigated her into a place of safety. There is a touch of romance in such findings that never fails to render them amusing and even exciting reading; and as stories they are often rich in a high kind of marine characteristics.

One of these yarns, I remember, impressed me greatly at the time. The master of a vessel, called the

Fides, sighted a Dutch barque water-logged. On approaching her, only one man was to be seen on board. He proved to be the skipper, who said that his crew had refused to remain by the vessel, and had left him alone in her. He was brought aboard the *Fides*, but had not been there ten minutes when he begged to be sent to his water-logged barque again. His entreaties were so moving that the captain of the *Fides* yielded, and he was once more put in possession of his wreck and left there. Next day a vessel, called the *Ballater*, took him off, and the wonder was that the poor fellow had ever managed to keep his life on the deck of the wave-swept hulk. Here, in the most obscure form in the world, is an exhibition of the sailor's loyalty to his ship so great as to make a truly heroical figure of that Dutch captain. Narratives which recount the meeting with derelicts and their conveyance to port often reveal some of the best qualities of the sailor—I mean his indifference to peril, his capacity of determined labour, his triumph over forces whose antagonism would leave most landsmen helpless and hopeless. Such was the story of the *Caledonia*, a prize crew from which took charge of the brig *Emily*, and, after ten days of fierce battling with violent gales of wind in a vessel jury-rigged and half full of water, were eventually forced to abandon her. Such was the voyage of five men in the derelict barque *Thor* of Tvedestrand, laden with scrap-iron and oil-casks ; they had to rig a jury-rudder to get her to sail, and for nearly a fortnight struggled with heavy weather and baffling winds, eventually being ship-wrecked near Youghal, and narrowly escaping with their lives only to witness the craft they had desperately laboured to save go to pieces among the rocks.

Not very long since a ship-rigged vessel of nine

hundred tons was proceeding on her voyage to one of
the West India Islands. The weather had been calm
and thick through the night, with a long swell rolling
up from the westwards, and the morning broke with a
fiery sun, red as that luminary is at his setting, and
a mountainous heave of the sea that in the wake of the
orb rolled in billows of molten gold, giving a kind of
dreadful splendour to the hazy morning, with its faint
and tarnished sky and the sickly green of the swelling
and foamless deep, and the stubborn belt of haze that
hung like the greyish shadow of rain upon the horizon,
save where the sun loomed like a blood-red shield as he
floated heavily out of the deep. There were a hundred
signs to betoken a gale at hand, and preparatory measures were accordingly taken aboard the ship. All the
light canvas and the mainsail were furled, and single
reefs tied in the topsails. Never was such rolling. The
draught of air had no weight to steady the vessel; she
fell into the hollow of the swell, and from side to side
she swayed as each ponderous liquid fold caught and
hove her over, the water bursting inboard in smoke
through her scupper-holes, the shrouds creaking with
the tension of the strain as though they would draw the
chain-plates like pliant wire, and every beam, strong
fastening, and bulkhead added their groaning notes to
the general clamour of the labouring hull and the beating
canvas. By nine o'clock the sun had vanished under an
expanse of slate-coloured cloud that hung over the whole
surface of the deep; but yet another hour elapsed
before the gale burst, and then it came along in a voice
of thunder and over a surface of milk-white waters.
With the upper topsail halliards let go and hands by
the lower topsail sheets, the ship leaned down to it until
the foam was up to a man's shoulders in the lee scuppers;

but they managed to get her to pay off, and presently she was speeding like an arrow on the wings of the tempest, piling the foam as high as her figure-head, her main-topsail blown in rags out of the bolt-ropes, and sheets of spray fogging her decks like bursts of vapour from a boiler.

The next thing to do was to bring her to the wind before the sea rose; the crew went aloft to stow the topsails and frap what remained of the main-topsail upon the yard; and after a little there was the ship with nothing on her but a small storm trysail, bowing and shearing at the huge surges which the storm had lifted in cones and pyramids, and which were now pouring and breaking with a terrible roaring noise. All day and far into the night the storm blew without intermission, but it broke in the middle watch, and then fined down so rapidly that at eight o'clock in the morning the ship was pursuing her course under whole topsails and topgallant-sails, and curtsying over the long heave of the sea, whose green seemed to sparkle after the purification of the tempest, and whose beautiful arching coils were brilliant with the diamond-like flashing of the foam chipped out of the emerald acclivities by the keen teeth of the clear, fresh north-east wind.

Shortly after noon the watch on deck had come out of the forecastle after eating their dinner, when a small brig was made out right ahead, apparently standing athwart the ship's hawse. On approaching her it was seen that she was drifting, and that though there might be people aboard, she was not under control. Aloft she was in a state of great confusion, her foreyards squared, and her after-yards braced as wildly as the leeches of the canvas would allow. The davit falls were over-hauled to the water's edge, and all the boats were gone.

Here and there ends of her running rigging trailed overboard, and as she rolled heavily in the trough of the sea, the sound of her flapping canvas threw a wild and melancholy echo athwart the breeze. The master of the ship loudly hailed her, and all eyes were eagerly fastened upon the brig to observe if there were any indications of life in her. Possibly nothing so heightens the mournful and tragical suggestions of an abandoned vessel as the loud hail of a passing ship and the deathlike stillness following, unbroken save by the hollow beating of canvas, the drowning sob of swelling water, and the creak of straining timbers.

It was very evident that nothing alive was in the brig, and the master of the ship, after consulting with his mate, decided on sending a boat. Accordingly, the second mate and a couple of seamen went over the side, and, after some hard rowing and careful dodging of the seas, they gained the brig, and scrambled upon her deck. They found that she was damaged to an extent that could not be imagined by inspection of her from the ship. Her galley and cabin skylights were smashed in, bulwark stanchions were started, and, in addition to various other injuries, there were three feet of water in the hold. Whether she had drained this water into her from the deck or whether it was due to a leak could not at once be ascertained; it was certain at least that her hold was full of cargo, and that it was of a nature that would not enable her to float should the water gain upon her. These facts were reported by the second mate, who added that he could find no papers belonging to the vessel, and that she had been stripped of all her provisions.

"It seems a pity to leave her knocking about here," shouted the captain. "It'll be another man's job if we don't tackle it. Do you see your way ᴖo carry her to Fayal?" then distant about four hundred miles.

The second mate conversed with the two men who were with him, and, after a little while, called out, "Ay, we'll risk it."

On this the two seamen were ordered to come alongside, when some provisions, water, a sextant, chart, and other needful articles were lowered into the boat. With these they put off, receiving a loud encouraging cheer from the rest of the ship's crew; and, reaching the brig's side, hoisted out the provisions, and hooked on the boat and dragged her up to the davits. The ship stood by for awhile, watching the plucky fellows, and perhaps suspecting that they might repent their undertaking, for even with a dry bottom the brig might have been reckoned a big navigating job for three men. She rolled heavily and continuously, her canvas striking the masts with loud reports, and making the light spars buckle, and as she lifted her shining sides out of the bright green seas the water was seen to gush from her bulwarks in a manner to prove the wrenching they had undergone from the recent tempest. There was no show of misgiving or repentance, however, on the part of the men. Having hoisted their boat they turned to and trimmed the yards, clapping the jigger on to the topsail halliards, and giving everything a good spread. The little vessel took the wind, slightly heeled, and came round to her course for the Western Islands, and the last thing the ship, as she filled and stood on her voyage, saw of the brig was the second mate at the wheel, the two men toiling at the break-pump amidships, and the little vessel under fore and main topgallant sail heavily swinging over the long ocean swell, throwing the foam from her deep round bows, and looking but the merest toy amid the vast surface of undulating waters which leaned away into the furthest reaches of the sky.

A crew of three men leaves, with one at the wheel, only two to do the ship's work. Four or five seamen would not have been too many to hand that brig's main sail alone, and a gale of wind might therefore oblige the second mate and his two companions to put their helm up and run for it, and leave the canvas to blow away with a blessing upon it before they could bring the vessel to. Four hundred miles seem but a short voyage nowadays; but a head wind might enlarge the period of such a journey into weeks, in which case, unless these men met with help—which, though very likely, was by no means certain—they were bound to perish of starvation, as the quantity of provisions supplied to them by the ship could not, however economically used, outlast four or five days. It is just because a sailor would keenly understand all the heavy risks and difficulties comprised in such an adventure as these three men had engaged in, that the courage implied in this and many other attempts of the same kind to save property found at sea deserves a good place in the annals of naval heroism. A half-hour's spell at the pumps satisfied them that by regular application the water might be kept under, though there could be no longer any doubt that the vessel was leaking either from a started butt or some puncture below the water-line. A tarpaulin was found and secured over the broken skylight, as a provision against dirty weather; the galley fire was lighted, and the decks cleared up, and there being an old reel-log near the wheel, along with a sand-glass, they managed among them to heave it—the second mate at the helm holding the glass—and discovered that the brig was making a little less than four knots. But the weather

kept fine, and this supported the men's courage, as did
also their assurance one to another that they were bound
to be well rewarded for the risks they were running.
They had another spell at the pump, and then fetched a
bit of the ship's beef that had been put to cook in the
galley-copper, and bringing it aft with some biscuit, made
out a tolerable meal, the mate steering with one hand
and eating with the other.

The day passed quietly, but the wind was light, and
the progress made was small. The duty of keeping the
pump going at regular intervals grew exhausting, but it
was absolutely necessary that the quantity of water
should be kept under the depth found in the brig when
she was boarded, and every hour throughout the day the
harsh clank of the pump might be heard, ceasing after
an interval when the men, pale with fatigue, and with
the sweat streaming from their faces, flung themselves
upon the deck breathless and spent. The breeze
freshened at sunset, and the topgallant-sails were taken
in. The night came down very dark, with a few misty
stars here and there, and a flavour in the swing of the
wind as it blew in gusts over the bulwarks that was a
promise of bad weather. The weight of the water in the
little vessel, coupled with the cargo, that came flush with
the main hatch, sunk her deep, and as the sea rose her
behaviour grew wild. The billows tumbled against her
weather-bow, and such was her inelasticity that at times
she would not rise to them, but let them roll over her
forecastle, burying herself pretty nearly as far aft as her
foremast, and flooding her decks to the wheel. Fortunately her upper works were staunch, or she must
have been drowned again and again by the seas which
tumbled in tons' weight over her head. The men made
shift to stow the upper topsails before it came on hard,

but they could do nothing with the lower canvas, which must blow away if it would not stand. This the fore-top-sail did shortly after ten o'clock in a squall of wind; the weather sheet parted, and in a few moments the sail was in rags, increasing the roaring noise of the gale and the crashing sound of the sea by the fierce whipping of the tattered cloths. Amidst all this confusion and wild scene of the black heavens and glimmering heights of water, the men betook themselves again and again to the pumps, and the metallic ring of the working brake flung a dismal note of shipwreck into the harsh uproar of the warring elements. It is difficult to realize a sterner picture of struggle, a more furious array of perils. Here were three men as crew of a vessel which wanted a good nine hands to work her, exhausted by pumping, and yet obliged regularly to apply themselves to the pump to keep the vessel afloat—forced by this work, or by having to tend the helm, to remain unsheltered upon the decks over which the seas were bursting in whole oceans; wet through to the skin, without the means of obtaining a warm drink, and without the chance of preserving a dry stitch even were an opportunity afforded them to change their clothes; a black and howling void overhead, and below a huge broken sea, in whose thunderous hollows the little vessel laboured like a drowning thing, one moment upright and becalmed by the towering coil of a rushing surge, the next on her beam-ends on the summit of the liquid height, with the full force of the gale howl-ing through her rigging, and the spray from the breaking heads of the near combers sweeping over her decks upon the breath of the black and ringing wind like a furious snowstorm.

In the limits assigned here it is impossible to do justice to this struggle. To make it a conceivable thing to the landsman's intelligence something of photographic minuteness is wanted in the reproduction; the picture of the men leaving the pumps and crawling along the deck to the wheel, their talk, their postures as they sat crouching and listening to the infernal din in the ebony void on high—a hundred such matters, indeed—together with the outline of the vessel, revealed for a breathless space, as she swooped into a trough with a headlong shearing of the bows that made the water boil in whiteness which flung a kind of twilight round about, in which the ink-like configuration of the straining and beaten fabric was thrown up as though a gleam of pallid moonshine had broken through the dense vapours of the storm and fallen for an instant into the swirling and creaming hollow in which the brig lay weltering. That the deeply-laden and half-drowned vessel should have outlived that night was a real miracle. Fierce as had been the preceding storm encountered by the ship, this gale had at times an edge in it that the other wanted. Happily, like its predecessor, it was short-lived, and blew itself out soon after daybreak, though it left such a tremendous sea behind that for several hours after the wind had sobered down into a topgallant breeze the brig was in the utmost jeopardy. The rolling was so frightful that the men could do nothing aloft. The mate refused to allow them to leave the deck, expecting every instant to see the mast go over the side. It was almost impossible to stand at the pumps; sometimes the little vessel would literally *dish* a sea over her rail that swept the two seamen off their legs, and forced the mate, who grasped the wheel, to hold on to the spokes for dear life; and it was as much as their necks were worth to let go for a moment. By noon, however, the swell had greatly subsided, and the men made shift to set the main and upper fore-topsails and topgallant-sails, and to board the foretack. The mate also got an observation which enabled him to set his course. But the night that was passed had almost done for them; they could scarcely stand, and crawled about like sick men; and such was their pass that when the mate, laying hold of the pump, sung out to one of his companions to come and lend him a hand, the reply was that if the pumping was to depend upon *him*, the blooming hooker might as well sink at once, as there was not strength enough left in him to kill a flea; and it was not until the mate and the other man who stood at the wheel had consumed twenty minutes in entreaties, curses, and other marine rhetoric, that the exhausted creature was induced to " tail on." Fortunately for the poor fellows the wind had shifted into a quarter favourable for their voyage; they dried their clothes, cooked some beef, and managed to snatch sufficient rest between the intervals of pumping to give them back something of their strength. Everything went on well until they were about forty miles distant from Fayal, when the wind backed and blew a fresh breeze right ahead. This was maddening enough. They braced the yards hard up, packed all that they could hoist upon the vessel, and swore that, come what might, they would not slacken a halliard nor touch a sheet though it should blow fit to prize the old butter-box out of the water. It was not long after this that a steamer hove in sight, and, probably suspecting a case of distress by the look of the brig aloft—for the rags of the lower fore-topsail still fluttered upon the yard—slowed her engines to speak the little vessel. "What ship is that?" was asked. The name was given and the circumstances related. The steamer then offered to give the brig a drag towards Fayal, but when it was understood that a share in the salvage

would be expected, the second mate sung out no, they
wanted no help, they had scraped through it all right so
far, and were willing to venture the remaining risks.
Thereupon the steamer proceeded, but had not sunk her
hull when the wind again shifted, and enabled the brig to
look up for her port with the breeze full abeam; and
within nine hours from the time of having been spoken
by the steamer, a pilot had boarded her, and she was
safely moored at the west end of Fayal Bay. The valut
of the brig and cargo proved to be sixteen hundred
pounds, and when the award came to be made, four
hundred pounds were given to the owners of the ship
that had boarded the brig, one hundred pounds to the
master and crew of the ship, and a substantial sum to
the second mate and his two men.

A CHANNEL INCIDENT.

THE captains of the steamers which ply as passenger and cargo vessels between London and the French ports are a class of men familiar in a more or less degree to most of us, and it is probably this familiarity that prevents us from dwelling, with the emphasis that is deserved, upon the singular skill they exhibit, day after day, and year after year, in carrying their ships through what may be fairly called the most dangerous waters in the world, with scarcely a misadventure to vary the chronicles of their little voyages. By night and by day they are threading the intricacies of the crowded river Thames, groping through white mists so thick that a buoy must be alongside before it can be seen; struggling against sudden bursts of furious Channel weather, which bring up the most abominable kind of sea that a sailor can tumble about in—short, roaring cross surges which seem to knock the very breath out of the paddle steamer, sloping her funnel like the *bâton* in the hand of a band conductor, submerging one paddle-wheel to let the other revolve like a windmill out of water, and blowing up in storms of snow from the sponsons, whilst the worried vessel pitches savagely into the narrow hollows, flinging up her stern like the hind legs of a colt that takes fright at a passing train, her tarpaulins streaming with wet,

the escape-pipe blowing as she reels, a few sea-sick passengers wet through aft, two or three seamen in oilskins
dodging the seas forward, and the skipper on the bridge
holding on to the rail with both hands, and wondering
what that confounded old "Geordie" right ahead is up
to, coming along with square yards and his patched
boom-foresail bellying out like a sailor's shirt drying in
the forestay, as if the whole of the Channel were his
private property, and it was his duty to run over anything that got in his road.

Take the trip to Boulogne alone. In fine, clear
weather it is all plain sailing, no doubt. But if a passenger wants to appraise the merits of these captains
rightly, let him quit the pitch-dark deck, and a night so
black and thick that it is a positive relief to the eye
when a shower of sparks breaks out of the funnel and
blows away into the ebony gloom to leeward, and go
below into the bright, warm cabin, and overhaul a chart
of the mouth of the Thames and the adjacent waters as
far as the South Sands Head Light. Why, the sight
is bewildered by the mere look of that chart. It is as
though a spider had got foul of an ink bottle, and had
been cleaning its legs on a large sheet of white paper.
West and East Girdlers, Margate Sands, Long Sands,
Sunk Sands, Goodwin Sands—it seems to be all sand;
whilst the soundings are more alarming still—eleven
fathoms here, and close against it, one fathom—the
English of which is blue lights, rockets, hovellers, life-
boats, and Board-of-Trade inquiries. Jones, asleep in
his little state cabin, knows nothing of the maze of
perils through which he is being steered; he will rise in
the morning and take his seat at the breakfast-table,
and in the composed features of the brown-faced, hearty-
looking captain who sits modestly eating a rasher of

bacon, he will find no trace or hint of a vigil which began at London Bridge and which will not terminate until Boulogne is reached, though perhaps—the Goodwins being astern, and neither the Varne nor the Ridge being very much in the road—the hardest part of it may be said to be over.

But the dangers of the English Channel are by no means limited to shoals and foul weather. If those were all, the captains who safely carry hundreds upon hundreds of passengers to and fro in the course of the year, would have to abate something of the praise to which their excellent skill and remarkable vigilance entitle them. In truth, a danger more to be feared than shallow water and tempestuous weather is collision. I am not speaking of the daytime and fine weather; though even in the daytime and in fine weather collisions at sea will happen through a dozen circumstances more absolutely unavoidable than the most apparently unavoidable railway collision ever attributed by a coroner's jury to pure accident. It is the thick and silent night that is most haunted by this deadly peril. There is no wind, but a drenching drizzle drops unseen, save in the haze of the cabin skylight, from a black heaven that seems to rest its ponderous burden on the slender mastheads of the creeping steamer. It is the English Channel, the great maritime highway that leads to all parts of the world, and now as ever it is crowded with shipping; and through this mighty shadow, full of hidden life and hidden danger, those captains I am writing of must bring their vessels, day after day, week after week. They must not lag, for time is precious to their owners. Their unscathed emergence year after year must surely savour of the miraculous to any man who will but give his mind to the character of the dangers through which these sailors steer their vessels in safety. As a sample of this particular peril of collision, let me give an instance—a recent one. It may remove reference from all risk of misapprehension if I say at once that the steamer was from Bilbao, bound to a North country port.

She was abreast of Beachy Head when the night fell, and the fresh southerly wind, suddenly shifting to the westward in a little squall, dropped. During the latter portion of the afternoon the weather had been slowly thickening, but when the wind went the haze rolled up all round like smoke, blackening the moonless night until the very foam breaking away from under the counter was a scarcely perceptible glimmer upon the inky surface that melted into the midnight void within a biscuit's throw from the vessel's side. There were a few passengers, who vanished with the daylight and might be seen, by peering through the cloudy skylight glass, seated at the cabin table, the lamplight bright upon them, and making the picture of the irradiated interior, by contrast with the breathless blackness on deck, like a magic-lantern show. There was no gleam of phosphorus, no pallid streak of foam, to define the presence of the deep; but the soft seething of the passing froth, resembling the escape of steam heard thinly and at a long distance, filled the ear with a permanent note, and the dull vibration of the engines could be lightly felt. The haze was as wetting as rain; and the bullseyes over the lighted interior glimmered like emeralds in the decks upon which the mist was crawling as the vessel carried it along. There is a mystery in the hushed blackness of a night like this at sea which may be enjoyed in the open ocean, where the imagination lets itself loose upon the hidden leagues of

waters, and finds a kind of life in death in the mere
capacity of sentience amidst such a universe of shadow;
but it comes with an element of fear in a narrow sea
studded with quicksands and alive with vessels. The
eye struggles with the darkness in vain. Every instinct
sympathizes with the blindness that has fallen upon
you; but the strained ear catches no more than the sob
and fret of passing water and the chafing of gear as the
vessel sways upon the indistinguishable folds of the swell.
A man coming up out of the cabin of that steamer might
have reckoned the vessel deserted and left to her own
guidance. The wheel was amidships, and there was no
familiar binnacle-lamp to relieve with its soft mist of
light the eye that strove to pierce the darkness aft. To
know where the captain was, or whether there were any
hands on the look-out, it would have been necessary to
sing out or go about the decks and upon the bridge
groping.

Presently, what looked to be a composant—a small
trembling point of light—hovered in the blackness on
the starboard bow, and a moment after there crept out
under it a dull green smudge, as faint and baffling in
the thickness as the wavering flame of spirits of wine.
A steamer's lights; but all that was visible of her was
a deeper darkness in the air where she loomed, a row
of illuminated scuttles like the beach-lamps of a little
town seen afar, and fibres of radiance striking into the
foggy air from the bright light on the fore-mast. A
deeper fold of darkness seemed to overlap the night as
the invisible steamship swept by; the pulsing of her
engines thinned down, and the wash of the bow-wave
melted into the vague, haunting undertone of chafing
water—a sound coming you know not from where. On
a sudden the decks rang with a loud and fearful cry,

"There's a vessel right ahead! Hard-a-port! Hard-a-port! mind, or we shall be into her!" Crash! You could hear the sound of splintering wood, followed by a whole chorus of shrieks, whilst a dozen orders were volleyed out in hoarse notes on the steamer's decks. "What is it?" "Where is she?" "Get some lights along, in God's name!" A bright red flame threw out a wild radiance over the steamer's side: there was a rush of men to see what it was, and there, gliding past the steamer, every outline distorted by the crimson, flickering, streaming fires of a flare-tin held on high by one of her men, was a French three-masted smack, her decks apparently full of people, shrieking altogether, and in every conceivable posture of entreaty and terror —a dreadful picture indeed, standing out with terrible distinctness in the red light of the flare against the liquid pitch of the sea and the sky. Their shouts and cries were in the rudest *patois;* it was impossible to distinguish their meaning amidst the hubbub on the maimed and broken hull, as it veered swiftly astern, the mainmast over the side, the wild light flashing up the crowd of white faces as the flame from the tin broke out in a blood-red fork of radiance, and the whole fearful picture vanishing as the light suddenly expired, and the night rolled its inky tide over it. The steamer's engines were instantly reversed and the iron fabric stopped. The passengers came rushing up out of the cabin, increasing the distraction of the darkness by their eager, terrified inquiries to know what had happened. The chorus of shrieks astern was silenced, and only faint, single, most melancholy shouts broke the terrible silence upon the sea, proving but too conclusively that the vessel had foundered, and that these cries came from swimmers.

Meanwhile every lamp and lantern aboard the steamer that could be collected had been brought on deck, and you could see the dark figures of seamen struggling to get the boats overboard, rushing aft, and vociferating promises of speedy help into the blackness astern, some bending on lanterns to ropes' ends, and letting them drop over the side, and flinging ends of line overboard for the clutch of such swimmers as should reach the steamer; whilst the cries of the captain and mates and the shouts of the crew were made deafening by the pouring and hissing of steam up in the blackness overhead. It always seems an eternity at times like this before the boats are overboard; something gets foul; the oars have been taken forward to be scraped, and cannot be found; a kink in the fall has jammed in the davit-block; there is no plug, and a dozen voices are shouting all at once for something to take its place. But two boats at last were launched, after an interval of about five minutes, and pulled slowly away for the spot where the smack had foundered, a hand in each bow holding a lantern and keeping a bright look-out for those black spots which should denote the heads of swimmers and drowning men. A silence as of death fell upon the steamship as her boats left her. A crowd of people stood in the stern watching the two spots of light upon the water, breathlessly listening for any sound that should indicate the rescue of even one man. The lanterns over the side flung a short space of radiance upon the sea, and men were posted along the rail to watch for any approaching swimmer who should have been missed by the boats.

"Are you finding any of them?" bawled the captain of the steamer, sending his voice in a roar through the hollow of his hands.

"Ay, ay, we're picking them up," came back the answer in the merest thread of sound.

Ten minutes went by, and then suddenly there arose a shout from one of the men stationed at the port bulwarks.

"Here's a man swimming here!" and in a breath there was a rush to the side.

"Get another light over!"

"Fling him this life-buoy!"

"Pitch a coil of rope to him, but mind you don't hit his head, or you'll sink him!"

Half a dozen splashes told that these various orders had been executed. "He's got hold of my line!" sang out a voice, and as the rope was gently hauled in, a seaman, jumping into the bight of a rope, sprang overboard, and in a few moments both men were dragged over the side.

The half-drowned French smacksman fell down in a heap the instant he touched the deck. He was dressed in heavy sea-boots and oilskin leggings, and how he had managed to swim the distance from where his vessel had foundered to the steamer was a miracle not to be explained by any known law of specific gravity. He was carried into the forecastle, unable to articulate; but another quarter of an hour went by before the boats returned.

"How many have you?" shouted the captain, as they approached.

"We have four, and the other boat has five. There are women among 'em," was the answer.

They came alongside, and one by one the poor creatures were handed up. There were three women, dressed in the picturesque costume of the Boulogne fishwife, but draggled, streaming, with closed eyes, and a quick, suffocating breathing, half dead. Most of the others were in the last stage of exhaustion; but one was able to speak, and as he stood a moment in the lantern-light answering the captain's questions, a more moving object could not be imagined. The water drained from his fingers, his hat was gone, and his iron-grey hair—for he was an old man—lay in a tangled mass over his eyes; and there was a most heartrending expression of horror and despair in his face.

He said his vessel had left Boulogne early that morning. There were four women and ten men and boys on board. He owned that they had had no lights burning. He trembled like a freezing man, and was then led below, with his hands to his face, sobbing as if his heart would break, and moaning in his rude French that amongst the drowned were his wife and boy.

"Are you sure there were no others afloat when you came away?" asked the captain of the mate, who had charge of the boats. "One man swam to us, I must tell you, and we have him aboard."

"Sure, sir," was the answer. "We pulled round and round, but there was nothing to be seen. The people were saved by the mainmast that was left afloat when the smack went down. Those who were drowned missed it, otherwise it was big enough to keep all of them up."

For another twenty minutes the captain lingered, peering into the darkness, and keeping one boat overboard ready for the first sound. But the deep was as silent as the tomb, and nothing disturbed the deathlike stillness, unless it were the murmur of the men forward talking over the tragical incident, and the quick, passionate whispers of the passengers, as one would suddenly say, "Hush! what was that?" and another,

"See! is not that something moving out yonder?" Nothing more could be done. Very reluctantly the captain quitted the stern of his vessel and gave orders to get the boat on board, and in a little while the steamer was slowly moving again through the blackness, her decks wrapped in darkness and silence, whilst the haze floated like steam round the masthead light, and the water gurgled like the cry of a drowning man as it eddied round under the counter and went away in a pale glimmer of froth into the midnight gloom astern.

This little incident will, I believe, fairly set before the reader one of the perils against which those particular captains to whom I referred in the beginning of this article have to contend. Here is a fishing-smack, lying becalmed, without a light showing, on a night made pitch dark by a drizzling haze. How could such a collision be averted, short of the captain of the steamer bringing up?—a remedy which his owners most assuredly would not think the better of him for adopting. I repeat that having regard to the difficult navigation of the mouth of the Thames, as far south as the southern limb of the Goodwins, to the mass of shipping of all kinds that is always crowding these waters, to the perilous weather to be found there, and to the negligence, foolhardiness, and indifference which are characteristic of the seamanship of scores of the men—English as well as foreigners—who have charge of small craft navigating that sea, the manner in which the masters I am speaking of carry their steamers from port to port, year after year, showing always the same clean bill of health, implies an amount of skill and vigilance which any one acquainted with the navigation and dangers of the English Channel from the Nore to the Bullock Bank will own cannot be too highly praised.

I FELL once into conversation with a smack-boy—a York-shire lad—who told me a story which I privately declined to believe until I saw the printed report of the inquest, and had confirmation of his narrative from other hands. Men who go to sea meet with strange accidents, and perish through causes which landsmen would ridicule as impossibilities in marine novels; but seldom do a vessel's crew encounter such a disaster as that which befell the people of the smack *Apostle*, of Hull. I wish I could tell the story as the fishing apprentice gave it me. No painter could imagine a finer study than the figure of the lad in his blue knitted overall, his big boots, his sou'-wester, the hinder thatch of which forked out from the back of his head like the tail of a gull on the wing, his young face as he talked warming up into a kind of passionate awe and fear, as it might in his sleep when the dreadful circumstance stood out in the sharp con-figuration of a dream; whilst now and again he would pass the back of his rough hand across his forehead to rub off the gouts of sweat which gathered there. How-ever, I can do no more than translate the lad's yarn, and make it complete, in its way, by facts I got from others. The *Apostle*, then, was a smack, belonging to Hull. Will Stevenson was her master, and John Butler her

mate. Besides these she carried two other men and a
boy—the lad who told me the story—making in all five
souls. She left Hull, however, with only four men,
for the boy did not join her until she had been out
cruising a week, when he was sent to her in a steamer.

Life on board a smack is but a dull affair, and such
excitements as it has are all against the fisherman. It
is tedious work drifting for hours with the trawl overboard; but what is to be made of it when, as sometimes
happens, the trawl is got aboard and the net found torn
to pieces by a piece of sunken wreck or something of
that kind, and all the fish gone? Or take a gale of
wind blowing for a week, keeping the fisherman waiting
and waiting for a spell of moderate weather to fetch his
ground. To be hove-to in a smack in the North Sea is
such a dance as you must endure—not for a day, but for
several days together—to understand. Who that has
rolled in a big steamer across the tempestuous stretch of
waters which wash our eastern coasts has not watched
from the reeling, spray-swept deck the spectacle of some
dandy or cutter-rigged boat, jumping as if by magic into
the arena of the green, pelting, and foaming amphi-
theatre, with her storm jib-sheet to windward or well
amidships, a slender band of dark, close-reefed mainsail
tearing at the quivering gaff, whilst she tosses the high
spring of her bows at the rushing snow of the surges,
chopping sharply down into the livid vortex and making
it flash up in white spume that smothers her like the
smoking spray of a great waterfall, vanishing until her
gaff is hidden, and nothing shows but the jerking vane at
the masthead behind the glittering ridge of the sea that
runs at her with the roar of a goods train sweeping
through a tunnel; and then springing afresh to the
height of the thunderous surge until some fathoms of

her keel forward are exposed, and leaning down upon
the slope of the mountainous wave, and under the giant
pressure of the ringing gale, until her mast seems
parallel with the water and her dark shred of canvas a
mere black patch upon the snow-storm under her?

One wonders, looking at such a sight, how the big-
booted fellows aboard of her hold on; how they manage
to cook their food; by what inconceivable art they
contrive to "fetch" their bunks, or sleeping closets,
without numerous ineffectual struggles, first of all, to
hit the holes. But, in truth, no class of sailors make
less trouble of dirty weather than fishermen. With his
tiller securely lashed, the storm jib slatting a moment
or two as the reefed mainsail swings the little craft into
the wind, then shoving her nose round again as the sea
runs hissing away under her, the air forward dark with
flying foam and the water draining overboard in bucket-
fuls with every send, the smacksman sits cosily in the
companion, pipe in mouth, keeping one eye on the look-
out and the other eye on the time when one of his mates
shall come and take his place, and send him below to
toast his hands at the little stove, whose ruddy glow
pleasantly tinges the darksome twilight of the cabin, and
enables him to find, without groping, another pipe of
tobacco before he lies down.

Daybreak on Friday, the *Apostle* being then very
nearly five weeks out from Hull, found the smack with
her trawl over the weather quarter and near the north-
east end of the Dogger Bank. There was a fresh
breeze blowing and a middling sea running, and the
smack, surging to leeward with the trend of the waves,
rose and fell with the regularity of a pendulum. Many
miles distant to windward was another smack, apparently
heading for the same ground over which the *Apostle* was

dragging her trawl; otherwise the sea was vacant, and
the greenish dawn, flinging a sickly tint into the sky,
but leaving the water dark by contrast, and throwing up
the great circle of the horizon until the ocean resembled
a black and solid disc centring the huge concavity of
the heavens, made the immediate aspect of the deep
indescribably wild and melancholy. Indeed, there is not
a more desolate scene in the world than daybreak at
sea. The shadow of the night still hangs in folds upon
the water, and the dim illumination in the east only
serves to accentuate the chilly sullenness and grim
bleakness bequeathed by the black hours, the last of
which is drawing away in gloom into the west. But
the sun is a noble magician, and one stroke of his flashing wand converts the mystery of the dawn's vague hints
into a glorious revelation of blue heights and sparkling
waters. The *Apostle's* trawl had been over all night, but
a further short spell of drifting could do no harm, and
might furnish out another trunk of fish, and the interval
would give them time to get breakfast. So the little fire
in the stove was stirred into a good blaze, the coffee
boiled, and the two men at rest in their bunks routed
out for the meal. Fishermen are usually well fed,
and that is one reason, I suppose, why they appear to
relish their food in a manner you shall not find in any
forecastle. They have generally a good freight of fish to
pick from, and they are not slow to boil a cod or cook a
big sole when fancy and appetite prompt them. Somehow or other, to me, the smoke that comes blowing away
out of the little chimneys which pierce their decks always
savours of good cheer, and I was not at all surprised,
on looking over some victualling accounts shown me by
a smack-owner, to discover that the fishermen's sea-
larders—many of them, certainly—are stocked with a

liberality that must make owners very anxious indeed
to know how much fish there is aboard, when their
vessel's number or burgee comes within reach of their
telescopes.

Breakfast done, the master gave orders for the trawl
to be got in, and all hands tumbled up on deck to help
at one of the few heavy jobs which happen aboard
fishing-smacks. I have already said there was a fresh
breeze blowing, and the vessel, though hove-to with her
jib-sheet to windward, leaned down freely under the
weight of the reefed mainsail. The sea was regular,
but ran quickly, and every lift of the surges helped the
wind to lay the little craft along, until at times her lee
gunwale was flush with the water; but, like all boats of
her class, she would right with great vehemence, jumping to windward like a goaded creature of instinct, and
making the decks, slippery with wet, extremely dangerous
even to practised feet. They say that a fisherman's
walk is two steps and overboard, and any one would
have thought the saying a true one who had seen this
jumping bit of a fabric—sparking like a shrimp in and
out of the hollows of the tumbling waters—and watched
those big-booted, clumsily-moving, powerfully-built men
striding about the decks and making ready to drag the
great trawl in.

The process is very simple. The dandy-wink is
manned, the beam secured, and the net is then dragged
in over the side. The *Apostle's* men had succeeded in
getting in the net to the cod-end, as it is called. All
five hands were employed on this job, as it is one that
demands the united strength of such little companies as
smacks carry. They leaned over the rail to grasp the
net, but the vessel at that moment burying her lee side
through the lift of an unusually heavy sea, one of the

men lost his balance and went overboard, and the net
bellying out and sending away as the vessel rolled to
windward, in the twinkling of an eye the other three
men whose hands grasped the meshes were torn clean
over the beam and buried in the sea alongside, leaving
only the boy on deck.   It was done in a breath.   There
was no time even to raise a shriek.   One moment there
were all four men leaning over the side, the net securely
inwreathed about their fingers and waiting for the signal
from the master to drag together; the next they were
floundering in the water alongside, struggling, desperately clutching at the sinking net, and drowning.
There was a portion of the net on deck, and to this the
boy—who preserved an heroical presence of mind in
the midst of this appallingly sudden and dreadful disaster
—clung, that the men might not drag it all overboard
(and so have nothing to hold by) in their wild and
overhand grasping at the deadly, deceptive meshes which
floated and sank under them, and clogged the free action
of their limbs, and clung to them like masses of seaweed, settling them lower and lower as new folds of it
were swept by the water around them.   The net being
to leeward, the tendency of every sea was to belly it out
and increase its weight, whilst also setting the whole
mass of it further and further away from the vessel's
side; but this weight was beyond description increased
by the men who battled with the fury of strong dying
creatures in the deadly envelopment of the trawl.
Every now and again a sea would break under the
vessel and bury the poor fellows in foam; and then, as
the smack swept down into the hollow and leaned
heavily to windward, the drag of the hull upon the net
would strike it up again, and the four smacksmen would
reappear with dusky despairing faces, their eyes pro-

truding as they strained for breath. Robust as the boy
was, here was a conflict it was impossible for him long
to engage in. He held to the net with as manly and
resolute a heart as ever an English lad brought to a
struggle for life ; but the weight of the bellying net and
of the men clinging to it, increased as it was tenfold at
times by the swing and rush of the smack upon the sea,
must have taxed and presently exhausted the strength
of a dozen such as he ; gradually as he failed the net
was torn foot by foot away from him, though every time
it was wrenched from his hand he grabbed at it again,
and held on with clenched teeth until another swoop would
unlock his fingers as you might snap a clay pipe-stem.

Suddenly turning his head—for hitherto he had been
engrossed by the dreadful struggle in the water just a
fathom or two away beyond him—he spied the smack
that had been sighted at dawn, about half a mile to
windward. She was manifestly heading for the *Apostle*,
and the boy shouted to the miserable drowning men
that help was coming, and urged them to hold on. But
it was doubtful whether they heard the lad's voice.
Close upon the water the seething and hissing of foam
would be deafening ; moreover, their eyes were glazing
—death had his hand on their throats ; they presented
a row of asphyxiated faces, now and again revolving in
the eddies amid the trawling gear, sometimes thrown up
until their bodies as high as the waists were out of the
water, in which posture they would remain poised with
uplifted arms that gave them a horrible appearance of
entreaty, then vanishing utterly, to emerge a few seconds
after as the roll of the vessel swung them up and out.
The boy's strength was now completely exhausted, and
also he had to let go in order to signal to the approaching
smack. The whole of the net then went overboard.

About an hour had passed since the men had fallen into the sea, during all which time this most shocking tragedy was being enacted, whilst the boy with magnificent courage protracted his shipmates' lives by maintaining his hold of the net.   But the moment he let go the net veered out to its full sweep, and an instant after one of the men sank and rose no more.   The smack was now within hail.   The boy rushed to the weather side, and shouted out the dreadful story with such strength as remained in him, at the same pointing frantically at the water where the drowning men were.   The dreadful scene was by this time visible to the crew of the vessel, which proved to be a Yarmouth smack called the *Esther*. They tumbled their boat over the side; a couple of hands jumped into her and rowed at once for the perishing fishermen.   The boy ran back to the lee side of his vessel to encourage the poor creatures, but, looking, he discovered that the third man was gone; the master and mate only were to be seen, both clinging to the gear and scarcely living.   The little boat—hardly better than a walnutshell in such a sea—came along fast; but before she could come up to the master, he let go his hold and floated away, face down and arms hanging lifeless, upon a running wave.   A few strokes of the oars, however, brought the rescuers abreast of him, and he was seized and lifted into the boat, which then returned and took off the mate from the gear, to which he clung like a mass of black seaweed torn from the rocks.   Calling out to the boy that they would see to him presently, the Yarmouth fishermen rowed back to the *Esther* with their dreadful freight, but when they came to hand the men up over the side they found that the master was dead.   The mate was carried below, stripped and dried before the cabin stove, then wrapped in rugs and laid in a bunk. But he was little more than a corpse when rescued, and the skipper of the *Esther*, going presently to see how the poor fellow fared, found that he had expired. This was the last of the four seamen who a couple of hours before were full of life and hope and heartiness. Meanwhile the master of the *Esther* had sent three of his men aboard the *Apostle*, and two days after the disaster both vessels arrived at Yarmouth.

I know not how this simple little narrative may affect others, but the relation of it moved me deeply. That four English sailors should meet with death so unexpected, so full of anguish in its protraction, so bitterly cruel throughout a long, long hour's suffering, is perhaps significant only as another illustration of the perils of the deep. It is just one of the brief and simple annals of the poor sailor. But I cannot but think that the behaviour of that young apprentice—named Frederick John Graham—makes it worthy of record. Those who have any acquaintance with English fishermen are only too painfully well aware that the relations between owners and apprentices are by no means of a cordial kind, and in several places I hear of the clergy and others taking up the cause of these boys, and asking the public for funds to help to give them homes and to educate them into some knowledge of religion and morality, and out of the deplorable ignorance in which they are suffered to live. I am well aware that some apprentices are decidedly trials to smack-owners. They will run away with their master's clothes. They will refuse to go to sea in the hope of being taken before a magistrate and sent to prison instead. But, nevertheless, I cannot quite satisfy myself that smack-owners—taking them as a body, granting

many exceptions—treat their apprentices with the consideration that even the most hard-worked and ill-paid
servants in other walks of life expect and extract from
their masters. One does not want them to act the part
of schoolmasters, and teach the boys to read and write;
but upon what principle do they oppose the efforts of
others who are willing to perform that duty? and why
do they find something obnoxious in homes established
to furnish smack apprentices with certain comforts and
harmless recreations—calculated to keep the lads out of
the streets when they come ashore from a voyage—
which smack-owners themselves do not apparently see
any reason for providing? For these and other reasons,
therefore, the endurance and hearty English spirit of
Graham may be thought a proper subject to hold up to
applause; for, accepting the lad as a type, the public
may witness enough merit in the hardly-used and
laboriously-worked community to which he belongs to
justify them in giving a helping hand to the humani-
tarians who are struggling to make the lives of the
apprentices when ashore happy and useful to themselves; whilst the smack-owner will recognize in this
narrative of Graham a spirit to which he is by no means
unaccustomed, though he needs perhaps to have it more
diligently emphasized than he has yet found it, before
he will accept the hint it offers to his forbearance and
to his humanity as the owner—in a most literal sense—
of lads who, taking them all round, are the most friendless beings in the world, with the whole machinery of
the law against them, and only here and there a few
seaside dwellers to take their part by endeavouring to
give some little wholesome sweetness to their existence
when out of their vessels.

AN impressive story of the destruction by fire of a full-rigged American ship in the North Atlantic has been told me. Certain features of it combine to make it an incident certainly worthy a longer record than is usually devoted to maritime disasters, and altogether it yields such an idea of the horror of fire at sea as is not often to be got from stories of misfortunes of that kind.

A certain Wednesday in August found the *R. B. Fuller* a little over three weeks out on her voyage from Cardiff to Valparaiso. She was freighted with coal, and carried a crew of twenty hands, being indeed a ship of 1360 tons register. A vessel of that size, unless maimed by short fore and mizzen topgallant-masts, is sure to make a handsome picture on the water under full sail. The Americans rarely mutilate their ships, but, on the contrary, with sky-scrapers and moon sails, pile their canvas to the heavens, and, mixing plenty of cotton with their sail-cloth, carry a yacht-like whiteness aloft that will shine upon the horizon like a peak of ice brilliant with snow.

The weather had been fine all day, with a beam wind, and the deep, long, black-hulled ship, leaning under the weight of her cloths, slipped softly along her course over the trembling and flashing blue. What

witchery is there comparable to such sailing? No sense
of delight that is born of freedom and movement sur-
passes the joyousness kindled in the spirits by the swift,
smooth rushing of a lofty sailing-ship over the swelling
bosom of a great ocean, all sky above, all sea below,
and between, the music of the clear, glad breeze.

The sun sank and the night gathered, the wind fined
down, and the American ship, with spars erect, floated
over the dark waters, in which the starlight seemed to
flake away in small coils of quicksilver. Over the side
nothing could be heard but the tinkling of the ripples
at the stem; aloft there was not a stir, unless it were
now and again the muffled chafing of the foot of a sail
upon a stay or the rattle of a reef-point upon the
canvas. Forward all was in shadow, with the figure of
a man on the look-out; whilst aft the mate on duty
paced the deck, pausing sometimes to take a peep at
the compass-card, where the binnacle-lamp glistened in
the brass centre-bit of the wheel, and shone upon the
face of the officer as he stooped to observe the indication
of the card.

The captain, Mr. Thomas Peabody, had left the
deck about three-quarters of an hour. He was asleep
in his cabin, when, shortly after ten o'clock, he was
awakened by a feeling of suffocation, and perceived that
the cabin was full of smoke. Moreover, the atmosphere
was charged with a deadly, nauseating, gaseous smell
that gave an iron tightness to his throat and filled his
body with an unendurable prickly sensation, as though
strong mustard had been rubbed into his skin. He
rushed on deck, where the fresh air at once revived him,
and not immediately perceiving anybody about, shouted
for the officer of the watch. The chief mate came running out of the darkness forward, and before Captain

Peabody could address him, cried out that the ship was on fire. The news spread as if by magic, and in a few moments the decks were alive with the crew hurrying out of the forecastle.

Of all cries, none thrills through the heart of a sailor like that of fire. Human helplessness is never so felt as at such a time. The ship is a burning volcano, from whose cabin the red flames may soar presently, making a wide circumference of air scorching hot with a furious play of withering flame. The mate said that he believed the fire was in the hold under the cabin. Forthwith there was a rush to the hatches, which were immediately closed; calking-irons were fetched, and the air was busy with the hammering of mallets. It was a sight to see the men. There was no lack of determined courage among them, but the cry of "Fire!" was ringing in their ears; they toiled in quick impulsive rushes, with feverish haste, glancing to right and left, knowing not in what part of the ship the fire would first show itself in flame. Every ventilator was closed, and the cabin shut up, in the hope of stifling the fire, and the crew then gathered in a group in the waist to watch and wait and see what their work would do for them.

Presently somebody called out that the smoke was still breaking through.

"Look there—and there, sir!"

It was hard to guess how it could escape; the hatches were closed and calked, every aperture securely blocked, and yet there was the smoke breaking out from all parts of the vessel as steam rises from the compact earth. On this the carpenter's chest was overhauled, and by order of the captain the men fell to work to bore holes in the deck. As the solid planks were pierced the smoke belched forth in puffs, mingled with a pestilential exhalation of gas that forced the seamen to work with averted faces. The pumps were then manned, the hose got along, buckets dropped over the side, and all hands turned-to to drown the fire by discharging water into the glowing cargo. Clouds of steam came up through the holes, regularly followed, as the white vapour thinned, by spiral columns of black smoke which wound round and round to the height of the maintop, where the light breeze caught and arched them over. No flames were as yet visible, but the men knew that the ship was full of fire, that at any instant the hatches might be riven and shrivelled up by a discharge of flame, and therefore when the captain gave orders to lower the boats there was a rush to the davits.

When the boats were in the water alongside, the captain, desiring to save certain articles, called the mate and four seamen to accompany him to the cabin; but they had not been there a minute when they suddenly ran out, some of them vomiting blood, and all of them complaining that their heads were swelled so that they were like to burst. Indeed, but for their speedy flight, they must have dropped dead in an atmosphere that was rendered virulently poisonous by the combined gas and smoke. A short spell of rest and fresh air recovered the poor men, and the crew then proceeded to victual the boats with such provisions as they could come at. The mainyards were braced aback, and the men entered the boats and rowed to a distance of about half a mile from the vessel, where they remained.

It was a fine night, very calm, and the ship, with her mainyards aback, lay steady. Hour after hour went by, but no flame showed itself, though there was a gradual thickening of the smoke from the deck, and the seamen could observe it hanging in a shadow over the

mastheads of the vessel and to leeward of her. Gazing
at her as she stood like a marble carving upon the dark
sea, it was difficult for the men to realize that her hold
was a concealed furnace; that by taking off one of the
hatches and looking down they could have beheld an
incandescent interior, a red-hot surface like a lake of fire,
with blue and green flames crawling over it, and masses
of smoke, repelled or consumed by the intense heat of
the central spaces. But for the shadow overhanging her
glimmering heights, there were no signs that anything
was amiss with the ship. Surveyed from the low level
of the boats, she looked a majestic fabric out there, a
brave sight in the faint, fine starlight. It was a long,
weary, and bitter vigil for the poor fellows to keep.
They would not leave the neighbourhood of the vessel while
she remained afloat. They could not tell what might
happen. If she burst into flames the light she made
might bring them help. Or the fire might die out and
so give them their home to return to. Whilst she was
there, she was, in a manner, something to hold on to;
for it was a fearful thing to look away from her into
the mystery of the darkness around, and to think of
being left to struggle amid that black and fathomless
desert of water in open boats, which brought the mighty
deep within reach of their hands.

Slowly the long hours went by, and then the dawn
came, and the sun uprose. With the first of the grey
light every eye was turned upon the ship. They could see
the shroud of smoke that overhung her, yet not a spark
of fire had been visible throughout the night, and this,
now that the sunshine was on the sea, begot a hope in
the men that, though to be sure the smoke crawled
thickly from the ship, the fire was not so bad as they had
feared, and that a long and resolute struggle might

enable them to conquer it. Accordingly the oars were thrown over, and the boats headed for the vessel. The boat occupied by the captain was the first to get alongside. He jumped on board, and was followed by others; but the heat of the decks striking through his boots made him put his hand to the planks. It was like touching hot iron. He walked to the cabin, but on feeling the door he withdrew his fingers with a groan. The whole fabric was full of fiery heat; whatever touched the flesh gave it pain; the very ropes which lay coiled over the belaying pins were too hot to handle; the pitch was bubbling in the seams; the air between the bulwarks resembled the atmosphere of a furnace; in the haze of the heat every object seemed to revolve like a corkscrew; and the men in the boats said that feeling her side, even to the level of the water-line, was as bad as putting the hand upon a boiler full of steam

A cry from one of the seamen who had come over the side in bare feet, raised a kind of panic among those already aboard. "Over with you," was the shout, "before she bursts into a blaze!" and in mad haste the poor fellows dropped over the bulwarks, seized their oars, and resumed the same distance from the ship that they had occupied all night.

Soon after this a small breeze of wind arose. It seemed to penetrate the vessel, for with the draught there soared up a thick body of smoke. Her passage to leeward was perceptible in the short, oil-smooth wake to windward of her; but the drift of the boats was the same as hers, so that the men had no need to use their oars to maintain their distance. There was now weight enough in the wind to blow the smoke clear of the decks before it rose a foot above the bulwarks, so that the picture of that full-rigged ship remained there in its completeness. As the time passed the men would see a fountain of sparks hove up occasionally in the smoke. It was dismal work sitting and watching that fine ship smouldering. All that the men possessed was left aboard of her; they had come away, most of them, in their shirts and trousers, many without shoes, and there in those three boats they sat looking at the burning vessel, silent in the main, often glancing around them on the look-out for a sail, and holding on to the thwarts or gunwales as the boats jerked and toppled sharply about on the bit of a sea that the wind had raised. A little before noon those who had their eyes on the ship perceived the mizzenmast to sway to and fro a moment; then suddenly it fell with a crash; a rush of smoke, like a monstrous balloon, hovered over the quarter-deck and concealed the ruin; but it soared into the air, and sailed away on the wind under a sudden furious discharge of sparks, which resembled the explosion of a mass of rockets, and when the vapour had settled down it was seen that the mizzenmast was over the side, the vessel a wreck aft, whilst forward the sails were dusky and red, as though iron-stained, with the blowing of the sooty coils and the fire of the glowing sparks.

Until the night came down no further alteration took place in the appearance of the vessel. During all those long hours the men sat crouched in their boats, watching their burning ship and searching the sea for the help that did not come. The second night rolled down dark, with windy clouds drifting across the skies. Here and there the phosphorus shone in the curl of a breaking surge. The half-clad men shivered under the fresh night wind; but the ship whilst she stayed there was a beacon. If they quitted her, what was there to do? She was a dreadful signal upon the dark sea, and might yet bring succour, and so they stayed. But the darkness had not gathered an hour when a tongue of red flame darted out of the deck abaft the mainmast. It threw out a great light, like the flash of a big gun, and the men could see one another's faces in it. It sank and seemed to expire, and then there rushed up a body of crimson sparks which clearly defined the dense and swelling volume of smoke that blotted out the heavens in the south-east; but speedily the flame swept aloft again like a serpent, wreathing itself around the mainmast; then forward and apparently out of the fore hatch sprang up another pillar of fire, and presently there were tongues and lances of flame crawling and hissing all over the doomed vessel, gliding in serpentine convolutions along her bulwarks, over her stern, around her bows, limning the configuration of her hull with burning pencils, filling whole leagues of the darkness with light. The stays, the shrouds, all the gear connected with the bowsprit and jibbooms, caught fire; the yards were kindled; the whole outline of the vessel was scored in fire upon the night; every detail of the standing masts and yards and sails, the crosstrees, outriggers, and tops—all the furniture of the ship's decks, the boat-davits, the catheads, the martingale, the spritsail yard, were expressed in flame. It was like the picture of a ship drawn in fire upon a black curtain. Not a sound came from the men in the boats. They watched breathless, full of amazement, thoughts of their serious position being overwhelmed by the dreadful but magnificent sight of that noble ship. When suddenly the burning vessel opened, a flame such as might go up from Vesuvius soared into the air, making a roaring noise upon the wind; there was a sound of the falling of the burning masts and yards; and then, in a breath, the whole terrific picture vanished; it

disappeared as you might blow out a candle; the boom
of an explosion came dully up against the wind, and
there was nothing but the stars and the black sea and a
dense shadow in the south-east where the smoke from
the foundered ship was heavily sailing away.

If ever loneliness was felt at sea it was felt by those
men when that great light went out, and left them in
darkness and dread and uncertainty. But enough if I
say that after tossing about for two days and nights,
they sighted a sail to the westward, which they chased
until they were sufficiently near for her people to see
them. She proved to be the London barque *Paracca*,
whose captain gladly received the poor fellows and
treated them with the utmost humanity.

SEA-SICKNESS.

MANY will remember the terrible description of Mr. Aaron Bang's pangs of sea-sickness in "Tom Cringle." It is fortunate that everybody whilst suffering from nausea is not so demonstrative as the West Indian planter. The horrors of a rough passage between Calais and Dover would be fearfully increased were the prostrate passengers to bewail amid their throes the wines and dishes which old Neptune exacts from them. And yet one has only to consider what kind of heaving sea it was that set the West Indian howling for brandy-and-water to commiserate the poor old epicure's noisy anguish. Sailors will appreciate the affect upon a passenger's stomach of a heavy gale of wind dropping as if by magic and leaving the sailing vessel—for Tom Cringle flourished before the days of steam—rolling upon a tremendous swell. A steamer whose screw or paddles are revolving and driving the hull through the water will not, amidst the heaviest sea, give you the same sensation you get from a vessel tumbling about on a strong, fine-weather swell, not a breath of air to steady her or give her way. The steamer in a measure escapes the worst of the seas by sliding out of them; her bows are lifting clear of the washing coil whilst her lee sponsons are buried, and she half jumps the intervening hollow as her paddles thrust her from the summit of the surge. Often have I watched this behaviour in swift steamers, and seen them take a bow or beam sea as a horse takes a hurdle.

But the motion of a vessel becalmed amid a heavy swell is one of the most uncomfortable of all sea-experiences. Let the merest relic of nausea linger in the human breast, and this movement shall make a full-blown anguish of it. I have heard of stewards, men who have made a dozen voyages round the world—whose stomachs were as immovable in a gale of wind as the ship's figurehead;—I have heard of such men, I say, in a heavy breathless swell, tumbling down among their dishes too sick to stand, rolling about among the crockery and echoing with their groans the spasmodic gurgling of the water as it sobbed in the scupper-holes or washed up full, green, and sickening over the glass of the scuttles or the cabin windows.

This sort of tumblefication is fast becoming a thing of the past among passengers, very few of whom nowa-days make their voyages in sailing ships, although it is by no means yet an extinct feature of the emigrant's progress from the old world to Australia and New Zealand. At such times as this the ship is as sea-sick as any of the yellow and haggard sufferers who moan in her cabins; squeaks and cries and the rumbling of a disordered internal organization resound in her hold. Over she leans like a fainting creature, and the bubbling wash of water alongside delivers a note full of nauseating suggestion; the beating of the canvas against the masts sends a shiver through the hull; down drops her counter amid a swirl of gurgling eddies, the stern-post complains, the rudder jars, the wheel chains harshly strain; and then up, slowly and giddily, mounts the after end of the staggering fabric,

making the pale and helpless holder-on there feel that
his brains are descending into his boots, and that his
bowels are rising to fill the emptiness of his skull, whilst
sharp reports of crashing crockery break out through
the skylights, the cask that has broken adrift on the
main-deck rolls to and fro and defies the pursuit of the
three or four seamen who dodge about after it and go
sprawling over one another into the scuppers, the pigs
under the long-boat scuffle and snort, chests and boxes
fetch away in the cabins, the sailors flounder over the
cable range as they stagger out of the galley with hook
pots of tea in their hands, and the sea-blessings showered
out by the cook as he chases his dishes and pans and
burns his fingers in his efforts to save the cuddy dinner,
can be heard by the man at the wheel and the youngster
who is shifting the dog-vane at the main-royal masthead.

This, I say, was an old experience; but it was a time
to try the stomach whilst it lasted. Think of three or four
days and three or four nights of it! In these days if you
are sea-sick you at least have the satisfaction of knowing
that the ship is always going ahead, and that the day,
if not the hour, when your nausea will have terminated
may be pretty accurately fixed. And yet what man
hanging over the side or prostrate on his back and
execrating existence can get satisfaction out of the
thought that, bad as his sufferings are, they might
be worse by being protracted? I believe there are some
people who, when once their heads are fairly over the
rail, or when what Thackeray calls the "expectaroon"
is between their knees, are inspired by such a loathing
for life that they are not to be moved by the wildest
threats of destruction. Once, in crossing from Calais to
Dover, I noticed a vast pile of luggage, unsecured by a
single lashing, heaped up on the fore-deck. All was

well until we got clear of the French coast, when a small beam sea set the vessel rolling. In a few minutes the bulwarks, from the sponsons to the eyes, were crowded with people of both sexes and various nationalities, all engaged in raising their voices in the most dismal manner, wiping their cheeks, and casting bloodshot glances around them, only to direct their gaze again with hideous rapidity upon the giddy white water that rushed in a spinning dance aft while they exploded in loud roars. I looked with alarm at the nodding pile of luggage, feeling sure that an extra lurch would tumble the whole over and seriously injure the unhappy sick people on one side or other of the vessel. I spoke to a French sailor—they were all Frenchmen aboard that steamer—and advised him to secure the luggage. He merely shrugged his shoulders and made off. I addressed another, who could not or would not understand me. Thereupon I went up to the sea-sick people, and touching first one and then another, I pointed to the tower of luggage and advised them to go further aft, out of the way of the boxes, lest they should tumble upon them. They must have seen their danger as plainly as I, but not one of them offered to move. They kept a tight hold of the rail, merely turning their lacklustre eyes upon me with an expression in them, half imploring, half savage, as much as to say, "Let the boxes come! Let us be crushed! What stops the boxes from falling?" Fortunately the second sailor I accosted perceived by this time that if the luggage was not secured the top boxes bade fair to go overboard when the stronger sea of the mid-channel was reached; and so among them the Frenchmen bound the boxes to the deck by ropes, and by so doing, in my humble opinion, saved several valuable sea-sick lives.

In this same journey I was amused by an aspect of
sea-sickness, or let me say a condition of it, that will
be familiar to many who make short passages by water.
Going forward of the funnel, where smoking is not pro-
hibited, I took notice of a gentleman wearing an eye-
glass. He was clad in a yachting coat, embellished
with brass buttons, and he was smoking a large cigar. A
very stout Frenchman was asking him some questions
in broken English. I heard the gentleman with the
eye-glass say that he believed there was a pretty
middling sea on outside; but "if you're afraid of being
sick, mounseer, you should smoke, sir. You should do
as I do. Nothing like tobacco for settling the stomach;"
and he gave a horribly confident laugh. The corpulent
Frenchman withdrew with a groan, and lodged himself
in the gloom under the bridge near the engines, the
vibration of which caused his immense body to quiver
like a jelly on a supper-table when people are dancing
overhead, and there he lay so clamorously ill that the
firemen dropped their shovels below to come up and
look at him.

Meanwhile I kept my eye on the gentleman who
believed in tobacco, and when the steamer took the first
of the seas I saw him seize hold of a shroud or a funnel
stay and set his legs wide apart. He continued puffing
at his cigar for some time. but the intervals between
removing and lifting it to his mouth grew longer and
longer; presently it went out, but he took no notice.
He had his glass in his eye and his face looked forward;
he was deplorably pale, and I never could have believed
that such a trifling thing as a brass button and so prosaic
an object as a nautically-cut coat could become, on
occasion, more cuttingly ironical than anything a man's
friend could say of him. The eye-glass gave this gentle-

man an unusually glaring expression; he never shifted
his gaze—I should say that he never winked. There he
stood with his legs wide apart, the extinguished cigar
in one hand and the other supporting him with a death-
grip, staring with horrible intensity at nothing. I knew
perfectly well that if that man were made to shift his
posture or speak he would rush to the rail.

It was a brave fight; but it could not last. A young
coloured gentleman, the ashiness of nausea visible in
his dark skin, suddenly jumped up from under the pile
of luggage, where he had been screening himself from
the wind, and, bolting to the side, expended himself in a
howl full of the deep throaty noise that is peculiar to
negroes. It was irresistible; the man with the eye-glass
let go, and staggered away, with his cigar gone and his
hands extended. I feared that he would find no room,
for the bulwark was lined with sufferers; but, with the
selfishness of acute suffering, he plumped with all his
might between a couple of Frenchmen, squeezed the
aperture between them open with his elbows, and fixed
himself there; and there he remained until the water
grew smooth near the English cliffs, and the steamer
went forward on a steady keel.

It is difficult to understand why people should find
anything diverting in sea-sickness, than which surely
nothing can cause more suffering. Of course, if a man
will give himself airs ashore or on smooth water, use
nautical words, and deride the misgivings others are
honest enough to confess to, then, indeed, if we find that
marine gentleman with his head in a basin, or with his
face over the side and his hat gone, we have some
excuse to laugh at him. There are people who never
will own that they are sick at sea, just as there are
people who deny with indignation that they snore in

their sleep. Such folks deserve our ridicule. For what
is there to be ashamed of? I have known old sea-
captains quit ships newly arrived from around the
world and be ill on a voyage from London Bridge to
Hull. If such men can shout for the steward without
blushing, it is hard to know why Jones, of the Middle
Temple, or Smith, of the Stock Exchange, or Snooks,
the celebrated novelist, should sneak to the side and
feel humbled if his fellow-sufferers see him blue in the
face with his pocket-handkerchief half-way down his
throat. It may be that people laugh at sea-sick sufferers
because of the enormously and by consequence absurdly
levelling character of the malady. One might be the
most compassionate creature living and yet find it impossible to stop laughing at the debasement of the high
and mighty personage who, when he came aboard, people
whispered was the Right Honourable So-and-so, or the
acute and famous Mr. Justice Somebody Else. He sits
aloof, he is full of dignity, he scarcely raises even a
condescending eye from the book or paper in his hand
to glance at the other passengers, who sit doggedly, if
humbly, waiting for the wheels to go round, inside and
outside. I say that a man must be more than human
if he can help laughing when the high and mighty
personage changes colour, when he puts his paper down
and rolls his eyes about, when nothing seems to keep
his head on but his shirt-collar, and when an invincible
horror of life gleams in that gaze which has grown
hollow with surprising rapidity. Alas! no amount of
reputation, no social importance, no eloquence, which
in other places might affect the heart and even improve
the understanding, can save him. Yonder in the bows
is a poor little cockney, a second-class passenger, in a
shabby coat and his trousers half-way up his legs, sick

I

beyond the power of description; there is no bench long enough on that vessel to furnish room for him and the great man at once if the water were smooth; but Nausea has waved her wand, and the humble little cockney and the high and mighty personage are brothers and equals, fellow-sufferers, with all distinctions vanished between them as, with yellow faces, the cockney forward, the great man aft, they overhang the rushing foam with open mouths, the tears pouring from their eyes, and anguish inimitably expressed in the curve of their backs and the occasional kick-up delivered by their legs.

More pathetic, perhaps, is the newly-married couple, though many a cruel laugh and jeer have been directed even at them. But nothing is sacred at sea. Sentiment that is full of poetry in drawing-rooms, among flowers, under the moonshine, among hedges, takes another character among rough waters.

I remember once crossing fifty miles of sea in company with a young gentleman and his bride. They were returning, I took it, from their honeymoon. They sat together upon a small, uncomfortable bench fixed against the inside of the paddle-box, whence they commanded a fine view of the action of the engines, and where the smell of the oil-cans hung steadily in the wind. They both knew they were going to be sick, and sat with hands locked, two devoted hearts bent on suffering together. The steward—a pale, large, sandy-haired man—considerately anticipated their wants by placing a couple of basins at their feet. The dismal implements made but a melancholy foreground for the impassioned pair, and I wondered how they would like to have had their photographs taken in that posture. A quarter of an hour sufficed to make the picture tragical. The wife leaned across the husband and the husband held on to her.

His heroic devotion was immense; I could hear him in guttural accents pouring consolation into her deaf ears amid the intervals of his own convulsions, and when an unusually heavy roll to leeward caused both basins to slide away out of sight under the bench, I never beheld anything more touching than his struggles to replace them without letting go of his wife.

Happily, however, the heart is occasionally steeled against such objects of misery as this by spectacles of selfishness and fear in the last degree contemptible. I particularly recall a gaunt Frenchman with a spiked moustache, who, long before nausea afflicted him, refused to stir from his seat to help his miserable, prostrate wife, and who answered her murmurs to Emile to put something under her head and something over her feet, by fierce commands to her to hold her tongue. This wretched man was himself seized with nausea, and so great was his fear—either excited by the somewhat heavy sea that washed alongside the vessel or by his sufferings, which to judge from the noise he made, must have led him to suppose that, bit by bit, the whole of him was going overboard—that after every explosion I could hear him shrieking, "Maman! maman!" like a girl.

What is the remedy for sea-sickness? I wish I knew—most cheerfully would I impart the secret. There are many prescriptions, from the ice of Dr. Chapman to Jack's lump of fat pork attached to a ropeyarn; but nothing seems to answer the end designed. Nor is it very remarkable that the wonderful vessels which were to put an end to nausea should still leave the "expectaroon," even on their own decks, the useful piece of furniture passengers have for generations found it; for whilst clever gentlemen have shown us how the effect of the rolling and pitching movement of a ship upon the head or stomach may be overcome by pivoted saloons and swinging accommodations, they have entirely failed to produce any kind of mechanism to obviate the consequences of those movements of a vessel in a seaway which are alone responsible for sickness; I mean the heave up and the swoop down. If a ship oscillated on an immutable basis, a cot or a balanced chair would effectually stop nausea; like a wineglass on a swinging tray, the passenger could always maintain a posture perpendicular with the horizon. But what is to qualify the sensations which follow the swoop down into the hollows and the roaring heave up on to the summits of the seas? Everything in the ship must accompany her in her falls and in her risings; and it is this motion which sends people rushing to the side, which sets them roaring for the steward, which causes them to loathe life and to lie with their heads anywhere and their feet anyhow.

I cannot help thinking, however that imagination contributes something, and often a very great deal, to sea-sickness; otherwise how are we to account for people suffering from nausea actually before they step on board the vessel that is to carry them? If a sea-sick man could be sent to sleep his sufferings would cease; yet the vessel goes on rolling, and if it is this movement, affecting the stomach, that causes nausea, I cannot quite see why the stomach should not be as sympathetic in sleep as in waking. Any way, I believe that a person could be made to forget to be sea-sick by having his imagination intensely occupied or his fears excited. Let a vessel full of sea-sick people drive ashore, or catch fire, or be in collision; let the captain bawl out, "We are all lost;" it would be interesting to conjecture how much sickness would remain aboard that ship. A good prescription might be a profoundly exciting novel: some hideous mystery so distractingly complicate as to make one sink all thoughts of waves and stewards in the eagerness to discover whether the figure Sir Jasper sees was really a ghost or his first wife, and whether it was her ladyship or the groom she ran away with who shot Signor Squallini in the throat and did the fine arts a real service. But it is better to be sea-sick than in danger; and, if the novelists can do nothing for us, I am afraid there is no alternative but to go on feeing the stewards and building swift vessels.

A LOG EXTRACT.

The following entry was made in the official log-book of a ship named the *Oxford*:—"Fifth November, 1882, Sunday, 4.0 p.m., lat. 35° 39' S., long. 18° 53' E., W. Waters, A.B., while furling the mizzen-topsail fell from the yard into the sea, striking the half round of the poop in his fall. A lifebuoy was promptly thrown him, the ship brought to the wind—it blowing a fresh gale from the S.W., with thick weather and a heavy sea at the time. The port lifeboat was at once lowered, and proceeded under the charge of Mr. A. Bowling, second mate, to pick up the man. Owing, however, to the shock sustained by him in striking the ship, and his being encumbered with oilskins, etc., he sank before the boat could reach him. After an unsuccessful search, the boat returned to the ship and was with difficulty hoisted up, owing to the heavy sea which half filled her. Everything was done that could be done to save the poor fellow. (Signed) J. Braddick, Master."

Now, here is the whole story, as who would not suppose? The sailor dropped overboard, a boat unsuccessfully searched for him, and then the ship braced her mainyard round and sailed away. But extracts from log-books, I have taken notice, are like the little box which the fisherman in the "Arabian Nights" found upon the sea-shore; when it was opened a wonderful creature shaped itself out, and its figure filled the sky. I particularly realized this when Mr. Bowling gave me a sketch of the yarn of which Captain Braddick's log is the briefest hint. Why, what a world of adventure, of heroism, of peril grows up out of these marine entries! Is it four lines about a ship rescuing a crew from a sinking vessel; or about a captain coming across a smack's boat in the middle of the North Sea, with nothing in her but a little crouching, starving boy; or about a brig found drifting helplessly, with her crew, dead of frost, lying upon her deck? Assuredly in those four lines there is the making of a thrilling volume to any man who shall faithfully put his hand to the work and, exaggerating nothing, relate merely the adventure as it befell, and how it came about and ended, and what the actors in it said, and did, and thought. Here, in very brief form, is Mr. Bowling's own yarn, told with my pen, of an incident as common pretty nearly in its way at sea as the sight of froth blowing into a hollow, or of the curve of the bow-wave flashing green and glass-smooth from the shearing cutwater.

"We left Calcutta on Sept. 4, 1882, with a full cargo, bound for the port of London. All went well—if by well you'll understand nothing extraordinary outside spells of bothersome head winds, dead calms, and now and again a twister over the quarter to give us legs— until came Sunday, Nov. 5, on which date you'll see by the extract from the log-book where we were; the glass stood low, and in the morning there was a kind of wild wet light in the sun when he sprang up from behind the dull-coloured sea, and the lustre that came along with him seemed to roll on the top of the swell as if it was burning oil lying there instead of being the up and down flashing of fair weather, when the light sounds the very bottom of the ocean with its silver lead-line, as you may see for yourselves if you'll watch the break of day under a pure sky and over clean blue water. We were under topgallant-sails, on the starboard tack, the wind about west, with weight enough in it to swear by, and a slow gathering of haze all along the horizon over the port quarter—south-west the bearings would be about—and a thick, deep-breathing swell coming out of it, tumbled by the wind into a bit of a sea that washed with a stormy noise along the bends, and made the ship as uncomfortable as an old cab on a road full of stones.

"I had charge of the deck, and not liking the look of the weather, I went below to tell the captain about it. He had been up pretty near all the night that was gone, and was in his cabin taking some rest. But there's very little rest for shipmasters, who need to have as many eyes as you find in a peacock's tail, that they might close two or three of them at a time, if ever they're to get the amount of sleep that all other kinds of people, barring nautical men, find needful to keep themselves alive on. Well, sir, I called the captain and told him that the weather looked threatening, and straightway he came on deck and took a squint around. The wind was freshening slowly and surely, and the topsails and topgallant-sails, out of whose cloths the wet of last night's squalls of rain were not yet dried, were stretching as if they would burst under it; and the water to leeward washed like boiling milk all along the scuppers as the ship was rushed by the pressure, taking the seas with a floating jump, and making them roar as she split them with her sharp stem and sent them seething in white smothers on either hand. There were clouds crawling up out of the thickness in the west and south, and passing like smoke over the mastheads, and there was a look of racing about the whole ocean with the sailing of those bits of vapour, and the pelting of the ship, and the wild hurrying rolling of the seas, along which there were sea-birds screeching as they skimmed in their low flight through the driving spray in pursuit of us.

"Well, sir, the fore topgaliant-sail was furled and the watch lay aft to roll up the mainsail; but not for long did we hold on with the main topgallant-sail; that was clewed up soon, and the wind freshened as sail was diminished; so that, although half stripped of canvas, the ship was heeling to it as before, whilst there was the hard look of a gale of wind in the sky that you saw grey between the scud; and the thickness was blowing up nearer and nearer, making a mere biscuit's-throw of the horizon, so that the seas looked lumping things as they rolled, all of a sudden like, out of the haze, and were under the ship and standing up on either hand of her almost as fast as they seemed to be formed. We were now under topsails and foresail only—of the square canvas—when on a sudden there comes a bit of a lull, and a sort of silence aloft that sounded strange after the roaring, and a great noise of washing waters all around; and then plump sweeps up the wind in a wild out-fly out of the south-west, driving the ship forwards until the foam of the cutwater looked to be smothering her head. All hands were called to shorten sail, the three upper topsail halliards were let go, the starboard braces rounded in, and the helm shifted to bring the ship to her course. Four able seamen and four boys went aloft to furl the upper mizzen-topsail. You know the old story: the light hands well out, the older hands in the slings and quarters, and the sail swelling up like a

sheet of iron to the wind that blew fair into it in a storm
betwixt the two yards. I had my eye on those men I
am speaking of, when a blast like a squall swept the
canvas out of their fists, and in a breath one of them
fell with a twirl and a toss of his clenched hands off the
yard, striking the half-round of the poop a blow that
came along with the yell of the wind in a frightful thud;
and with that, rebounding as a ball might, over he goes
into the yeast and froth alongside. It is a horrible
thing to happen; it will stop the breathing of the
strongest for a minute. The fellows on the yard roared
out, 'Man overboard!' I sprang aft, and had a life-
buoy in my hand in an instant, which I threw fair, as
I prayed and believed, to the yellow patch of sou'wester
that I saw dark on the foam of the side of a sea; but
the wind blew the light thing, like a feather, to leeward
of him. But he was swimming—there was life in him,
though, man, you should have heard the thump of his
fall, and then thought of him struggling there with
his great sea-boots full of water, and his heavy oilskins
dragging him down, and a rushing of froth over his
head every time that a sea swept him up into the snow
of its breaking crest. Well, sir, we went to work
smartly; the hands came tumbling down from aloft,
and the ship was brought to with her main-topsail
aback, whilst half a dozen of us were obeying with mad
haste the order to clear away the quarter-boat ready
for lowering.

"Meanwhile a hand remained in the mizzen-topsail
yard to keep the poor fellow in sight, and he was
shouting that the man was swimming, and swimming
strong; that he didn't seem to see the life-buoy, but
that he was struggling bravely; and I, seeing this too,
and driven half mad by the pitiful sight of that sailor

and shipmate fighting the whole ocean, as I may put it, and battling it with an English seaman's courage, sang out, 'Who's going to volunteer for the boat?' There was no hanging back; it was just a leap to see who should be first. As fast as they could tumble in, there they were, six of them, the pick of the crew—merchant seamen, sir, whom we're being taught to despise; there they were, I say, with the others handling the falls, and every one looking as if the saving of the life of the man astern was his business and nobody's else; for he was a shipmate, and that means a brother at sea, sir, when the forecastle holds real sailors.

"It was four o'clock in the afternoon, and the mist was driving between the masts. I was in charge of the boat, but try my dead best I could not help her being badly stove before we got away, and the water came in fast as we headed for the spot where the man was last seen. You must go through it to realize the difference between the deck of a ship pitching and rolling, no matter how heavily, and the feel of an open boat released from her side in the same sea. The solid deck you're fresh from makes the contrast fearfully sharp, and I can well believe what I remember reading in your yarn of the wreck of the *Indian Chief*, that the survivors of her crew when in the lifeboat owned to being more frightened by the fearful tossing and jumping of the buoyant craft than they were when in their foretop, with the hull of the ship going to pieces under them. We could only pull four oars, for two men had all their work in baling the boat, one with a sou'wester and the other with a sea-boot, those being our balers. My duty lay at the helm, in watching for the man and looking out for the seas. Bitterly cold it was, the sun going down, the haze thick around, and the ship a mere heaving darkness upon it when we had measured but a few lengths from her. I looked narrowly about me, but could see nothing of the man. Sometimes a lump of green water tumbling over the foam would show like his head, and my heart would leap: but the next moment the clear sea would roll away from the blowing froth and explain what the deception was. We pulled to the buoy, but it was empty.

"Then one of the men said, 'Supposing even Bill had not been hurt by the fall, surely he couldn't live in such a sea as this.' And another said, 'Think of his wraps and oilskins, sir. The best swimmer in the world couldn't hold up all these minutes under such drags.' But they spoke not as if they wished to give up, but as if preparing themselves for the disappointment. Had he hurt himself more than we could know? Was he broken and dying when he touched the water, and were his struggles there the despairing efforts of a broken and dying man? We strained our eyes, but could see nothing save the boiling heads of the seas which came roaring down upon us and threatened with every desperate swing to fill the boat. Still we kept up heart. 'Another pull, boys! impossible to go back without him!' I would cry, whilst the two fellows in the bottom were chucking the water out over the side, and the thickness stood like a wall around.

"Well, for three-quarters of an hour did we hang about, pulling in all directions, and thinking only of finding and saving him; and then we gave up and looked round for the ship. I could not see her. I sung out to the men, 'Do you see the ship?' and they turned their heads upon their shoulders to look; and the chap in the bow cries out, when we were standing nearly end on up the side of a sea, 'There she is, I think.'

"Well, to be sure, I could see her, but it might as well have been the thickening of the mist that way as the ship, for she made a shadow scarcely noticeable, and I looked with dismay at the distance that lay before us to row over, and at the water that was coming into the boat as fast as the two men could bale it out, and at the terrible sea around us. We had got into such a situation that the seas ran right abeam, and every send drove us to leeward, and sometimes the mist swept down so thick that there was never a man of us all who could see the ship, though, thanks be to Heaven, it did not come to our losing sight of her for good. It was a bad job for us that the heaving and straining of the boat caused her to leak worse and worse. But for her leaking I could have put the two men who were baling her to the oars, and they would have been just the sort of help we wanted; instead of which they were scarcely able to prevent the boat from filling. It would, however, have been destruction to us to have set more men than those two at the job they were on. Every moment was precious; the afternoon was fast waning; in a short while the night would be upon us, and I knew quite surely that if it came before we fetched the ship we were doomed men. Oh, sir, it was a fierce bit of labour. In the midst of our struggles a squall of sleet blew down and hid the whole surface of the ocean to within our own length of us; but it cleared off, and when it was gone the mist thinned somewhat, and gave us a better view of the ship, at whose peak we could see a colour streaming as a signal of recall. Never was any man of us nearer to death in his life than he was during the time we occupied in reaching the vessel. That we did reach her you may reckon, or I should not be here to tell you this story. But by the hour we had pulled across her head and dropped along the port side of her, the water in the boat was up to the thwarts, we showed scarce more than our gunwale, it was almost dark, the sea had increased in volume, and the wind was blowing half a hurricane. We were fairly exhausted when we gained the deck, but humbly grateful as we were for the preservation of our lives, ne'er a one of us could cast a look over the quarter in the place where our shipmate had gone down, and where the darkness of the evening now lay, with the white foam showing with startling clearness upon the sides of those black rushing hills, without feeling that our thankfulness would have been deeper had we been allowed to rescue the man whom we had been very near to losing our lives to save."

LONELINESS has many forms. It is Selkirk, imprisoned in an island, with nothing but the wash of the surf to break the shocking stillness; it is the mountain-climber missing his way, and passing the long night amid the tremendous silence of towering hills and black valleys; or it is the loneliness described by Byron, that of a man solitary in crowds. But what sense of solitude can equal that felt by shipwrecked men in a small open boat, surrounded by a universe of waters, with no other chance for their lives than such as a passing ship may bring? It is not the first hour, nor yet the first day; the agony of such a trial lies in the slow maddening of the mind by fruitless expectation; the deception of the white shoulders of clouds, which look like ships as they seem to linger a moment upon the horizon before sailing above it; the straining of the aching sight against the pitiless, vacant sea-line; the sense that death is close at hand, though a hundred deaths may have been suffered before the skeleton's clutch is upon the sufferers.

No kind of human anguish is more terrible, and no stories catch a tighter hold of the imagination than those which relate it. Generations have shuddered, and generations will yet shudder over the grand and soul-moving description in "Don Juan." The raft of the *Medusa* is an immortal horror. The narratives which are at once the most fascinating and depressing in the marine records are always those which concern the sufferings of human beings adrift in an open boat in the midst of a great ocean. The deep is unchanging in the misery it works. Our ships are of iron; they are propelled through the calm sea by an irresistible power faster than a gale of wind would drive them; they are of proportions so colossal that many of them could sling the "tall schippes" of our forefathers over their sides, and stow them on skids as they stow their boats; and yet just the same sort of sufferings are endured now by mariners as were experienced by them in the days when a vessel of thirty tons was reckoned big enough not only to seek the North-West Passage but to hunt the unnavigated oceans after continents.

I heard once a story that seemed fitter for the lips of an ancient mariner, like Coleridge's, than the mouth of a seaman who lives in an age in which the Atlantic is crossed in eight days, and in which the Cape of Good Hope has been pretty nearly extinguished by a narrow water-way across a hundred miles of sand. The hearing it took me back in imagination to the days of the ship *Thomas* of Liverpool, the *Lady Hobart* packet, the Yankee ship *Peggy*, the French East India Company's *Prince*, and I know not how many more old craft which ages since became phantom vessels, to be wrecked again and again upon the dark and noiseless oceans of tradition.

"My name," began my informant, "is William Pearce. I have used the sea for above eight and twenty year, have sailed in all kinds of ships in all sorts of capacities—boy, ordinary seamen, sailmaker, bo'sun's mate; crossed the Atlantic seventeen times, and been round the world eight; been shipwrecked thrice; likewise overboard during seven hours of darkness, and picked up at daybreak with my head in a lifebuoy; know pretty nigh the best and the worst of the weather that's to be found at sea; and am, therefore, capable of taking my oath to this, that of all the bad jobs that ever I was in or that ever I heard of any other sailor being in, there's nothing to beat the sufferings us men of the schooner *Richard Warbrick* had to endure when the foundering of that vessel obliged us to take to the boat.

"The schooner sailed from Runcorn with a cargo of coals for Plymouth. She was twenty years old, and a trifle over a hundred tons burden. There were five of a crew, and nothing particular happened until we were abreast of the Bristol Channel, when there blew up a heavy gale of wind from the east'ard. There's no call to describe it; it was of the regular kind, full of wet, and raising a sea a sight too big for a vessel of one hundred tons pretty nigh chock-a-block with coal and with twenty years of hard use in her hull. However, we scraped through the gale and two or three more that followed fast, until one morning we were somewhere betwixt the Scilly Isles and the Cornish coast. It was dark, thick weather, blowing and raining hard, the sea rough, bitter cold—as you may calculate it was, the month being January—and everything invisible that was more than half a mile off. The wind was east and north, and we were ratching along under very small canvas, when, being turned in, as it was my watch below, and the land o' Nod close aboard, I was roused up by a loud cry on deck and a tremendous crash. I tumbled up as fast as ever I could pelt, and found the schooner going down and the men getting the only boat we carried overboard. It was no time for questions. You could feel

K

the vessel settling under your feet, just like standing on soft mud and sinking in it. The seas were washing over the deck, and growing heavier as her bulwarks sank lower. There was nothing but white water to be seen on the starboard bow—no rocks, nothing showing above the froth ; but I didn't want any one to tell me that we had run foul of the Seven Stones. There was no time to do more than launch the boat and roll into her. Daly was the last man in, and scarce had he jumped when the schooner plumped clean out of sight, going down like a deep-sea lead, so suddenly that it took my breath away.

"There's no sensation worse than that a man feels when he looks for the ship he's been forced to abandon and finds her vanished under the sea. The ocean never seems so wide as then. The whole world appears to be made of water. Sailors are a class of men little given to talking, and when they come clear of such jobs as this they say next to nothing about it, and so people think that either they're men without the capacity of feeling, or else their sufferings were not equal to what might be supposed. Had people who take these views been in that boat along with us, they'd look sharp in altering their opinions. The suddenness of the disaster—our being one moment safe, and the next tossing on the sea in a small boat, with the schooner gone, nothing saved but what we stood in, not a morsel of food nor a drop of drink of any kind, the wind blowing fit to freeze the eyes out of our heads, every mother's son of us soaked to the skin, and drifting fast away towards the Atlantic—took our senses away for a spell. We sat holding on and staring like daft men. The captain was the first to rally.

"He called out, ' A bad job ; it's a bad job, lads ! ' several times, and then said, ' No use letting her drive too fast. We mustn't let her blow away into the ocean ; '

and with that we lashed the two oars to the painter and flung 'em overboard.

"This brought her head to wind and slowed her drift; but, for all that, every hour was carrying us further and further towards the open sea, and away from the Scilly Isles and the Cornish coast, which were our best chance, so that all the hope that was left us was being picked up by a passing vessel. Yet there could be no worse month in the year than January for that likelihood. How long were the gales and the frost going to let us last? We were far to the nor'ard of the fairway, in a part of the sea that every vessel was bound to give a wide berth to. The weather, as I have said, was so thick that you couldn't see half a mile off, and though of course it was sure to clear in time and open out the horizon, so that vessels could have a view around them, the question was where should we be when it came on fine?

"Unlike a good many others who have gone through such dreadful messes as this, our sufferings began the moment we tumbled into the boat. In the lowest latitudes that ever I was in I never felt such cold. Had the water been fresh our clothes would have froze into coverings of ice. The air was full of spray, and squalls of sleet came rolling up. We sat in the bottom of the boat in a lump, to keep her steady, and for the shelter of one another's bodies, and those who were to windward—that is, in the fore part—would shift from time to time, and others take their place. We had no mast nor sail, nothing but the two oars we rode to. It was a Monday, and all through the daylight we sat lifting our eyes above the gunwales, and trying to pierce the haze for a vessel. It was blowing about half a gale of wind, and it kept steady. Now and then we'd ship a dose of water, and bale it out with our caps; but it kept our feet soaking, and I reckon it was worse than being without boots at all. The boat did well, and the oars were a kind of breakwater, and helped her. After four in the afternoon the night drew on. We never could get used to the darkness. The daytime was bad enough, but the night made our sufferings maddening. The wind, when the sea was black, would take the feel of solid ice; we couldn't see one another, and that made talking a kind of foolishness, and so we never spoke, which caused every one to feel himself a lonely man upon the sea. Likewise the noise of the water would sound stronger. In the daytime I took no notice, but at night I'd find myself listening to the crying of the wind up in the dark, and the hissing that rose all over the ocean from the breaking of the waves.

"I don't know what my mates did; but that first night I never closed my eyes, never tried to shut them, never thought of sleep. I saw the dawn come, but the haze was too thick to let the light show on the horizon; it was overhead as well as around, when the morning broke; there was no darkness that you'll find hanging in the west at daybreak. Indeed, I believe the sun was up above the sea before any light came, so thick it was. All the men were awake, and dreadful they looked, as of course I did. One of them was named Burke. I noticed him at once, and thought he was dying. He lay athwartships with his back against the starboard side of the boat, and there was a strange working in his fingers, like the movement of a woman's hands opening a skein of thread.

"The captain said, 'For God's sake look around, lads, and see if there's anything in sight.'

"The sea ran high, and made it dangerous for any

of us to stand up, for fear of capsizing the boat; so we
hung over the gunwale with our chins on a level with it,
and stared into the driving smother with all our might:
but there was nothing to be seen but the breaking seas
when we were hove up, and the water standing like walls
on either hand when we dropped into the troughs. All
at once Burke sat up and began to sing out for a drink
of water. He talked as if he believed we had it and
wouldn't give it, which was the first sign of his insanity.
The captain tried to pacify him, speaking very kindly,
and seeking to cheer him.

"'We have outlived a day and a night,' said he.
'Keep up your heart, mate; we may have a thousand-
ton ship under us before it comes dark again.'

"But Burke kept on crying for water, saying that he
was dying for it, and pointing to his throat; and then,
falling on all fours, he puts his face to the salt water
washing about in the bottom of the boat and sucked up
several mouthfuls. Well, it seemed to do him no hurt,
and he lay quiet. Soon after this I spied something
knocking about in the sea a few fathoms astern, and
called the skipper's attention to it. He said it was one
of some kegs of butter that had been aboard the
schooner, so we pulled the oars in and dropped down to it
and picked it up. We broke it open and ate the butter
in fistfuls, being mad with hunger; but it was as salt
as brine, and the effect of it was to make our thirst
raging. The knife we had used to open the keg lay in
the bottom of the boat, and Burke, on a sudden turning
over, seized hold of it, jumped up, and fell upon the captain. He hit him once, but the knife didn't pierce
through the thick jacket the skipper had on, and, before
he could raise his hand again, we dragged him down and
kneeled upon him.

"There was no worse part in all that dreadful time than this. The madman's face was a terrible sight; almost black it was. He snapped about him with his teeth, and his cries and curses were things it brings the sweat upon my face to talk about. Think of our situation, mad with thirst ourselves and struggling with a madman, a killing north-easter blowing like knives through our frozen bodies, the sea leaping and roaring around us, and nothing between us and the bottom but the little old boat we were in. We were too weak, and in too much suffering ourselves, to remain holding the madman down, and finding him quiet we let go, and squatted one close to another for warmth; but scarcely had we hauled off from the poor wretch when he jumps up and throws himself overboard. 'Mind!' shouted the skipper, 'one's enough!' fearing that if we all got to the side Burke had leaped from we should upset the boat. I was the nearest, and as he came up close I leaned over, and got him by the hair, and dragged him into the boat. He was pretty nigh dead, and gave us no more trouble.

"Well, sir, the night came down a second time, finding us living, but without the looks of live men. I made sure I should never see another daybreak. My thirst was not so sharp as it had been; but I don't know whether the dull throbbing in my throat, the kind of lockjaw feeling in my mouth, the burning in my tongue as though it were a lump of hot iron, was not more torturing than when the craving was fiercer. All night long it blew a strong wind, with now and then a squall of sleet and rain, and hour after hour two of the men, Parsons and Daly, were groaning in the bottom of the boat. When the light came, I looked to see who was alive, and my eyes falling on Burke, I called out, 'Dead!' The captain leaned down and felt him, and said, 'Yes, he's gone. He's the first. God have mercy upon us!' and catching hold of my shoulder he stood up to search the sea, but the haze was as thick as it had been all the time, and he threw himself down with his hands over his face. Presently, looking at the body, he said, 'We must bury him; but first, my lads, let us say a prayer for him and for ourselves.' We all knelt while the captain prayed, and when he had done we lifted the body and let it go overboard.

"The madness that thirst creates broke out strong in Daly and Parsons when the body was gone, and down they dropped as Burke had, and lapped up the salt water in the bottom of the boat like dogs would. The captain implored them not to drink, but they never heeded him nor me, who likewise entreated them. However, no harm seemed to come of it. Well, sir, there's no need for me to describe that Wednesday nor our third night in that open boat. Thursday morning came, making the fourth day, and to our joy the weather cleared, the wind shifted and moderated, and the sea went down. We got the oars in, rigged up one as a mast, and two of us having oilskin coats on, we joined them so as to form a sail, made a yard of the other oar, and putting the boat before the wind, which was blowing a light breeze from the south'ard, headed, as the captain judged, for the Irish coast. All the day long we kept a wild look-out, as you may reckon, for any passing ship; but never once, not in the furthest distance, did such an object heave in sight. We might have been sailing in the middle of the Pacific. Nature in us was almost numbed. We had come to such a pass that we were too faint and exhausted to feel the craving of hunger and thirst. At least I can speak for myself, and it's in that way I account for my suffering less at the end than I did at the beginning of the dreadful time we went through. It was still cold, but nothing like the bitter cold of the gale and the heavy seas and squalls. We reckoned by the sun that the wind hung steady, and we let the boat slip before it; that was all that could be done. If we were to sail at all we were bound to keep the breeze over our starn, seeing there was nothing to draw but a couple of oilskins secured to the oar.

"But the coming on of Thursday night was like the bitterness of death itself, sir. Indeed it was. All day long we had reckoned upon sighting something before the sun went. Every hour we had hoped and prayed and believed would heave up some sort of vessel to come to our rescue; and therefore, when it drew up black, only a few stars among the slow clouds, and we were brought face to face with another long winter's night, my heart failed me altogether; I felt that there was a curse upon us, and that we were doomed men, singled out to die of famine, the most cruel of deaths, because the longest. Think of ninety-six hours in an open boat, in January, in the Chops, a north-east gale blowing most of the time, with never a morsel of food except the salt butter, and no drink but the salt water washing in the boat! And yet when the Friday morning came we were still alive, the captain steering, doubled up with faintness and the cold, his knees against his mouth, and his head lolling for want of strength in his neck; Daly and Parsons lying still as dead men under the thwarts, and me in the bows, too weak and broken-hearted even to cast my eyes around the sea to notice if there was a vessel in sight.

"The morning passed; the afternoon passed. Were we to go through another night? The sun was within half of an hour of his setting when Parsons, who was leaning his breast on the gunwale, stood upright and pointed. His mouth was full of froth, and as he tried to speak the foam flew out of his lips, but no words he spoke; it was naught but a kind of death-rattle in his throat. We all looked in the direction he pointed to, and saw a large sailing-vessel heading right down for us. How we watched her! all of us standing up, never speaking, and only moving with the roll and toss of the boat. It took her an hour to approach us, and then she hove us a line; but her people had to sling us aboard. None of us could move. Nothing but the excitement of seeing her had allowed us to stand. The moment the line was in the boat and we were alongside, we all became as helpless as babies.

"The vessel's name, sir? She was the Austrian barque *Grad Karlovak*, commanded by so humane a man that I feel fit to cry when I think of him and his kindness to us poor miserable shipwrecked English sailors. That's the story, sir, or as much of it as there is any call to relate. Five days and four nights in the month of January, in an open boat, most of the time blowing heavily! The tale's known at Plymouth—it's known at Runcorn—it's known to Mr. Hopkins, the agent of the Shipwrecked Mariner's Society at Plymouth. And I'll tell you somebody else it's known to, sir—some one as'll swear to every word of it; and that's me."

WAITING FOR A SHIP.

The Shipping Office in Tower Hill is a place where seamen, firemen, stokers, and others assemble in the hope that captains in want of crews will come and pick out the best men among them to "sign on," as it is called. I was induced to visit it the other day by hearing a sailor complain bitterly of the filthy state of it. "Neglect," said he, "is our lot; but the condition of that shipping office beats my time. It's all dirt and Dutchmen, and if ye want to see something to make you reflective, just trot down the steps and take a turn round the yard the next time you're passing that way." When finally I did trot down the steps I found myself in a kind of courtyard, flanked on the one hand by the shipping offices—grimy doors, leading into gloomy interiors—and on the other hand by a species of shed, partitioned into stone rooms, with hard and painful seats against the walls, and unwholesome draughts of dampish wind eddying about them. It was a gloomy day—rain had fallen, and pools of muddy water gleamed here and there in the yard; the brown and stooping London sky threatened more wet, and flung a shadow that made the shipping office and its yard and its condemned-cell-like rooms under the shed an unspeakably cheerless, depressing, and miserable picture. Some sixty or seventy men stood or moved about in groups in the yard, or were seated in the cells under the shed. I was hardly prepared to witness so large an assembly, and remained near the steps for a little while surveying them. A few of them were decently attired—one or two respectably and comfortably dressed in good clothes and clean linen ; but a large proportion of them were, so far as their costume went, little better than scarecrows. Some were clad merely in shirt and trousers, with their naked feet thrust into old shoes or boots ; here and there was a red or blue shirt, or a figure buttoned up in such a manner as to suggest that under the ragged old coat there was no shirt at all. "And is this," thought I, "the British sailor of the nineteenth century?—is this the original of those rubicund features, those flowing breeches, that tarpaulin hat on nine hairs, those well-polished shoes twinkling in the light-hearted measures of the hornpipe, which are offered by novelists, dramatists, and theatre lessees as accurate representations of the jolly tar we are so fond of joining in choruses about, and whom we gaze at with such patriotic enthusiasm as he hitches up his breeches, turns his quid, and smites his timbers?" Every crowd of human faces is full of variety, but no crowd that ever I looked at had the variety submitted by the countenances of these sixty or seventy men who were "waiting for a ship." The negro's face—flat, bland, and open-mouthed—was, of course, not wanting. Square cheeks, hollow cheeks, high cheeks ; complexions black, brown, and yellow; eyes of every pattern and shade—from the small, twinkling blue of the North-country to the filmy and red-webbed optics of the gin-soaked Cockney—combined, with the different build and shapes of the men, the appearance of their clothes, the various head-coverings, to make up a truly singular scene. I stepped forward and got among a little bunch of men, of whom, addressing myself to one, I asked what sort of shelter that dirty and wretched shed and those bleak and stony cells offered in the winter, when the wind blew with an edge and the sleet and rain fell. No notice had been taken of me before, but on my making this inquiry the eyes of the whole group were fixed upon me, and half a dozen voices answered at once. The meaning of the replies was lost in the confusion, but the noise was like a signal; for I can truly say that within a few seconds of my having asked that question every man in that yard and every man that had been lounging in the cells had gathered about me, so that before I very well knew what was happening I found myself—pretty tightly squeezed—in the centre of a mass of men, the outer portions of whom pressed eagerly upon the inner to hear and see what was going forward. It was like a mutiny on a large scale, and when I looked around at the mass of faces, and tasted the tobacco-laden breath of the near people blowing hot against my cheeks, I felt that nothing was wanted to complete the suggestion of revolt but the gleam of a score of sheath-knives flourished in the air. " Give me a little room, my lads," said I, working with my elbows ; and, having freed myself somewhat, I said, "There seems no lack of men here ; captains ought to find no difficulty in manning their ships."

" They don't want Englishmen ; it's Dutchmen they take," shouted two or three voices.

" Here's a man," called out some one, pointing into the left of the crowd, "who's been walking this yard for five months."

" Five months, as true as the words I use is English," bawled a hoarse voice. " But they won't have me because

my name's Johnson. If it was Unks von Dunks I'd ha'
been woyaging o'er and o'er again in the time I've been
kicking my heels about starving here."

"Scoffen von Romp would do as well," said a man
near me. "Don't matter what the name is so long as it
sounds Dutch."

"By Dutch I suppose you mean foreigners of all
kinds?" said I.

"Ay, they're all Dutchmen!" was the shout.

"But why is it that Dutchmen are preferred to
Englishmen?" I asked.

The hubbub raised by this obliged me to hold up
my hand and entreat silence; but it would not do.
Every man's mind was full of the grievance, and, amid
the chorus of replies, I barely succeeded in catching
such answers as—"Dutchmen 'll ship for two pound a
month!" "Dutchmen 'll eat anything!" "Englishmen
won't put up with the messes Dutchmen 'll swallow!"
"Skippers can rope's-end Dutchmen, but they durs'n't
serve Englishmen so!" "It's the Dutch crimps as
does it!" and so forth.

It was difficult to hear these cries and watch the sea
of surging heads and faces around me with unmoved
gravity. There was something to touch the very dullest
capacity of appreciating the ridiculous in the astonishing
contrasts of physiognomies, and in the multifarious expressions which adorned the poor fellows' countenances;
but I am not sure that the appeal made to my laughter
did not owe much of its force to the sorrowful element in
it—to a quality of pathos lying close to humour. Many
of these faces had a pinched look, that was painfully expressive of want, if not of positive starvation; and sad
indeed, it seemed to me, was the sight of it in men who
carried the manners of real seamen, and who appeared

to me to be fit for any forecastle afloat, and for any duty
that a sailor is expected to understand.

"I suppose you all come here with certificates of
conduct in your pockets?" said I, when the hubbub had
ceased.

Instantly a crowd of fists were thrust under my nose,
filled with documents, and "Here's mine!" and "Here's
mine!" "V. G. every one of 'em!" was roared out in
twenty or thirty voices. I looked at some of these
certificates, and found the letters "V. G." (very good)
endorsed on the backs of all that I examined.

"D'ye want to ship, sir?" sung out a fellow whilst I
was glancing over these papers. "I've got two V. G. certificates in my pocket, and as I've not had anything to eat
to-day you shall have 'em both for a couple of shillings."

"Are certificates often sold in this fashion?" said I,
of a quiet-looking man standing alongside of me.

"Sold!" he exclaimed indignantly; "what's to hinder
'em? If a man sticks to the name that's on the certificate, who's to know? and so ye get men shipping themselves with false characters, no more fit for sailors' work
than if they wos greengrocers."

"Perhaps that's one reason why skippers and owners
prefer Dutchmen to Englishmen," said I. But this raised
another storm; they shouted that more rascality went
on in that way among Dutchmen than British sailors;
that the reason was not that, but because, as I had
heard, Dutchmen shipped for wages no Englishman would
look at, and put up with food, accommodation, and treatment which no Englishman would endure, and likewise
because there was a deal of underhand crimping work
going on between the foreign boarding-house runners and
mates and captains, and so on.

Here the emotions of these sixty or seventy men

brought them pressing so heavily around me, that my
anxiety to hear their statements was swamped in the
labour of breathing and the struggle to liberate myself.
I bawled to them to make way, as I wanted to have a
look at the rooms under the shed; on which they drew
back and let me out, though they followed at my heels
as I passed from one room to another, talking and arguing hotly, calling marine blessings down on the heads of
all Dutchmen, and wondering what good it was nowadays being born an Englishman, when even a Finn,
whom, in the olden times, no sailor liked to be shipmates
with, was thought a better man? The rooms were
middle-sized, damp, dark, and dirty compartments, and
were meant to serve as waiting-rooms for the unhappy
creatures who thronged the bleak and frowsy yard in
the hope of being engaged by captains. It was like
being in the dungeons in the Tower of London—which,
by the way, stood close at hand—to pass through these
death-cold apartments and view the legends, dictated
by hopeless waiting, roughly scrawled in pencil upon
the walls. Dirt and soot everywhere!—on the ceilings,
on the floors, on the walls, on the benches, in the very
atmosphere that filled the cheerless haunt. A strip of
grating ran through the floors, disclosing the outline of
a hot-water pipe; but it looked, in that grave, the very
corpse of a heating apparatus; and when I asked if ever
these stone rooms were made warm by that old, mouldy,
dirt and soot covered contrivance, the only answer I got
was a loud growling laugh, as if, exquisite as was the
joke, it was likewise very offensive. And this, thought
I, as I stood gazing with mingled astonishment and dis-
gust at the picture of grime, neglect, and dirt, is the
great London shipping office, the medium for the vast
and ever-growing port of London for the transaction

of business between the masters and crews of ships !
Who are these men who come here in the hope of obtaining employment by manning the fleets we are never
weary of extolling as the source of Great Britain's wealth
and power, that they should be used in this manner—
furnished for their long, weary, and often hopeless waiting with accommodation fouler, unwholesomer, colder,
more soul-depressing than the worst prison that ever
excited the horror and provoked the denunciations of the
philanthropist ?

"Has this place," I asked, " been long in this condition ? "

"It used to be kept a little more decent," was the
reply; "but it's been falling from bad to worse for many
a month gone.   Considering the fees * we sailors have to
pay, it's a shame that we should have to put up with a
place which no farmer who values the lives of his hogs
would stow 'em in.   I've been day after day down here,
from the opening hour till the closing at four o'clock, for
six weeks, hoping to be engaged ; and I tell you, sir, that
a man need be to be born a gutter-snipe, used to sleeping
all his life under railway arches and the likes of them
places, not to feel the effects of such a slum as this upon
his spirits, when day after day goes by and he has to
keep on waiting here for a captain to single him out.
You are seeing it now in summer, when the air's warm ;
think of it in winter, sir, with the slush a foot thick, and
the wind blowing into those waiting-rooms fit to turn
your marrow into ice."

The Board of Trade is responsible for the conduct and
keeping of this office.   Have the officials of that great
department any conception of the state of the place ?   Is
it ever visited by them ?   Do they know anything more

* This was written in 1881.

about it than that it is situated somewhere in the neighbourhood of Tower Hill? Nothing more disgraceful is
to be found in London.

By degrees the men left me, to resume their weary
trudging up and down or to draw together in groups;
on which, finding that I should be able to converse without the risk of suffocation, I went up to a well-looking,
decently-dressed sailor-man, on whom I had had my eye
for some time previously, and asked how long he had
been waiting for a ship.

" It will be three weeks to-morrow," he replied.

" What are your certificates? "

" I have four in my pocket," he answered, producing
them; and I found that he had served in the several
capacities of boatswain, sailmaker, and able seaman
aboard sailing-vessels belonging to some of the best
firms in London.

" How long have you been at sea? "

" Thirty years," he replied.

" And is it possible," said I, running my eye over his
neat suit of pilot cloth, his clean blue shirt, and silk
handkerchief, and admiring his unmistakably sailorly
appearance, and the frank expression in his tanned face,
" that in this age, when one hears so many complaints
of the difficulty of procuring good seamen, that a man
who has been thirty years at sea, filled responsible posts,
and holds honest vouchers to his efficiency and good
conduct, cannot get a ship! What countryman are
you? "

" A Scotchman—an Aberdeen man."

" Wouldn't the last ship you were in take you
again? "

" She discharged at Cardiff, and is now for sale. My
wife lives just out of the Commercial Road, and that's

L

why I'm in London," he answered. "I had only been home a week when I tried to get a ship again, for I'm a poor man."

"What are you willing to ship as?"

"As anything; I'm too poor to choose, sir. I'll go as A. B. if I can get the berth. But this hanging about is eating up all our little savings."

"Why can't you get a berth?" said I.

"Because the captains won't take Englishmen," he said.

"What are their objections?"

"Oh," said he, "objections are easily made if they're wanted. Captains say that English crews desert, that they're loafers, bad seamen, expect more wages than they're worth, and that the best of us are no better than vagrants, turnpike sailors, who'll never work so long as there's a police-magistrate within hail, and who'll soger * when they're at sea. That may be true of some, but it's false if said of the rest; and, depend upon it, sir, it don't account for eighty per cent. of the men employed in the mercantile marine being 'Dutchmen.' Our argument— the English sailor's argument—is this: There are a lot of foreign boarding-house keepers in London. We'll take one of 'em. He has, say, twenty Dutchmen in his house, who pay him, each of 'em, sixteen shillings a week. Well, sir, most of these men have no means to last their expenses much beyond a fortnight; so the boarding-house keeper or runner says, 'Look here, my lads, you can't stay here. I must get you a ship, and you'll pay me five shillings apiece out of your allotment notes for doing it.' To this they're agreeable. The runner then goes down to a ship with his pocket full of his men's certificates, hands them, along with a bribe, to

* Loaf, skulk.

the mate or master, who brings 'em to this office, and the Dutchmen, who've been told by the runner to come to Tower Hill, are called in to sign articles. It pays the runner, who gets five shillings a man for shipping them, besides his other expenses out of the allotment note, which he discounts at about fifty per cent.; and it answers the purpose of the skipper, who pockets the bribe, and comes down to find a crew all ready cut and dried for him; but it leaves us Englishmen out in the cold, kicking our heels about, starving many of us, and standing no shadow of a chance against the underhand roguery that goes on."

"This is a grave charge to bring against captains," said I.

"Grave or not," he replied, "go and ask the opinion of British seamen all round the coast, and see whether or not this crimping swindle is understood by them and taken as the evil that's filling English ships with foreigners."

"But this kind of rascality is provided against, for the Act says that any person who receives any remuneration whatever other than the authorized fees for providing a seaman with employment incurs a penalty of twenty pounds."

"Act or no Act," he answered contemptuously, "it's done every day; it's done every hour."

"Can't you Englishmen catch one of these 'Dutch' crimps and make an example of him?"

"It's carried on so that it's hard to prove," he replied. "Dutchmen won't give evidence against one another; besides, the men sail away and are lost sight of, and there's no seeing how to get at the runners."

"What is the remedy, then; what is it you want?" I asked.

"We English sailors want this," he said; "we ask that captains shall come to the Shipping Office and pick crews out of the crowd; not go and take certificates from crimps, and come down to find a crew ready beforehand, to step in as they're called in. Give us a fair chance along with the Dutchmen. If already eighty per cent. of the crews in English ships are foreigners, what's to happen later on when there'll not be an Englishman found in the forecastle of a ship that flies the red ensign? Why, the whole breed of sailors 'll die out. Talk of Jack being a skulker, a scaramouch, a no-sailor! What's the good of abusing him if you don't give him a chance? It was said not long ago that owners meant to ship black crews, so hard did they find it to get Englishmen to act honestly by their employers. But look at this," said he, pulling a newspaper cutting from his pocket—"look at this account of three Arabs, two Egyptians, and a negro locked up for thirty days for refusing to serve as firemen after they had signed articles; receiving three pounds apiece in money, and then striking because they wanted a month's advance; getting it, and then refusing duty because they said they couldn't get the allotment notes cashed; receiving the money from the captain, and still refusing duty, and threatening to cut the captain's throat. Those were black men. Suppose they had been Englishmen? Dutchmen! why, sir, the most dreadful mutinies that ever happened have taken place aboard vessels manned with foreigners. Captains and owners know that. And does any man suppose," he continued, speaking with great warmth, "that if England should find herself at war with foreign nations, the Dutchmen who man her merchant ships wouldn't carry 'em into the enemy's ports? Why, in crowding our forecastles with foreigners, sir, we're striking the heaviest blow that could be aimed at this nation; we're stopping all chance of recruiting the navy with seamen to fight our battles; and we're putting our property into the hands of strangers who hate us, and who'd betray us by running away with it at the sound of the very first gun that was fired in anger." And so saying he touched his cap, and left me to make my way out of the gloomy, dirty, melancholy haunt, followed as far as the steps that led up to the street by several men petitioning me to "do something for them," "to get 'em a ship," "to help them out of this starving life."

Sailors are men of strong prejudices, and will often take wrong-headed views of things. To what extent my informant spoke the truth, those who have a wide knowledge of the inner life of the mercantile marine will judge. But certainly I cannot persuade myself that shipmasters act the part in relation to the foreign crimp which my seaman charged them with. I will go further, and assert that the shipment of foreign seamen is due, not to the British captain's dislike of the English sailor, but to his owner's order that he shall man the vessel with "Dutchmen" only. But these admissions must still leave the current system of crowding the English forecastle with foreigners an unmixed evil; nor do they affect the British sailor's declarations as regards the energetic agent the foreign crimp, runner, or boarding-house keeper is allowed to be in the recruiting of our mercantile marine. The subject is one that will probably in due course command attention. It is as unreasonable as it is impolitic that the "Dutchman" should be caressed and honoured with the full confidence of British employers while the English seaman, willing to work, is left to starve or decay. From shipmasters and mates, at least, some sympathy should be expected for him, for they are largely sharing in the neglect he is visited with, and finding themselves ousted out of their berths by foreigners. The English sailor has many faults, but he certainly is not so bad but that he may be made better if something of the old good will is shown him, and something of the old helpful hand extended to him; and, let his demerits be what they will, depend upon it he is the man who should be found aboard an English ship, and that a fair specimen of him is worth as many " Dutchmen " as he has fingers.

SHOULD owners allow captains to take their wives to sea with them? Opinions vary among master mariners on this head. Some think that a man has as much right to be taken care of at sea as ashore; that shirts, buttons, and linen want as much looking after in a ship as in a house; that captains are always the better for having their wives with them, because when in port they have an inducement to stop by the vessel and spend their evenings in the cabin, instead of roaming ashore at nightfall and bringing up in bad and perilous anchorages; and they also reason that a ship and cargo are bound to be rendered the safer by the captain's wife being on board, as the skipper is sure then to be vigilant and keep his weather-eye lifting. Of course a cynic might say that so far as regards the safety of the ship, and the inducements to the skipper to spend his evenings when in harbour aboard of her, a good deal must depend upon the lady as wife and companion. I once met a captain who told me that he questioned whether an insurance could be effected on his ship and cargo were it to be suspected that he had any intention of carrying his wife to sea with him. "We're always quarrelling," said he—a remark that saved me from asking him more questions. But what do the wives think? Are owners' objections to their accompanying their husbands agreeable to them? It is quite possible for a woman to love a sailor without loving the sea; and though owners deserve no praise for their hard and fast rule touching captains' wives, as there is not an atom of sentimental regard for the ladies in it, I cannot but think it a good rule, as it saves many a woman from following her husband into a life to which nothing could have courted her but the sense of wifely duty. After all, what sailor would willingly subject the woman he loves to the perils of the deep by taking her with him voyage after voyage? The farewells, it is true, are hard to say; the shot is often low in the locker, and she and the children will have a hard job to scrape through the months while father is absent: but then she is safe, there are no gales of wind to affright her, no mutinies, no collisions; the little home can never be water-logged, nor can there ever arise the need of taking to the boats and perishing of famine after a week of unspeakable anguish. There have, indeed, been many heroines among captains' wives, many brave and some truly heroical acts performed by them whilst at sea with their husbands. Nothing, for instance, in its way was ever more striking than the conduct of the wife of the captain of the *Edgar*. All the crew, with the exception of the captain and mate, were prostrated with sickness. The ship was homeward bound from Senegal, and the captain and mate had to work in the engine-room, whilst the wife steered. In this way the vessel was safely brought home, though, as was related in the newspapers at the time, seven of the crew died of the fever on the voyage. Here, perhaps, was a valuable ship saved by a captain's wife, for without her it is difficult to imagine what the other two

could have done; and those skippers who think owners
unjust in forcing them to go to sea *en garçon* should
quote the case of the *Edgar* as a very strong commercial
argument—the only sort that is likely to prove successful—in favour of their views. But, as Lord Bacon
said of dancing, so may I say of such instances as this :
The better the worse. The greater the marine dangers
in which women distinguished themselves, the more
resolved should husbands be to guard their wives against
the like risks. If it were always fine weather; if charts
were always perfectly accurate; if there were no fogs
and no shoals; if there was no danger in iron pyrites;
if all surveyors were above suspicion; iron ships as
well constructed as they are highly classed; stevedores
scientific people; and if vessels were built by rules of
common sense instead of being the fragile products of
a system of economy rendered vicious by insurance;
then, indeed—the maritime millennium having arrived
—might all skippers laudably combine to agitate until
owners gave in, and allowed wives to ship with their
husbands. But, while the ocean and all the conditions
of the ocean—wrecks, leaks, piecework, blind rivet-holes,
"boat iron," storms, thick weather, and all the rest of
it—remain as they are, captains who are good husbands
will keep the ladies ashore. It is only men of the Billy
Taylor type who deserve to be followed to sea; and it
is only the Hannah Snells of this world who should
attempt such pursuits. Over and over again one is
reading of the wrecks in which the captain's wife, and
too often, alas! the captain's little child, lose their lives.
The poor things are always called "passengers," and it
is usually the "passengers" who seem to be drowned.
Here is one of these stories related by the captain himself; and, taking it as a typical thing, which all seamen

may know it to be, I will ask, is it not well that owners —no matter the reasons which influence them—should object to their captains taking their wives to sea with them?

"The steamer I commanded was a schooner-rigged vessel, built at Low Walker, and you may call her tonnage in round numbers 500. She left a North-country port on a certain day with a crew of seventeen hands and a cargo of coal, our destination being Cronstadt. My wife was on board, and this was the first voyage she had made with me. We had been married two years, and in that time I had made several trips, as you may imagine; these voyages—as I suppose I must call a trip across the North Sea, or a run along the Mediterranean —occupying only a few weeks. Every time I started, my wife wanted to go too; the owners had no objection, but I had. I told her the sea was all very well for lady passengers who had to cross it, but it was no place for a woman to make a home of. She would do far better keeping house ashore, and making all ready for my return; and so I would put her off. But when it came to this trip, she pleaded so earnestly, saying that she loved the sea, that the run would do her good, that she felt terribly lonely when I was away, and that her place was at my side let me be where I would, that I could no longer refuse. 'Very well,' said I, 'for this once,' my notion being that one voyage would do more for my wishes than fifty years of arguing; and so she came aboard. Well, sir, at the start we had fine weather. It was in the spring; the air was sharp, but the sky was blue and the sunshine strong and cheerful; and my wife heartily enjoyed it. There was no sea-sickness to baulk her relish; she was too much a sailor's lass for that weakness. We were not much of a ship; you know

the regular type, high bows, wall-sided, Plimsoll's mark
well awash, you may take your oath, the flying-bridge
over the chart-house, and the pole-compass forking up
like a scarecrow above that. But my wife thought the
vessel made a fine sight—merely, I expect, because I
commanded her. Poor girl! poor girl! often I'd come
on deck and see her leaning over the side, when she'd
call to me to admire the line of froth there—as if that
was a thing an old fist like me would take notice of;
and if a vessel passed she'd stand and watch it with a
look of delight, as though nothing more beautiful was
ever seen, though it might be an old sailing collier, sir,
with nothing showing over the rail but a red night-cap,
or a steam-waggon after our own pattern. But much
as she enjoyed the water, her presence never gave me
pleasure. I remember going below on the very night
on which the ship was lost, and looking at my poor lass
as she lay sleeping, and I recall that the sight of her
worried me to a degree you'd scarcely think likely. I
was for ever wishing her back home, snug and secure in
the little house that she always had ready and bright
and cheerful for me to return to. You might almost
think such wishes unnatural, but I see them in their
proper light now, and reckon there's a world of truth
in that old saying about coming events casting their
shadows before them. It was a Tuesday afternoon.
The weather had changed in the forenoon, and at mid-
day it was blowing a strong breeze from the north-west.
It had grown as cold as January, and now and again
when a squall drove up there'd come a shower of hail
that was like heaving a bucket of shot on to the decks.
I had kept the patent log towing astern, our course
being a trifle to the north of east, and on hauling it in
at noon I found that we had made about a hundred and

seventy miles run since quitting our port. There were no sights to be got, for, though the morning had opened fine, the sky was now as thick as mud. All this time the wind was freshening up into a gale. I put the log over again, keeping the vessel on the same course, under sail, and her engines going full ahead. The wind was well abaft the beam, the sea a following one, and there was nothing to stop the ship; she drove along handsomely, whitening the water all around her, and for a couple of miles astern, and making excellent sport for my wife, who stood holding on and taking in the scene with her eyes like diamonds, and her cheeks like roses. I never could have supposed that there was so much to admire in the sea as she had found. To me it was hardly much more than a waste of salt water that was to be crossed as soon as possible, full of hard work, exposure, poor pay, and heavy anxiety. My poor lass knew nothing of that part of it, except the pay. I think, had time been given her, and we'd been making a long voyage, she'd have converted me into a kind of poet, and taught me to see beauties even in thick weather and strong head seas.

"Well, sir, by this time there was thick weather enough. It was three o'clock, a gale of wind on the quarter, the sea out of sight half a mile ahead, lost in a haze of rain, and the steamer pitching heavily as she swung over the stormy tumble. Nothing could have been more annoying than the thick weather; the gale was good, the sea did no harm; we were getting an extra two knots out of the ship; but the haze was like your being in a hurry, mounted on a swift horse, with your eyes blindfolded. However, I was determined not to slow down. Despatch is everything nowadays. It is all very well to talk of risk, but if a man's situation

depends upon his pleasing his owners by being sharp,
sharp he must be, and take the odds as they come.
Better lose a ship and let the owners touch the insurance than make a losing venture by tardy delivery.
So, as sailors say, we 'held on all,' keeping the canvas
aloft and firing up below, and racing through the smother
in proper modern fashion. Darker and darker it grew,
and the wind came along more fiercely. My poor lass
was frightened, and came up to me and asked what
made me rush the ship when scarcely her own length
was visible. I said we couldn't stop the vessel; the
wind was after her, and she was bound to go. 'But
you may run into another ship,' said she, 'and not
know she is there until you have struck her.' 'Ah,
Polly,' said I, 'that sort of calculation belongs to a past
age. Certificates would be of no use if they were based
on such reckoning. All that we skippers have to do is
to drive on. If there were to be any trouble over a
tardy delivery, do you suppose this thick weather would
be taken as an excuse? Others who left, perhaps, after
we did, will have arrived before us; and the luck of one
is expected to be the luck of others.'

"It stormed up harder after nightfall, and was then
as dark as a vault. I was on deck from eight till twelve,
going into the chart-house occasionally, but never into
the cabin, and at midnight I hauled the log in, and found
we had run about a hundred and twenty miles since noon.
The course, east by north half north, seemed to me correct.
It was as I always steered on this run, and so I held on,
putting the log overboard again; and I was going below
for a minute to see after my wife, when there was a noise
like the explosion of a gun forward, and some one sung out
that the fore trysail had blown away. This was a small
matter; but it was good as a hint. We took in the other

canvas, and went rolling and pitching along under steam, averaging about seven knots, but shipping a good deal of water forward, which washed about the decks and made walking difficult and uncomfortable. At four bells in the middle watch I went below to get some rest, leaving the chief mate in charge. Everything was right, as I supposed; a hand on the look-out on the forecastle, plenty of water under and around us, and nothing to cause anxiety but the haze. My wife was sound asleep. I lay down, completely dressed, on a locker, but could get no rest. This was unusual; a sailor, they say, can sleep anywhere, and amid any sort of disturbance; and I for one in former days have been able to sleep when it was impossible to hear a voice calling the watch, in consequence of the shrieking of the storm on deck and the groaning of the vessel below. I had a foreboding, an uneasiness in my mind; there was nothing to account for it, but it kept me awake, and presently it found me standing looking at my wife, wishing her to wake up, that she might talk to me, yet unwilling to arouse her. At that moment the ship struck—I felt the grind of her forefoot along the stony bottom; she heeled over, with the engines working their hardest, and I knew that she had come to a dead stop, not only by the manner in which I was thrown forward, but by the thunder of the seas breaking over her decks. I rushed up and heard the men shouting. It was still very thick, hailing and raining in torrents. I sung out for the mate, and he came to me, and I told him to get the wheel put hard aport, whilst I bawled down to the engine-room to keep the engines going. No attention was paid to this, for the engineers, firemen, and the others, thinking the vessel was going down, swarmed up on deck, and, without heeding my commands, turned-to to help the rest of

the crew to get the boats over. My notion was that all
hands meant to abandon the ship, and would leave my
wife and me to our fate if we did not bear a hand to
join them; so I ran below, and found my poor lass
dressing herself and in a terrible fright. I did not wait
to answer her questions, but, catching her by the hand,
ran on deck with her. Great heaven! what a night,
what weather, what a scene for any poor girl to be
dragged into! I heard the cries of men alongside, and
understood by that that one of the boats had been stove
and the men in her thrown out. I shouted, 'Here is
my wife, men; for God's sake, take her with you if you
intend to abandon the ship.' The chief engineer answered, 'Bring her here—there's room in the starboard
lifeboat.' I ran with her to the side, and, looking over,
saw the boat with seven or eight men in her. I called
to the men to look out, and I then put her over, giving
her a kiss as I did so, and bidding her have no fear;
and the men caught her, and sung out to me to let go
the painter. I answered no, it would be better to let
the boat veer astern and ride there whilst I endeavoured
to find out the condition of the ship; and they agreeing,
I carried the end of the painter aft and made it fast.

"I now called to such as remained on board to join
me, but only three men came, amongst them my two
mates; all the others had got away, were drowned, or
were in the boat with my wife. We could do nothing
till daylight came, and sat crouching out of the reach of
the water that was flying in heavy masses over the ship.
It was as much as I could do to see the boat astern; but
every now and again I'd crawl aft to notice if she still
lived, and then come back again to the others thankful
to the Almighty that she was making good weather of it,
and might still save my lass's life. But how am I to

describe my feelings as I reflected upon what she was suffering in that open boat, pelted with the hail and rain, the deadly cold wind penetrating her poor body, tossed like a nutshell upon the roaring seas, and never knowing but that the next moment would find her struggling in the water. Well, sir, the daylight came, and showed us that we were hard and fast upon a dangerous reef off the Jutland coast. We could see the land there looming upon the haze about four or five miles off. The ship was full of water and bound to go to pieces, though she was still holding well together in spite of the terrible pounding of the sea. I went to the stern to hail the boat and say a word of comfort to my wife; and when the men saw me they sung out, 'Let go the painter, captain. We must take our chance of driving ashore; it's killing work here.' My wife put out her arms to me, and I heard her cry, 'Oh, don't leave him behind!' The boat had already as many as she could well carry. Perhaps the men feared that I would try to join my wife, and drag the boat alongside, which might end in sinking her; but I had no thought of that kind, the gig still remaining, and was about to tell them to hold on and keep the shelter of the wreck for a spell, as the weather might moderate presently, when a man in the bows cut the painter. A heavy sea taking the boat as he did this, swung her up and around; she plunged into the hollow, and the water rolling between, prevented me from seeing her. But as it passed it hove up the boat again bottom up, the black keel just showing among a smother of foam, with here and there the upright arms of a drowning man. It was done in a moment; it was all over in a moment; it left me staring like a man struck dead by lightning and holding the posture he was killed in. The chief mate,

catching me by the arm, cried out, 'She's going to
pieces, sir. For Heaven's sake, let's get away. We're
doomed men if we linger.' I broke from the horror and
grief in me, and went to work, not so much to save my
own life as to help the others to save theirs. Had I
been alone I should have thrown myself down and
waited for death. The shock I had sustained had driven
all instincts of life out of me. Well, sir, we got the gig
overboard, and that we were saved you may suppose, as
I am here to tell the story. Four other men got ashore
besides us, making ten of the crew drowned besides my
lass. Oh, sir!" cried the poor fellow, covering his face
and speaking amid convulsive sobs, "why did she insist
upon accompanying me? Why did she not keep to our
little home ashore, and be there to cheer and comfort
me when I came back from this shipwreck, a ruined
man! My certificate has been suspended—I cannot get
a berth—and I have lost the darling of my heart, the
truest wife that ever man had. Why did she insist?
why did she insist?" he repeated; and, rising like a blind
man, he left me speehless in the face of a grief it was not
in the power of human sympathy to soften.

SEA SONGS.

CONSIDERING that Great Britain is an island, that immense numbers of the inhabitants live in seaports, that the sea is within at hour or two of the metropolis, that there is always an abundance of sailors "knocking about" ashore, and that pretty nearly all our wealth as a nation is owing to our seamen and our shipping, it must be owned that many of those notions of Jack and his life ashore and at sea which may be found among the greatest maritime people on the face of the earth, are in the highest degree extraordinary. Is it possible that the sailor is still supposed to have nothing to do at sea but to sit down with a pipe in his mouth and let the wind blow him along? Are there people yet living who imagine that on Saturday nights at sea cans of grog are handed about, roaring nautical songs sung, and wives and sweethearts toasted? Is it even in this day of steamboats believed that a sailor cannot express himself without loading his language with marine terms; that he cannot speak of "walking," but of "steering;" that the right-hand side ashore is the "starboard;" and that he cannot step backwards without making "sternway"?

Where do these highly nautical fellows live when they are at home? I never have the luck to come across them. In some seaports you may still see here and there, over a public-house, the sign of the Jolly Tar: a figure in flowing breeches, tarpaulin hat on "nine hairs," a bottle of grog in one hand, and a great red nose, set in the midst of a shining face. Who was the original of that fellow? He is not a man-of-war's man, and most certainly he is not a merchantman. I take it that he is nothing more nor less than the embodiment of the landsman's notion of the sailor obtained to a large extent from marine novels, but mainly from the English sea songs. You might walk the whole of Great Britain over without meeting with the counterpart of that effigy, unless it lay in some turnpike impostor who gets a living by swearing he has been shipwrecked. If the merchant seaman is to be typified, he must not be dressed in loose breeches and an open-breasted shirt. If his language is to be imitated, it must not altogether consist of "hard-a-lee" and "haul the bowline." And if his life at sea is to be pictured, one must drop all reference to cans of grog, and have nothing whatever to say about Saturday nights and sweethearts and wives.

But how can landsmen be ridiculed for their absurd ideas of the sailor when for years and years writers who profess to know all about him have persisted in reproducing the same stereotyped likeness—the same drunken, singing, good-humoured, sprawling mountebank, shouting out for more grog, bawling inane verses about his Poll and his Sue, clamouring the purest "slush" about the Union Jack, and talking inconceivable nonsense about topgallants and handspikes? Of course the likeness is accepted by those who know no better, and songs are sung about Jack which no sailor can listen to without astonishment that ignorance so profound should be also so widespread.　I remember a man who was much applauded in his day as a singer of nautical ballads, saying to me, "To-morrow I have to sing 'Tom Tough,' by desire.　Can you tell me, sir, what attitude I ought to adopt when I come to—

> 'So I seiz'd the capstan bar,
> Like a true, honest tar,
> And in spite of tears and sighs,
> Sung yo, heave ho'?

Do I pull or do I push, sir?"

What did it matter?　Whether he pulled or whether he pushed would have been all the same to his audience. Who but a sailor at a concert would notice that a vocalist thought it all right when he roared out—

> "And at the bosun's call,
> We m n the poop downhaul,
> And furl the main jibboom, lads,
> So, boys, so"?

Apparently, let the words employed be as nonsensical as they will, so long as there is plenty of "yohing" and "heaving" and "so-hoing," the song is accepted as extremely nautical and peculiarly expressive of the free and open character of the sailor.

I was once in a house much frequented by seamen, when there entered the room in which I was sitting an elderly man of a somewhat sour cast of countenance, dressed—not, believe me, in that flowing rig in which all kinds of sailors are popularly supposed to go clad— but in plain black cloth and an unstarched, striped cotton shirt, with a cravat round a stand-up collar. He had the look of a man who had been at sea all his life, and consequently no marine exterior could be less suggestive than his of "So-ho's" and "Heave ho's," and "Pull aways."　He called for half a pint of ale,

and filled his pipe, and sat smoking and listening to
a conversation between two men relative to a collision
in which the vessel they had recently left was concerned.
By-and-by he began to grope in his pockets, and
presently produced some sheets of songs, which he held
out at arm's length the better to inspect the highly marine
figure who, in sailor's shirt and jacket, with straddled
legs, immense belt, and lifted hand, embellished the
titlepage of the cheap collection. He took a long look
at this striking figure, frequently removing his pipe
to expectorate, and then very leisurely began to examine
the songs.

I saw by the movements of his lips that he read
little bits here and there, and now and again I would
catch him stealing a glance at me, as though he had
something on his mind, but was too shy to address me.

"What have you there?" said I.

"Why," he answered, reverting to the titlepage,
"something I paid a penny for just now—bought it
from a chap who stood alongside a row of 'em fixed
against a wall. They call it the 'Sea Songs of Great
Britain.' It's full of queer spelling, and it's all about
Jack, whoever *he* may be, if this be'n't him," and he
pointed to the absurd straddling woodcut.

He went on reading for a short time, his pipe in his
hand, and his mouth opening wider and wider, until,
coming to the end of the song, he looked at me and said,
" Well, I'm jiggered ! "

"What's the matter?" I inquired.

"Dibdin—Dibdin!" said he, "d'ye know anything
of that gent, sir?"

"Only as the greatest nautical song-writer this
country ever produced," I replied.

"Yes," said he, casting his eyes upon the page,

"I see he is a nautical song-writer; but was he ever at sea?"

"Not as a sailor, I believe."

"Mates," he called out to the others, who had stopped talking and were listening to his questions, "what d'ye think of this for a nautical job? It's called 'My Poll and my Partner Joe;'" and he read slowly and hoarsely—

> "I did my duty manfully while on the billows rolling;
> And night or day could find the way,
> Blindfold, to the maintop-bowling."

He paused and looked around him.

"'Blindfold to the maintop-bowling!'" he ejaculated. "Which end of it, d'ye reckon, mates? Would he come down the bolt-rope to the bridle? That must have been it, otherwise what manfulness would he have had occasion to talk about? But listen to this, boys— evidently the work of another nautical man. It's called 'The Storm.'

> 'Now it freshens, set the braces;
> Quick, the topsail sheets let go!
> Luff, boys, luff; don't make wry faces!
> Up your topsails nimbly clew!'

'Set the braces!' How's that job done, d'ye know? And when they was told to 'Luff, boys, luff,' did they let go of the wheel to 'Up their topsails nimbly clew'? It must have been a bad storm, that. I wonder they didn't ship a capstan bar in a lee scupper-hole to keep the ship upright."

"You mustn't be too critical," said I; "it's the music of those old songs that makes them beautiful."

"I've got nothen to do with the music," he said warmly. "It's the words I'm looking at. What's the music got to do with the sense? See here!" he cried.

"What's the name of it? oh! 'The Boatswain Calls,'"
and he read—

> "Come, my boys, your handspikes poise,
> And give one general huzza,
> Yet sighing as you pull away
> For the tears ashore that flow,
> To the windlass let us go,
> With yo, heave ho!"

He let fall the paper on his knee and stared at me.

"Well, that is certainly very poor stuff," said I.

"Poor stuff!" he exclaimed. "Why, it ain't even
that. Ne'er an omnibus driver but could do better.
How can they pull away if they've got their handspikes
poised? and what's the windlass got to do with pulling
away? And hear this—

> 'If 'tis storm, why we bustle; if calm, why we booze,
> All taut from the stem to the stern.'

Booze in a calm! Why, there's naught going but
liquor in these blooming rhymes. And 'All taut from
the stem to the stern'—did the chap who wrote that
have the least glimmerin' shadder of a notion of what
he meant? But stop a bit; here's a song called 'Poor
Jack'—

> 'Though the tempests topgallant-masts smack-smooth should smite,
> And shiver each splinter of wood,
> Clear the decks, stow the yards, and house everything tight,
> And under the foresail we scud.'

What d'ye think of that, boys?" said he, addressing
the others, who were on the broad grin. "Did ye ever
hear of a topgallant-mast going smack-smooth? One
lives and larns. I always thought that was a job for
the lower masts. And, I say, how d'ye relish stowing
the yards? He can't mean atop of the booms, for he
keeps the foresail on her to scud with; but perhaps

the foreyard's stowed too, and the reefed course is set
on the flying jib-stay.   But follow this—

'For,' says he, 'd'ye mind ye, let . . .'

—something; here's a word left out—

'. . . 'ere so oft,
Take the toplifts of sailors aback!'

Does he mean topping-lift?   If so, that's a queer sort
of thing to be taken aback.   Why, if he goes on in this
fashion he'll be reefing the mainsheet next."

All this was exceedingly amusing to me.   It was too
good, indeed, not to encourage.

"Nautical blunders seem uncommonly cheap," I
said.   "You appear to have got a wonderful lot for one
penny."

"Look here!" he cried, bursting into a laugh as his
eye lighted on another ballad :

"'Twas in the good ship Rover'—

that's the name of it—

'That time bound straight to Portugal.
    Right fore and aft we bore ;
But when we made Cape Ortugal,
    A gale blew off the shore.

'She lay, it did so shock her,
    A log upon the main,
Till, sav'd from Davy's locker,
    We put to sea again.'"

Only a Harley or a Robson could do justice to the
seaman's face as he looked at me after putting down the
paper—there is nothing in words to convey the sour
astonishment and contempt in his expression.

"'Right fore and aft we bore!'" he presently
exclaimed.   "Did any man ever hear the like of that ?
What sort of course is it ?   How's her head when she's

bearing right fore and aft ? And then think, arter lying like a log upon the main, of putting to sea again without going into harbour first ! "

" I doubt if ye can beat that," said one of the other sailors.

" Think not ? " answered the old fellow quickly, " then what d'ye say to this out of a song here wrote down as ' Spanking Jack ' ? —

> 'One night, as we drove with two reefs in the mainsail,
>   And the scud came on lowering upon a lee shore,
> Jack went up aloft to hand the topgallant-sail,
>   A spray washed him off, and we ne'er saw him more.' "

" What is wrong there ? " I asked.

" Wrong ! " he shouted. " Did ye ever hear of a square mainsail with two reefs in it ? and a square one's meant if anything is meant at all, by the hallusion in the verse to the topgallant-sail. And what's intended by the scud coming on louring upon a lee shore ? Scud comes from windward, don't it ? And what's a spray ? "

" Quite enough water to wash off such a sailor as Spanking Jack, I dare say," I remarked.

" Ay, you're right," said he, with a grin. " But I'm not done yet. Here's something in the ferocious line, called ' The Demon of the Sea '—

> ' With equal rage both ships engage,
>   And dreadful slaughter's seen ;
> The die is cast—a ball at last
>   Has struck his magazine.

> ' And now appall'd, his men they all
>   Stand mute in deep despair ;
> The pirate, too, and all his crew
>   Were blown up in the air.'

What d'ye think of that for a nautical bust-up ? Think of standing in mute despair after the ball had struck the magazine! How long did the chap as wrote this wash reckon it takes powder to hexplode arter it's fired? Instead of being appalled and standing in mute despair, they should have taken to the boats; for, ye see, that convenient magazine was bound to give 'em plenty of time. And they calls this," said he, turning the pages backwards and forwards, " 'Sea Songs.' It's the likes of this that is offered to shore-going folk as correct representations of the mariner's calling, hey? Ain't it true to life? Here's a bit for ye—

> ' William, who high upon the yard,
>   Rock'd with the billows to and fro,
> Soon as her well-known voice he heard,
>   He sigh'd and cast his eyes below.
> The cords glide swiftly through his glowing hands,
> And quick as l'ghtning on the deck he stands '

What sort of cords did he come down by—the signal halliards? And isn't it quite conceivable that, being on a man-o'-war, and aloft on duty, he should drop his job to come down to his Susan without leave of the officer in charge? Wonderfully true to life, sir, ain't it, ispecially them bits about the sailor boy capering ashore, and jolly tars drinking and dancing at sea, as if cargoes consisted of nothing but casks of rum which sailors are allowed to broach whenever they want to be merry?"

He turned to the rude woodcut, and had another long look at it; then, suddenly twisting the sheets up in his hand, he thrust one end into the fire, singing out as he looked around him:

"Anybody want a light?'

This sour seaman was, of course, a very hard and exacting critic, belonging to a class of sailors who, when reading about the sea, should they come across the least oversight on the part of a writer, will fling his book or poem or song out of window, and vote the author a lubber and utterly ignorant of all that concerns the calling. I remember, when I wrote an account of the wreck of the *Indian Chief*, a sailor gravely told me he was cocksure the whole yarn was an out-and-out lie, because I had made the chief mate escape from the mizzenmast by getting into the maintop by the mizzen-topmast stay. No doubt I should have done better by sending the mate to make his way into the top from the topgallant masthead; but just because my sailor was sure that the mizzen-topmast stay of the *Indian Chief* set up half-way down the mainmast, he refused to believe the story of the wreck. Yet it is quite possible to read many of our English sea songs with wonder and ridicule without necessarily bringing to them the sourness and severity of judgment I found in the old seaman. The present generation of writers are not worse sinners in respect of accuracy than the past; but I am bound to say that their blunders are to the full as numerous. The production of a sea song is by no means conditional on a man's having been to sea. The finest marine lyric in this or any other language, "Ye Mariners of England," was written by a man who had no knowledge whatever of the sailor's calling. There is nothing false in that glorious poem, no absurd references to bowlines and topsail sheets, and other words of which few landsmen have the least idea of the meaning. But can as much be said of Allan Cunningham's popular poem, "A Wet Sheet and a Flowing Sea"? It is just possible that the poet may have used the word "sheet" rightly, and meant the song to refer to a small fore-and-aft vessel that when heavily pressed down might wet her sheets; but Jack, when he hears that ballad, is strongly disposed

to believe that the writer thought that a " sheet " was a
sail, and this being his suspicion, he could never sing the
song with the least relish or enjoyment of even the
beautiful air with which the words are associated.   By all
means let landsmen continue to write sea songs ; but if
they desire a larger audience than shore-goers for their
compositions, if they wish to hear of their verses in the
forecastle and learn that they are popular among sailors,
let them rigorously avoid all technicalities, all the stupid
old clap-trap about cans of grog and " Yeo, heave ho,"
and " So ho ! " and the like.   For a song may be as salt
as the sea itself, and yet be as free from the stereotyped
nauticalisms as a page of " Hamlet."   Indeed, the real
English sailor is not one-third as nautical as he is supposed to be ; and the numerous inanities dedicated to his
rollicking enjoyments when at sea, his Sues and Nans
ashore, are about as true to his real character as the
public-house effigy of him, on one leg, in shoes, and
round hat at the back of his head, is like the original.

AN HOUR'S ROW.

THERE is not a more painfully diverting sight in the whole world than that of a cockney with a face as yellow as a London fog, a tall hat at the back of his head, his coloured shirt-sleeves rolled above his elbows, tugging upon the sea at a small pair of oars in a rather heavy wherry. He has no idea of tides, of waves, of winds, or weather. He looks to leeward for squalls, and over the stern for any other news of the sea. The current that dangerously and helplessly sweeps him away from the land delights him by a sense of velocity. The waves which rise and threaten to fill the boat gladden him with the sensation of going "up and down." I once took the trouble to watch a cockney get into a wherry and row himself out to sea. I kept a very powerful glass bearing upon him, and had his face within reach of my hand, so to speak, when he was two miles off. There was a strong tide setting to the east-ward, in which direction lay the North Sea. He went away very fast, and with my eye to the telescope I found myself smiling in sympathy with his radiant enjoyment of the speed at which his boat was going. He did not feather his oars, but rowed with prodigious contortions of his body, carrying his nose aft until I thought he would tumble upon it in the stern sheets, and then lying back

at an angle so acute that I was constantly watching for
his heels, whilst his oars flourished themselves in the air
like a pair of tongs in the hands of a clown. I was sure,
by the expression in his face, that he believed it was his
fine rowing that made the boat go so fast. He did not
know that the tide was helping him at the rate of very
nearly three and a half land miles an hour.

At last he thought it was time to turn back. He let
go one oar to pull at the other with both hands, and so
he got his boat's head round. He still smiled and looked
confident, and rowed unintermittently for about ten
minutes, in which time he had gone astern about the
sixteenth of a mile. Then he stopped and took a look
over the bows. His face was no longer radiant, but, on
the contrary, very much puzzled, and even slightly dis-
tressed. He rowed hard again, and then stopped and
took another look. This time he seemed horribly
frightened. Indeed, examined through the telescope,
his yellow face was a curious study. The emotions of
his soul were finely expressed, and every time he stopped
rowing to turn his head and gaze at the land, a fresh
passion was depictured on his fog-coloured lineaments.
Eventually a couple of boatmen went to succour him,
and with much difficulty towed him home. He stepped
on shore very defiantly, and, instead of rewarding the
boatmen for their services, expressed his gratitude by
offering to row either of them for a pound.

It is plain that hardy and dexterous landsmen of this
kind must occasionally meet with exciting adventures on
the deep. An experience not so commonplace but that
another touch or two would have raised it into tragical
dignity was encountered not very many days ago by a
plain, honest, decently-educated Londoner, a City clerk,
aged forty-four, who, being afflicted with the delusion

that he could row, put forth in a wherry along with his
wife and child. He told me the story, begging me to
print it as a warning to others, but at the same time on
no account to mention his name nor the port at which
he embarked on his disastrous voyage. As nearly as I
can remember, this is how his story went.

"I don't know," he began, "whether I shall ever
live to keep a servant, but it would be more sensible for
me to hope I may never live to feel the want of one.
Any way, when a man can't afford to keep a servant,
then, if he has a baby it must always go along with the
wife; and this being so, when I offered to take my wife
out for an hour's row we were bound to carry the baby
with us. The baby was weaned six weeks ago. It's a
small thing to say, but worth taking notice of, as it made
our troubles harder, as you'll hear. I never professed
to be an oarsman. I had in my time pulled a pair of
sculls on the Thames, and got along middling well—well
enough to enable me to say to my wife on this occasion,
' Look here, Sarah, there's no need to take a man. A
man will be a shilling extra. I don't say I can feather;
and I don't know, if I were to row with other men,
whether I should be able to keep time. But I'm quite
competent to pull in a boat by myself.'

" ' Very well, William,' said she; ' if you think
there's no danger, an hour on the water will be very
enjoyable. But we don't want more than an hour.'

" ' Certainly not,' I answered; ' an hour is eighteenpence.'

" The baby was dressed and fed, my wife put on her
hat, and we left our lodgings for the place where the
wherries lay. As we went along my wife suggested that
we should carry a few buns with us.

" ' What for?' said I; ' we shall be back for tea.

We're sure to eat the buns, and they'll destroy our appetite for the shrimps.' That was my reasoning. It was very shortsighted; but what should a man who is cooped up in the City of London for eleven months in every year know about the sea and how to provide against its dangers?

"We were pursued by four or five boatmen to the landing-stage, where I selected what looked to me a nice light wherry. It was five o'clock in the afternoon. We meant to be home by six. The sun was still very hot; but the boatman who helped us to get into the wherry said we should find a cool air on the sea. I removed my coat and waistcoat, and turned up my arm-sleeves and set my hat securely on my head. My wife sat upon a cushion in the hinder part of the boat, and the boatman put on the rudder and told my wife to lay hold of the strings—I don't know what sailors call them. But she said she would rather not touch them, as she had no idea of steering, and besides, the baby kept her hands employed.

"'I can steer,' said I, 'with my oars.'

"On this, an old man with a long stick with a hook at the end of it, pushed the boat off. There was quite a crowd of other boats—empty boats—in the way, and I was a good deal confused by the shouts of the boatmen telling me what to do. We ran into several of these boats, and twice I let one of the oars fall overboard, which gave me a great deal of trouble to recover. We got clear of these boats, and I was rowing pretty steadily when, to my surprise, I found the boat's head turning and aiming for the pier. I endeavoured to remedy this by rowing more strongly with one oar than with the other, but the wherry would insist upon going the wrong way, and I had come to the conclusion that there was something seriously amiss with the boat, and was about to put back and exchange it for another that would go straight, when I perceived that the rudder was inclined, in consequence of my wife sitting on one of the strings connected with it.

" When this was freed the boat went straight, and I pulled vigorously for the open sea. We had several alarms, however, before reaching the open water. First, there were three boats full of schoolboys, splashing about with their oars, who kept on screeching to me to mind where I was going. Then a man on the pier roared to me to keep clear of the tug. Then, again, we were nearly run down by a smack.

" ' I certainly don't call this enjoyment,' said my wife faintly, striving to soothe the baby, who had been awakened by the boys, and was crying at the top of her voice.

" I made no answer, but continued rowing with great resolution, and, as I flattered myself, with a dash of science, too, all things considered, earnestly looking over my shoulders to see where I was going, until my neck was as stiff as an office-ruler. At last we got out of harbour into the open sea.

" There was a large steamboat arriving from some place or other; there were numbers of people on the pier, but all watching the steamboat and thinking about her, and so nobody took the least notice of us. The water was quiet, with what nautical men call a swell that lifted and sank us; there was a nice wind that cooled the air; I saw two or three wherries at anchor in the opposite direction to that I was rowing in, and I fancy the people in them were fishing. Very far out at sea were some ships, but the only vessel near the harbour was a smack that came out soon after us, and, filling her sails, pushed quickly past us. One of the men upon her

N

called out something as the vessel went by, but I didn't catch what he said.

"My wife now agreed with me that this was real happiness. There was a delightful quiet in the air, to enjoy which a man must live for eleven months every year in the bustle and noise of the City; the town looked beautiful in the afternoon light, the tops of the white cliffs as green as new silk, and over and over again, after rowing a few moments, I would hang on my oars and look at the houses in the distance and the different objects changing their shapes or shifting their places. As I had pulled the oars very leisurely indeed, I calculated that it would not take me more than a quarter of an hour of steady pulling to cover the distance I had been lazily traversing; I mean I reckoned that I could cover in a quarter of an hour the distance I had slowly come in three-quarters. That would make the hour; but my wife was enjoying the air and the sea so thoroughly that I thought it would not greatly matter if we broke into another hour. This was a treat we didn't often get. My wife flattered me by saying I rowed very well, and made the boat go wonderfully quick, considering I put very little strength into the oars. I thought so, too, indeed, and was surprised to observe how rapidly, in proportion to my exertion, the land had receded away from us. By this time the pier was only a black line upon the water, and the people upon it invisible.

" 'You'll be facing the shore, Sarah,' said I, 'when I turn the boat to row back, and you'll be much interested in seeing the various objects growing bigger and bigger as we approach the land.'

" 'No wonder people are fond of the water,' said she; 'I could stop here for weeks.'

"Poor woman! I doubt if she'd say that now.

"It was six o'clock when I turned the boat's head. I never doubted that I could row back in twenty minutes, and reckoned that the extra half-hour would be well worth the money. I rowed at first with a good deal of energy, and my wife was delighted at the manner in which I made the foam fly with my oars. Indeed, I worked too hard; the exertion soon tired me, and I perspired at every pore with the heat. It was slightly distracting that the baby, who had been sleeping very quietly, should now wake up and cry for what I suppose you might call her tea, if you can give regular names to milk-and-water administered about seven times a day.

" ' I am sorry, William,' said my wife, ' that we have stopped longer than the hour.'

" ' Oh,' said I, knowing that the child was running in her head, ' baby will do very well until we get home; we shan't be long now;' and again I exerted my strength and toiled like a champion rower.

" ' It's very curious,' said I, giving up after about ten minutes, and feeling quite exhausted, and panting for breath.

" ' What's very curious?' said my wife.

" ' Why,' said I, pulling out my watch, ' here it is twenty minutes past six, and the land seems rather farther off than it was before I turned the boat's head towards it.'

" ' Yes,' said she, growing a little pale; ' I've been noticing that, too.'

" ' Perhaps it wants a steadier stroke,' said I, wiping my forehead; and, settling to the oars again, I rowed for another ten minutes, and then looked over my shoulder. I could not be deceived. Row as I would, I not only could make no way, but the boat actually lost ground. I could not conceive of a current in the sea; a tide was

an intelligible thing to me in a river, but I could not
realize that the great body of water we were floating on
was moving in a contrary direction to the land. There
was nothing about to give me the idea; no buoys, or
anything of that kind. All that I understood was that
the harder I rowed towards the land the farther we fell
away from it. I was heartily frightened, and pulled
in the oars to stand up and look around me. My wife
began to cry and the baby roared as babies can when
they are particularly wanted to keep quiet. There were
some ships, as I have said, a long distance off; and
there was the smack that had passed us, two or three
miles distant; but there was nothing near us. I put
my hands to my mouth and shouted towards the land
as hard as ever I could, flattering myself that there was
a faint chance of the smooth water conveying the sound.
I then stood waving and flourishing my hat for at least
five minutes.

"'Oh, William, what will become of us?' cried my
wife, sobbing piteously.

"I was much too upset to answer her. I had hoped
that we should be noticed by some of the people who
keep a look-out on the pier; but as the time went by,
and the sun sank lower, and I could see no signs of
anything coming to our rescue, my spirits fell, and I
sat down and stared blankly at my wife. I put out the
oars again, but was so wearied that I soon gave up
rowing; besides, I felt that we were being carried away,
and that the oars scarcely hindered our progress towards
the ocean. All this while the baby was giving us the
greatest trouble with its incessant crying. My wife
filled up the pauses of its screams by anticipating all
the horrors which might befall us. She assured me
that she could see nothing before us but death from

starvation, unless the sea should rise and upset the
boat and drown us, or unless a passing vessel should
crash into us when the darkness fell. What could I
do? We were in one of those situations in which it is
simply impossible for people to help themselves. I
could not row; we had no sail, and even if we had had
a sail I should not have known how to use it; I had no
means of calling attention to our position except by
waving my hat or flourishing an oar, which seemed an
idle thing to do, considering what a speck the boat
made upon the water, and how far off we were from
everything but the miserable sea.

"Sure enough, presently the sun sank, and though
the twilight lasted a good bit, yet the water soon grew
dark, and speedily after sundown the coast grew faint,
and the ships in the distance were swallowed up in the
gloom. When the night fairly came the wind got up,
not very much, but enough to disturb the water, and
the wherry began to slop about horribly. What was
worse, it blew off the land and helped to carry us
farther away. How I cursed my folly for not having
brought a man with me! The crying of the poor
hungry little baby and my wife's moans and reproaches
were just maddening. It was very fine overhead, the
sky full of stars, but there was no moon, and the sea
looked as black as ink. I could see the lights on the
land, and could even very faintly hear the strains of
a band of music playing on the cliff, for, as I have told
you, the wind blew from the shore. I pulled out my
watch, but though I held it close to my nose I could
not see what time it was. I kept on looking around
in the hopes of observing a passing vessel, but,
though no doubt some must have passed, I did not see
them.

"My wife was continually saying, 'Oh, William, what shall we do?'

"'Do?' said I. 'What *can* we do? We must sit here and wait.'

"'Wait!' she would cry. 'What is there to wait for?'

"'For daylight, if for nothing else.'

"'But what will daylight do for us? We have been lost in daylight, and when daylight comes where shall we be?' and here she would hug the poor crying baby and wish herself dead, and so on.

"Lord, what a time it was! The sea kept the boat rocking incessantly, so that it was impossible for me to stand up. The dew fell like rain, and my clothes were as heavy as if I had been exposed to a shower. My wife said her limbs felt like pieces of iron, and that she had the cramp in every joint, which I could easily understand, for I, too, suffered atrociously from having to keep seated and to balance myself to the tumbling about of the wretched little wherry. By degrees we lost sight of the lights on shore; and we felt as if we were in the middle of the Atlantic. Once or twice I thought of taking to the oars again, but when the lights disappeared there was nothing to aim for. How we passed the hours I can't tell you. The baby would wake and cry until she cried herself to sleep, then wake and cry herself to sleep again, and so on, hour after hour. My wife and I fell silent; we had exhausted all that *could* be said, and we sat there like two statues. To my dying hour I shall remember the gurgling and sobbing noise of the water splashing against the boat's side, and the dreadful silence overhead and around, above the water, as I may say.

"It must have been past midnight, when I thought

I heard a kind of groaning or rumbling sound in the wind. I could not imagine what it could be, until, looking into the darkness on my right hand, I spied three lights upon the sea—one green, one red, and one white—this last much higher than the others. Soon after there was a heavy noise of washing water, and just over the white light there was a shower of sparks, and presently a great black shadow stood up on the sea and blotted out the stars behind it. I was weak and worn out—terrified to a degree by the swift approach of this steamer—and though I managed to shout, my voice seemed to stick in my throat. The great vessel swept past us not above twenty yards distant; saving those lamps she was all in darkness, and soon after she had gone by I thought the wherry would have upset in the waves the steamer had left behind. My wife screamed as the boat sprang up and down, and every instant I expected the sea to rush into us. I shouted again to the steamer, hoping that I might be heard. This time my voice carried well, but nothing came of it; the steamer rushed on, and was soon out of sight.

" The dawn was just breaking, when I saw a vessel making a black mark against the pale green light in the place where the sun was coming. It took me some time to find out which way she was going, but presently the rising sun made her plain, and I saw that she was a small smack, and that she aimed directly for us. I managed to stand up in the wherry and flourish my hat. There was no coast to be seen—nothing visible upon the sea but that smack. So far as water went, we might have been in the middle of the biggest ocean in the world. I perceived before long that the smack saw us, for she lowered one of her sails, and came along slowly. I looked at my wife to see how this adventure had served her, and it seemed to me that she had aged twenty years. Her face was hollow, her dress draggled and limp with the dew; she was a most melancholy object to look at. I hardly knew her, indeed; and she was equally astonished by my appearance, as she afterwards told me. Who could suppose that a night spent in an open boat at sea would work such a change in people's looks? As for poor little baby, she had been crying on and off all night, and, being pretty nearly perished with hunger, she was a distressing thing, truly, for us parents to see. It was nearly three-quarters of an hour before the smack came close to us, counting from the time I had first seen her. A great man in yellow clothes bawled out, ' What's that boat, and what do you want?' You might have supposed he would guess our want by our appearance.

" ' We've been carried away to sea,' I answered, in a faint voice, for I felt as weak as an infant and just fit to cry like one, ' and we've been in this boat all night.'

" ' Where do you come from?' he called.

" I told him, and he answered, ' We'll tow you in. Look out for the end of the line;' and another man threw a rope at me.

" I caught it, but did not know what to do with it; seeing which, the first man told me to keep hold, and dragged the wherry up to the smack, and then got into her and attached the line to the boat.

" ' Will you sit here or come aboard?' he asked.

" ' Oh, come aboard, certainly,' I replied; so he took the baby and passed it to a sailor on the smack, and then helped my wife up, and then me.

" So here we were, saved; but faint, broken-down, feeling as if we had been dug out of the grave. Luckily they had a few tins of Swiss milk in the cabin, and so poor little baby got something to eat at last. Also they

gave us some corned beef and bread, which we devoured
gratefully, after the manner of shipwrecked people.
The captain of the smack laughed when I told him we
had originally started for an hour's row.

"'How much do they charge you for an hour?'
says he.

"'Eighteenpence,' I answered.

"'You have had a good eighteen-pennorth,' said
he. 'You may thank the Lord, master, that ye're alive
to pay even eighteenpence. D'ye know how many miles
you've drifted from your port?'

"'No,' said I.

"'Well then,' said he, 'you've drifted eleven miles.
There's the coast—you can calculate for yourself;' and
he pointed to the white cliffs, which were visible from the
smack's deck, though not from the boat. A fearfully
long distance off they looked, to be sure.

"'William,' said my wife at this moment, 'I'll never
come upon the water again.'

"'Nor I, Sarah,' said I; 'at least without a man.'

"'Man or no man,' said she, 'I'll never venture
my life again.'

"'And I have no doubt she will keep her word,
though it won't cost her a very great effort to do so,
for I am quite sure I shall never attempt to make her
break it.'"

"And so," said I, "you got home safe?"

"Yes," he answered; "the smack landed us in about
two hours. The boatman wanted to charge me for
twelve hours' use of his wherry; but I got off for half a
sovereign, which I thought cheap, as he talked of having
the law of me."

And here terminated this middle-aged City clerk's
narrative. The moral of it is not far off, and may be

found without much hunting ; and that a little musing over it shall not be without value, any man may judge for himself if he will but take his stand upon a British pier and watch the typical seaside visitor enjoying " an hour's row."

THE PLEASURES OF YACHTING.

STEAM has played sad havoc with the beauty of our naval and merchant vessels; but, though it has not spared our pleasure fleets, it has left untouched numerous graceful fabrics among the yachts of the country, and sail-power may survive for many years yet in the most beautiful form it has ever been moulded to by the genius of man. There is a story told of a butterfly alighting on the breast of a dying girl and taking wing at the very moment she expired, and soaring into the blue sky with the sunshine sparkling on its bright wings. I thought of this tale the other day when I spied the hulk of what appeared to have been a sailing frigate or an old East India merchantman towing up Channel. There was a strong, clear wind, and the water flashed like a prism, and I was gazing with interest at the poor old dismasted hulk when a fine schooner yacht, beating to the eastward, swirled up under her stern. A noble sight was that pleasure vessel. Her lee rail was almost flush with the foam which swept like a storm of snow under the gleaming milk-white curve of her lower cloths; to windward her sheathing was hove high, and the yellow metal glittered like new gold as it glanced through the network of spray and the shining emerald-green fibres of water which leapt about her glossy sides. She might have been the very spirit of the old dismantled sailing ship, leaping into bright and beautiful being as the most exquisite and the completest expression of marine grace. It would have gratified the most morose sailor to see her. Here was a sight to comfort Jack for the loss of the noble sailing ships of his younger days. The grand piles of canvas, the little skysails topping the swelling pyramids, the magnificent sweep of jibbooms bearing their marble-coloured cloths in layers like a heap of clouds, the ringing minstrelsy of the wind among the taut hemp that resembles a spider's web as you look at it against the sky of the horizon— these things are gone, or fast going; the ocean will soon be bare of them, and the star-like shine of sails upon the sea-line smothered by the long black coils of furnace smoke. But while such yachts as that whose flashing progress I watched remain afloat the sea will still possess her English beauties.

It is the owners of such vessels who are perpetuating all that is fair, all that is memorable, of the traditions of our English ship-building yards. The survival is a very fit one. It seems proper, indeed, that the stateliness and elegance of the sailing vessel should come into the keeping of men to whom the deep is its own exceeding great reward—as poetry was to Coleridge—who traverse it for love only of its caressing waters and the glorious life of its noble expanse, and who make it the framework for marine pictures into whose idealization enters all that money, fine taste, and devotion to what is beautiful and harmonious can furnish.

Surely to those who love her for herself the sea is a bountiful and great-hearted mother. The fascination the ocean exercises over the mind cannot be expressed in language; and happy is the man who, yielding to her spell, counts himself one of her sons as a yachtsman.

Mercantile Jack may profess to despise such seafaring as a fresh-water job; but, nevertheless, let him own that he envies the sand-white decks, the snug forecastle, the easy life, the glorious runs under blue skies and over tumbling and silver-bright waters. No other form of "sailorizing" yields so much unalloyed pleasure. Privacy is the first grand privilege. You will get that in your yacht, but you will get it aboard no other kind of ship which ever I have heard of. No amount of passage-money will save you from worry and companionship you may not be in the humour to enjoy on board the finest passenger vessel. It is hotel-life: you are a number; you have luggage; you are making the voyage for a direct object; in short, you have a destination, and the having a destination makes one of the main differences between yachting and going to sea in any other way.

A yacht is a man's home. He need never be in a hurry. Like Jefferson in "Rip Van Winkle," he lives about in spots. He may leave a good deal to his skipper, but he is always master; he owns the craft which others steer, and never a humour can come into his head which he may not indulge without having anybody to argue with him. It is a fine thing to be lord of the sea in this fashion. A captain of a big ship is a great man, but he is a sort of a slave also. His business is to make haste, and obstacles vex his soul. The patent log that he tows astern typifies the condition of his mind. A head sea is an affliction, and most of the wonders of the deep are great nuisances to him. He wants to sight nothing. He objects to excitements and adventures. All that he prays for is fine weather and so many nautical miles a day. These are the penalties of having a destination.

The bliss of yachting lies in the having to go no-where in particular, and one port being as good as another. If you can't weather a point, then there is nothing to do but put your helm up and come back again. The barometer seldom tells lies, and one of its safe readings, which makes yachting so delightful, is "Keep the harbours aboard." That certainly may always be done in the English Channel, and not for this reason only does one cease to wonder that it should be the most popular of all yachting waters. Much has been written about yachting in the Scotch lakes and northward among the isles. Such cruising might suit a man who is easily sea-sick, and who is never so comfort-able as when his tow-rope is aboard a tug. But the yachtsman who has the instincts of a seaman will choose the wide waters of the English Channel, pushing away to the westward until the Atlantic swell is under his forefoot and his white sails mirrored in water as blue as the heavens. The Channel is a sea of itself, and most of the changes of the sea may be felt and enjoyed on its breast. Here you will get breezes which toss a yacht prettily enough, and the calms are made beautiful and soothing by the gentle swell that runs out of the vague horizon, and keep the water flashing and fading under the sun. Once to the westward of the North Foreland, there is no finer space of water for yachting, and no-where more beautiful shores and nobler coast scenery. It is a great maritime highway, too, always full of ships, and so crowded with marine interests that the yachts-man is never weary of looking over the side of his vessel. Given a strong and sweeping wind from the southward of east, with the sharp blue sky which that sort of breeze makes ; and let the sun still be soaring, and the atmosphere so transparent that the coast stands along like a photograph; and let your mainsheet be eased, and the white heights of the North Foreland on your starboard quarter, the whole of the grand old Channel is under your bowsprit. Though there be no cups to win, there shall be a hundred races to run as you go ; and, keeping to leeward of the Goodwins, every jump of the yacht unrolls a glistening length of white, and green, and brown, and golden shore.

Indeed, there is not a little sport to be got out of the unpremeditated races of yachting. I remember once coming up Channel, homeward bound, in a fine clipper ship. We had the wind abeam, and fore-topmast studding-sail out, and we went ahead of everything like a roll of smoke, until, coming abreast of the Isle of Wight, a powerful yawl—as superb a yacht as ever I saw—came frothing and buzzing along, with her main boom almost amidships, and Dunnose like a blue shadow over her stern. She ratched like a phantom to windward of us, and then, settling herself upon our weather quarter, starboarded her helm, eased away her sheets fore and aft, and overhauled us as if she had a mind to tow us. She was in a smother of foam. It must have been up to a man's knees in the lee scuppers. She showed us the whole of her deck—a lady sitting in the companion, coolly ogling us through a binocular glass ; three or four yachtsmen aft, squatting under the weather rail. But the view she offered was not prolonged. She forged ahead of us like a " bonito," and in a couple of hours was a small leaning white pillar upon the horizon dead over our bows.

These are the unpremeditated matches I mean, and I have known some of them to be run with as wild a desire for triumph as ever a regular yacht-race kindled. They used to make one of the heartiest pleasures of

yachting; but nowadays where is the foeman worthy
of the steel of the slashing yawls, and cutters, and
schooners? Nearly everything that floats goes by
steam, and for a yacht to race a steamer would be
as sensible as to make up a Derby of locomotives and
thoroughbreds. Yet those crank racers, with their
enormous spread of cloths—though they be things of
beauty—are certainly not a joy to everybody. They
are very proper to take prizes, but those who love the
sea most wisely will least envy the privileges of the
owners of such craft. Sailing with your mast at an
angle of fifty degrees, half the mainsail dark with
water, the froth hissing and seething and bubbling up
to the lee side of the skylights, all hands holding on to
windward and wondering what's going to happen next,
may be exhilarating to some souls, but it is a mad sort
of yachting. These crank and nimble spinners give you
no chance of looking about. They are a fine sight to
watch. I know nothing more exciting to witness than
a great narrow-waisted yawl, almost on her beam ends,
hurling through an ocean of foam, jumping the seas
until half her keel is out of water, then burying her
bows in the storm of froth as if she were about to
dive out of sight, her metal to windward looking like
a sheet of polished gold, with the sunshine sparkling in
the wet of it. But to be aboard! Decks that one can
walk on may be an unsailorly prejudice, yet they are
comfortable; and the obligation to stick to windward
and to hold on with clenched teeth grows tedious and
even fatiguing if too long imposed.

But the word yacht is a generic term, and comprises
many different kinds of vessels. The middle kind between the knife-like racer and the motherly, lubberly
tub, is the best for those who go down to the sea in

pleasure vessels, not to do business, but to enjoy the
freshness and wonder and beauty of the ocean. There
are scores of them afloat, superbly modelled craft, whose
lines would have made the old Baltimore clipper-builders
green with envy. I will name no names, but will think
of a yacht I have seen—a schooner, near about 150
tons by yacht measurement, with magnificent spars
exquisitely stayed, a bow bold about the figurehead,
but fining away with delicate keenness at the forefoot,
with such a swell of the side as promises stability in a
gale of wind, but arching thence to the keel in a conformation so tenderly sinuous and beautifully clean that
a sailor would want to know no more to enter her in his
mind as one of the fastest vessels of her class. This
she is, but she gives you a beam as well as speed.
There is plenty of room to walk about her decks ; there
is no fear of falling down the forehatch for want of a
gangway to get into the eyes of her ; the coils of her
running-gear are never in the road. Is there anything
more tenderly beautiful than a vessel of this kind
slightly leaning under her cotton-white cloths, her
polished and swelling heights of canvas softly shaded
at the leeches, the brass-work on her deck full of blinding crimson stars which wink like bursts of fire from
the mouths of cannon watched from a distance, as the
lift of the swell veers the brilliant metal in and out of
the sphere of the sun, whilst a line of froth streams
past her like a shower of silver dust upon the sea, and
the gentle moaning of water at the stem mingles with
the vibratory humming of the wind in the vessel. This
is the sort of vessel in which a man can take his ease
and enjoy all that the sea has to offer. And this, too, is
your ship for Channel cruising. She would carry you
round the world if you had the mind to try her. She'll

creep into the wind's eye with the luff of her foresail
blowing to windward, not shivering, but standing out
full of wind that way, whilst the after half is drawing
and doing its work. I know her to be a typical boat,
and that is why I describe her. Whilst such craft as
she remain afloat, the grace of the sailing vessel in its
most beauteous form survives, and steam may be defied
to demolish a lingering but most noble marine ideal
realized.

Owners of yachts do not all take the same view of
the delightful pastime. Between the yachtsman who
never seems so happy as when he is out of soundings,
and those sailors who creep from port to port, and take
a three weeks' spell of rest in every harbour they succeed
in making, there is a prodigious stretch, filled up by a
surprising variety of tastes. But the harbour-haunting
yachtsman grows rare. His excursions to sea, even out
of sight of land, are every year more frequent. He
learns to hear a music in the wind that's piping merrily,
and the threat of lightning in the horned moon ceases
to scare him. This is as it should be. Yachting is
surely but a sorry entertainment when warps hold your
vessel against a stone or wooden pier, and no livelier
recreation offers than bobbing for flounders in the mud
at the bottom of the water alongside. Our English
summers are not very long, and there is much to be
seen, much to inspirit the mind, much to invigorate the
body. The warm and brightly-coloured sea, for many a
league enriched with verdant and dazzling and tender
stretches of coast scenery, courts the fortunate yachtsman with promises which it never breaks. It is not
racing only, it is not sailing only; it is the calm day
sleeping under the rich azure heaven; the water a
breathless surface of molten glass, shadowed here and

there where the shallow soundings are; the horizon
streaked with floating wreaths of vapour or darkened by
the blueish smoke of a long-vanished steamer; the coast-
line some miles away swimming in the haze of heat, and
the water in the south blending with the flood of light
which the sun flashes into it. Here and there is a
motionless smack, with her reddish sail reflected without a tremor under her; or a distant ship whose white
canvas seems to be melting upon the faint light blue
over the horizon. Or it is the summer night, with a flood
of moonlight shivering the ripples, whilst on either hand
the sea stretches away in solemn darkness touched faintly
in places by the lustre of the glorious planets unpaled
by the moonshine. A soft breeze murmurs over the
water, and keeps the spectral canvas on high sleeping,
and a narrow wake goes away astern into the darkness,
with fitful flashes of phosphorus in the circling eddies,
in the run of the ripples as they break near the silent
hull.

Small wonder, indeed, that the sea should court men
as it does, and fascinate them too. Happy the man who
can take the pleasure it yields as a yachtsman, and in
his own beautiful vessel can traverse its glorious waters
as idly, and freely, and gaily as the wind that impels
him.

A DRUNKEN SHIP.

In one of Edgar Poe's stories there is an account of a crew clinging to the bottom of their capsized vessel, and watching a ship approach them. She comes yawing and steering very wildly, but there are people aboard, and the poor sailors are full of hope; until on a sudden an insufferable smell is borne to them by the wind, and they discover that the figures lolling upon the ship's sides are putrifying corpses.

This tale of horror as well as of imagination came into my head some time ago, when I read the evidence that had been tendered in St. George's Hall, Liverpool, by a certain pier-manager and coxswain of the lifeboat belonging to a north-western town. He said that at about half-past five in the morning he was roused out by a man who told him that there was a vessel drifting ashore. He hurried down to the beach, and saw a barque of between 300 and 400 tons a short distance off under lower topsails. There was a fresh breeze from the westward. He watched the vessel a few minutes, and perceived that she would sometimes fall off so as to bring the breeze on her quarter, and then round close to the wind, like Poe's dreadful ship, and that she was coming ashore as fast as ever she could drive. The lifeboat was launched when this strangely-behaved barque was within a hundred and fifty fathoms of the beach, and on the boat getting alongside, a strong smell of rum and water was found to pervade the atmosphere. A man got on to the rail and dropped into the boat, and the coxswain said "he seemed stupefied, took no notice of anything, and did not speak." This was the skipper. The rest of the crew tumbled into the lifeboat and were conveyed ashore, while the barque took the ground and became a total wreck, nothing being saved but some sails and a few stores.

Such a very unusual circumstance as that of a well-found barque sailing ashore, as one might put it, of her own will, was sure to have a queer story behind it. And assuredly the story *is* a queer one, making one of the most disgraceful narratives to be found in the modern marine annals. It shall be told by a specimen of one of those plain, honest, English seamen who captains say are no longer to be found, and whose extinction, they declare, obliges them to ship "Dutchmen." I will not give this excellent man his name, glad as I should be to do so, for the punishment inflicted on the captain and mate by the court that inquired into their conduct would render a large public identification a needless supplementary penalty. The certificate of competency held by the captain has been cancelled, but to the mate there has been granted a twelve months' chance of reformation, and this alone should explain the reason for suppressing all names.

"The barque was a vessel of 340 tons, and we had a crew of ten men, not counting the captain and mate. We were bound for Quebec, which, I reckon, should make a ship's course about west by south; but on this, as you'll take note presently, all mariners don't seem to be agreed. The whole of the crew, saving me and

another whose name shall be Bill, were drunk when the
barque left Liverpool. Speaking of the fo'ksle, I don't
mean to say there's anything unusual in this. Drink's
grown with legislation. In old times, when there was
less law, there was less lush. It's a teetotal age, this;
nothing but water going in vessels, and the consequence
is that men newly shipped, knowing that there'll be no
grog betwixt this and the next port, go in for a bout of
drinking to serve them, as it might be, for the whole
voyage. See 'em come aboard, sprawling and roaring,
too sick to stand, rolling below, and leaving the ship to
sail away with no one but the idlers—and them drunk,
too, maybe—to do her work for twenty-four hours or
longer. If I was an owner my ship shouldn't be a tee-
totaler. Every day, at noon, there should be a can of
rum on the capstan for the men—a tot apiece; but I'd
make this rule, that any man as came aboard in liquor
should have no grog served out to him for the rest of the
voyage. That would stop the drunkenness ships carry
away from the ports, and all the dangers which a
drunken crew brings on a vessel that's got to grope her
way down rivers and along channels full of peril.

"Well, there was ten of us, and eight were drunk.
I'm speaking of forrards; I'll come aft presently. I
never saw men worse in liquor. You remember them
Scotchmen that used to stand at tobacconists' doors,
taking a pinch of snuff?—dummies they were, you'll
recall. Well, think of giving one of 'em a shove, and
seeing him fall. If ye can fix such an object in your
imagination you'll comprehend the sort of helplessness
of my eight shipmates. They lay in the fo'ksle as
lifeless as bits of timber; and this being the condition
of the barque, we were towed out with a pilot aboard,
and then, when abreast of the Nor'-west Lightship, were

left to shift for ourselves. The mate was aft, me at the wheel, and Bill forward. There was not an inch of canvas on our vessel, and no one on deck excepting those I've mentioned. Whilst we were towing, the mate came up to have a look at the compass now and again, and then I noticed that if he wasn't downright slewed he didn't want very many more nips to settle his business. He goes lurching along till he comes abreast of the main rigging, and here he lays hold and sings out, 'All hands make sail. Tumble up, my lively hearties! Bear a hand with your hair oil and your silk stockings, my sweet and noble fellows!'

"But nobody took any notice except Bill, who sings out, 'There's no tumbling up aboard this galliant vessel, sir—leastways, forrards; there's naught but tumbling down.' At which the mate bursts into a loud laugh, swaying upon the rope he had hold of as though he meant to swig off on it. Then, looking up and around, he sings out—

"'This ain't a steamer. The sails must be loosed and the yards hoisted, bully, if the Liverpool gells are ever to clap eyes on us brave mariners again; so jump below among them dreadful drunkards and rout 'em out. Rout 'em out, do you hear?'

"Well, Bill did as he was told, and after a bit he managed to shove two or three of the crew through the scuttle on to the deck. They stood blinkin' in the light like owls, rolling up against one another with their hair over their faces, and their clothes looking as if they had been put on upside down.

"'Now, then! now, then!' sings out the mate, who couldn't keep his legs without holding on; "what's the meaning of this here dissipation? There's no drink allowed aboard this tidy little ship. There's nothing

but the teetotal lay to be found in this handsome
hooker.   Milk and water, my bully sailor lads! that's
the tap if ever ye want to end as philosophers.   Loose
the fore-topmast staysail.   Loose the spanker.   Get the
main-topmast staysail on her.   Lay out, some one, and
loose the inner jib.'   And he rattled order after order as
though he'd got a ship's company of fifty men to do his
bidding.

"How the drunken fellows scraped through the job
I'm sure I don't know.   It was a bad look-out for us two
sober men, but for the life of me I couldn't help laughing
to watch the sailors Bill had managed to shove on deck
go aloft.   Talk of hanging on with your eyelids!   Again
and again I expected to see 'em all drop overboard; but
I suppose their instincts for holding on were there,
though their senses were gone, and the same mental
henergy it was, no doubt, as enabled them to get the
gaskets adrift and loose the lower topsails.   When those
sails were sheeted home—the jib, staysails, and spanker
being already set—the drunken men refused to do any
more work; they rolled over to the scuttle and disappeared, the mate looking on, but too intoxicated to
act.   The skipper all this while never showed himself.
I asked the mate what course I was to steer.

"'Course?' said he; 'why, keep the vessel's head
followin' the jibboom, can't ye?'

"'Easy enough,' says I; 'but where's the jibboom
a-going?'

"'No impudence!' he cries out.   'Smother me if I
know what the British sailor's a-coming to.   It's all
drink and jaw nowadays.   What's become of all the old,
'spectable, sober seamen?—tell me that, you terrapin.'

"There was no use arguing with a man who couldn't
stand without holding on.   I says, 'I'm not going to

steer this barque all day—'specially as we seem bound to nowheres. My trick was up and out a long spell since.'

" 'And d'ye think,' says he, ' the vessel don't know her way without you? Hook it forrard, afore I skin yer.'

"I let go the wheel and walked forward. I looked behind me as I went, making sure that he'd take my place. But the deuce a bit. He was leaning against the rail, and shook his fist at me when I turned my head, and there was the barque without any one steering her, her fore and aft canvas full, but her topsails aback, and her whole company, saving two, so drunk as to be incapable. It was a good job that old Drainings was not so drunk as the others, otherwise we should have been obliged to light the galley fire and get ourselves supper. We were not disposed to take this job upon ourselves, so we hauled him on deck and gave him several buckets of water, which appeared to wash some of the fumes out of his intellects, and he then turned to—in a very staggering fashion, sartinly—and got us some tea, being scared by our threats to drown him out of hand if he didn't tend to our wants.

" Me and my mate hung about the deck forrard watching to see if the skipper showed himself, but he never appeared, which, taken along with the condition of the mate, made us suppose he was drunk too; but we couldn't have swore to this without getting a sight of him first. I says to Bill, ' Here's a pretty look-out. What's to be done? No one at the wheel; no one in charge; everybody drunk, and the night coming along.'

' There's nothing to be done,' answers Bill, ' except to turn in and take our chance. It won't do for us to take command of the barque. If there's to be a mess, let it find the skipper boss, not us. I don't want no magis-

trate's job, for one.   We're but common sailors, and
common sailors have but a poor chance now when it
comes to law, and the fight's between them and the
captain.'

   " This was a middlin' sensible view; but still, life's life,
and I couldn't quite see my way to turn in aboard a drifting ship, and take our chance of all going well throughout the night.   So, calling old Drainings, who was
getting his senses and beginning to understand the
muddle we was all in, we lighted our pipes and had a
long confab, the end of it being an agreement that the
three of us should keep a look-out, turn and turn about.
There was to be no steering—nothing but looking.   Well,
I kept the first look-out, and in all them hours I never
see either the captain or the mate on deck.   The breeze
was small, and the ship lay steady enough, her topsails
aback and her staysails drawing.   Two or three steamers
drove past, and I'm pretty sartin they'd have been into
us if I hadn't taken the precaution to get the side lights
over.   Bill relieved me at six bells, we having settled for
his turn to follow mine, so as to give Drainings time to
sleep off the rest of the rum that worked in his system.
When I went below the fok'sle was as hot as an oven,
such a smell of liquor about as would have made you
think yourself in a public-house, and all hands snoring
so loud that you might have reckoned the barque was
sailing ten miles an hour, and that noise the sound of
the water rolling away from her stem.   I turned in all
standing, ready for whatever might happen, and fell
asleep, and when I woke it was to the tune of a desperate
hammering on deck.   It was broad daylight, and, when
I tumbled up, I found the mate beating the deck and
bawling at the top of his voice, ' Up with ye, you
drunken swine ! up naked, every mother's son of you,

and don't stop to dress !' he was roaring, filling up his meaning with more oaths than he had fingers and toes. He was just in the same condition he had been in all along, rolling and sprawling here and there, and fogging the air all about him with the smell o' spirits.

"Old Drainings was at the wheel, and I spied the captain aft, holding on to a backstay with one hand and shaking his other hand at Drainings, who grinned in his face. Though pretty near the whole ship's length was betwixt us, I easily saw that the captain was as drunk as his mate. By-and-by he turns his head and sings out for the mate to lay aft. The mate goes, and the skipper, fetching him a thumping whack on the back—meant for love and good fellowship—casts his arm round the other's neck, and down they tumble below, for another reviver, no doubt. Drainings left the wheel and came forrard.

"'I can't help laughing at the old man,' says he. 'Never heerd such nonsense as he talks. But, all the same, what's to do?' says he. 'We shall be driving ashore if we don't mind. Have any of the men recovered?'

"'I've not had time to see,' I answers, and I dropped down the fo'ksle hatch to have a look. I stirred them as was on the deck with my foot and made some of them talk to me; but there was not one man among them as was of any use. They had not only come aboard steeped to the eyes in drink, but had brought a quantity of lush along with them, and two or three empty black bottles knocking about 'splained how it was that sleeping in all night hadn't made these scowbanks fit for duty.

"Well, I don't want to make an endless job of this yarn, or I'd give you the particulars of that day and the night as followed. By that time most of the men had recovered their senses, and me and Bill took care, as fast as ever we could get 'em to sit up and listen, to 'splain the quandary the vessel was in, and our danger. This sobered 'em quicker than water would have done. They came on deck and took a look around, saw nobody at the wheel, no one in charge, and nothing on the barque but what we had made shift to hoist after the tug had left us.

"This was the afternoon of the third day. The weather looked dirty in the south-west, and shortly before five o'clock the wind breezed up hard. Luckily we was under small canvas. I says to the men, 'The best thing we can do is to haul down the staysails and heave her to. There's no telling where she's been drifting to all these days. No sights have been taken, the log never hove, no reckoning of any kind kept. Whether we're off England, Hireland, or Scotland I'm not going to calculate; but one thing I'm certain sure of, we shall be having one of them kingdoms close aboard of us before long; and so I reckon our business is to slow down this here drift as fur as we can, whilst we see if the captain means to take charge and sail the vessel to Quebec, or keep drunk and send us all to the bottom.'

"Everybody being agreeable, we hauled down the staysails and backed the foretopsail. There was no watches, the crew hadn't been divided; however, we formed ourselves into two gangs, and agreed to keep watch and watch till the morning; then, if things remained as they was, we arranged for some of us to go aft to the captain, and, if he refused to do his duty, to hoist a distress signal, and 'splain our situation to the first ship as came along. The deuce of it was, ye see, there was ne'er a man forrards as knew anything of navigation. Had we turned to and seized the skipper's instruments and charts they'd have been of no use to us. Well, next morning arrived, and found the barque still drifting and the weather as thick as mud in a wine-glass. All hands assembled, and we held a sort o' parliament, and then it was agreed that I and another should go aft and inquire of the captain what he meant by this conduct. 'Cordingly we lay aft, and going into the cabin found the mate lying there drunk, though not incapable. He asked us what we wanted; but we took no notice, pushing on to the captain's berth. We hammered on the door, but getting no answer opened it, and saw him lying sound asleep and kinder stupefied in his bunk. We laid hold of him and hauled till we'd roused him up.

"'Captain,' says I, 'we've come aft to ask what you mean to do with the barque. She's drifting anyhow, and all hands feel their lives to be in danger.'

"'Pooh, pooh!' says he, stretching his arms and gaping, 'it's all right. Have a glass of grog?'

"'No,' I says firmly; 'we don't want no grog. What we require is to know what you mean to do?'

"Instead of answering, he lay back, turned over and shut his eyes; so, seeing that there was no satisfaction to be got, we came away and went forrards again. The men were now thoroughly scared. They said they warn't going to stand skylarking of this kind, and if the captain didn't turn to and take charge and sail the ship back to Liverpool, they'd knock off work. I went aft once more with this message, but though I nearly dragged the captain out of his bed, I couldn't make him understand, nor even rouse him up. So I walked up to the mate and told him of the men's resolution.

"'I don't care,' says he; 'it's no business of mine. I'm not going to do anything without the captain's orders.'

"We was in a regular fix. The weather was so thick that it would need a ship to come very close to make out any signal we might hoist; we none of us knew where we were, in what direction to steer, what to do with the barque if we took charge of her. Whilst we were debating, the mate came out, and orders us to square the yards.

" 'What for ? ' says the crew.

" 'Why, for Liverpool,' he answers.

"We turned to with a will, the mate standing at the cabin door looking at us. We held on E.S.E. till about midnight, when we spied a light on the port quarter, and the mate said it was the Chickens off the Calf o' Man. It proved to be nothing of the kind, but Morecambe Bay light. At daybreak the land was plain to be seen about four miles distant, and the captain, who was now on deck, gave orders for the helm to be put up to let her drive ashore, which she did, the lifeboat coming out when we was close on to the beach, and taking us all off. The first to drop into the boat was the skipper; he wasn't too drunk to do that.

"What d'ye say to this tale of the sea, sir ? What'll the public think of merchant sailors after hearing it ? Should you think proper to print it, I'll allow that there'll not be a landsman as won't reckon it an out-and-out twister, spun from the winch o' your own invention. But, that there may be no doubt about it, just add what the finding of the Court was as inquired into this business: 'Neither the master nor the mate attended properly to his duties in navigating the vessel. They were both under the influence of drink during the voyage. The vessel was not navigated with proper and seaman-like care. She was stranded owing to the utter neglect from drunkenness of both master and mate. The Court considered that this was about as gross a case as ever came before a court of inquiry, and found both master and mate grievously and wrongfully in default.'

"Mild enough, sir. Had the Court been aboard, you may take your oath they'd have drawed it considerably stronger."

NOT very far from the London Docks, and within a stone's throw of that refined and odoriferous thoroughfare known as Leman Street, Whitechapel, there is situated a large, fine building, with entrances commanding two streets, and a summit that towers very nobly among the adjacent roofs. Once upon a time the Royal Brunswick Theatre stood where that house now stands, and vestiges of the old structure still linger in the form of some pillars or columns at the main entrance, and various underground avenues, in whose atmosphere, despite forty years of very strong marine flavouring, there seems to lurk to this hour a kind of ghostly smell of ancient orange-peel. The house is known far and wide as the Well Street Home for Sailors, and I once accepted an invitation from the manager to overhaul the premises, and judge for myself to what extent the Home improves upon the comforts and privileges the sailor flatters himself he may obtain at a common seamen's boarding or lodging house. I must own that I approached the place with a certain amount of foregone prejudice. Establishments known as Harbours of Refuge, Seaman's Sheet Anchor, Ports of Call, and the like, all mariners who will not sham piety for the sake of a coat, or a plug of tobacco, or a meal of bread and meat will keep to windward of. Jack objects to this

kind of classification. He dislikes to be dealt with as
something apart from the ordinary run of mortals ; to be
preached to in language which the minister may fondly
imagine to be the dialect of the sea ; to have tracts doled
out to him in the form of marine allegories, as if he
could comprehend no other allusions to life and death,
and sin and virtue, than those which referred to heaving
billows and storm-driven barks and broken tackle ; and
when ashore, to make one of a flock of seamen, to meet
nobody but seamen, to go to prayers in a church filled
with seamen ;—to be treated, indeed, as if he ought to
carry a badge or number on his back, as if his whole
class were socially tabooed. So, thinking this Well Street
Home to have something of the old unpleasant and ill-
judging form of charity mixed up in its composition, and
considerably disturbed in mind by the first four lines of
its forty-seventh annual report, I entered the Dock Street
entrance, never doubting but that I should meet with
plenty of features to account for the sailor's preference
for the grimy, frowsy, and squalid lodging-houses, of
which there were some dozens in the neighbourhood.

I found myself in a very large hall filled with seamen.
There was perhaps hardly a nationality that was not
represented. Englishmen and Scandinavians were
plentiful ; but in numerous places were black and yellow
skins, the sight of which carried the mind thousands of
miles east and south, and brought up visions of skies
different indeed from the brown heavens which were
careering in gloomy folds over the chimney-pots visible
through the windows. In a few moments I was joined
by the manager, and we proceeded to inspect the premises.
In a manner it was like surveying St. Paul's Cathedral.
Big as the building looked outside, it seemed four times
as large again when I began to roam about it. Room

led into room, wing conducted into wing, until methought Whitechapel itself might seem to lack area enough for the accommodation of this most ramified and capacious interior. Behind a glass front stood a porter wading through several huge piles of letters in search of those expected by some dozen men, who eagerly waited while he looked.

"The correspondence here must be enormous," said I, "judging by those samples."

"It is enormous," answered the manager. "Thousands upon thousands of letters and telegrams are received and distributed in the course of the year."

We entered a large room with a circular counter in it, behind which were several clerks hard at work over their ledgers, while a number of seamen were drawing or paying in money.

"This is the bank," said the manager; "here we receive such moneys as the men choose to deposit, and credit them with the wages which they have to receive from the ships they have been discharged from. Here, too, we cash their allotment notes, and what we do in that way you may guess by looking at that long box there, that is full of allotment notes which are maturing at various dates."

"But," said I, "I thought the allotment note was only made payable to a relative or to a savings-bank. This is not a savings-bank?"

"Oh," he exclaimed drily, "there are two kinds of allotment notes. One is, as you say, payable only to a relative or a savings-bank; the other is an illegal document, sanctioned by the Board of Trade, February, 1868—here it is in the corner: you see their imprimatur?" said he, handing me one of the notes.

"What is the meaning of this," said I, "at the

bottom of the note?—'Caution.—The Merchant Shipping
Act does not provide summary remedy in the case of this
note.'"

"Only a confession that a blunder was made," he
answered, "when the Act was passed. The advance
note was said to encourage crimping; accordingly the
allotment note was substituted. The seaman protested,
as he found the note practically useless. Instead of
rescinding or modifying the Act, an illegal concession
was made by the issue of notes payable to anybody, like
the old advance note. The issue is sanctioned by the
Board of Trade, who compromise with their official
conscience by giving the holder of the note to understand
that he cannot recover upon the note by summary
remedy. The old advance note was made payable three
days after the man had sailed in the ship; in the present
note the shipowner protects himself by making the note
payable fifteen days, or in some instances thirty days,
after the man has sailed. This may not increase the
risk, but the delay in payment causes the holder to charge
a heavier rate of interest for cashing the note, so that
practically the Act leaves the sailor as much at the
mercy of the boarding-house keeper as he was in the
days of the advance note. We have hitherto charged
nothing for cashing these notes; but we shall have to
do so in self-protection, for we are perpetually losing
money by them, and the law, which sanctions their issue,
yet deprives the holder of all means of recovering on
them."

So much for British maritime legislation, thought I.
Here are people, willing to pay the sailor the amount
his note is worth without any deduction whatever, obliged
to own that they can no longer act in this liberal manner,
because the law prevents them from dealing with the

dishonest clients who rob them! Will the day never come when the hidden part of our gigantic marine interests will be capably represented in the House of Commons?

"And pray," said I to the manager, "where are your bedrooms?"

He led me a short distance, and presently we came to a stand at the bottom of what I may call a shaft of galleries of a very curious skeleton-like appearance. The highest tier was probably about seventy feet. Every fibrine-looking gallery or platform ran the whole length of the wing, and was flanked on either hand with rows of little bulkheaded rooms called cabins, all of them numbered, and every one containing an exceedingly comfortable wire-wove spring mattress, slung by a species of metal triangle from the ceiling. I found that there were three of these gallery shafts situated in wings of the building, and capable of comfortably accommodating and bedding between five and six hundred persons. One of those gigantic ranges of cabins, dedicated to the late Admiral Hope, struck me as exceedingly handsome and curious. The lower berths here are devoted to the mates and captains. They are large, airy, superbly ventilated; but these are the characteristics of all the cabins. At one end of this fine division is a marble tablet inscribed to Admiral Hope, with handsomely carved coloured flags on either side. To see these cabins, the manner in which they are poised one above another, the stairs leading up to them, the delicate tracery of the platforms, and observe the seamen coming out of their rooms and descending the steps fifty and sixty feet above your head, is to get a new theory of human existence. I never saw anything more comfortable, more clever, more strange. I mounted to one of these galleries with the manager, and seeing a cabin door open put my head in. The place was in gloom, and I was about to withdraw, when to my astonishment I observed what looked like two little half-moons glimmering in the dusk. I stared, and was amazed to find a negro lying upon a chest, reading. I saw the whites of his eyes the moment he rolled them up to look at me, but the rest of him being black was not to be discerned at once. I asked him what he was reading.

" The Bible," said he, showing the book.

He was newly arrived at Hull from Barbadoes, he said, and had come to London to look for a berth as steward aboard a ship bound to the West Indies. He was a handsomely spoken, well-mannered young fellow, pronouncing his words with the finish of a man of culture.

We next visited the dining-room. This was a great department with rows of tables stretched along it, all covered with white linen and hospitably furnished with good glass and cutlery. At a large centre heating contrivance stood a carver flourishing an immense knife over a big pile of joints of roast beef. Sirloins, ribs, topsides, were mixed up, but the manager said that did not matter, as there would be little enough to be seen of them presently. A number of waiters ran in and out, setting dishes of potatoes, vegetables, puddings, bowls of soup, and such matters, on the table, and it needed nothing but a loving cup and a flourish of trumpets to make the thing look like a civic feast. Presently a bell was beaten, the seamen came tumbling in, and in a trice every table was crowded, and all hands eating their hardest.

" There is plenty of independence here, apparently," said I, looking round at the rows of " shell-backs "—and

I appreciated the term when I marked the taut curve of their shoulders—working away with spoons and knives and forks.

"Independence!" exclaimed the manager. "Why, no hotel confers more privileges. We are in reality a club. We were originally called a Home, and have stuck to the name; but I think it would be better had we borne the title of Club, for there is something in the sound of a home that savours of charity, and charity is a thing most seamen object to."

"What are your charges?"

"Fifteen shillings a week to the men, and eighteen shillings to mates, who eat in a room to themselves."

"Do you mean to say," I exclaimed, "that you give these men a bedroom apiece and feed them after the fashion I now see for fifteen shillings a week?"

"Yes," said he, smiling at my surprise. "And we go a little further even than that; for if a sailor arrives here without clothes or means, we dress him and put money in his pocket, and repay ourselves by deducting the amount, without a farthing of extra charge, from the allotment note he receives from the ship in which, in numerous instances, we procure him a berth."

"And may the men do as they like here?"

"As if they were in their own house. We close at half-past twelve; but there is a night porter, and a man is admitted at any hour."

"So that, practically, this is nothing but a first-class hotel worked at a cost that enables the very poorest seamen to use it?"

"Exactly. Our sole object is to provide the sailor with a comfortable home while he is on shore, help him in every way that he will allow, and so keep him clear of the boarding-house people—the wretched men and still more wretched women—who prey upon him, drug him with vile drinks, cruelly rob him, and often turn him adrift with scarcely a stitch on his back. Come, sir; more remains to be seen."

He took me downstairs into a ready-made clothing shop belonging to the Home.

"The tailors in the neighbourhood," said he, laughing, "more especially those who pay women commission to bring sailors to their shops, don't love us for this invasion of their rights or wrongs; for our charge for clothes is very little above the price they cost us, and a man may get here for two pounds ten a suit he would have to pay eight or nine guineas for to a boarding-house tailor. I may say the same thing of the bar we have opened. There were some murmurs at first among the directors; but, sir, we found lemonade and coffee would not do. They drove the sailors to the public-houses; for the men would have their glass, and if they could not get it here they would go to low places for it. Jack must be treated sensibly, as a man with brains. To stop his grog at sea is one thing, but to put him upon cold water ashore is merely to drive him to those who live by plundering him. The result of opening a bar here has been to extinguish half the public-houses in the neighbourhood, and you may believe me when I say that our people know their business too well to suffer any approach to intemperance in this Home."

"Well," said I, "I came here expecting to find a lot of false and mischievous sentiment mixed up in the administration of the place. I see that Jack's character is understood among you. You treat him as a rational man, and he respects you for it. No wonder the same people return again and again."

"There is no need for a man to do anything here he

does not like," said the manager. "We have serious, sober, steady fellows among us; for them there are prayers morning and evening, and all may attend who will. But there is no obligation to be present. So at church—yonder it is, close to the Home, you see—we muster a good congregation; but there is no compulsion. Whatever can be done to reclaim those who need it, to help to set men right, to teach them to lift up their thoughts, we attempt; but there is no forcing of religion —nothing to induce hypocrisy on the one hand, nor to excite aversion on the other. We say, ' My lads, here are your opportunities, take them if you will; but take them or leave them, we wish to do our duty by you, to make your lives ashore happy and comfortable, to keep you to windward of the low and nauseous snares which are everywhere set about for you, to come between your simplicity and the acts of the miscreants who find their account in your easy-going natures.' That is about the amount of our theory," said the manager; "and if we are not greatly successful, it is because the job we have set ourselves to perform is a very, very large one."

From the dining-room we went to the basement, where I was shown a number of capital bath-rooms, fitted with a plentiful supply of hot and cold water; a laundry and drying-rooms; store-rooms filled with joints of meat, loaves of bread baked on the establishment, white as milk and of a flavour that made one think of farmhouses and Mrs. Poyser; sacks of flour, potatoes, and other things of that kind; and an immense kitchen, with a wonderful array of ovens and boilers for cooking by steam; everything as polished and bright as a new bell, and not the smallest feature anywhere discernible that did not exhibit the completest signs of anxious and attentive supervision. This Well Street building may be called a Home, and in a sense may answer to that character, but in reality it is nothing but a fine, admirably managed marine hotel or club, filled with bedrooms a good deal more comfortable than many a one in a hotel that a man has had to pay five or six shillings a night for; providing liberal meals in the shape of breakfast, dinner, tea, and supper, and furnishing the seaman with all the comforts of a first-rate club for the extraordinary moderate charge of fifteen shillings a week. What does such an institution replace—or rather what is it designed to replace? I suppose there is no part of the sailor's shore doings more talked about and less understood than the life he leads at the greasy little boarding-house kept by a crimp or a tailor, or, worse still, by old women and abandoned daughters. I stood gazing at one of these houses—a broken-down bit of a hole, with an evil, swaggering look in the posture of its door, and with dirty, stained white blinds in the windows —and thought what a wonderful, dreadful book might be made of the scenes that had taken place in it. A sailor-man was at my side, and I fell into a short talk with him.

" Do you regularly stop at the club ? " I asked.

" Yes; it is my home whenever I am in London. I have used it for years, and so have scores of the men you see."

" A pity all sailors are not equally alive to their own interests," said I. " Here they are made really comfortable for a few shillings a week; money is advanced to them, clothes furnished to them at cost price, a hundred little comforts placed within their reach, and friends are at hand to help them to a berth if they find difficulty in getting a ship."

" Perfectly true," said my companion.

"What attraction beyond the privileges and happiness
a residence in this club-house offers can they discover,"
said I, pointing to the miserable little boarding-house we
confronted, "in such a den as that?"

"Most of the men you find in such places are forced
into them," replied the man. "All about here is filled
with touts and runners and their bullies. Sailors are
watched coming ashore. They may want to put up at
this Home; but the boarding-house runners are at hand
to tumble 'em into cabs, drink is given them, the girls—
and such girls!—are called in to help, and if the men
are obstinate they are fallen upon and beaten; and, to
such an extent is this kind of intimidation carried on,
that, however anxious a man may be to rescue a shipmate from the hands of those rascals, he'll think twice
before he does it, for so sure as he attempts to interfere
and bring a man to this Home, so sure is he of being
fallen upon and half killed when he's alone and the
night's come. There's not a policeman hereabouts but
is full of stories of such work."

"And what, pray, is the sailor's life in the low sort
of lodging-house?"

"A vile debauch, as a rule, caused by the temptation
thrust upon him. It would be difficult to make respectable people understand how he's robbed. I knew a man
who was brought to one of these dens and asked to
'shout'—that is, to stand a drink all round. He did so,
and was made drunk. Next day he was charged for
eight 'shouts,' the people swearing he had ordered the
liquor, and that it was not their fault if he was too intoxicated to remember. That's only one sample. Abandoned
women are kept in the pay of the slop tailors to bring
seamen to their shops and press them to buy, and a
single purchase at such places is enough to ruin a poor

man. There are, no doubt, respectable boarding-houses, but they are few and far between ; the most of them are kept by rascally men and women, who, taking the sailor as a simple-hearted fellow, fresh from a spell of salt water, and willing for a bit of a frisk, ply him until they have peeled him, and then kick him out. It was not long ago that a pencil-scrawl was brought to this Home. It had been chucked out of a lodging-house window by a man to a friend who was passing. It stated that the people of the house had stolen all the writer's clothes, and it begged the manager to send up a suit that the man might get away."

"Such things must be known to sailors ?" said I.

"Ay," he replied, "and a good deal more."

"And yet many of them persist in putting up at those haunts ?"

"I can't account for it," said he. "Here's such a chance as any gentleman with plenty of money in his pocket might be glad to take ; and yet there are sailors who'll carry their bags or chests to the lodging-houses, as certainly knowing that they are going there to be robbed of all they have as that their feet are upon dry ground."

I have only ventured to write down a very little part of what I was told about these lodging-houses. I will not pretend to be ignorant of much of the inner life of those places ; but I own that some of the stories related to me filled me with horror and astonishment that such deeds should still be doing in this enlightened age of marine progress. But is it not strange that so truly valuable an institution as this Well Street Home, which counts bishops, marquises, admirals, and captains in abundance among its directors, should be deliberately neglected, and even viewed hostilely, by the Board of

Trade, whose efforts to promote the interests of the sailor it helps to a degree no one would credit without close and careful investigation of its theory and practice ? Why, for instance, should the Board of Trade decline to licence a shipping-master in connection with this Home ? Surely the directorate should abundantly guarantee the character of the duties such an official would discharge. What conceivable object can the Board of Trade have in objecting to the Home endeavouring, by legal means, to obtain employment on board ship for the numerous highly respectable men who use the institution, and who must often want help to obtain a berth ? The Home asks for no State help ; it is self-supporting ; it has extinguished a number of low public-houses and crimps' haunts in its neighbourhood ; it is doing a great work ; and no man who values the sailor can read the list of gentlemen whose names are associated with it without an emotion of gratitude to them for the generous, wise and humane part they are playing. Surely it is the duty of the State to co-operate with the endeavours which the working of this Home exemplifies, and to omit nothing that may tend to lighten the labours of its exemplary officials and advance the truly national purpose for which it was originally established.

" Sir," said a middle-aged master of a merchantman to me a few days since, laying down his pipe in order to grope with both hands at once in his waistcoat-pockets, " I should very much like," said he, looking now at one hand and now at another as he produced a number of odds and ends before lighting upon the things he wanted, " to have your opinion upon some documents which I cut out of a morning newspaper, and must have stowed away somewhere with such uncommon carefulness, that dash my wig if I know where I've put 'em! "

I waited whilst he groped and slapped himself, and explored a weather-beaten pocket-book. Finally returning again to his waistcoat, he produced with an air of triumph three newspaper cuttings, which, after putting on a pair of spectacles to read them first himself, he handed to me one at a time.

One was headed " Thanks." The writer said that he considered it a portion of his duty to publicly express his deep gratitude and that of his surviving shipmates to Captain Townshend and the crew of the barque *M. J. Foley,* " who not only rescued us from a miserable death by frost and starvation, but did everything in their power, by the kindest possible treatment and self-

sacrifice, to mitigate our intense suffering and supply
our many wants." The writer added that nautical men
would fully appreciate the meaning of the addition of
nineteen persons to a small crew in the winter-time;
"but in this case my men were well fed, and we were
sorry to be the means of every one being put on a limited
supply of water." The writer of this letter, brimful
of honest, sailorly thanks, signed himself, "Abraham
Evans, chief officer of the late *Bath City* (s)."

My friend the shipmaster kept his gaze attentively
fixed upon me whilst I read this newspaper extract, and
on my putting it down called out, "Kindly now cast
your eye over this document," and handed me a second
cutting.

This was headed " *Elba*, brig," and was a request to
be allowed to thank Captain Jacob Backer, of the Nor-
wegian barque *Sarpen*, for rescuing the eight men who
signed the letter "from our water-logged vessel, when
only 2 lbs. of putrid meat stood between us and starvation. He gave us food, clothing, medicine, and every
attendance, and was most ably seconded by his kind-
hearted crew; and in the seven days we were on board
his vessel he made us in a great measure forget the
privations we had undergone."

The third extract was of a similar character, signed
by three survivors of a crew of fourteen souls.

"Well, sir," said the shipmaster, as I handed him
back the third and last cutting, "what do you think of
these documents ? "

I replied that they were expressions of gratitude
honourable to the saved and to the savers, and that it
was a pity such illustrations of the humanity and gratitude of seamen did not obtain more publicity than was
generally given them, as not only was there nothing

nobler in the world than the marine stories which the
letters he had given me to read touchingly testified to,
but that the interest of the sailor could never be better
served than by landsmen again and again dwelling upon
the bitter perils of his vocation, and upon the scores of
illustrations of the magnanimity and generosity of his
simple heart.

My friend the shipmaster listened to me very attentively, as though I had given him a new view of the
subject; but, shaking his head suddenly, as if to clear
his mind of all matter that was not in it before, he
said, "Ay, it may be as you observe, and I'm not
the man to tell you that sailors are likely to get
more than what they ought to want. The point's
this : If it's a beautiful thing to read such pieces of
gratitude as these documents contain, how much more
beautiful would the reading of them be if it was to
be known what impediments, that have grown up like
mangrove bushes from the lack of a proper Christian
civilization to cut 'em down, a ship's captain has to
contend with in order to gratify his instincts as a man
of feeling and compassion. It's all very well," said he,
striking a match and holding a flame in the hollow of
his hand as though a stiff breeze were blowing, " for
landsmen to read those letters of thanks and to feel
touched, and to talk of the generosity of sailors and the
like. Why—since the laws which govern folks are made
ashore, and not at sea—why, after they've done wiping
their eyes over the humble thanks poor sailors give to
them who save their lives, don't they turn to and give a
hand to the cause of humanity on the ocean by letting
captains know that the laws of the British nation, any-
way—leaving other countries out—will never let a man
who does a noble act suffer for it as much, ay, and some-

times more than if he did a wrong? You hear of ships passing vessels in distress—taking no notice—pushing on, as if in a hurry to get out of sight. There is nothing in the marine reports which set my teeth more on edge than those yarns—nothing! But I'm master of a ship; I know the duties and responsibilities of that position. I've tried to do good, have hauled some fellow-mortals out of the very jaws of death, and have been so made to suffer for my humanity that when I think of it there comes into my mind a bitterness that makes me curse the ill-luck which drove me into the track of the sinking ship and her perishing crew. These are strong words, but if I don't justify them you shall force me to eat 'em. Give me your attention for five minutes. I'll try not to keep you longer; and if I should lose my temper and talk a bit stronger than you may think there's need for, take no notice, but just quietly go on listening till I've done; and then, should I fall a-swearing, maybe I'll have got you into a frame of mind fit to join me.

"In the middle of last October my ship sailed from a certain port—there's no need to give any names—in ballast, bound on a voyage across the Atlantic. The weather was promising enough for three or four days after we got away; moderate, north-easterly winds which, crank as we were, enabled us to carry a fore-topmast studding-sail, and we drove along prettily enough, nothing happening to call for remark. But this sort of thing was too good to last; accordingly, at midnight or thereabouts on the fifth day of sailing, I was roused by the mate, and, hurrying on deck, found half a gale of wind blowing, everything in confusion, vessel almost on her beam ends, everything let go, and as much shindy aloft as would furnish out noise for a

battle-field. It was a squall with a storm behind it.
However, bit by bit we managed to roll up the canvas
and save our spars, and when daylight broke we found
ourselves under a lower maintop-sail, tumbling upon as
savage a sea as was ever rolled up in a few hours by a
gale in the Atlantic.

"This was the beginning of a deal of delay. The
gale kept us humbugging about in one place—allowing
for that lee drift which you'll expect of a ship in ballast
—for hard upon a week: then better weather came. We
shook out reefs, mast-headed the yards, and crawled a
trifle to wind'ard; but the slant was a short one;
another gale came along and lasted three days; and
so it went on, sometimes fine and most often foul, until
at the end of thirty-six days we found ourselves a good
deal closer to Europe than we were to America.

"Well, sir, the thirty-seventh day proved moderate;
a breeze from the W.N.W., a heavy swell running to
show that either a gale had been blowing or was coming,
and pretty clear weather, with a little glimmer of sunshine now and again streaming through the cloud-rifts;
enough to improve our spirits. I came on deck at half-past
seven, and was taking a look at the weather and wondering if the swell that was making the ship roll like an
empty cask was to signify more bother, when I was
hailed by the mate, who sung out that there was a dark
object upon the water, a point on the lee bow. I took
the glass and made out the hull of a totally dismantled
vessel—apparently a barque, but all that was left of her
masts were three stumps barely showing above her topgallant bulwarks. She was water-logged—like a pancake
on the swell that hid her with every send; and after
taking another look at her, and not doubting from her
appearance that she was abandoned, I put the glass

Q

down, water-logged vessels being by no means rare objects in the North Atlantic.

"We were swarming along over the swell at about three to four knots an hour, and as we should pass the hulk pretty close to windward, I reckoned that if there was any poor miserable creature aboard her we were bound to see him as we drove by. However, I had scarcely put the glass down five minutes, and was standing looking over the taffrail, when the mate again hailed me, and on my going to where he stood peering through the telescope, he put the glass into my hand and told me to look yonder, for there was a boat full of men, heading directly for us. I looked, and sure enough saw a whole boat-load of human beings lifting and falling and coming towards us. It was more like an apparition than a real thing, for when I examined the wreck again I could not conceive how such a number of men had managed to keep by a hull which offered them no refuge aloft, and over whose decks the water rolled in shining masses, as she swung into the hollows.

"As the boat approached, we backed the mainyards, and lay waiting for her to come alongside. By this time I could make out no less than fourteen men, and a sadder freight of human beings I never want to see again. Their white faces, their streaming clothes, their gaunt, hollow looks, the languid movement of the oars, and, above all, the manner in which those who rowed kept their faces turned towards us upon their shoulders, as if they feared we should vanish if they did not keep their eyes fixed upon us, was a sight the most iron-hearted man could not have viewed without pain and grief. We bore them the end of a rope, and dragged the boat alongside; and I wanted no better assurance of the character of their sufferings and of the lamentable condition they were then in than their slow, weak motions as they caught the line, and got their oars in and stood up. One by one we lifted or helped them over the side—fourteen of them, sir. Some of them were too weak to answer our questions. My men took the seamen forward, holding them up as they walked, for they could scarcely use their limbs; and I carried the captain and the two mates into the cabin, where we furnished them with food and dry clothing, and then got them to bed.

"All this while we remained hove to with the wreck bearing about a mile distant from us on our lee bow. My own crew consisted of eleven hands only, and the job of helping the rescued men forward had given them work enough until the poor fellows were below. I went on deck, and found the mate singing out to the hands to swing the main-topsail and get way upon the ship. I stood looking on, full of thought. Presently the sails were trimmed, and I called the mate over to me.

"'Do you know,' said I, 'that we have been very nearly forty days at sea?'

"'Ay, sir,' he answered, 'I know it only too well.'

"'We're provisioned, Mr. ——,' said I, giving him his name, 'for one hundred and ten days, counting for our crew only. But if you add fourteen to eleven you get twenty-five, and that's the number of people our provisions must now serve for.'

"He grew very thoughtful, and took a long look round at the weather.

"'I fear,' continued I, 'that it will merely be tempting Providence to pursue our voyage with all these extra men aboard in the face of the ill-luck that's dogged us for near upon forty days. If we're to make no more headway than we've already done in the same time, I'm afraid,' said I, pointing to the wreck that was slowly drawing abeam of us, 'we shall be as badly off here as if we turned to and shipped ourselves aboard yonder hulk.'

" ' That'll be about it, sir,' said he. ' The harness cask, to say nothing of the scuttle-butts, is much too small for fourteen extra hands, unless we're to get a gale of wind astern of us.'

" ' Which we've got no right to expect,' I answered.

" However, before I decided I thought I'd first take counsel with the captain we had rescued, and, on his waking up much refreshed in the afternoon, I put my position before him, and asked him for his opinion. He never hesitated when he heard how long we had been at sea and for how many days we had been provisioned. But I'm not sure that even his advice would have settled my resolution—for what can be more trying than to have to give up and go back, after beating about and toiling to get across for over a month ?—had it not that same evening breezed up ahead with a stormy appearance. It was just as if the weather said, ' No, you don't.' I took a look, listened a moment or two at the men singing out as they clewed up the topgallant-sails, and then told the mate to get his helm over and head the ship for the homeward passage.

" Now, sir, though it was disagreeable enough to have to go back after consuming so much time in getting forward, I was a good deal comforted by reflecting upon the cause that was sending me home. It was a cheerful thing, likewise, to see the men who had come aboard half-dead gradually recovering their health and spirits, and testifying their gratefulness by not only lending a hand with a will, but by striving to take all the work they could come at out of the hands of my

crew. Besides, I will frankly own to you, sir, that I
was buoyed up by the belief that any money difficulty
that must follow my useless trip into the Atlantic—
useless, I mean, in the commercial sense of that word—
would be in some degree met by the owners of the craft
whose people I had saved, and if not by them, then by
the 'authorities'—a sort of strange people who come
into one's head when one falls into an expecting mood,
and stop there as if they were real and had all the dis-
position and power you fancy of 'em, though to my mind
there's no illusion to equal 'em, and ne'er a word in the
English dictionary that makes a man fiercer to come
across after he's got, by writing letters and calling, to
find out the true meaning of it.

"The nearest port was a French port, and there we
arrived after a pretty quick run, and landed the rescued
men, of whom I'll say this—that their gratitude was
such, that if they could have turned their bodies into
gold so that we could have made sovereigns out of their
flesh they'd have done it cheerfully. Well, sir, after I
arrived in England, the first thing I did was to represent
what I had done to the owners of the barque whose crew
I had saved. I told them that I had been obliged to
abandon my voyage in consequence of the assistance I
had rendered, and that by so doing I had not only lost a
voyage, but consumed the whole of my stores. No notice
was taken of me; and when I complained to a friend
who knows a good deal about the law, he said the
wonder would have been if any notice *had* been taken,
as I had no claim whatever on the owners of the barque
for the rescue of the crew.

"'But,' said I, 'd'ye mean to tell me that there's no
Act of Parliament, no statute, no sort of general understanding, no kind of provision—call it by what name

you will—to protect a man from suffering heavily in his pocket because he goes out of his way to save fourteen human lives?'

"'No,' says he.

"'And must I,' says I, 'be compelled to pay off my crew—which I've done—and ship another—also done—and accept a twopenny freight to the West Indies to enable me to reprovision my ship—all which I've had to do—with never a living being in this whole wide world made responsible, either as the manager of a fund set apart for such cases, or as the owner of the wrecked vessel, or as the British Government itself, whose business it should be to encourage acts of humanity shown to those sailors it's always bragging about and leisurely looking after, for the loss I've been put to?'

"'Well,' says he, 'on reflection I think ye might drop a line to the "authorities"'—you know who he meant, sir: 'there's a fund called the Mercantile Marine Fund, out of which, I think—mind, I only think—the "authorities" may, if they think fit, pay a certain sum, whatever it be, in satisfaction of salvage where nothing more valuable has been saved than fourteen human lives.'

"'Well,' says I, 'I'll write to them;' and so I did. And what do you think was the result?

"I cannot imagine, I replied.

"I got no answer, said he. "I got no answer," he repeated, passionately; "and there's no more chance of my getting an answer than there is of—" he paused, and added, "I was going to say than there is of my stopping to pick up more shipwrecked mariners—but God forgive me for the fancy! It's not in my head, sir. But, putting all sentiment aside, wouldn't you consider mine a hard case? And is my loss made the lighter to

me because I am asked to reflect whether I *ought* to
expect the authorities, or the owners, or anybody else to
pay me for saving fourteen men from a dreadful death ?
Here, sir, you have one of the difficulties—one of the
hundred difficulties—master-mariners have to contend
with, as little known to or understood by landsmen as
Jack comprehends the business of an attorney. It's not
for me to suggest what should be done. But when next
you hear of shipwrecked sailors being abandoned by a
passing ship, don't be too quick to condemn the captain
as a coward and a villain for leaving his fellow-beings
to perish miserably, but say to yourself, ' His heart was
with them, and he'd have saved them if he had dared;
but British civilization said, '' Whatever you do you do
at your own risk. If no harm befalls you, good and well;
you shall pass by and nothing more be said or heard of
your act; but if you lose money, don't look to *me*," says
British civilization, '' for the only answer you'll get will
be that you're an impudent fellow to expect to recover
any loss you incur in the service of humanity ; " and so
the skipper, knowing this to be true, sails away, holding
that his wife and children at home must not be beggared
that a perishing crew may be rescued.''

Thus speaking, my friend the shipmaster rose
abruptly from his chair, pulled his hat down to his ears,
and impetuously wishing me good day, left me to lapse
into a very brown, I may almost say a very black,
study.

"I DON'T know what country he hailed from, I'm sure; but, thank the Lord, he wasn't an Englishman," said a smacksman, in the most fervent manner, to me the other day, speaking of Osmond Otto Brand, who was executed on the 23rd of May for the murder of an apprentice named William Papper or Pepper. At any other time than this I believe the story of that miscreant's barbarity would have deeply stirred the public mind; but of late days * murder has become a common thing, much talked of and freely practised. People's capacity of being horrified gets dulled by iteration of shocking news, and the significance of any one item in a blood-red catalogue loses value as a particular impression. Whatever effect, however, may have been produced by Brand's crime on the lay mind outside the district where the murderer and his victim were known, there can be no doubt of the impression it has made upon smack-owners and smacksman all round the coast. There is scarcely a fisherman who has not the horrible story off by heart, who does not view the atrocious cruelties practised by the foreign smack-master as a foul disgrace to the fishing industries, and who does not indignantly lament that the men who helped Brand to slowly kill the miserable apprentice were not hanged

* 1882.

along with their skipper. One result of Brand's crime was to cause some questions to be asked in the House of Commons. There was also some talk about the whole subject of fishing apprentices being considered by Government. If it is to be dealt with it will be as well, perhaps, first to give the Hull murder time to drop out of memory. To adopt it as a text for legislation would assuredly be to mislead honourable members who vote without looking very deep into the matters on which their opinions are challenged. If the condition of the smack apprentice is an improvable feature of current life, it is not so merely because Brand slowly tortured Pepper to death. We must shelve all thoughts of that murder, and ask questions without the least reference to it. What is the life of a fishing apprentice at sea? What is it ashore? How is he fed and clothed? What is the nature of his relations with the owners' interests? What is the average character of the men with whom he is thrown? These and other questions I will endeavour to answer from inquiries I have made into the inner or hidden part of the lives of a body of lads of whom the public know less than they know of any other kind of seafaring people.

I once wrote an account of a voyage in a smack in the North Sea. One such journey is enough for a lifetime, and the recollection of it makes me here declare—and I am sure there is not a sailor living who will contradict me—that of all the several forms of seafaring life there is absolutely none comparable in severity, exposure, hardship, and stern peril to that of the smacksman. His vessel is a small one; his cabin a little darksome hole; his working hours are full of harsh toil; he has to give battle to the wildest weather, to struggle on for bread through storm and snow and frost,

through the long blackness of the howling winter's night,
through the grey wilderness of a foaming ocean swept
by winds as pitiless as the hand of death. No legislation
can alter these conditions of his life. Philanthropy will
have its cod and sole and turbot. The fish must be
caught, but caught in such a manner that those who
shoot their trawls for them catch other things besides—
a wild roughness of bearing, a defiance of civilized instincts, a sense of outlawed and neglected life that
brings with it a fixed conviction of social immunity.
"I'm a fisherman myself, sir," a man once said to
me; "and I'll allow that there are many well-mannered, sober, steady men among us; but, taking us all
round, you'll not find a coarser set of human beings
in the world; and, if you want to know the reason,
you've only got to look at yonder smack, heading away
into the North Sea, where, maybe, she'll be heaving and
tossing about for weeks, with ne'er a proper influence
in the shape of books or company for the men to
come at."

Take now the fishing apprentice. He comes to this
severe, coarse life, himself most often of the coarsest.
He is fresh from a reformatory, from a union, or, worse
still, from the gutter. His associates are men who were
themselves apprentices; lads who came one knows not
from where, the refuse of the street manufactured into
marine objects by the owner's boots, and breeches,
and coats; and hammered into sprawling, unwieldly
smacksmen by the hard blows of their calling. They
know all about dandy-bridles and trawl-warps; but
they do not know how to read, and they do not know
how to write, and they do not know how to think.
Their home is the public-house when ashore, and they
take the morals of that sort of home to sea with them.

The apprentice comes among them, gets knocked about, picks up their oaths and their shore theories, and imitates them masterfully enough to be able to hand on their conditions with an added flourish, when he is out of his time and has boys under him to swear at. Now, what is legislation going to do here? You have the roughest life in the world; the roughest lads in the world recruits its ranks. What is to be done, short of what a few philanthropists are endeavouring to do, to prevent them from being the roughest men in the world? I cannot see that the smack-owners are to blame. They must have apprentices. They will take the best of such boys as they can get; and it is really carrying idealism too high to expect that these men, who have to work hard themselves, who have to be down among their vessels, seeing that their men do not run away, that they are properly engaged in preparing for the voyage, and so forth,—I say you cannot expect that these men, who come home of a night tired out, should turn schoolmaster and parson to their apprentices, and set them to moral jobs, when they are ready to abscond—with their master's clothes also—if they are not allowed their evening out after being at work all day up to their knees in mud, scrubbing the vessel's bottom. No one with any knowledge of the smack-owner's calling, of his hardly earned money, of his risks and anxieties, will envy him. Boys are boys all the world over, and that smack-boys should be peculiarly troublesome is not hard to account for on reference to their antecedents—that is, the antecedents of most of them. "The law has come between us and the boys," was said to me, "and makes our case harder than it was. We have no remedy now. Time was when we could send a constable after a lad when he was

off; but the law has stopped that. We have got to wait
a couple of days, and then apply for a warrant, by
which time the boy's t'other end of England. Take the
case of a vessel about to start. A boy refuses to turn
to. I'm on the spot, and call a policeman, and in his
presence repeat the order. Boy still refuses. Policeman then walks him off afore a magistrate, who fines
him, and I have to pay the fine if I want to get the
vessel to sea; for if I don't pay then the boy's locked
up, and the vessel detained two or three days whilst I'm
seeking another boy." The hardship is clear enough,
though I for one should be heartily sorry to see it recti-
fied by a return to the old and brutal system of locking
up lads in gaol at the will of the smack-owner. Let me
briefly place the case of the owners before you with
regard to their apprentices. To begin with, the lads
come from all parts, as I have said, and are bound
apprentice for terms of three, five, or six years. If
bound by institutions such as workhouses, reforma-
tories, and the like, a certain sum of money is paid with
them—in some cases £10, enough to purchase an outfit.
I asked a smack-owner what he reckoned to be the
average yearly cost of a lad's clothes, and he said £8.
"A pair of sea-boots alone," said he, "cost £1 16s."
Boys, however, when they first go to sea do not get sea-
boots, but "bluchers," the cost of which is about 12s. a
pair. When the lads are in harbour the smack-owner
has to house them. In many instances they sleep in
his own house, or in lodgings provided for them. If
they do not take their meals with their masters they live
as well; dining from the same joint and getting much
the same fare as he has for tea and breakfast. There
may be exceptions to this; but it is a practice so
general that it may be taken as a rule. When ashore

the owners also keep the boys furnished with a little pocket-money. The lad, for instance, who acts as cook at sea gets, when in harbour, 6*d.* a night, the deck-boy 9*d.*, and the third-hand apprentice 1*s.* These payments are made during what is termed "settling time;" but, in addition to this money, the owner gives them the small fish caught during the voyage, called "stocker-bait," the produce of which yields each lad an average sum of 1*s.* a week all the year round. Whilst in port the apprentice's work mainly consists in scrubbing the vessel's bottom, touching her up with the paint-brush, preparing nets for the next voyage, etc. At sea the lesser duties are assigned him. Suppose a smack carries three boys; the youngest will probably act as cook. When the net is hove up his post is in the hold, where he coils away the trawl-warp, which done he returns to his cooking. The deck-boy's post is on deck when the men are below taking their meals. He steers the vessel in the morning until noon or 12.30; then gets his dinner, and turns in. The duty of a third-hand apprentice is that of a man. He is commonly within two years of his time; and, though he is still an apprentice, he is generally treated as a well-seasoned and fully developed smacksman. Talking recently with a body of smack-boys, I asked them what sort of grub they got aboard.

"Good enough, master."

"What do you have for breakfast?" said I.

"Well, we has the choice of tea or coffee or cocoa; we has roast fish and butter and soft tack—as long as it'll last—and then we has biscuit."

"And what do you get for dinner?"

"Why, fresh and corned beef for a spell; and when that's ate up we has fish, and suet pudden, and cabbage

—as long as it lasts—and carrots and parsnips when they're in, and 'taties."

"And your tea?"

"Tea's the same as breakfast."

"Do you get any supper?"

"Ay, master; 'twixt eleven and one, 'cording as the watch is called, we has cheese and pickles and biled fish, or if there's any cold meat left we has that."

When it is considered where these lads come from, this fare is scarcely of a kind to justify them in grumbling and running away. Indeed, of all seafarers, smacksmen live the best. When Jack is gnawing upon a piece of junk, and knocking his biscuit upon the deck to get the worms out of it, the fisherman is regaling himself with the best of the produce of his trawls, or fattening himself on hearty fresh beef and—if it be Sunday—on good plum-duff. The apprentice fares just the same. And even in other ways he is better off than if he were in a ship's forecastle; as, for instance, in the matter of clothes, the owner being obliged to keep him well furnished in that respect, and to equip him with garments a hundredfold warmer and better than those which most sailors take to sea with them. The whole truth is, so far as I can judge, the comfort and happiness and prospects of the smack apprentice depend upon his own conduct. Owners, like all other employers of labour, want the best hands they can get, and smacksmen are glad to have smart and willing lads along with them. It is a rough life—the whole marine calling is a rough life, and there is none rougher than a fisherman's. If a boy is dull and slow, obstinate and sulky, he will be shoved and kicked about, and that would be his lot in any ship he went aboard of; but if a boy is willing, does his best, lends a hand cheerfully,

and is a steady lad, then he will be well treated, the
men will like him, the owner favour him, and before
long he will find himself in command. He has inducements to persevere and behave well such as no other
ship-boy gets that I know of; for if he has served his
time honestly, and shown such promise as the smack-
owner wants to see, then, when he is out of his time,
he is furnished with £20 worth of clothes, and a
sovereign or two for his pocket. I am aware that all
smack-owners are not so liberal, and I have heard of
some men sending their apprentices, when out of their
time, adrift in the clothes they stood up in, and forcing
them to seek work from other masters. But the rule is
to treat a good lad liberally when out of his time.

Whoever has examined into the fishing industry must
be well aware that smack-owners have substantial cause
of grievance in respect of their treatment by their
apprentices. An owner told me that a boy came to him
for a berth; the lad was in rags and starving, and so
filthy that the owner would not send him to his house
where his apprentices were. He walked with him to
the Sailor's Home, had him bathed and scrubbed and
fed, paid nearly a pound for him for seven days at the
Home, purchased for him some clothes that cost over
£2, and then on the morning of the day on which the
vessel was to sail the boy ran away, and the smack had
to be detained until another lad could be shipped.
Instances of such behaviour are numerous, and might
really account for, if they should not justify, a very much
harsher discipline and sterner kind of treatment than I
have been able to discover. For always let us remember
that the smack-owner has, as a rule, been a fisherman
himself, gone through the mill, suffered all the hardships
of the life, and, though ashore, has to work harder for

his living than ever he did when at sea. He is in this position, that he is only able to insure for total loss. He belongs to a club whose members subscribe in proportion to the number of vessels they severally enter. "Only yesterday," said a smack-owner, "one of my vessels came in; she had lost fifteen fathom of warp, two main-bridles, dandy-bridle, trawl-warp tackle, two trawl-heads, a trawl-beam, a ground-rope, mortices, head-line, and other gear. I have to bear all that. There is Mr. ——. In one night of storm his loss amounted, in insurance of other vessels which had foundered, to £245, together with eight sets of gear, valued at £60 a set." It is a vocation full of risk; scores of men may be beggared by a gale; and, seeing the important part that smack apprentices play in the fishing interests, it is reasonable that we should survey the question from every point of view, before hastily forming conclusions on the basis of such an incident as that of the recent Hull atrocity. Of course, there are savages and bullies among smacksmen, as there are the whole wide world over, whether among landgoers or seafarers. But whatever might have been the state of things in former days, I do not believe that, at the present time, there is half the ill usage to be found aboard smacks that I know exists at sea in other kinds of vessels. The crime of the murderer Brand necessarily gives a malignant colouring to every smack-master's report of having lost a boy by drowning whilst at sea; but the old salt maxim, "A fisherman's walk, three steps and overboard," should go a long way in explanation of many of the disasters that befall smack-boys. An accident aboard a smack happens in a breath. A lad dips over the side for a bucket of water; the vessel is sailing fast, the bucket pulls the lad over the rail, and he is astern and drowned before the fellow at the tiller can sing out. Or a boy goes to look over the stern to see the white water running away; the boom jibes and flings him into the sea. I should very gravely question whether a deliberate murder could be done without some one of the men reporting it. No doubt black deeds have been perpetrated in fishing-smacks. For instance, a story is told of a lad who was frying some fish; through his neglect the fish were burnt, whereupon the skipper, smelling the fumes, bundled below, seized the boy's hands, and thrust them into the boiling fat. The instant he was released, the boy rushed on deck and flung himself overboard, and was drowned. One might conceive of a man hating another and jogging him into the sea on a dark night. But the statistics of loss of life among smacksmen and smack apprentices at sea must reduce such dreadful possibilities to a very small number; and of that small number it is rare indeed to find one to which any better basis can be furnished than suspicion. So far as the professional life of the smack apprentice goes—his treatment at sea, his food, his clothes, and the like—it is difficult to guess, having regard to the unavoidable roughness and hardship of his calling, how his position is to be improved. You cannot make a drawing-room of a smack; there will be always hard work and hard words where there is hard weather; and there is not much hope of polished airs and genteel behaviour amongst a race of men who sleep in holes at which a blackbeetle might stand aghast, and who are boxed up for many months together in the year in a bit of a fabric whose forecastle is full of raffle, and whose hold is full of dead fish. But ashore no doubt something may be done for the lads to advance them morally, and make real men of them when they come to be men. It would be well if there were a few more

Smack-boys' Homes than there are. There is one in Ramsgate the theory of which is exceedingly good. The manager writes to a school or reformatory for boys, the conditions of acceptance being that the lads are healthy and strong and of good character; also that enough money be paid down to furnish each youth with a fishing outfit and a Sunday suit. The boys being got together in this fashion, the smack-owners are asked to take apprentices from them. This many of them do, I believe, on the understanding that the boys lodge at the Home when in port at a cost of 2s. a day each. By this means the lads are brought under a certain moral influence. They are watched over by the clergy associated with the Home, attend service in a chapel that adjoins the building, and are provided with the means of harmlessly amusing themselves in the evenings. The sole objection is—and it is a commercial one—the expensiveness of the arrangement to smack-owners who have several apprentices. "If I had but one apprentice," said an owner, "2s. a day would be cheap enough; but I have ten, who at 2s. a day per boy would be a good deal dearer to me at the Home than I find them in my own house." This is a point I will not deal with, but in all other respects I know of nothing that can be advanced against smack-boys' homes. Smacksmen make fine sailors; the navy and the merchant service ought to have no better recruiting field than the British fisheries, and therefore something of Imperial signifiance should enter into consideration of the smack-boy's moral and material welfare. You are not going to make him a refined person, but you can teach him to write and read, to have a reverence for God, to think of himself as a responsible being. An early training of this kind will not impair his hardiness, but it will put him higher than he is as a human creature. The lower orders of smack-owners let him run loose of a night when he is ashore, he is quite uncared for, and in the prison days he passed a good deal more of his time in gaol than at sea. "Making every allowance for second or third convictions," says the Rev. J. E. Brennan, of Ramsgate, writing in 1878, "we are not far from the truth in stating that 50 per cent. of these boys go to prison during some part of their service." These incessant punishments naturally led people to infer the worst of the fishing life. "Think what a calling it must be," they would say, "when boys actually beg to be sent to prison rather than on board these smacks." But Mr. Brennan justly, I think, attributes the lads' defection to their neglected condition, to the absence of all suitable guardianship. "The scenes of drunkenness and sin," he writes, "of which some of these lads are cognizant I will not describe. Let it suffice to say that many a pure-minded boy has in a few months become utterly corrupted, and his character, it may be, utterly ruined for ever." He is writing of the boys of one town; but his remarks are equally, and even more, applicable to such places as Grimsby and Hull and Yarmouth. Here, then, is the real evil. It is not that the boys are maltreated at sea to any extent outside the proverbial rough usage of the marine life; it is not that smack-owners—the majority of them certainly—do not feed and clothe them well, nor that they exact unreasonable share of labour from them; it is that, when ashore and during the evenings, they wander about, fall into bad company, acquire habits of intemperance, become unspeakable nuisances to the police, to the inhabitants, and to their own masters, run away, and leave owners in the lurch and practically now without redress; and so, in a large proportion of instances, end in becoming untrustworthy men, worthless sailors, people whom nobody will employ. Smack-owners, as I have said, cannot be expected to look after the morals of the lads; their hands are full of business, they come home wearied, and, even with the best will in the world, they must lack in ways it would take too much space to explain here the opportunities to care for the boys as they are cared for at a Home. What is really wanted is a Home wherever there are fishing-apprentices, an institution conducted with something of the self-sacrificing spirit that characterizes the Ramsgate Home; where the boys can be comfortably housed and tended at a small expense to their employers; where they may be educated and helped and rewarded for their merits as seafaring lads; and any one truly concerned in the welfare of our mercantile marine, and who holds that we should neglect no source from which we may derive the forces that keep our nation dominant upon the sea, will believe that the State could make no wiser disbursement than in helping in the establishment of such institutions, and contributing to them until they become self-supporting.

I NEVER pass Gravesend without thinking of poor Mrs. Henry Fielding's dreadful toothache, and the trouble her husband and the surgeon, "the best reputed operator in Gravesend," took to persuade the suffering lady to keep the hollow tooth a little longer. To what extent has the old town changed since the author of "Tom Jones" surveyed it from the deck of the little old vessel that carried him to Lisbon to die there? Much should have happened in a hundred and thirty years; yet in one respect Gravesend remains unaltered; it is still, so to speak, the same old point of nautical departure; ships still "drop" down abreast of it, and bring up to receive their passengers; and yet it remains the one spot of English soil which, when left astern, makes you feel that the great ocean is all before you, and that your voyage has commenced indeed. But is not human nature the same in all ages? Fielding's description of sitting at dinner and being startled by the bowsprit of "a little ship called a cod smack," driving in through the cabin window, and his account of the sea-blessings showered upon each other by the crews of the two vessels, might stand for a picture of to-day's river life. "It is difficult," he says, "I think, to assign a satisfactory reason why sailors in general should, of all others, think themselves entirely discharged from the common bands of humanity, and should seem to glory in the language and behaviour of savages." His opinion of Jack as a gentleman was not ill founded. But what would he think now if living, and with the memory in him of his uncouth sea-swab of a skipper (who, to the delight of posterity, fell upon his knees at last and begged Fielding to forgive him), he should step on board the 4000-ton steamer that lay abreast of Gravesend, with blue-peter at her masthead, on the day I happened to find myself in that town?

Not much imagination is needed, I think, to extinguish the monster fabrics which day after day lie floating motionless abreast of Gravesend, and refurnish the broad and quivering stretch of waters with the marine phantoms of olden times. The Indiaman of 500 tons is viewed with astonishment at her prodigious dimensions as she lies straining at her hempen cable, the sunshine sparkling in the big windows which embellish her huge quarter-galleries, her stern towering out of the water like a castle, a wondrous complication of head-boards and massive timbers distinguishing her bows, long streamers whipping from every masthead, and rows of cannon bristling along her tall, weather-tossed sides. You have little pinks, and snows, and cutters of fifty tons burden which have made part of a convoy from the West Indies, and have outweathered the heavy Atlantic surges as bravely as any Cunard liner of to-day does. Here, too, are colliers, "ships of great bulk," Fielding calls them, though there is scarcely a skipper of an old boom-foresail *Anna Maria* or *John and Susan* now afloat who would not hold them capacious only as long-boats. To appreciate all that the present means, you must step back and then look

ahead. Only the other day I saw a Blackwall liner
towing up the river. It is not so very long ago when
that ship would have been thought a wonderfully large
vessel. Handsome she is, with her painted ports and
frigate-like look, though her main-royal mast was un-
comfortably stayed aft when I saw her, and she wants a
prettier stem-piece ; but as to her size, she seemed little
more than a toy as she swam past the line of huge
towering iron hulls. You think of the scene of the river
as Fielding surveyed it, then as you remember it
twenty years since, then as you see it now ; and your
wonder is, What will the end be should the end ever
arrive ? What will be the bulk and vastness of the
fabrics in the good time coming ?

"The new docks," said a waterman to me, pointing
across the river with a finger like a roll of old parch-
ment, "are to start from yonder p'int, and end right
aways down there ; " and the sweep of his finger
seemed to embrace some leagues of the opposite low,
flat, treeless, and mud-coloured shore. Assuredly all
that can be given will be wanted. Our marine
giantesses are multiplying faster than they drown ;
and it seemed to me that there was something prophetic
in my waterman's finger when he made the gesture of
it to signify miles instead of acres. But many changes
must take place and a long time elapse before Gravesend loses its old distinctive tradition as a point of
departure. Think of the thousands of eyes which have
grown dim as they watched the old town veer away
astern, and of the thousands of hearts which have leapt
in transport as from mouth to mouth the cry has gone
round, "Gravesend is in sight." No other place—I am
speaking, of course, of vessels bound Thames-wise—
gives one such a sense of home as this. Jack may have

the English coast in view pretty nearly the whole way from the Isle of Wight as high as the South Foreland; he may bring up in the Downs, and have Deal and Walmer close aboard, and hear the church bells ringing, and see the people walking on the beach; he may take his fill of Ramsgate and Margate as he rounds the great headland; but somehow or other it is not until Gravesend has hove in sight, and he sees the shipping abreast of it, and the river curving into Northfleet Hope, that Jack feels home is reached at last; that the voyage is as good as over, and that in a few hours the noble ship that has carried him in safety through storm and calm, through sunshine and blackness, will be at rest, silent as the grave—as though, after the long and fitful fever of the deep, she was sleeping well.

These are the gayer thoughts, for they come with the hurricane-chorus that breaks from the forecastle of yonder ship as her crew get the anchor, now that the first of the flood has come, and the tug alongside is already to forge ahead and tauten the hawser. "Oh, when we get to the dockyard gates!" shout the poor fellows gleefully, with as much voice as a voyage from San Francisco has left in them; and you think that to-night there will be some middling salt and tough yarns spun in more than one grog-shop, whilst already Jack's most unlovely Nan—as Charles Dickens only too truth-fully described her—is overhauling her few penn'orths of finery in anticipation of the treats which are to be got out of a fund made up of £3 10s. a month.

But Gravesend appeals most from the other side of the picture—the outward-bound side. I was favoured with an immense illustration of this. A big steamer, with a black-and-white funnel, lay abreast of the Gravesend pier, with her decks literally choked with emigrants. She should have sailed the day before, I was told; but the emigrants—mainly foreigners—had rebelled; declared they had been promised a steamer belonging to another company, and refused to start in the vessel they were packed aboard of. Some one on the Gravesend pier told me that a thousand people had been put into her that morning. There was hardly room for a pin along the bulwarks. Clustering masses of human heads blackened the rail, as though all the crows in Kent had swooped down upon that great iron steamship, and were taking their ease upon her sides. I had no excuse to board her, but I managed to gather a good idea of her living freight by taking a boat and pulling round her. I had seen a very similar class of foreign emigrants in a North-country port, and had made a short voyage in company with five or six hundred of them, but that crowd did not impress me as this did. There was something very pathetic and melancholy in the postures and looks of this large con-course of people, who overhung the water, and gazed, with little of movement among them, at the shores on either hand. The thought of this mass of human souls afloat on the deep with nothing between them and eternity but a thin surface of iron, combined with the speculations as to the future into which the mind was irresistibly impelled; the new lands which awaited them; the long—perhaps everlasting—separation from their mother country; the numberless interests they represented; and the rapid growth of that amazing Western Empire, whose humanizing and civilizing progress was strangely illustrated by the embarkation of this immense assembly—the freight of a single ship, too!—for its ports, contributed to make the picture of the *Holland*—for that was the name of the steamer—a truly impressive and memorable one. It was a warm, sunny afternoon; far down the Hope, trending north-wise athwart Gravesend Reach, were the white heights of Cliffe, sparkling like marble in the brilliant radiance; the long stretch of water was crowded with shipping, whose bunting and variously-coloured sides filled the eye with colour; Gravesend lay in a heavy mass of grouping close down to the water's edge, with a lumber of huddled houses to the right of the new Falcon Hotel, here and there a window flashing back the sunlight, and the church bell ringing a pleasant farewell to a Penin-sular and Oriental steamer, whose head was being canted towards the north shore by a tug that she might have a clear road before her engines were set in motion; whilst, some distance up the river, vessels which had passed Gravesend twenty minutes before were fading upon the blueish haze of smoke from tall chimneys and fog from the marshes, the spars of the Blackwall liner looming huge and vague above the land which concealed her hull.

The very beauty of the picture furnished an element of melancholy to the crowded steamship, and the rows upon rows of faces which were all steadily gazing land-wards. I watched the Peninsular and Oriental steamer get under way, and contrasted her with the emigrant ship. The big deck-house or saloon of the former, with the two funnels rearing out of it, gave her, to my eye, a somewhat heavy look forward; but it was something to remember to run the eye from her almost unpeopled decks—nobody to be seen but some men in uniform on the bridge, a Lascar in a turban squatting in the after-awning, holding a little white flag in his hand, and one or two figures in the forward part of the ship—to the motionless black hull of the emigrant steamer, teeming

with life, and the bulwarks literally creeping with faces.
It is a responsible thing to carry mails, to be answerable
for a mass of specie, and for the lives of a number of
gentlemen and ladies ; but think of standing on the deck
of a steamer on a dark night, and reflecting that under
your feet lie sleeping a thousand human beings, not
counting your crew, and that the very existence of this
vast company of fellow-creatures depends upon your
vigilance, judgment, skill as a seaman. I believe the
sympathy and wonder of any man who saw that
crowded vessel and gave attention to the sight, would
have gone to the captain—to the seaman who was to
hold all those lives in his hand, so to speak. Who
would willingly accept such a responsibility? and who,
finding men equal to the discharge of these enormous
trusts, would not gladly lend a hand to smooth their
path for them by denouncing and demanding the re-
moval of whatever unfairly obstructs and harasses
them—the action of unjustly-constituted courts, the
decisions of empirics, and of people who could not tell
the difference between a gin-block and a dead-eye, the
iniquities of the modern ship-building yard, and the
hundred small red-tape worries which makes the shipmaster's life a burden to him ashore?

How much Gravesend is a point of arrival and
departure I was reminded as I stood overhanging the
stone projection and looking down on the landing-steps.
From a large sailing-ship towing up the river, a waterman's boat shot away and made for the Gravesend pier.
In it was a middle-aged man, bronzed with the suns and
winds of four months, and dressed in clothes which it
scarcely needed a tailor to guess were of an Antipodean
cut. His luggage was heaped about him in the bottom
of the boat. I watched him land, and followed him as

he came up the steps, when a rush was made by a little
group of people dressed in mourning, and in a breath a
woman, tossing up her black veil, was in his arms, and
sobbing on his shoulder. Those sombre garments threw
a shadow upon the happiness of this meeting; but still,
he had come back, he was well, and by-and-by the dead,
never to be forgotten, let us hope, would be buried indeed,
and the living heart reassert itself. The watermen
seemed to know when that ship had left her port on the
other side of the world, and so I found that this man
had been four months in making his way to England.
And how much longer had he been absent? But then
think of the glory of the green trees and fragrant
beauties of our English May to this traveller fresh from
one hundred and twenty days of salt water! Figure
the flavour he will find in a cut from a prime sirloin! the
sweetness of " soft tack "—ay, even such bread as is now
baked—after the bilious little bits of dough manufactured in the galley by the baker, and sent aft under the
satirical title of " rolls ! "

Scarcely had the sunburnt man and his friends disappeared, when there came a little figure that I could not
view without lively concern and compassion. This was
a small midshipman, resplendent in the newest of
uniforms. The buttons glittered on his tiny jacket, and
the brand-new badge on his cap shone like a freshly
minted sovereign. There lay his ship a short way down
the stream—a good-looking iron vessel, very long and
very narrow, without an inch of that " swell of the
sides " one loves to see, as I had taken notice when she
slewed on her heel to the first of the flood and gave us
a view of herself end on, with double topgallant yards,
skysail poles, and the capacity for an immense spread of
lower cloths. The poor little chap took a long squint at

his new home, and then a peep at the lady alongside of him, who, from the strong family likeness between them, I reckoned at once to be his mamma. She had been crying, her eyes were red, but she looked at her youngster with a kind of quivering smile now, for it would clearly not do to capsize his sensibilities at this most trying point. He had insisted upon going to sea, no doubt, much against poor mamma's will. He had fine notions of the marine calling, I dare say, all acquired by days and nights of study of nautical romances; and here he was ready to sail away, handsomely brass bound, mamma red-eyed at his side, bravely fighting with her heart. Hundreds of men have gone through this, and something betwixt a laugh and a sigh will come from them when they think of this little brass bounder and look back to their first voyage. What ideas had the young fellow formed of the life? But, alas! what mariner has not allowed his boyhood to gull him in the same way? "There is," says Dana, "a witchery in the sea, its songs and stories, and in the mere sight of a ship and the sailor's dress, especially to a young mind, which has done more to man navies and fill merchantmen than all the pressgangs in Europe. I have known a young man with such a passion for the sea, that the very creaking of a block stirred his imagination so that he could hardly keep his feet upon dry ground." These sentences recurred to me as I watched the little midshipman. But for how many days was the spell of the ocean's witchery to lie upon him? Probably, if they had head winds down Channel, he would be sick of the life and longing to be ashore in a warm bed, with his mother to tuck him up, and a good breakfast to go downstairs to next morning, before they were abreast of the Start. "Oh, my golly!" said a negro whom I met at Gravesend, selling flowers, "S'elp me, sah, as I stan' here, I'd gib dis basket—yas, ah would—and all de close horff my back, for a good blow-out of lobscouse!" But that little middy will have to be a black man if he wants to enjoy sea-fare as my negro-friend did. A few days of dark and evil-looking pork, and salt beef out of which he might cut models of ships for his friends at home, and "duff" made of copper-skimmings, not to mention the being routed out in his watch below, and having to tumble up aloft in a night blind with storm and rain, are pretty sure to disillusion him. But his buttons are new, and his hopes are young and fresh; there is no tarnish of salt water on either as yet; so let him take his mother's yearning, passionate kiss, and bundle into the boat and be off. She could not bear to see him row away, and the moment he went down the steps she hurried off; whilst he, to show what a man he was, squatted himself in the stern sheets, and pulled out a short wooden pipe and lighted it. In a few minutes he was out in the stream. I watched him get alongside his ship, trot up the gangway ladder, and vanish in a kind of twinkle of new brass and gilt over the side.

It is these constant comings and goings which give Gravesend its interest and its memories. One hour it is a party of people newly arrived from the bottom of the world; another it is a couple of drunken firemen tumbling into a boat, and shoving off for some lump of a steamer that lies abreast of the Obelisk or Denton Mill. But, in spite of the heaps of nautical conditions which beset it, Gravesend cannot be called wholly marine. It may be thought fishy, but it certainly is not salt. Contrast it with Deal, which it resembles in its lower streets. The wind may pipe never so merrily, but there is no shrewd briny pungency in the shrilling gusts as they

sweep round the corners. The boatmen have a fresh
water look. Their sou'westers and jerseys cannot de-
ceive the practised eye. They can handle an oar capitally;
but they have not the toughened and bronzed and
Channel-tossed look of the fellows whom you encounter
lolling in blanket trousers over the Ramsgate piers, or
arguing in groups at the entrance of the Margate jetties,
or heightening the picturesque appearance of the Deal
and Folkestone shingle. Yet I cannot conceive of any
place better calculated to delight a man of maritime
studies and scenes than Gravesend. You may linger all
day on the queer-looking roofed-in pier, with the old
barge moored against it, and never feel weary. Hour
after hour unfolds the canvas of a never-ending panorama of shipping. Picture after picture goes by—the
great ocean steamship, the little ratching ketch, the
sturdy old collier, the white and shining yacht, the large
and loftily rigged ship, the eager tug hissing through the
trembling current, and all the life and light and colour
and wondrous transformations of the river take a certain
character of remoteness akin to unreality, as though
what you gazed at was nothing but a series of noble
paintings, indeed, from the quietude that prevails about
you; an atmosphere of lazy stillness broken by the
muffled, rushing sound of the current sweeping under
the pier, the dulled voices of men conversing outside the
wooden structure, and the straining noise of boats as
the tide sets the little craft chafing one another's sides.

A CHAT WITH A FISHERMAN.

A FEW days after the dreadful gale that had wrecked whole fleets of smacks belonging to the eastern and north-eastern ports, and drowned many hundreds of fishermen, I was visited by a Hull smacksman, who came to tell me that he had lost a son in one of the vessels which had gone down on the Dogger Bank during the storm, and to inform me of the misery and destitution into which the widows and children of the poor drowned men were plunged. He told me in a rough, plain, earnest way how his son was to have been married to a young girl on his return, and how the poor lad had saved up a few pounds to purchase a little furniture for the home, which she was preparing, when the news reached her that the smack in which her sweetheart was had gone down with all hands; how, in house after house, down whole streets, there was a constant sound of wailing and moaning, with misery and hunger indoors, amongst the weeping women and the sobbing children; and, said my fisherman to me, though God knew he was a poor man, yet such was the suffering he had witnessed, so unspeakably great was the calamity that had overtaken the fishing population of Hull—and of other ports, but he spoke of Hull because he belonged to it—that, had the thirty shillings he subscribed to the fund for the relief of these widows and orphans been the last bit of money he had in the world, he must have given it and taken his chance for himself.

The subject was a deeply interesting one to me, who had lived among fishermen, written about them, knew their heroism well, their hardships, the simple-heartedness of them. We got talking about the smacksman's life, his risks, of various features connected with his calling; and, as the subject is one that has been commended to the British public in an appeal for charity for those whom the frightful storm bereaved, I offer no excuse for repeating in print some of the observations made by this smacksman on his own vocation. His reference to what is known as the "boxing system" enabled me to lead off with my questions. The term boxing, I may say, is applied to the conveyance of fish in boats from the smacks to the steamers which bring the fish home. As the vessels fill up with fish they transfer them to steamers, which, by relieving them of their freight, enables them to remain for weeks on the fishing ground.

"Is it a fact," I inquired, "that smacksmen object to the boxing system?"

"It is, sir," was the reply.

"Why?"

"Because it's dangerous to life, sir. It keeps men working for a considerable time in open boats in all kinds of weather. It answers the owner's purpose; he shares in the profits of carrying the fish, and it enables him to keep his vessel at sea as long as it is possible for her to remain there; and by this means the men are deprived of all home comforts and of the management of their families."

"What is the size of the boats employed in carrying fish from the smacks to the steam cutters?"

"Well, their length'll be about 20 ft., breadth 6 ft., and depth 3 ft."

"And these boats the men have to launch in heavy weather?"

"Yes, often in weather that may be called heavy. The risk is increased by the peculiar circumstances under which the men are placed whilst working at the boxing system; for you'll hear again and again of their shoving the whole of a night's catch into the boat at once, in order to secure a quick despatch and obtain the earliest possible market."

"How is the Dogger Bank relished as a fishing ground?"

"Well," he replied, "it passes by the name of 'The Cemetery' among us. In the winter time, I don't suppose a there's more dangerous place in the world. With strong winds from the N.E., veering to the N.W., there come the heavy seas from the Atlantic—if you can call the ocean to the norrards of the North Sea by that name—which strike the rising ground of the bank and turn the water into a boiling caldron. It was there where the smacks went down. The seas just coiled over and fairly broke upon 'em, smothering 'em, smashing in their decks, stamping 'em out as you might grind a beetle out of sight with your heel."

"Are your smacks supplied with barometers? I mean by that, have they any means of knowing when to expect foul weather?"

"No, sir; they're not generally supplied. One firm owning about twenty sail of vessels, who always work on the single-boat system in winter, provide their vessels with barometers. I should think they must be very useful instruments," said he, speaking as though he had never been shipmates with one; "and I may here add that none of those twenty vessels alluded to were lost. The majority of us smacksmen have nothing to tell the weather by except practical experience."

"But couldn't the admiral signal—couldn't *he*, at least, be furnished with a barometer?"

"No doubt," he replied. "But smacks get scattered, and it would be best for each master to understand the weather for himself. The admiral is more for rallying of us. He has his job cut out for him after a storm. His general scheme is to fall in with a steam carrier, and then sail to the ground from which he's been driven by the gale, expecting the rest of the fleet to do likewise; but it often happens that many days pass before they're able to get together, and this brings heavy losses among the fishermen, who, having no ice, are forced to find the admiral before they can start fishing afresh."

"What difference is there in the mode of fishing among the Hull, Grimsby, Ramsgate, Penzance, and other smacks?"

"Vessels belonging to Hull, Grimsby, Ramsgate, and Lowestoft use the trawl net; but the Penzance boats are what is called 'drifters,' or herring boats."

"I asked that question," said I, "in order to inquire what kind of fishing—that is, which sort of voyage—is most in favour among smacksmen."

"Why, in winter time we like best the single-boat system—when a smack goes out and gets what fish she can, and returns. This system does not require us to use small boats. It pays just as well as the other system, and is less dangerous in other directions than that of doing away with 'boxing,' as it leads to vessels scattering, and helps in that manner to lessen the risk of collision We don't object to the boxing system in summer, but it oughtn't to be practised in winter. That's what we think."

"Smack-owners manage to secure themselves, don't they?"

"Well, yes, by what's termed mutual insurance, which provides for total loss and for damage to a certain amount apart from fishing gear. Masters don't much like these here insurance companies. They're too despotic. I'll tell you what they do, sir: they won't allow a master the right of defending himself against any charge that's brought against him before them. Why, they think nothing of suspending a man from acting as master for a couple of years, perhaps for nothing worse than an error of judgment which the Board of Trade Commissioner would have been satisfied to reprimand him for."

"Do smacksmen make a provision for their families by any method of insurance or clubbing?"

"Yes, sir," he answered; "as a rule they do. There is a Fishermen's Widow and Orphan Society, which, for payment of one shilling a month, pays a widow £20 or £25, according to the time her husband has been a member; and there is also a Friendly Protection Society, numbering at Hull 700 members, which gives sick pay for certain periods and £12 at death. Both these institutions do a great deal of good. Many fishermen also join the local friendly societies."

"But a large number, I suppose, do not subscribe, and it is the widows and children of those who have been plunged into immediate destitution by their husbands' death?"

"Yes, sir. But it is not always possible to subscribe; there are too many of us, and some go without work for weeks."

"What is the average tonnage of the Hull and Grimsby smacks?"

"About seventy tons."

"What is your opinion of them as seaworthy vessels?"

"Well, sir, the build and behaviour of them are first rate; but a great many are ill found, and are in a bad state as concerns leakage; and I can assure you that among us fishermen there is a strong feeling that there ought to be Government inspection of fishing vessels by practical men."

"Will you explain to me the meaning of shares, and how they are proportioned?"

"It's in this way," said he: "the net proceeds are divided into eight shares; the master takes $1\frac{3}{4}$ share, the mate $1\frac{1}{8}$ share, and the owner $5\frac{1}{2}$ shares, out of which he has to pay three boys or casual hands, who receive together on an average about £2 2s. a week, and he has also to find his vessel's outfit."

"Is it true that smacksmen object to lifebelts?"

"No; they don't object generally. Some do, on the ground of their being too cumbersome to work in. They ought to be worn in 'boxing.' There's a particular danger in that system which I forgot to mention: it's that of collisions, which are constantly happening owing to the men being anxious to get their fish on board the steam cutter, to do which they all sail to her as close as they can, with their boats in tow and two hands in each boat."

"And what other special dangers are there," said I, "connected with your calling?"

"Well," he replied, "answering that question, as concerning the single-boat system, which I've explained, I can but say that what the smacksman has to contend with are just the ordinary perils of a seaman's life, such as shipping heavy seas which wash us overboard, and being dragged into the sea whilst drawing water, hauling in the net, and the likes of that. But the boxing system adds to these dangers by the risk of collision, the capsizing of boats, and the uselessness of the casual hands, the best of them preferring to ship in vessels on the single-boat system."

"Your casual hands, as you call them, touch the apprentice question. What is your opinion of smack-boys' homes?"

"Why, that they're a great advantage to all fishing ports and to the lads themselves, if the homes are properly managed."

"Can you say that smack-boys are ill-treated at sea?"

"No, I can't, sir. There are a few exceptions, but my experience is that the boys are treated with uniform kindness."

"To return to the question of loss of life," said I, "amongst smacksmen, what proposals have you to offer to diminish it?"

"Well, sir, if I had my way, I'd totally abolish the boxing system from the end of September till the end of March. That alone would greatly reduce the death-rate among fishermen; and I'd also have Government inspectors to survey the vessels, and see that they were found, and equipped, and ballasted, and so on."

"And now," I asked, referring to the vessels which trade among the smacks in spirits and tobacco, "what can you tell me about the system called 'coopering'?"

"Why," he answered, warming up, "my opinion of 'coopering' is that steps ought to be taken to put a stop entirely to such degrading traffic. If it could be put an end to, it would be a blessing to all concerned—particularly to the men. It 'ud make your hair stand on end to hear of some of the awful things I and scores besides have witnessed—many of our men having, in their drunken fury, jumped overboard, and in many instances been drowned, and in hundreds of cases 'coopering' has been the means of causing the men at sea to fall out and fight almost to death's door. I'll explain how it's carried on. The trafficking craft is in most cases an old vessel that has been condemned in England and sold to some foreigner for the purpose of carrying on this trade—some one hailing from Hamburg, Bremerhaven, Antwerp, or some port along the Dutch, German, or Belgian coast. This man—or call it these people—get their tobacco, cigars, liquors, and the various other articles they deal in, in large quantities from agents in the different ports they visit, at a very low price. The articles sold are of a very inferior quality—especially the drink, which is chiefly rum and gin of a very common and fiery nature. The prices charged, as a rule, are—for shag tobacco, 1s. 6d. per lb.; cavendish, 2s. per lb.; cigars, from 6s. to 12s. per box. Gin and rum are sold at 1s. 6d. per bottle; brandy, 2s. The smacksmen generally arrange to take a little money to sea with them for the purpose of buying tobacco, to save paying 4s. per pound for it at home. In my opinion, this traffic would receive a blow if fishermen were allowed to get their tobacco out of the bonded stores."

This, it will be seen, coincides with the report of the Sea-Fishing Trade Committee, who called attention in strong terms to the evils of "coopering." Not only, was it stated, do these boats lead to the bartering of ships' stores and gear for drink, "but they bring about the demoralization of the hands and even of the skippers serving on board smacks, and directly lead to risk and loss of life. We have it in evidence that they are floating grog-shops of the worst description, and that they are under no control whatever."

There was little more that I could think of to ask my intelligent friend. In reply to my inquiry as to the value of smacks at various ports, he said the question was difficult to answer, "as there's a vast deal of difference among the smacks belonging to the ports, and likewise in the damage done 'em, for its damage that counts heavily in the support of them. The cost of a new smack at Hull and Grimsby, with all the modern appliances, will be about £1500; the average worth of smacks at those ports is about £900, and the cost of their fishing-gear about £70."

"And a Hull smack's earnings?"

"Between £800 and £900 a year—I mean the gross earnings."

"Smacks are being constantly run down by vessels. Do they want better lights? What is the reason of these frequent disasters?"

"As a rule," he answered, "smacks carry very good lights; but there is room for improvement. I'm one of many who strongly advise that smacks should carry more powerful lights than they now use. If smacks are very often run down—and true enough that is—it's mainly because of the bad look-out that's kept aboard vessels navigating the North Sea. There are captains who don't respect our lives. They see us lying-to our nets, they know we can't get out of the road; but on they come, never shifting their helm, and if they pass by without striking us, and we call to 'em to know where they're coming, all the answer we get consists of brutal curses."

Apparently, then—and I say it not alone on the evidence of this man, but on the assurance of many others engaged in the fishing trade—the measure that is required to diminish the loss of life at sea among the valuable class of men employed in the North Sea fishery is the suppression of the boxing system during the winter months. And another most important step would be the supervision of smacks by qualified inspectors appointed by the Board of Trade. At present I do not know of any law to prevent an owner from sending, or to punish an owner for despatching, to sea the craziest old smack that can be kept alive by long and frequent spells at the pump. It is certainly most anomalous that close attention should be given to the loading, construction, and equipment of ships belonging to one section of the English marine, whilst another section that finds occupation for many thousands of men and boys is utterly disregarded by the State in all things saving the exhibition of lights.

Dr. Johnson once said that the full tide of human life was to be seen at Charing Cross. The full tide of human commerce begins a few bridges lower down. A man should count it a real privilege that, for the modest sum of fourpence, he is able to survey such an illustration of the wealth and power of this Empire as may enable him to form a very clear and true conception of the aggregate commerce and industry of the United Kingdom. To embark at London Bridge on board a fourpenny steamboat, bound to Woolwich, is, in my humble judgment, to be conveyed through the most wonderful series of transformation scenes that the world has to offer. What is comparable to that passage? No one who has entered the Sidney Heads but will remember the astonishment and delight inspired by the miles of blue water studded with fairy islands, the jasper-like reflection of clouds in the glass-clear depths, the rich tropical vegetation of the shores, the gleaming spars of shipping lifting their delicate tracery into the darkly-pure blue. Passages of strange and shining beauty recur like haunting memories of fragments of Eastern story to those who have threaded the waters of the Nile or the Hoogly; and recollections of the Peiho are made delightfully picturesque and impressive by visions of uncouth junks moored in the rushing stream, by glimpses of distant temples, by remembrance of soft winds aromatic with spices.

But the Thames! Its scenery is the work of human hands. An atmosphere of yellow light gives magnitude and a vagueness of outline to the leagues of waterside structures, and an obscurity to the horizon in which the monuments of industry fade with a simulation of immensity that cheats the senses into a belief of immeasurable remoteness. The great ships are in the docks far down the river; but though the steamers which lie in tiers upon tiers in the Pool, and far beyond the limits of that reach, are for the most part but of middle size, yet the mind loses all sense of their individual dimensions in the overwhelming impression produced by their collective tonnage. One journey through this magnificent stretch of stream is a large education. The flags of a score of nationalities colour the sombre heavens with their green and blue and yellow and white folds. All the countries in the world appear to pass in a kind of review as the ear catches the hundred tongues, and the eye the hundred faces, and the nostrils the hundred scents wafted from the holds of ships whose greyish spars seem yet to retain the heat of the equatorial sun, and whose sides are fretted with the wash of the surges of the great oceans.

I once took fourpennyworth of travel aboard a Woolwich steamer, for the sake of renewing some old recollections. I will not say that a better kind of steamer would not have made the voyage more comfortable. The dexterous and watchful skipper, who stood upon the bridge carrying his freight of human lives through the intricacies of blundering barges and the bewilderment of swinging ships and capricious tugs, by light motions of his arm and soft asides to the boy, who furnished them

with ear-piercing echoes, seemed to me to deserve a
stouter ship. The funnel-casing had much the appearance of an aged saucepan whose bottom has been burnt
to the thinness of a sailor's shirt. I thought to myself,
"Suppose we should tip some of these old barges our
stem by mistake? Assuredly we should crumple up
forward like a sponge-cake; and how should we manage
to save our lives?"

I looked everywhere, but there was not so much as
an old cork to pitch overboard in case of accident. Even
the seats, rotten as the hinges were, were not likely to
come away in a hurry. But there was too much to be
seen to permit me to bother over the crazy, quivering,
admirably handled, and most dangerous old machine that
was running us from pier to pier against a strong flood
tide. Once clear of London Bridge we were in a complete lane formed by moored or anchored steamers.
They were very much alike—little beauty amongst them;
some of them well-decked, with their gangways out,
showing the covering-board close to the water, and
making the structures, with their tall afterdecks and topgallant forecastles, look as if they were in course of being
built, instead of newly arrived from voyages long and
short. But all such characteristics were lost in the
thoughts of the immense mass of tonnage here submitted. Where did it end? where would the last of these
steamers be lying? To right and left they stretched,
with lighters alongside, steam winches rattling, the
vapour of donkey engines blowing out in volumes, some
in semi-discharged state, with a heavy list to port or
starboard, with frequent alternations of the flags of
Denmark, Sweden, France, the Netherlands—I know
not what other bunting—amid which our own red ensign
counted as twenty to one.

The whole commerce of the world seemed to be here, but in truth the Thames' show of it was only just begun. On either hand, trembling in the distance, in the vacant places between the buildings, could be caught the hair-like outlines of the masts and rigging of ships, with their house-flags twinkling in tiny spots of colour ; and still as the fleets of steamers held us in their interminable lane, did there heave up out of the remote sky more lines and threads and tapering tremulous heights of shipping. But the wealth of industry and the prodigious achievements of British commerce were not more noticeable in the vast assemblage of steam and sailing vessels than in such minute particulars as the little panting screw-tug with a chain of deeply-laden coal barges in her wake, every ebony mound embellished with a recumbent figure in shirt-sleeves, a sooty pipe in his mouth, and his face to the sky. The familiar Thames wherry was also here to add its touch of interest to the wonderful scene— the old waterman resting on his oars, and squinting over his shoulder at the passing tug, in whose tumble, as she goes by, the little boat begins to flounder, while the tall hat of the rower shortens and enlarges with the reeling of the wherry like an optical illusion.

As the lines of steamers dwindle the river widens ; and when we come to the bend of a long reach, it opens into a metal-coloured surface of gleaming water trembling with the speeding of its own rushing, though it retains polish enough to serve as a mirror, and to hold under each vessel the dark, inverted shadow of a phantom ship. Here we come across a long, low, iron four-masted craft, with painted ports. Even a sailor who has never been shipmate with more than three masts at a time might gaze with something of astonishment at the complex tracery that crowds the air over that immensely long and narrow hull, and wonder how long it would take a man to find out where all those ropes lead. It is not enough that there are four masts; there must be double topgallant yards too, making eight sets of braces where in former times three were found enough. But these are progressive days in ship-building. By-and-by we shall have five-masted full-rigged sailing ships, no doubt, with new Board of Trade rules for the examination of candidates in square-rigging. Let us hope that there will be also rules for the proper manning of such craft; for it struck me, as I looked at that big four-masted ship, that if her complement is assessed on the basis of her tonnage, without reference to the number of cloths she spreads, it must go desperately hard with the cook and the butcher's mate in a gale of wind.

Father Thames, once a god, might more fitly be termed a goddess, under the title of Commerce; for this assuredly is the presiding spirit. It quickens with life the smallest and craziest structure by the water-side; the very ebb and flow of the noble stream seem obedient to its laws, and its shadow is in the air and upon the face of the waters. I cannot imagine any one of those skippers of the Woolwich and Greenwich steamboats, who pass up and down the river some scores of times in the course of a week, so intimately acquainted with the wharves and warehouses and the uncountable features of industry which crowd the bank for miles and miles as not to behold something new, something he has never taken close notice of before, every time he directs his gaze with attention to the shore on either hand. The billy-boys and barges squattering like mudbanks hard against the slimy piles; the giant cranes poising tons' weight of burden in the air; the vast warehouses, with the long and powerful steamships snugged securely alongside them; the endless procession of wharfage teeming with hurrying figures full of business—these and countless other features of the scene furnish the apparently limitless lines of steamers and other craft with such a background as completes the deep and stirring significance of their multifarious aspect. It is a vast picture of motion—of great vessels coming, of great vessels going, of lighters swirling up swiftly with the tide broadside on, of tugs speeding in quest of towage jobs, of passenger steamers driving through the steel-coloured current with a glancing of silver at their keen stems and a whirl of snow sluicing in a broad torrent from under their counters. Now it is a big ocean steamship, of some three or four thousand tons, leisurely making for Gravesend, as trim as a man-of-war to the eye, her sides and funnel spotless, her scuttles twinkling like diamonds in her black length as they catch the sparkle of the passing water; whilst in vivid contrast there comes towing past her a full-rigged ship fresh from some Antipodean port, her brave hull covered with the scars of the conflicts she has waged with distant seas, her canvas carelessly rolled up on the yards, her rigging slack, and a crowd of men forward and aft engaged in pointing out one to another the familiar scenes ashore.

Ay, pathos is not wanting even amid so prosaic a scene of commerce as the reaches of our noble river exhibit. You find it to a degree proportioned to your powers of perception and realization in some such an object, for instance, as that ship yonder, newly warped out from one of the docks and all ready to begin her voyage. The hearty shouts which rise from her decks, the active little figures aloft, the bustle and business in her, cannot impair the pregnant suggestiveness of her leave-taking. You think of the people aboard who have said "Good-bye" to their friends, perhaps for ever. Poor Jack, sitting astride on the fore-topgallant yardarm, catches hold of the lift, whilst he turns his head in the direction of where he reckons Stepney or Poplar lies, and, as he thinks of his wife or sweetheart and the perplexities of the new allotment notes, he discharges a stream of tobacco juice into the air, and, with a melancholy countenance, wipes his mouth with the back of his hand and goes on with his job. There may be plenty of bustle and loud calls, but there is bound to be a share of sorrow too. It is not long since the skipper took his wife to his heart, and his head is full of her and the youngsters as he paces the quarter-deck, sometimes pausing to peep over the side at the cluster of boats round the gangway ladder, and sometimes singing out to the mate, who has his hands full forward. Indeed, it is impossible to look at an outward-bound ship without sympathy and a kind of respect that comes near to being reverence in some minds. What will be her fortune? you think. She holds herself bravely on the bosom of the calm river; the current wrinkles itself sharply against her solid bows, and breaks away along her side in a cadence like the tinkling of bells. Who can doubt that tears are being shed in her darksome interior? It is hard to leave the old home. The glimpse of the church spire through the open scuttle brings up memories which tighten the throat. When shall the next meeting be? and when time brings it about, will not absent faces and a change in the spirit of old associations make it sadder than this going is? Pray God that no harm befall the stout ship! As you sweep past her your hearty hope is that prosperous winds may attend her, and that in the new country fortune and happiness await those whose sad eyes dwell fixedly on the land that will be far astern of them before the sun has thrice sunk beyond the deep.

It may be that thoughts of this kind are suggested more by sailing than by steam ships, because the existence of the propeller does to a large extent mitigate the bitterness of the contemplation of distance. But let no in-shore dweller flatter himself that the sailing vessel is very nearly extinct. She may have one leg in the grave, but the other seems to me still to possess an astonishing amount of animation. The hulls of the vessels in the docks on the Blackwall side of the river are not, for the most past, visible from the water; but, unhappily for steamers, there is not the least difficulty in telling, by the look of spars bristling out of a hidden dock, which are steamships there and which are sailing vessels. Some of these days, perhaps, when the right kind of moral shall have been drawn from broken propeller shafts and twisted rudder-heads, the difficulty of distinguishing between the rig of a sailing ship and the rig of a steamer may prove very much more considerable than it now is; but, as this matter is at present ordered, the towering masts, the immensely square yards, should leave even a ploughman in no doubt as to the character of the vessels to which they belong.

The number of sailing ships which crowd the docks on either side the river must prove a real surprise to people who believe that it is all steam nowadays. Let ancient mariners be consoled by this assurance: there is plenty of steam indeed, but there is a deal of canvas too, so that all Jack's work does not lie in the bunkers yet, and there must still be a large demand for seamanship of the old sort.

I am not sure that the wonder of the river does not owe quite as much to the sailing ships as the steamers. The tall spars, the magnificent spread of yards, the black lines of shrouds, the beautiful tracery of intersecting running gear, added to the shapely hulls which support these towering fabrics of hemp and steel and wood, make a most noble and impressive sight, and give, so to speak, a final touch to the teeming, opulent, commercial inspirations of the great river. Lower and lower yet down the grand old stream the spirit of enterprise is settling, and the day is not far distant when the projected dockyards at Tilbury will veritably transform the quaint old town of Gravesend into the sea-gate of London. It is almost startling to contemplate that time. One thinks of Gravesend now as a mere break in the departure from the Thames. Will the chain of docks end at Tilbury? At Gravesend, apparently, they are thinking otherwise! and reckoning—somewhat against their own hopes—that if the Tilbury Docks people play at leapfrog with the Albert Dock proprietors, the latter company will repay the compliment and land themselves some distance lower down yet. The limits of the Port of London, however, will, I believe, be reached by within a quarter of a mile by the promoters of the Tilbury Dock undertaking,* so that one cannot say in this case that there is room enough for all. Unquestionably the docks which are nearest the sea will be the docks best liked; and owners will profit at the expense of tug-masters and pilots.

Meanwhile Gravesend may be complimented on its prospects. But what do the watermen think? They are loud just now in their complaints of the steam ferries. They say that they are not allowed to board the ocean steamers, even to put Gravesend passengers ashore. Everybody must go to Tilbury first. How much of their vocation will be left when the new docks are opened? But assuredly if some old interests vanish, many new

* Since this was written other limits have been defined

interests will start into life under the magic wand of
the harlequin Progress. One may look for a complete
transformation of the low, flat, treeless shore of Tilbury
Ness and an ever-increasing clustering of industries
along the banks of those reaches whose skirts now
mainly consist of mud. Our fourpenny voyage will
have to be extended if we are to compass all the wonders
of our river below bridges. The New Zealander who is
to muse over the ruins of St. Paul's may come as soon
as he likes, only it is quite certain that his meditations
will not be excited by any spectacle of decay. Life and
industry were never more active on the Thames than
now—enterprise never more bold, speculation never
more prophetic. The time is not remote when Gravesend, which I may say for centuries has been thought of
as a port of call, will be connected with London by lines
of edifices and piers and wharfs, as Blackwall is connected, and future passengers by the little Thames
steamboats—which, it is to be earnestly hoped, in the
good time coming will be considerably more river-
worthy than they now appear to be—will be conveyed
past a continuous panorama of commercial life and
marine interests to limits which will make Gravesend
and the opposite shore the actual sea-gate of the Port of
London; in other words, the entrance to a scene of
civilization comparable to nothing that we can imagine
even by the building up of fancy from the wondrous
facts at present submitted to any man bold enough to
adventure upon a fourpenny voyage down the Thames.

I CLIMBED the steep hill that runs from the Belvedere railway-station, pausing now and again for breath and to glance at the summer beauty of the distant green land through which the river toiled, like a stream of quicksilver sluggishly rolling, and presently, passing through a gateway, found myself in a fine park-like stretch of grounds, shaded by a multitude of tall far-branching trees, in the midst of which, and upon the highest point of the billowy soil, stood a spacious and exceedingly handsome mansion. There were circular seats affixed to many of the trees, and upon them I noticed several bent and aged figures leaning their breasts upon stout walking-sticks, and holding themselves in very quiet postures. Here and there, walking to and fro near the house or upon the grass under the trees, were similar figures, all of them bowed by old age, though some of them paced the turf with a certain nimbleness of tread. They were dressed in pilot-cloth trousers and sleeved waistcoats, with brass buttons, and ancient as these men were, yet it was wonderful to observe, even where decrepitude was at its height, how the old sea-swing and lurching gait of the sailor lived in their hobbling and determined their calling, as though the word "seaman" had been branded upon every man's forehead. I stood looking at them, and at the house and at the great trees, beyond which the distant prospect was

shining under the high sun, for many minutes before
advancing. The sense of repose conveyed to me by the
shadows of the trees, the restful shapes of cattle upon
the slopes beyond the mansion, the motionless postures
of the old men seated, and the movements of the few
figures who were walking, cannot be expressed in words.
I listened. There was no note of human life in the air;
no sound broke the fragrant summer stillness but the
piping of birds in the trees, the humming of bees and
flies, the silken rustling of leaves. The landscape was
like a painted picture, save where here and there, upon
the far-off shining silver of the river, a vessel slowly
gliding broke the still scene with a fugitive interest. I
walked to the house and entered the spacious hall, and
as I did so, a single stroke on a bell to denote that it
was half an hour after noon resounded through the
building. A number of ancient men hung about this
entrance, and I examined them curiously, for of all the
transformations which old age works in the human
countenance I never beheld stranger examples than were
submitted by many of these venerable seamen. Let me
own to a feeling of positive awe in my inspection, for
there was no face but that time had invested it with a
kind of sanctity. "How old are you, my man?" I said
to one of them. He turned his lustreless eyes upon me
and bent his ear to my mouth. I repeated the question,
and he answered that he was ninety-three. Years had
so honeycombed his face that such likeness of humanity
as there was in it appealed to the eye rather as a fantasy
than as a real thing. A sailor is usually an old man at
fifty, thanks to exposure, to hardship, and to the food
he has to live on. Many of these men had used the sea
for above half a century; some of them were drawing
near to a hundred years of age; little wonder, therefore,

that they should be mere dim and feeble vestiges of creation, and that vitality in conformations so decayed should excite the awe and reverence of those who explore the vague and crumbling features, and behold the immortal spirit struggling amid lineaments which have the formlessness of the face of a statue dug from the sand which entombs an ancient city. I turned my eyes from these old men to the hall in which I stood. Pretty columns of malachite supported the roof; woodwork and ceiling were lavishly decorated; marine hints helpful to the prejudices of the decayed mariners were not wanting in the shape of models of full-rigged ships —men-of-war and East Indiamen of the olden time; through the door I could see the green grass sloping away into a spacious lawn; and the warm air, full of sunshine, gushed in sweet with the smell of clover and wild flowers.

In a few minutes I was joined by the house-governor, himself a skipper, and fresh from the command of a sailing-ship—a genial, hearty gentleman, and the fittest person in the world for the command of such a quarter-deck as this.

" The old men will be going to dinner at one o'clock," he said; would I like to see them at their meal? I answered "Yes;" so we stood in the door of a long, handsome room, fitted with tables and benches, and watched the aged seamen come in one by one, hobbling on their sticks, many of them talking to themselves.

" Have you any shipmasters among these men ? " I inquired. " Several," answered the house-governor; and he instantly called out a name. An old man approached us slowly; he was bald, with a very finely-shaped head and a long grey beard, and stood deferentially before us, his hands clasped, waiting to be addressed.

"This man had command of vessels for many years," said the house-governor.

I looked at the poor old creature, and received one of the gentlest, saddest smiles I ever saw on a man's face. I asked him how it was that he came to need the charity of this institution in his old age.

"I was in the General Steam Navigation Company's service, sir, for many years, and had charge of vessels running to Boulogne. But my memory began to fail me; I was attacked with dizziness, and had to give up. I had saved some money, and took a little hotel at Boulogne, on the Quay. I could not make it answer, and, being ruined and an old man, sir, I had to come here."

He broke down at this, his eyes filled with tears, and he turned his back upon me. I waited a little, and then, taking his arm, I asked him if he was happy in this house. Yes, he said, he was quite happy.

"You may talk to me without fear," I continued; "I am here to learn the truth and to speak it. Do they feed you well?"

"Very well, sir."

"Have you no complaints to make?"

"None, sir."

"You think this institution a good and honest charity?"

"God knows what we should do without it," he exclaimed, looking round at the old men who were taking their seats at the dinner-tables. Here the house-governor brought up some other aged men, whom he introduced as shipmasters. One of them was a North Shields captain, eighty years of age; he supported himself on two sticks, was a little, white-faced,

ancient creature, with strange silver hair, and he spoke
with a wistful expression of countenance. He had been
seized with paralysis by " farling doon " the main hatch
of his vessel. He told me in his rich, plaintive, North-
country brogue, how the doctor had measured his leg and
thigh with a tape—for some purpose I could not clearly
understand—and how the accident had flung him upon the
world, a beggar, and forced him to take a refuge in this
institution. Was he happy? Ay, it was a man's own
fault if he wasn't happy here. He was grateful to God
for the care taken of him. At eighty a man was " na'
langer a laddie," and with a bright old laugh he hobbled
hungrily towards one of the dinner-tables.

In a few moments two bells were struck, signifying
one o'clock, and all hands being seated, I followed the
house-governor to the bottom of the room to have a
look at the tables before the old men fell-to. The dinner
consisted of salt fish, butter, potatoes, and plain suet
pudding.

" This is Tuesday's fare," said the house-governor.
" On Sundays they get boiled beef, potatoes, and plum
pudding ; on Mondays, vegetable soup, boiled mutton,
and vegetables at discretion ; on Tuesdays, what you see ;
on Wednesdays, soup, boiled beef, and potatoes ; on
Thursdays, roast mutton, vegetables, and bread and
cheese ; on Fridays, salt pork, pea soup, and calavances ;
and on Saturdays, soup and boulli—not soap and bullion,
as Jack says, one onion to a gallon of water—but a very
good preserved soup, with potatoes or rice and bread-and-
cheese. Taste this fish."

I did so, and found it excellent ; so, likewise, was the
suet pudding. The potatoes were new. The beer was
the only doubtful feature of the repast ; it was thin,
insipid, and flat. I made haste to taste and approve,

for I could see that the old fellows were very hungry.
The governor left me, and went to the top of the room,
where, in a loud and impressive voice, he said grace,
bidding the ancient mariners be thankful for what they
were about to receive; they all half rose, and in one
feeble, rustling old pipe, sung out "Amen," and then,
like schoolboys, made snatches at the dishes, and in a
minute were eating with avidity. It warmed my heart
to see them. It made me feel that there must yet be
plenty of goodness left in this world, when—through the
benevolence of strangers and their large-hearted concern
for poor Jack—ninety-three old, very old seamen, tottering
on the verge of the grave, so poor and so destitute, so
feeble and so friendless that but for the benevolence of
those whom Providence had brought to their succour,
they must have miserably starved and died, were
clothed, and fed, and sheltered, and tenderly watched
over. I know not that I have ever been so moved as I
was in my passage through that dining-room. It was
not only the pathos that lies in the helplessness of old
age ; I could not but think of the great compass of time
these men's experiences embraced, of the changes they
had witnessed, of the sorrows and struggles which had
made up the sum of their long lives, and how eighty
and ninety years of privation, endurance, and such
pleasures as sailors take, and such ambitions as sailors
have, had ended in these bowed and toothless shapes,
clutching at their plain repast with child-like selfishness,
indifferent as death itself to the great machine of life
that was whirring with its thousand interests outside the
silent sphere of their present existence, and dependent
for the bread their trembling hands raised to their poor
old mouths upon the bounty of those who love the noble
profession of the sea, and who will not let the old and

bruised and worn-out seaman want for such help as they can send him. Here and there were men too infirm to feed themselves; and I took notice how thoughtfully their aged messmates prepared their meal for them. Some of those thus occupied were more aged than the men they assisted.

"Bless your honour, he's but a child to *me*," said one of them, in answer to my questions; "he's but three and seventy, and I shall be eighty-nine come next September."

One pitiful sight deeply affected me. It was an old man stone deaf and stone blind. How is the helplessness in his face to be conveyed?

"He's losing his appetite fast," said a seaman of about eighty who sat near him. "His senses is all locked up. Ye never hear him speak."

There were sadder sights even than this; but I dare not trust myself to write of them.

I followed the house-governor out of the dining-rooms into a large apartment, well stored with books, magazines, etc., the gifts of friends of the charity. This I was told was the reading-room. It looked on to the green grounds, and was a most cheerful and delightful chamber. Further on was another room furnished with bagatelle boards and side tables for cribbage, etc. There was a particular cleanness and neatness everywhere visible, and I asked who did the work of the house. The house-governor answered, "The inmates. The more active among them are put to washing down and dusting at ten o'clock, and they finish at twelve. This is all the work required of them. Throughout the rest of the day they have nothing to do but to lounge about the grounds and amuse themselves as they please in the bagatelle or reading rooms, or in the smoking-room, which is a large apartment in the basement." Mounting the wide stone staircase, and admiring as I went the singularly handsome and lavishly-embellished interior of the very fine building, I found myself on a floor devoted to the sleeping-rooms. These consist of rows of bulk-heads partitioning off little cabins, each with a door and a number, and furnished with a comfortable bed, and some of them were movingly decorated by photographs of a mother, a sister, a child, with humble memorials saved from the wreck of the past; such relics of the old home as a few china chimneypiece ornaments, a coloured picture, and the like, with here and there a sea-chest, though, as a rule, these little cabins, as they are called, were conspicuously empty of all suggestions of marine life. Now and again the opening of a door would dis-close an old man seated on his bed, darning a sock or mending a shirt. It might have been that they were used to the visits of strangers; but I could not help observing in all these old seamen an utter indifference to our presence and inspection, a look of deep abstrac-tion, as if their minds were leagues astern of them or far ahead, and existence were an obligation with which they had no sympathy, and of which they never took notice unless their attention was compelled to it.

"Here," said the governor, taking me into a room in which three or four old men were assembled—for dinner had been finished some time, and the seamen had quitted the tables—"is a veteran who has taught him-self how to write. Show us your copy-book, my man," said he, giving him his name.

The old fellow produced his book with a great air of pride, and I was struck by the excellence of the writing.

"Is this all your own doing?" I asked.

"Ay, sir, every stroke. It's been a bit of a job; for,

you see, when a man's nearing eighty ye can't say that his brain's like a young 'un's."

"This would shame many a youngster, nevertheless," said I.

"I'd be prouder if I could read it, though," he exclaimed, with the anxious and yet gentle expression that seemed a characteristic of the faces in this institution.

"Ah, I see," said I. "You can copy, but cannot read what you copy. Never mind! that will come too, presently."

"I'm afeard not," said he, shaking his head. "Writin's one thing, readin's another. I have learned to write, but dunno as ever I shall be able to read it."

The governor, with an encouraging smile, told him to persevere, and then led the way to one of the sick wards, where I found a very aged man in bed, and two others seated at a table.

"That poor old fellow," said he, pointing to the bed, "begged to be allowed to attend the funeral of a man who died in the institution a short time since; he was so much affected that he was struck with paralysis, and had to be carried back here. He was for years a shipmaster, had command of several fine ships, and is a man of excellent education. He has been in this institution some years." And then, addressing him, "Well, and how do you feel yourself now?"

"Mending, sir, mending," answered the old man. "It's death to me to be lying here. Why, for seventy-nine years I never had a day's illness, never took a ha'porth of physic."

"You must have patience," said the governor; "you'll be up and doing presently."

"Ay, the power of forereaching is not taken out of me yet," he answered, breaking into a laugh, the hearti-

ness of which somehow pained me more to hear than
had he burst into sobs.

There were more "cabins" upstairs, and in one
of them we found an old Irishman standing, lost in
thought, looking out of the window I addressed him,
and he answered me in a rich brogue. I never remember meeting a more winning old face, nor being
won by a voice more cordial and pleasant to hear. He
told me he had been in the *Kent*, East Indiaman, when
she was burnt. This was so long ago as 1825, and he
was then a hearty, able-bodied man. It was like
turning back the pages of the history of England to
hear him talk of that famous and dreadful disaster.

"There's another man in the institution who was
along with me in the *Kent*," said he.

I thought of the description given of the *Kent* by the
master of the *Caroline* as I looked at this ancient man.
"Her appearance was that of an immense cauldron or
cage of buoyant basketwork, formed of the charred and
blackened ribs, naked, and stripped of every plank,
encircling an uninterrupted mass of flame." Again and
again had I read the story of that terrible fire at sea,
thinking of it always as something deep-buried in
history, and infinitely remote; and now here was a
man who had been an actor in it, talking of it as if
it had been but of yesterday, quavering out his "says
I's" and "says he's," and eager to let me know that
if he liked he could tell me something about the behaviour of certain responsible persons on board that would
not redound to their credit. It was pantaloon with
harlequin's wand in his hand; the faded old picture
was touched, and became a live thing, the seas rolling,
the ship burning, the terror and anguish of nearly sixty
years since growing quick again under the magic of this

ancient man's memory, and in the presence of a living witness of that long-decayed night of horror.

Of such a charity as this of the Royal Alfred Aged Merchant Seamen's Institution how can any man who honours the English sailor and values his calling hope to speak in such terms of praise as shall not seem hyperbolical? Not for one instant will I say that as a charity it is superior to others which deal with the sick, with the destitute, with the infirm, with little children. "There is misery enough in every corner of the world as well as within our convent," Sterne's monk is made to imply by his cordial wave of the hand. But I do claim for this institution the possession of a peculiar element of pathos such as no man who has not beheld the aged, the stricken, the helpless, the broken-down men congregated within its walls can form any idea of. As you survey them their past arises; you think of the black and stormy night, the frost and snow, the famine and the shipwreck—all the perils which sailors encounter in their quest or carriage of that which makes us great and prosperous as a nation; and then reflections on the dire ending which must have befallen these tempest-beaten, time-laden men but for the charity that provides them with a refuge break in upon you, and you feel that no words of praise can be too high for such an institution, and that no money dedicated by generous hearts to the alleviation of human suffering can be better directed than to the exchequer of this aged seamen's home. Ninety-three old sailors are at present lodged in the institution. The house is big enough to accommodate two hundred, but the funds of the charity are already stretched to their last limits, and many an old and broken-down seaman whom this home would otherwise receive, and

whose closing days would be rendered happy by all
that tender ministration, by all that pious kindness can
effect, must die in the cold and cheerless silence of the
Union unless the charity that is prayerfully entreated
for him is given.

On a fine, calm day from the height of the cliffs betwixt Ramsgate and Broadstairs you may spy at low-water time a yellow vein, like a thin winding of pale gold, a hand's breath this side of the horizon—the famous and fatal Goodwin Sands. I suppose there is no shoal in the whole world that a man whose sympathies are with sailors can view with more interest. Starting from the North Sand Head, which is almost abreast of Ramsgate, and looking east, the eye follows the south-westerly sweep of the Goodwins until the Downs are embraced with all their dim tracery of spars and rigging and faint sinuous lines of steamers' smoke beyond, whilst the giant South Foreland acclivity stares down upon the lightship abreast of St. Margaret's Bay, marking the extreme limits in the south and west of the deadliest stretch of sands upon the face of the globe.

Who can view the Goodwins without thinking of the treasures which lie buried in their heart, of the hundreds of ships which have gone to pieces upon them, of the thousands of human corpses which have floated out of their flashing surf to be stranded upon some distant beach, or to drift, maybe for days, upon the bosom of the tides, looking up with blind faces to heaven through the green transparent lid of their sea coffin? There is

no spot that has ever been the theatre of wilder human
suffering. Again and again as you sail past you see
forking up out of them some black gibbet-like relic of a
wreck a week, a fortnight, a month old. Something of
the kind is always visible, as though even on the
tenderest of summer days, when the blue water sleeps
around, and the heavens are a violet hollow, with a
rayless sun making gold of the sea in the west, the
deadly suggestiveness of that long sweep of yellow sand
should be as plain as when its presence is denoted amid
the black tempestuous night by the ghastly gleam of
boiling white waters.

I remember once passing these Goodwins and seeing
a number of little black figures running about them. A
pleasure vessel from one of the adjacent ports was lying
at anchor a short distance off, and her boat was against
the slope of the shoal. It was a very calm day indeed,
the sea just blurred here and there with small draughts
of air that gave the water in those places a look of ice,
with a pallid streak of the French coast beyond the white
mainsail of the pleasure-cutter, hove up by the refraction
of the light above the sea-line. I brought a small pocket
telescope to bear, and observed that those little black
figures running about like the savages Robinson Crusoe
saw were Cockney excursionists, engaged in playing
cricket. They played as if they wanted to be able to
talk of having played rather than as if they enjoyed the
game. Talk of contrasts! A man may be rendered
pensive by watching children sporting in a graveyard,
by mingling in a festivity held upon a space of ground
where once a famous battle was fought, and where the
feet of the merrymakers are separated from the bones
and skulls of warriors by a couple of spades' length of
earth. But to see those little black-coated creatures

U

running about after a ball on top of such an ocean burial-place that the like of it for the horror of its annals and for the number of those it has sepulchred is not to be found in this habitable world, might well have made the gayest heart sad and thoughtful for a spell.

As I leaned over the rail, looking at those happy pigmies—those lords of creation who, viewed half a mile further away, might have passed for a handful of black crabs crawling about—the scene in imagination changed, the darkness came rushing out of the east with a moan of approaching storm, the three lanterns winked like stars beyond the North Sand Head, and there was a sound of weltering waters and the seething and hissing of surf rising up through the gloom out from the whole length of the shoals. The wind rose fresh and eagerly, with a raw edge in it; the ebony of the swelling water was broken by the glimmer of the froth of breaking seas. I could hear the muffled thunder of the confused play to windward of the surf, with the shrieking of the blast overhead, whilst a deeper shadow yet gathered in the air. Then, with a blinking of my eyes, back would come the facts of the thing again, and yonder were the little figures merrily chasing the ball, the sea spreading like a sheet of silk to the yellow rim of the hard sand, and the blue sky bright overhead. Yet another touch of the magician Fancy's wand, and it was all howling storm and flying blackness and the steam of hurling spume again, with a sudden glare of lightning between, flinging out the shapes of the piles of whirling clouds like monstrous brandished wings going to pieces in the hurricane, and throwing up the black fabric of a big ship on her beam ends, her masts gone, and a fury of white water veiling her.

There are lifeboat coxswains who need but close their

eyes to see fearfuller things. Just where those little creatures are brandishing their tiny bats and flourishing their shrimp-like legs, the great ship struck, and four hundred men and women shrieked out to God for mercy in one breath. A man's fancy must be feeble even on the softest of summer days not to hear the crash of her timbers, the thunder-shocks of the smiting seas, the rending noises of hemp and wire and spar torn by the tempest from their strong fastenings; not to see the ghastly picture she makes in the wild gleam of the signal flare whose tongues of fire are blown horizontal, like streaming flags, by the furious breath of the storm, illuminating with a dull horrible crimson light the throngs of human beings who cry and struggle upon her decks, or hang, like streaming suits of clothes, in what remains of her rigging.

Is this an exaggerated picture? Alas! the pen never yet was wielded that could pourtray, in the barest form, any one of the countless horrible scenes which have taken place on that stretch of sands where one summer day I watched, leaning over the rail of a vessel, a number of light-hearted excursionists playing cricket.

Among the things which never can be known may be placed the thoughts which possess a man in the moment of shipwreck. Of the hundreds of published narratives none satisfies the reader; and of those who relate their experiences, how infinitely remote from the truth do their statements strike them as being when they put what they have written side by side with what they remember having felt! The reason is, I take it, because in no other situation is death more awful than upon the sea. It is commonly slow—at least, it gives time for anguish to become full-blown—and the hope of rescue must be very strong indeed, and well founded,

to qualify that agony of expectation, sinking into paralyzing despair, which confounds and in a manner stuns
a person stranded far out upon the water in a black
night, seeing nothing but the glare of lightning or the
spectral flashing of froth flying past, hearing nothing
but the grinding and trembling and dislocating noises
of the hull upon the ground.

It is supposed because sailors cannot or do not
describe the horrors they pass through that they lack
the capacity of expression. But you may put the most
eloquent writer now living, call him by what name you
please, on board a ship foundering amid a tempest or
going to pieces in a storm on such a shoal as the
Goodwins or the Sunk Sand, and when he has been long
enough rescued and ashore to recover the use of his
brains, you may defy him to write such a narrative of
the disaster as will come, to his own conscience and
memory, one jot nearer to the truth than the newspaper
paragraph of five lines in which the wreck was chro-
nicled. A man can describe what he has suffered in a
railway collision, in a house on fire, down in a mine
where there has been an explosion, in a theatre where
there has been a panic ; but put him aboard a ship and let
him clearly understand that he is going to be drowned,
and when succoured he can tell you little more than
that the waves ran mountains high, that some people
were brave, and that some people shrieked, and that
what he best remembers is catching hold of something,
and hearing the water in his ears, and being dragged
into a boat.

Very true is the old saying, " If you want to learn
how to pray, you must go to sea." So distracting, so
paralyzing, so utterly despairful are all the conditions
of shipwreck in its worst forms, that I cannot but think,

when a man is known to act bravely and coolly in that situation, unmindful of himself, thinking of others, encouraging and heartening them, the heroism he exhibits is of a kind not to be matched by any kind of courage a man may show in a position that lacks the overwhelming features which distinguish the foundering or the stranding of a ship.

Some days ago I met a seaman who had made one of the crew of a brig that a few months since was stranded on the Goodwin Sands, and went to pieces there. The circumstances of the wreck were so recent that I was sure it could not but be a very sharp, clear memory in this sailor; and, wanting to hear what sort of thoughts come into a man's head at such a time, and how he will act, what kind of impulses govern him, and the like, I carried this mariner to where a seat and a glass of beer were to be had, and conversed with him.

"She was a wessel," said he, "of 220 ton, and we was in ballast, bound from Can (Caen) to Seaham. All went well, nothen particular happening, I mean, till we comes abreast o' the South Foreland. It might then be twelve o'clock in the middle o' the night. The weather was as thick as mud, plenty of rain driving along, and the wind west, blowin' a fresh breeze. We was under upper and lower main-tops'l, lower fore-tops'l, and foresail."

Here he took a drink.

"And the weather as thick as mud, you say?"

"Ay, thick as mud in a wine-glass. The Sou' San'-head light was on our starboard beam, and ye may guess how clear it was when I tell you that that light took a deal of peering at to make out. As to the East Good'in, why, all that way was black as my boot: not the merest glimmer to betoken a lightwessel *there*. I was at the side, heavin' the lead, getting nine fathom, and then seven, and then eight, and then seven again. Right fair betwixt the Callipers and the Deal coast I'll allow ye'll get eleven and twelve fathom good till you come on to past the Downs—headin' up, I mean—and then it shoals down to height and seven and five and a 'arf. So in a night as black as a dead wall, when there's no moon, who's to know, when the last light seen has drawed out of view, and there's ne'er another to be sighted, where you are in that water? We was going along tidy fast, when a squall of rain drives right up over our starn in a wild smother, and I had just made seven fathom by the lead when the wessel took the ground, chucking me off the rail on to the deck. The skipper begins to bawl out like mad, 'Let go the main-torps'l halliards! Haul up the foresail! Let go the——' Wash at that moment comes a lump of sea right over the port quarter, cantin' our starn to the south'ard and smotherin' the decks. You didn't want to see—you could feel that the brig was hard and fast, though as the sea thumped her she'd kinder sway on her keel."

Here he took another drink.

"Well?" said I.

"Well," he continued, "what was to do now, master? Everything being let go aloft, the canvas was slatting like thunder up there, and though I'm not goin' to tell you it was blowing a gale of wind, yet it seemed to come twice as hard the moment we took the ground, and the seas to rise as if our falling helpless on a sudden had swelled 'em up with joy. We lay with our head about nor'-nor'-east, and over the starboard bow you could see the white water jumping. But that was all that was visible. The wind seemed to blow up the thickness all

round us, there was not a light to be seen, and looking
around anywhere away from the white water was like
putting your head in a pitch-kettle. Cold! master, that
was the worst part of it. I'll allow that in all sitivations
of this kind the cold's the part that's hardest to bear.
Somehow danger ain't so frightful when it's warm.
Can't explain it, I'm sure; matter o' constitootion,
perhaps: but I doubt if ye'd find much bravery among
the Hesquimos and the Roosians up near the pole, and
the likes o' them. Can't see how it's possible; but it's
only my 'pinion."

Another drink.

"Well," he continued, holding up the fresh glass of
ale I had ordered for him to the light, with a look of
pensiveness in the one bloodshot eye he kept open, "we
tarns to and makes a flare—a sort o' bonfire. But if we
couldn't see anything, who was to see us? However,
we kept all on burning flares, whilst first the fore-top-
gall'nmast came down with a run, causing us all to jump
aft out of the road, and then the main-topmast carries
away at the cap and falls with a roar over the side, and
set us all running forrard. I for one made up my mind
we was all to be drownded. I couldn't see no help for
it. The noise of them spars cracking and tumbling away
in the blackness overhead, and the shindy set up by the
slatting canvas, along with the creaking of the hull and
the washing of the water that came as white as milk
over the starboard rail, was enough, I reckon, to make
any man suppose his time had come, and that his ghost
was to be turned out of him. However, we took heart after
a spell, by noticing that the seas burst with less weight as
the tide left us, though every butt in her must have yawed
open after she had been grinding awhile, for she was full
of water and a few hours more of such dusting was bound

to have made staves of her. Well, at about half-past four o'clock in the morning, we being by that time pretty near froze to death, the weather thinned down, and we caught sight of the Gull Light shining—about three mile off, I dare say. What was to be seen of our wessel was just a fearful muddle; masts overboard washing alongside, the lower masts working in her like loose teeth with every heave, decks full of raffle, and the water every now and again flying over us as though detarmined if it couldn't wash us overboard it would keep us streamin' wet. When we spied the Gull Light we turned to and made another flare, and presently they sent up a rocket, and to cut this yarn short," continued he, having by this time emptied his second tumbler, and finding me slow in offering him a third, "just as the light was abreakin' in the east one of us sings out that there was a steamer headin' for us, and when the mornin' grew stronger we spied a tug makin' for us with a lifeboat in tow. Well, by this time there was little enough sea, and the lifeboat, letting go off the tug, came alongside, but two of our men was so badly froze up that they had to be lifted into her, and such had been our sufferings, though I'm not going to say they equalled what others have gone through on those cussed sands, that we couldn't have looked worse, with salt in our eyes and our faces washed into the appearance of tallow, had we been spendin' forty-eight hours on that shoal. We lost all our clothes, every bloomin' thing we had with us; and that same forenoon, just afore twelve o'clock, half a gale of wind sprung up, and by two o'clock there was nothing to be seen of the brig."

"And that's the story," said I.

"That's it," he answered; "every word gospel true."

"How did the others behave," said I, "in this awful situation? Pretty well?"

"It was too dark to see," he answered.

"Did you encourage one another?"

"Well," he replied, "the cook at first kept on singin' out, 'We're all drownded men! Lord have mercy upon me!' and the like of that, until the cold took away his voice. I don't know that there was any other sort o' encouragement."

"And what were your feelings," said I, "when the brig took the ground and the water washed over her?"

"My feelings?" he replied. "Why, that we was in a bloomin' mess. That was my feelings."

"How did the prospect of death affect you—I mean the idea of being swept into the black water and strangling there?"

"Are you chaffin' me, sir?" he asked.

"Certainly not," said I.

"Well," he said, "I'm blessed if I was asked such a question as that afore," grinning. "It's like a meetin'-house question."

"Didn't you think at all?" said I.

"Yes," he answered; "I thought what a jolly fool I was to be ashore on the Good'ens on a winter's night, gradually dyin' of frost, instead of bein' in a warm bed ashore, with a parlour to take breakfast in when I woke up. That's about it, sir."

A PLAIN red-brick building stands in the West India Dock Road, with the following lengthy name or description written along the front of it:—"The Strangers' Home for Asiatics, Africans, and South Sea Islanders." On the day I visited this house there were three or four people standing on the doorsteps, with faces which did more in an instant to express the character of the place than could have been effected by reams of reports of annual meetings and descriptive pamphlets. They were, it is needless to say, persons of colour, and of very decided colour too: one as black as a hat, another of a muddy yellow, a third a gloomy brown. They were dressed in European clothes: they might have belonged to nations which were in a high state of civilization when the Thames was clean water, and rolled its silver stream through a land whose scanty population hung loose and unclothed among the trees; but for all that, they had the look of wild men in breeches, and the very black person needed little more than a boomerang or a bow and arrows to give him the aspect at least of an unsafe object. I had, however, but little time to inspect these men, for a commotion in the hall of the building, coupled with an assemblage of some dozen or twenty people on the street pavement, called my attention to

a spectacle of real interest. This consisted of the starting
of a troupe of Javanese musicians for the place of
entertainment where they were then performing. There
were a number of men and four women—at least, I think
there were four women; yet it is possible that I may
have mistaken a man for one of the other sex, for some
of the men and women were very much alike, especially
the men. They streamed out in a great hurry, their
bright black eyes sparkling in their brown faces, the men
smoking short pipes of a decidedly West India Dock Road
pattern, and the women bundling along in such queer
raiment that it would be as hopeless to attempt to
describe its colours and cut as to catalogue the stock of
a rag-and-bottle merchant. A kind of large private
omnibus stood at the door, into which these strange
people got, some of them climbing upon the roof; and
striking indeed was the appearance of the windows of
the vehicle, framing, as they did, every one of them, a
dark, contented face, whilst the roof of the omnibus
was crowded with blacks and whites, like the keys of
a pianoforte.

"Who are those people?" said I to a Chinaman, as
the omnibus rolled away.

"Hey?" answered John.

"Those people," I said, pointing towards the retreat-
ing vehicle, "they are not sailors, are they? There are
women among them."

"No, no, not sailor, no, no," cried the Chinaman
with great earnestness, and wagging his head so violently
that he nearly shook his hat off. "Music-man, not
sailor; play tic-a-tic, tic-a-tic;" and here he screwed an
imaginary fiddle into his throat and fell to sawing the
air with his elbow.

At this moment I was joined by the secretary—a

gentleman, let me say at once, who, after spending many years of his life in India, is now gratuitously devoting his services to the poor Asiatic who finds himself homeless in this great wilderness of London, often penniless, and speaking a tongue with which he may journey from Mile End Gate to Hammersmith without finding an ear capable of comprehending a word he says. This gentleman told me who those queer-looking people were, how they were in charge of a Dutch *entrepreneur*, and how they were " putting-up " at the Strangers' Home because there, and at no other place in London, they were likely to meet people who, even if they did not speak their language, would impart a sense of home.

We now proceeded to inspect the building. As at the Well Street Sailors' Home, so here, the common room, if I may so term it, is the central hall, a large place furnished with seats and tables and heated by an immense stove. Here of an evening, when it is cold or damp out of doors, the inmates of the home assemble, and the bright lamps shed their light upon as many diverse countenances and costumes as there are nationalities to the eastward of Russia and in the great oceans which wash the Capes of Africa and South America. Strange, indeed, is the admixture to a European eye: the Hindoo sitting cross-legged on a bench listening, with dusky eyes rolling in his black attenuated features, to the pigeon-English of a round-faced Chinaman; a Malay endeavouring by gestures to make himself understood by a Kanaka ; a native of Ceylon smiling over the porcine gutturals of a couple of Zulus ; with here an Arab reis pacing the floor in lonely dignity, or a red man of a paternity indistinguishable in his features, which seem compounded of the Nubian, the last of the Mohicans, a dash of Polynesia, with a hint of Liverpool or Bristol, spelling over a volume full of murky and eye-confounding hieroglyphs.

"When this hall is full the sight is a remarkable one," said the secretary. "What with the hum of the strange languages—perhaps as many as twenty all going at once—together with the various faces and clothes, I assure you it needs no small effort of mind to convince one's self that one is still in London, and that just out of doors omnibuses are rolling, small boys calling out the evening papers, and policemen standing at the corners."

I felt the force of this, thinly peopled as the hall was, when I stood in it gazing around. Was it the strange haunting Eastern smells—vague fumes, as of a hubble-bubble recently smoked out; a lingering whiff as of curry; a thin, ghostly odour of bamboos, chillies, oil, nutmeg, and cedar-wood? or was it the turban, the pigtail, the almond-shaped eye, the black, bronze, and yellow skins of the few Asiatics who were seated in a body on a central bench, that carried my imagination out of the West India Dock Road into the tangled forests, the hot, blue heavens, the joss-houses, the sampans and junks, the rushing rivers, the jackalls, the dusky figures, the blue gowns and red or yellow shoes of the distant, spacious provinces of the sun? Hark to the sing-song chatter babbling from that Mongolian visage! What is the magic of it, that this hall, gloomy with the smoke of the great city blowing riverwards, should be transformed into a shining Eastern city, whose shores, rich with the green of tropical vegetation, are washed by a sea whose breast reflects a heaven of sapphire? The voice ceases; the spell is broken; the muffled roar of the toiling world outside breaks in and establishes one of the very sharpest contrasts in life—

that of the condition of an Asiatic, fresh from the hot suns and thick jungles of his own country, plunged amid the smoke, the turmoil, the unspeakable odours of the east end of London, incapable of making his wants known, languishing in misery and cold in the gloom of railway arches or some unfrequented court, feeling what solitude is in a sense never imagined by Byron. For the Asiatic's loneliness is that of the dumb brute; he has a language, but he might as well be voiceless, and, worst of all, he is the victim of the unnatural, ignorant, and wicked prejudice which finds in the coloured skin nothing but what is fit for derision, contempt, and cruel neglect. This was the lot of the Eastern stranger before a number of humane Englishmen banded themselves together to furnish him with a refuge. I own that the fine humanity of this institution affected me strongly as I stood looking at the knot of dark-visaged, strangely apparelled men, and considered what would be their fate if this Home were not at hand to help them, to receive them, to interpret their wants, and to assist them to return to their native countries. Time was when few tragedies were commoner than that of the finding the body of some coloured man who had made his way as a sailor or stoker to London, been robbed by the beasts of prey who wander hungrily round the dockyard gates, and had lain himself down in some corner of this opulent city to die of cold and hunger. Such horrors are things of the past, and honoured be those and the memory of those who have made them so. No Asiatic stranger need perish for the want of a friend in London now. The Home will receive him, and for a very moderate sum—which he may easily pay either from the wages due to him from the ship he leaves, or by the note advanced by the owners whose ship he joins

—feed and lodge him, and spare no trouble to restore him to his own country. Hence, to a large extent, the institution contributes to its own support. But the charges it makes are so small, the losses it incurs through the new allotment or bonus notes are so frequent, and the cases of absolute destitution it deals with so numerous, that it is bound to continue to be dependent upon outside help to a certain extent; and I believe that no one who has any knowledge of the work it is doing, no one with sympathy for the helpless of his own species, but will admit that there is not an institution in existence that better deserves the gifts of the charitable than this Home for Asiatic Strangers.

But all this time I am leaving the obliging and kind-hearted secretary waiting to show me over the premises. We pass out first of all into a space of open ground at the back of the building, of which a substantial piece has been converted into a flower garden. This the superintendent of the Home, who has joined us, contemplates for a while with silent satisfaction, and then, with considerable pride, draws my attention to it.

"It has all been done within the last two or three years," he says. "The Asiatics lend a hand, find old seeds knocking about the bottom of their chests, and plant them, but they never come to anything. They won't grow, you know, in this climate. Here's a sample," he says, pointing to a row of shoots which look like the first buddings of that patriotic vegetable the leek; "they were planted three days ago by those Javanese women you saw, and this is what they've already come to. But I suspect they'll end at that."

A balcony runs at the back of the house, and along it there was stumping a John Canoe, smoking something strange, whether a pipe or cigar or cigarette or piece

of cane I could not tell. He vanished through a door
when we mounted the steps, which I regretted, as I
should like to have examined the thing he had in his
mouth.

"This," said the secretary on our re-entering the
building, "is what we call the firemen's dormitory."
It was a large room with a bulkhead dividing it, and on
either hand of the bulkhead went a row of narrow beds
furnished with coarse coverlets and mattresses stuffed
with fibre. There was no carpet, and I ventured to ask
the reason, as the bare boards had but a cheerless look.

"Carpet!" exclaimed the secretary; "my dear sir,
these Asiatics wouldn't know what to do with such a
thing. They'd pull it up and make trousers of it. You
cannot conceive the strangeness of their habits and
customs. For instance, to give them a table-cloth
would be like ill treating them. Nothing bothers them
more than a fork; and you may see them eating eggs
with clasp-knives, which they pull out of their pockets."
Then seeing me eyeing the beds, he continued, "It
would hardly do to give the firemen fine linen to lie in.
Sir, they arrive here thick with grime, they foul whatever they touch, and it takes several days of hard
bathing to clean them."

There were several of these dormitories, each of them
divided by bulkheads, uncarpeted, and containing the
same kind of bedsteads, every one bearing a number at
its head. The Javanese troupe occupied one of these
dormitories, the men sleeping on one side of the bulkhead and the women on the other. I looked for their
luggage, but could find nothing but a fiddle and an old
sword. I think, if the public had seen where these musicians sleep, they would reckon the sight stranger than
any other part of the performance these Eastern people

were giving. There is one dormitory, however, upstairs filled with cabins similar to what they have at the old Sailors' Home at Belvedere. These are occupied, I was told, by the better class of Asiatics.

"And who might they be?" I asked.

"Why," I was told, "Japanese officers, stewards, Chinese carpenters, native doctors, and the like."

These are the "dignity men." They have a little room in which they may dine apart from the Lascars, Kanakas, John Chinamen, and the others; but, somehow, they don't seem to value exclusiveness, for most of them will quit their table to join the pigtails and half-castes in the big eating-room downstairs, where they find a relish in their rice and fish which appears to be wanting in the dishes in the other apartment. In one of the dormitories we came across a Javanese—one of the troupe—sitting cross-legged on his bed, ill with a cold in the head. His unsmoked pipe lay by his side, and he was listlessly handling some pieces of printed calico, though the use he meant to put them to I could not divine. There is a no more melancholy object than a coloured man suffering from a bad cold in the head. I saw him shiver, and then roll his eyes—black as ebony set in orange—upon the window, and I thought to myself, "How this harmless, coloured man, who speaks nothing but Javanese, and who belongs to a country where the air is radiant with beautiful birds and fragrant with delicious fruits, must enjoy the climate of the West India Dock Road!"

We struggled to impart sympathy by several kinds of gestures and motions, but it would not do; we could not get further than alarming him, and so we left him. In another dormitory we found a Ceylon man, a Madrassee Lascar, and a Japanese. The Ceylon man was a very handsome fellow, his hair parted down the middle, and he had as fine a pair of eyes as ever I saw in the human countenance, regular features, and a wonderfully good figure. He was reading an English book, and spoke English so well that, what with his correct utterance, the colour of his skin, and his striking face, a misgiving seized me.

"Are you a pure Cingalese?" I asked.

"No, no," cried he, with much anxiety in his manner; "my father was an English sailor!"

But the Madrassee man, in a measure, atoned for this disappointment. He was the real thing—just the sort of conformation to tumble about in a surf-boat, very black, very lean, with snow-white teeth, and a high long nose as thin as a hatchet. The secretary conversed with him in his native lingo, and it seemed to do the poor fellow good to talk. The Japanese had a wooden face, and had very little to say. Indeed, I always think that the people of his race and the Chinese view us and our works with a good deal of contempt. What a mean opinion they must have of our toys, of our paintings, in which the literal is sacrificed to the poetical; of our clothes, tea, head-dresses, coiffures, and a thousand other matters! They have a Chinese porter at the Home, who is dressed in a black coat and wears a hat. I did not speak to him, but I should judge, from observing the expression on his face when in a state of repose, that he has but a poor opinion of Great Britain. In another dormitory were a couple of Arabs mending shirts; and downstairs, in the scullery, I met a Zulu, who told me that he was a subject of Cetewayo, and had called at that King's lodgings when he was in London, but had not managed to see his Majesty. One of the suite promised to write and appoint an hour for an interview; but no letter ever reached the youth, and the

next thing he heard of Cetewayo was that he had sailed
for Africa. This scullery led into a large kitchen, very
well appointed, and in spick and span condition. Ad-
joining was the provision room, containing one large
sack of rice, a quantity of smoked herrings, a jar of
chillies, another jar of curry powder, and other Eastern
relishes.

"The mackerel is the favourite dish with our inmates, be they of whatever nationality they will," said
the secretary. "They consider it the finest fish that is
caught in European waters, and lament when the season
for catching them is over."

I asked what food they were supplied with in the Home.

"We have," he replied, "what we call three messes.
The first-class mess is sixteen shillings a week—this
includes a separate cabin; the second, without a cabin,
is fourteen shillings; and the third, which we term the
curry and rice mess, is ten shillings. The first two
messes comprise, for breakfast, fish or eggs, coffee,
bread and butter; for dinner we give beef or mutton,
with vegetables, and curry and rice always; tea, the
same as breakfast."

"The charge is small enough," said I.

"But they have other privileges," said he. "For
instance, there are hot and cold water baths downstairs,
for the use of which no charge is made. We also receive
and take care of their money and valuables—for some
of the people who come here bring real valuables, such
as jewels, with them, I assure you. Since last January
the amount deposited in money with us has amounted
to £2,285, of which I do not scruple to say that, but for
the existence of this home, the greater portion would
have been stolen from its owners by the crimps and
boarding-house people who haunt our neighbourhood.
That room you see there is our shipping-office; captains

come to us and select men for their vessels, and when the choice has been made we accompany the men to the marine offices, see them sign articles and that the advance is duly made. Indeed, we do all that we possibly can to help and protect these poor strangers."

"What I have seen assures me of that," said I.

"This," he continued, as we went upstairs and entered a large cheerful dormitory, "is what we call the ayahs' room. It is meant for native women who are brought home as nurses and discharged. Sad cases of destitution are often occurring. Not long ago a City missionary found a native woman in an empty house in Shepherd's Bush. He brought her here, and, having learnt the name of her mistress, we went to her, and were told that the ayah was insane, that she had been kept as long as possible, had at last refused to go, and was accordingly turned out. We took charge of her for awhile, but her madness increased, and we were forced at last to send her to a county asylum, where she now remains."

The inspection of this room exhausted all that was to be seen; so, bidding the cordial secretary farewell, and taking a lingering look at a knot of dusky men who were talking in the hall, I quitted this hospitable and most valuable institution, resolving to record all that I had heard and viewed, in the earnest hope that of those by whom this record of my visit will be read some may be induced to help an excellent charity by sending donations to the manager of the Strangers' Home, West India Dock Road, London.

PRINTED BY WILLIAM CLOWES AND SONS, LIMITED, LONDON AND BECCLES.